EAT, DRINK, AND BE MERRY

EAT, DRINK, AND BE MERRY

CHARLES ENGAR

ISBN 978-1-4583-3287-5

PROLOGUE

The master teacher fondly gazed at the expectant faces of his students. He contemplated how best to help them understand the pitfalls and dangers they would face as they, themselves, would soon be called to teach the wandering children of God. Their future students could easily become their tempters, if care were not taken to recognize the traps that could ensnare them as they spread the good news.

His concern was not so much for the masses of simple people who struggled to find enough clothing to keep warm and enough food to eat. He knew they, individually, were good, God-fearing people, who, unfortunately, could easily be led down a wayward path. What concerned him greatly were the self-appointed leaders of the masses; the religious hypocrites, who preached one thing to their congregations but practiced something totally different. These wicked men, who coveted power, influence, and wealth, deluded themselves into believing in their own self-importance. These were men who refused to see the inevitable consequences of their hypocrisy; their own eternal condemnation and the eventual destruction of their beloved city, Jerusalem.

He knew pitfalls and traps to ensnare his disciples would be laid by such hypocrites, as they would, most assuredly, view the gospel the disciples preached as a threat to their power and position. The gospel taught mankind to love, to sacrifice self for others, and to look for long-term rewards for short-term tribulations. Power and wealth, gained on earth, could never engender a path to Heaven.

The Son of God taught his disciples using a parable. "The ground of a certain rich man brought forth plentifully: And he thought within himself, saying, What shall I do, because I have no room where to bestow my fruits?

And he said, This will I do; I will pull down my barns, and build greater; and there will I bestow all my fruits and my goods.

And I will say to my soul, Soul, thou hast much goods laid up for many years; take thine ease, *eat, drink, and be merry.*

But God said unto him, Thou fool, this night thy soul shall be required of thee: then whose shall those things be, which thou hast provided?

So is he that layeth up a treasure for himself, and is not rich toward God". (*Luke, 12:16-21*)

Contents

PART ONE

CONSPIRACY

Chapter 1

The bleak, overcast, early-spring day, which was about half-over in Washington D.C., mirrored perfectly the current state of mind of the freshman senator from Oregon. Rick Benson, who had been elected by a paper-thin margin in spite of a last-minute campaign blitz against him by the president, came to Washington with unreal expectations and an equally unreal energy level. This promptly irritated much of the power elite who had made this schizophrenic city their home for too many years.

Compromise, a political catch-all term, which politicians of all stripes could use to justify just about any action, was not one of Senator Benson's favorite words. He abhorred what compromise had come to mean in Washington and considered his election a repudiation by his constituents of the current mode practiced in the nation's capital.

Earlier in the day, Benson had learned first-hand how out of sync his view of the term was compared to the beltway interpretation. He had been summoned the night before to a meeting at nine a.m. with Senator Jack Williams, a four-term senator from Texas. Williams, considered by the national media to be the dictionary definition of right-wing, was, undoubtedly, the best friend the military had in Congress. He was also a devout political enemy of the Democratic president. Williams felt it would be proper to have a cordial chat with the new senator from Oregon.

As a senior representative of his party's power in Washington, Williams was accustomed to junior colleagues, as well as representatives from the defense industry, responding to his summoning promptly and without questioning. After all, few people in Washington wielded the same degree of power to control virtually billions of dollars in defense spending as did Williams. Money meant power and over the years Williams had learned to play the power game like few others. As a result, his expectation was the freshman from Oregon would break whatever plans he had to meet with him and learn from the master player how Washington really works.

Benson did, in fact, have to change plans in order to meet with Williams. He had promised his wife, Kristina, shortly after arriving in Washington, he would take her and their three children to see the Smithsonian, and all had arranged their schedules to do that today. The Senate docket was virtually empty and the plans were a natural until the call came the night before. Benson had briefly considered telling Williams' secretary no, but decided against that, believing it wouldn't be prudent, politically, to get on the wrong side of such a powerful senator so soon. Little did he know then, his attendance at the meeting would end up causing a rift between the two men eventually having a profound impact on the future of the country.

What was particularly aggravating to Benson, he was forced to compromise one of his basic values. Ever since his marriage to Kristina twenty-three years ago, he had vowed that only under extreme circumstances would promises made be broken. Even a promise to take her and the kids to the Smithsonian, which might seem in today's self-indulgent world too insignificant to worry about, was significant to him. And to have to break his promise to his wife in order to politically placate the arrogant senator from Texas was truly galling.

Earlier, after arriving promptly at 9:00 a.m., Benson waited for fifteen minutes in the outer foyer before he was directed into the senator's spacious but overly decorated office. After exchanging congratulations and other pleasantries, the senator from Texas abruptly asked Benson why he felt like he had the responsibility to right all the sins of the country's capital overnight?

Before Benson could respond, Williams said in an emphatic tone, "I've had, at least, half-a-dozen senators in my office from both sides of the aisle. They all want to know who this smart-ass new guy is from Oregon. Doesn't he know anything about who pays the dues around here?"

Williams continued, "I'd like to think your problem has more to do with inexperience than uppity arrogance. I, and my distinguished colleagues, have been at this game a long time, in some cases before you had your first little horny thought as a pimply kid, and you'd damn well better come to that realization fast!"

Benson, who almost never lost control of his emotions, was restraining himself from spreading the senator's nose over his pompous, pock-marked face.

He started to respond but Williams interrupted. "Now, I don't have a lot of time to waste talking to you. You can do yourself a lot of good and demonstrate you're not as dumb as some folks in this town think by listening carefully to what I'm about to say. Your career in the Senate can either be successful or severely limited, depending on how many people become pissed off at you. After four short months, there are a lot of people that need un-pissing, if you get my drift?"

Benson opened his mouth to speak, but Williams cut him off again with a wave of his hand. "Senator, as you are aware, I, and some of my conservative colleagues, are trying to round up enough votes to override our limp-ass president's threatened veto of the *Williams/Hackett bill.* You have been more than a pain in the ass expressing your opposition on this. Our country sorely needs this bill to ensure we can meet any and all possible threats to our security into the next couple of decades."

Benson was fully aware of the *Williams/ Hackett bill.* It was probably one of the most expensive pieces of pork ever considered in Congress. Though not advertised, its main provisions allowed for the continuation of two obsolete military bases in Texas, as well as a multi-billion dollar, multi-year contract with Howard Aircraft Corporation to build a hundred, new-generation, stealth bombers. Howard Aircraft was located in Texas and was the single largest contributor to Senator Williams' re-election campaign.

Williams interrupted Benson's thoughts, "… but now is not the time to play the martyr. Now is the time to get on board with the rest of the team and get this bill passed." Williams condescendingly added, "Besides, a little humble pie on your part, showing us you can compromise when asked to do so, certainly will be a good beginning toward mending the fences you have damaged."

Benson lost it. "Who in the hell do you think you are, you arrogant ass? The people in Oregon, my friends, elected me to stop people like you from ruining our country. What gives you the right to do that? To make decisions that waste billions of dollars out of the pockets of honest, hard-working folks whose only hope for a good life is to trust that people like you won't screw them too badly." Benson, honestly afraid he was going to strangle the pineapple-headed curmudgeon from Texas, locked eyes with him and said emphatically, "You can take your bill and stick it up your fat butt!"

He turned and strode purposefully with clenched teeth out of William's office through the outer office without even a sideward glance at the startled secretary, sitting, wide-eyed, with mouth agape, behind her desk.

As Benson sat solemnly at his desk, fiddling with papers without actually looking at them, he realized what angered him the most wasn't what Williams had said, but that he, himself, had lost his cool and responded to Williams at the same gutter level. Benson always prided himself at his ability to communicate without profaning and felt personally ashamed he let his temper flare.

He visualized William's round, ruddy, pompous face, with purplish lips, mouthing the baloney about how important his bill was to the country. He thought, *Yes, it was important all right, to Senator Williams and a few rich, self-absorbed cronies in the military-industrial complex in his own state.*

The freshman senator worried how far the country had slipped since the experiment in representative democracy was launched by a handful of patriots risking their lives over two centuries ago. He remembered how his hope had been rekindled, immediately after the events of September 11, 2001. Then, the country briefly united in outrage at eighteen Islamic extremists, who, in their zeal to demonstrate their hatred of America, rode their flying bombs to glory. Within a few months, however, the realities of a self-absorbed America returned the public's psyche right back where it was before—what Benson intellectually referred to as the "what's in it for me" syndrome.

Senator Williams was a living manifestation of the corruption slowly corroding the magnificent experiment. The Republic was morphing into something else, where a small cadre of self-appointed elites presumed to run things, talking, as if their opinions were representative of the citizenry, regardless whether true in fact. The continuous bloviating, along with, periodically, providing a variety of entitlement sops to keep the masses blissfully happy, served to keep the elites in power.

Benson wondered if he had made a mistake coming back to this sterile city. Would it ever be possible to make a difference when all the power and money was controlled by jerks like Williams? Coupled with his broken promise to his wife and kids, his encounter with Senator Williams made this day truly one to throw into the trash heap.

Chapter 2

President Lebedov sat across the expansive mahogany table from Chou En Lo, the Chinese foreign minister. They had just finished two days of extremely fruitful talks. A tentative agreement had just been concluded on a plan that, if successful, would drastically alter the power structure in the world to their advantage.

Almost immediately upon assuming the presidency of Russia, Anatoli Lebedov had begun to covertly steer Russian foreign policy in a direction increasingly divergent from the West, particularly in the Middle East. He was quietly expanding relationships with radical Islam, including, not only the more extreme regimes in the Middle East, but the leadership of the most prominent Islamic terrorist organizations.

In addition, the president had focused on improving relations with his huge Chinese neighbor to the southeast. His effort, as demonstrated with the tentative agreement just reached, was paying dividends.

The recent collapse of North Korea and its absorption by South Korea, while at first glance, appeared as a setback for Russia and China in Asia, had turned into a real plum. The new Republic of Korea had become totally absorbed in its own rehabilitation, which resulted in a noticeable reduction in military collaboration with the United States. Korea no longer felt threatened by its immediate neighbor, so why continue spending billions for a military whose reason for being was greatly diminished? Reflecting the new reality, the last American soldier left Korea just a few weeks ago. China had also recognized the unification of the Korean peninsula as a net plus and was wise enough to not take any action to stop it.

The new thinking in Europe, encouraged by Lebedov, was Russia was a partner, not a potential enemy. NATO had ceased being a credible military threat. No American troops remained in Europe and European defense expenditures were imploding drastically.

In reality, both Lebedov and his Chinese neighbor shared a similar loathing for America, which, with some careful nurturing, could turn into a strategic plus for both countries. His proposal to the Chinese, which they had tentatively accepted, would turn their common hatred into decisive action that could restore Russia to its rightful place as a world superpower.

One thing Lebedov shared with his predecessor, and his new friends from China, was utter amazement at how eager the Americans and Europeans were to sell their newest technology to potential adversaries. Both Russia and China had long ago discovered the West was easy to fool. Tell them what they desired to hear, and they would give or sell just about anything you wanted. Lebedov was convinced capitalism's ultimate Achilles heel was its built-in greed. He thought Americans, particularly, were short-term thinkers. They invest in foreign plants and infrastructure, rape the cheap labor in Russia, China, and elsewhere, and make millions while it's easy to make—the future be damned! Lebedov thought to himself, *Well, if only the smug Yankees knew what a future they were buying.*

President Lebedov was certain the course he was embarking on was one his predecessor, the former prime minster, would have embraced. Prior to his untimely assassination, the prime minister had restored Russia's traditionally strong, executive-centered, government, reversing a decade-long slide into a culturally-unworkable democracy. His success made Lebedov's plans viable. Had a Chechen Islamist assassin's bullet not cut the prime minister's life short, he might even have considered a similar idea. Now, however, thanks to the previously laid groundwork, Lebedov could manipulate all the strings necessary to return Russia to its rightful place on the world stage. Even his predecessor's assassination by a Muslim extremist directly benefited the new president. Lebedov, a former Afghan and Chechen war hero, was elected by a huge majority, after the Chechen killed the popular prime minister.

President Lebedov was certain the Russian masses shared his longing to be a world power again. Years of economic doldrums, the psychological impact of losing the former Soviet empire, the rise of organized crime, and the demise of the Russian military had all served to turn the Russian population into vodka-guzzling schizophrenics with bad cases of depression. Restoring Russian greatness in the world, in Lebedov's view, would provide the healing balm so badly needed in his great country.

Chou En Lo passively watched the endless, patchwork landscape slipping under the wing of the Aeroflot jet as he contemplated the recently completed negotiations with the Russians. He thought Lebedov was an interesting man with a vision of the world's future that could, with some reservations, be embraced by the Chinese. But even with a shared vision and virtual agreement on the need to change the power structure in the American-dominated globe, Lebedov's proposal was frightening

China's economic expansion had suffered a severe setback two years earlier. Countrywide strikes by millions of workers and the resulting crackdown by Chinese troops, resulted in the death of thirty-five thousand workers. Worldwide condemnation had led directly to economic stagnation, although investments by the West were on the increase again. The foreign minister smiled inwardly, knowing America, and its comrades in Europe and Japan, couldn't resist the cheap labor for long, even if the labor force was now reduced slightly.

What was tempting, however, was the prospect, as proposed by the Russians, of having a cheap, guaranteed source of oil to lubricate the wheels of the recovering economy. This made almost any risk worthwhile. If the plan was successful, the Chinese economy would expand exponentially, and the conquests of Alexander the Great, the Roman empire, Genghis Khan, and even Adolph Hitler would pale in comparison to the new order in the world.

Chapter 3

The unseasonably warm breeze swirled the sand into a dozen mini-tornados in just about any direction Mustafa Mohammed looked. It seemed no matter how much effort he put into sealing the cracks in the dirty, ramshackle shack he and his family lived in, sand was always present in the food he ate, the bed he slept in, the mats he sat upon, and the tub in which he washed. The same winds creating the mini-tornados outside, forced sand through the tiniest cracks making life a constant misery.

He walked to the open door and peered through the shimmering heat as his three-year-old daughter ran as fast as her stumpy little legs could carry her away from her older brother, who was about to throw a hand-full of sand at her face. Mohammed yelled, "Hey! Anwar, leave your sister alone or I'll make you eat what's in your hand!" Anwar immediately let the sand filter between his fingers and mumbled something unintelligible to his sister.

Mohammed, his wife, and three small children, had lived in this corrugated-steel roofed oven for the past year, in a refugee camp situated on the outskirts of Al Karak, Jordan. It was close to the Jordan River, which separated Mohammed from his ancestral home in Hebron. Al Karak, ironically, was known mainly for the thirteenth century ruins of an infamous Crusader castle.

He had lived in Hebron all of his life, even becoming an Israeli citizen, albeit a second-class one. Events over the past decade, however, changed the course of his life. The ascendency of the Hamas leader, Mohammed Rashid, to the chairmanship of the PLO, triggered a cascade of occurrences quickly altering the Middle East landscape. Rashid, upon gaining power, almost immediately declared a new Palestinian state in the West Bank and Gaza with Jerusalem as its capital. He stated his immediate goal was the absorption of all of Israel into the new country, preferably without the Jews. It was surely the most short-lived state in the history of the world. One week after his declaration, the Palestinians no longer controlled any of the West Bank or Gaza, having reclaimed their former status as displaced refugees, mostly in Jordan and, to a lesser extent, Lebanon. The Israeli Army again demonstrated to the world its brutal efficiency when faced with a real threat to the country's continued existence.

The expulsion of the PLO and Hamas, along with over a million Palestinian supporters, was met with worldwide condemnation. Even Israel's erstwhile ally, the United States, joined the chorus. When the UN Security Council, however, sought to implement sanctions with teeth against Israel, the United States, again, incurred the wrath of the Arab world by vetoing the sanctions.

Mohammed was forced to choose his loyalty. When the Israeli Army forcibly expelled the Palestinians from the West Bank, it didn't matter what his citizenship was, he was still Palestinian. His former dislike for the Israelis had now grown into an active, consuming hatred. His constant struggle to find enough food to keep his family from starving was particularly aggravating, since he was forced to accept handouts from American aid workers. It was after all America who kept the Israeli balloon full of air.

Mohammed had recently been able to focus his encompassing hatred of Israel and America into overt action. He had become a member of a new branch of the Hamas paramilitary called Black October. A similarly named organization won eternal Arab adulation at the Munich Olympics in 1972. The name was even more relevant now since the Palestinian expulsions from the West Bank and Gaza occurred in the month of October. A small covert training base had been set up near Al Karak.

Initially his wife, Sarah, had been vehemently opposed to his decision to join Black October. Mohammed had just as adamantly insisted he had an obligation to his fellow countrymen, his family, and Allah to do what he could to destroy the infidels responsible for the destruction of his nation. When she had continued opposing him, a quick backhand across her face silenced any remaining protest. Besides, he reasoned, he wasn't going to be called upon to do anything suicidal—that was always reserved for the young, single martyrs.

Mustafa Mohammed had been involved in extensive training during the past three months, having become an expert with the Kalashnikov AK-47, automatic rifle. He had also been chosen, because of his quick grasp and obvious intellect, to join an elite group being trained in the use of explosives.

As a final exam, he, and four others, were given the assignment to bomb a Jewish tourist bureau in Hamburg, Germany the following week. After properly surveilling the target, they were to plan and execute the destruction of the building housing the bureau. If a few innocent Germans died as collateral damage, a term the West so often used to sugarcoat the killing of civilians, then so be it. After all, Germany was little more than a puppet for the great Satan, America.

The Air Egypt flight from Cairo to Hamburg was uneventful. Local ground winds in Hamburg made the landing somewhat of a nail-biter, but since Mohammed had never flown before, the whole flight was a nail-biter and a huge rush at the same time. If he hadn't been so nervous about the assignment, the flight would have been an amusement ride to never forget. The gnawing fear just under the surface, however, of the dangerous direction his life would take during the next few days, never allowed him the luxury of enjoying the ride. Part of him was exulting in the knowledge, unknown to the ignorant masses around him, he was a freedom fighter, fighting for his nation's freedom, while another part was riveted with fear. His firm faith, however, that Allah would protect and save him, either in life or death, gave him the courage to continue.

The next three days were spent carefully observing the human traffic in and around the tourist bureau. Though not overly busy, there always seemed to be five or six customers in the bureau at most times, particularly during the early evening hours. The bureau was located in the interior of a small mall on the main floor of a five-story, ten-year-old brick building. The first floor fronting the sidewalk was almost all glass, allowing shoppers to peer at the merchandise displayed provocatively to attract customers. The upper floors were occupied by several small businesses including a fair share of law and accounting firms. One of the accounting firms was even American.

The public area in front of the building, as well as other commercial establishments sharing the mall with the tourist bureau, were, by contrast, extremely busy. Particularly after work in the early evening, literally hundreds of people were swarming up and down the wide sidewalk and in and out of the mall.

One thing had particularly attracted the attention of the five bombers—the lack of security. Over the course of three days and nights of surveilling the building, only two police officers were observed, and they had merely stopped to purchase bratwurst at the shop next to the bureau. It appeared Europeans had become complacent regarding the threat of terrorism. It had been several years since the last significant terrorist activity in Europe had occurred. That would change.

The group had begun to think this was not going to be so dangerous after all. The cell leader, a Jordanian named Abdullah, had solicited everyone's agreement that the coming Friday, three days from the present, would be the target day. Before then, much planning and work needed to be done.

Chapter 4

Senator Jack Williams was furious, and the more he thought about it the more aggravated he became. Ever since his talk a week ago with the smart-ass freshman senator from Oregon, Williams had been seething. Then, this morning he had received a call from Senator Hackett who told him a small group of Republicans, lead by Senator Benson, had decided to split with the Republican leadership and join with a similar number of newly elected Democrats. Their stated goal was to oppose the politics-as-usual mentality of the beltway and forge ahead with their own agenda, based on the real needs of the American people. Williams thought, *What the hell do they know about the "real needs" of the American people? The people themselves don't know what their real needs are*.

In Williams' view, the most recent presidential election validated his opinion. The American people elected assuredly the most left-wing president in the history of the Republic. The senator was convinced President Papadakis was a committed socialist and was determined to turn the country into an American France. The national media, at least the networks, were slobbering all over themselves praising the new president. The same was true for labor unions, women's rights organizations, and gay rights activists; the president's agenda, so far, pretty well matching that of his left-wing nutcase supporters. Among other things, the recent passage of universal health care and gay marriage laws confirmed Williams' views. The people were fooled, which, in his view, was what happened when the establishment elite are ignored. The American people's pique against the political establishment resulted in this aberration and the consequences could be disastrous to the country. Likewise, the new senator from Oregon was an aberration, only he was a right-wing aberration. Williams, found himself occasionally envying the Chinese, thinking, *When the masses there forget who they are, the ruling class simply eliminates a few thousand of them.*

Williams was firmly convinced the words, American people, represented sort of a title bestowed upon the ignorant masses out there by the political elite, whose responsibility it was to make decisions for them, while telling them it was what they really wanted. He fumed inwardly. *Now this upstart nut from Oregon with his archaic moral values presumes to know what the American people really want. "Politics as usual" is what made America great. We won the cold war. We're the world's only superpower. How dare this wannabe from Oregon rock the boat!*

What particularly angered Williams was Benson and his group's adamant opposition to the *Williams/Hackett bill*, alleging the bill represented the worst example of pork-barrel legislation. The senator from Texas had just about reached the last straw. He had begun thinking of certain actions only a person in his position could initiate that could stop Senator Benson cold. Benson was going to learn a hard lesson others before had learned to their detriment; you don't get in the way of the power in Washington without severe consequences.

Later the same day, Senator Benson, at his small townhouse in Alexandria, was discussing the day's events with his wife Kristina. She was not only a good listener, but furnished reasoned, common-sense insight, which had been invaluable on more than one occasion. Over the twenty-three years of their marriage, her readiness to be Benson's confidant and trusted counselor, lover, and mother of their children had strengthened and deepened their relationship far beyond the dreams they shared years earlier when they first wed.

He had met Kristina a year before they married. Their meeting was the result of a blind date, which, in spite of the awful track record for blind dates, turned out to be inspired. Even more astounding, their first few hours together occurred at the Highland drive-in movie, hardly the place one would expect to meet a future spouse. To this day, Benson could not remember what the movie was. It wasn't love at first sight, but it didn't take long. She was an athletic and attractive brunette, a former cheerleader at a Salt Lake City suburban high school, who never left him struggling for conversation.

Their first few years together were tough financially but great in virtually all other respects. Rick did not come from a wealthy family. His dad was a junior-high-school, music teacher in Salt Lake City and his mother worked in a clerical position at the county board of health. He grew up never having enough money, so struggling financially was nothing new. Kristina worked fulltime at odd jobs while Rick was completing his undergraduate education at the University of Utah with a degree in political science.

He always had a deep-felt desire to get involved in politics and entered graduate school with that in mind. During his first year of graduate school, however, working toward a master of public administration degree, opportunity knocked when the Federal Bureau of Investigation recruited him. Pursuing the opportunity initially as much out of curiosity as a desire to join the Bureau, Benson passed all of the tests and interviews and received an appointment offer about a week before final exams at the end of his second semester. He did about as well as could be expected on the final exams, dropped out of graduate school, and became an FBI agent.

After moving around the country for several years including a three year tour-of-duty in Washington D.C. as an inspector, Benson and his family, three children by now, transferred to Detroit where he served as the assistant special agent in charge. He subsequently transferred to Oregon and was promoted to the special agent in charge (SAC) of the Portland field office.

After a couple of years, opportunity knocked again when the late senator, Christopher O'Brien, offered him a position as chief of staff. Benson agonized over the decision to resign from the Bureau only eight years before he was eligible to retire. The Bureau had been good to him, but politics had always been Benson's dream, and the opportunity would probably never be this good again.

The three years since that fateful decision went by like a blur. Two years after accepting his new role as the senator's chief of staff, his life took another sudden turn when Senator O'Brien suffered a massive heart attack and died within a week. After the initial shock, the senator's supporters in the moderate wing of the Republican Party, both in the state of Oregon and on the national level, urged Benson to run for the vacant office. He did, and, after beating what seemed like insurmountable odds, won.

It was apparent the people of Oregon were sick of the politics being practiced in the nation's capital. Over 80 percent of the Oregon electorate voted in the election, which was not only a record for the state of Oregon, but an obvious repudiation of the complacency rampant in the rest of the country.

Even after all she had seen during Rick's years with the Bureau, Kristina was still amazed and disgusted at the blatant corruption and unethical behavior that had infected the politicians and bureaucrats who ran the country. In her view, even the Constitution itself was in jeopardy. As her husband related the day's activities to her, she had to make a conscious effort to avoid exploding at him for being part of this corruption, reminding herself that he, and a few others who shared his values, were probably the last hope for America.

Chapter 5

Mohammed's heart was pounding out of his chest. The three previous days had kept him so busy he hadn't had time to be scared—until now. The plan Abdullah and his four comrades were to follow had been scripted months earlier and was outstanding for its simplicity. They had to steal a van, fill it with explosives, and simply drive it through the glass front of the mini-mall in which the Israeli tourist bureau was located. The passenger would start a sixty-second timer, get out with the driver, and run away from the mall. By the time the bomb detonated they would have joined the other three, and all five would be far enough away to observe their handiwork and not be hurt. In the confusion that would follow the crash, they were confident nobody would notice them running from the scene. If they were noticed, the witnesses wouldn't live long enough to tell anybody. Security in the area was virtually nonexistent.

Mohammed had been designated as the driver of the stolen van, and he, and a second terrorist, were now headed at about thirty miles-per-hour toward the glass front of the mall. The five-year-old Toyota van he was driving was carrying more than two hundred pounds of explosives.

He noticed the sidewalk in front of the mall was crowded with early-evening shoppers and businesspeople leaving work. Abdullah had chosen late afternoon as the prime time to strike to obtain the greatest benefit—in terms of potential body count. He had calculated correctly. Mohammed had been ordered to keep driving regardless of the number of people in front of the mall. If a few died under the van's wheels, what did it matter? They would all be dead in little more than a minute anyway.

Even with the hatred motivating Mohammed, he had to fight off a desire to slam on the brakes to avoid plowing into the crowd. So many innocent people! Just to the left, he glimpsed a young mother pushing a baby carriage right in front of the onrushing van. He stopped breathing, closed his eyes, and pressed on the accelerator. He could hear the thump of bodies being launched through the air, and thought he heard a metallic clank of the baby carriage as it rocketed off of the van. A second later the van crashed through the glass front of the mall.

Even before it had stopped rolling Mohammed and his passenger were exiting the van. His partner had actually set the timer before they bulldozed the crowd on the sidewalk, so they actually had something less than sixty seconds to distance themselves from the explosion. Neither needed much motivation to run like they had never run before. The van was packed with over two hundred pounds of high-yield Semtex explosives, immeasurably more powerful than the kerosene-fertilizer bomb that had destroyed the federal building in Oklahoma City in the early nineties.

As they exited the shattered front of the building, Mohammed couldn't help but notice the look of horror and confusion on the faces of the people that were now running toward the building. If the poor souls only knew what was about to hatch in the gut of the van they would be running in a different direction.

Mohammed sprinted as hard as he had ever run in his life. He had knocked over several people in his haste to get away from the scene, probably saving their lives in the process. After what seemed like several minutes, he spotted Abdullah and the rest of the cell sitting in an older-model, faded black Mercedes facing in the direction of the tourist bureau. He crossed the street and was about to reach for the rear-door handle when a huge explosion rocked his world. The blast wave was much stronger than was anticipated and threw Mohammed into the side of the Mercedes, stunning him.

His partner in the van was less fortunate. He was considerably more heavy set and, as a result, lagged significantly behind Mohammed. The blast launched him into the side of a light pole shattering his skull. He bounced off the pole landing in a rag-doll-like heap on the sidewalk, unconscious and barely alive.

Abdullah was shocked. He and the others had not anticipated the strength of the explosion. He regained his composure quickly, however, and ordered the terrorist in the backseat to get out and grab Mohammed. He calculated the battered form lying in a heap at the bottom of the light pole was dead, or would be shortly, and was not worth the risk of trying to rescue him. Once Mohammed was in the car, the driver made a tire-squealing U-turn and sped away from the horror two hundred yards up the street.

The world predictably condemned the attack on the German mall. Invariably though, after the initial headlines, the apologists who ran most of the governments in Europe began the twisted logic of blaming Israel for the bombing. It was, after all, the Israelis who expelled the Palestinians from their homeland, creating thousands of new oppressed freedom-fighters with no choice but to strike back.

The sheer magnitude of the carnage begged for military reaction by someone—anyone. Fifty-five Germans and five Americans lost their lives, as well as twelve Israelis. Hundreds were injured, many permanently maimed. Most of the dead and injured were simply passing by on the sidewalk in front of the building. The pressure was unrelenting on the United States to do something as a sop to the public outrage both in the United States and Germany.

The German government, of course, could not order a military response because of the convenient argument they were legally prohibited from doing such by their own laws. The Germans were more than happy to let the United States bloody its hands.

The Germans had not been able to positively identify the terrorist found dead on the street two hundred yards north of the bombing site, other than a general identification as a probable Palestinian.

The U.S. president decided a quick, relatively massive, one-time air strike on a known terrorist base would be a sufficient response. By ordering it, he could gain political points by appearing decisive, killing a few Arab refugees no one really cared about, and allowing the outrage to pass quickly so the world could go on making money. As it turned out, he need not have bothered to come up with a plan. Israel preempted any contemplated American action.

The Israeli Mossad had been developing raw intelligence that a new terrorist organization had recently been established and was training recruits at the refugee camp in the vicinity of Al Karak, Jordan. The Israelis, unlike the Germans, readily identified the dead terrorist as a member of Black October and drew up plans to retaliate against the camp at Al Karak. They felt an attack on the camp was justified, even though the actual location of the terrorist base at the camp was uncertain. Whether the people killed in the air strike were terrorists or innocent civilians didn't really make any difference. The message was what was important.

Forty-eight hours after the bomb exploded in the German mall, ten F15 Strike Eagles, flying out of the Ramon Air Force base in the Negev desert, obliterated a good part of the sleepy refugee camp near

Al Karak, killing over 350, including some terrorists, but mainly women, children, and old men.

President Lebedov was having a particularly good day. He had learned of the Israeli air raid in Jordan the previous evening. He couldn't believe how well events in the Middle East and Germany were furthering the plot he and Chou En Lo had set in motion just a few short weeks ago. He had suspected the Palestinians would do something sooner or later to tell the world how badly Israel and the West had treated them. He had not anticipated the scope of their action in Hamburg. Lebedov thought the Americans would respond quickly in a measured response of some sort. The Israeli response, instead, surprised him.

The bombing at Al Karak was such an exercise in overkill, even Lebedov was surprised at the level of brutality. His surprise, however, was more than offset by the increased antipathy toward Israel and its mentor, the United States, generated by the attack. The hatred exploding in the refugee camps in Jordan and Lebanon, was going to expand the fertile pool of eager operatives who would just need some money, resources, and a little direction to carry out his plan to change the course of the world.

He was amazed at how naïve the Americans were. He was fully aware of America's recent overtures to Arab countries and covert negotiations with some of the worst terrorist organizations. The American president seemed to believe he could buy the good will of the militants by a combination of money, sympathy, and apologies. Buying security with appeasement had never worked in the last century and certainly would not work in this one. Yet the United States was following the lead of its European partners in the same failed approach.

In Lebedov's view, the biggest threat looming in the new century to the hegemony the Americans and Europeans had enjoyed over the past several hundred years was the rise of militant Islam. Sooner or later the billions around the world, who had been the recipients of American and European colonialism and subjugation, were going to find a way to even the score. The most recent Israeli actions in Jordan inflamed an already explosive situation. Lebedov smiled as he thought, *I'm merely going to provide a needed service to these poor wretches, giving them, at last, an opportunity to finally strike back at their oppressors.*

Mohammed was pleased with himself, in spite of his initial misgivings about the extent of the carnage he and his fellow freedom-fighters had caused. Although the interrogation he, and the survivors of the action in Hamburg, endured in Cairo the night after the bombing was pretty intense, in the end, it was apparent the leaders of Black October were pleased with the worldwide reaction to the bombing. The world's leaders could no longer push the Palestinian suffering out of their consciousness.

As he lay in the lumpy bed contemplating the events of the past week, he realized this would be the last day he would enjoy sleeping in a bed, even a lumpy one, that wasn't full of sand. He was looking forward to seeing his children again and sharing his sand-filled bed with his wife.

Suddenly the door to his room slammed open, and Abdullah rushed in, his face distorted in rage. He yelled for Mohammed to get dressed. Before he could ask what was going on, Abdullah screamed, "The Jews have bombed Al Karak. Hundreds are dead!"

Five hours later, Mohammed and several other freedom-fighters rode into the refugee camp at Al Karak on the back of a World War II deuce-and-a-half. They could see the columns of smoke long before reaching the outskirts of the camp. The scene that slowly appeared through the smoke-caused haze was what nightmares conjured up, only to Mohammed and the others it was a nightmare from which they couldn't awaken. Mohammed's neighborhood, if you could refer to the bleak refugee camp as a neighborhood, was rubble.

He dismounted from the truck and made his way through the carnage to where his wife and children had lived a few hours before. He began to aimlessly dig through the rubble without really thinking he might find someone alive, but he could think of nothing else to do. As he pulled out a stone, lodged in a section of rubble that rose a little higher than the rest, the stack suddenly collapsed and exposed a tiny arm and hand sticking grotesquely up in the air. Mohammed knew instinctively it was the arm of his little girl.

Agonizing grief overcame him as he helplessly, pathetically prostrated himself atop the pile of stones and became racked with uncontrollable sobs. After several minutes he sat up and looked up into the sky. As he looked to the heavens his grief slowly turned into an ice-cold rage. With both fists shaking he screamed, "As Allah is my witness, you'll pay!"

Chapter 6

William Johnson, also known as Slick Willie by those who knew him well, was in the procurement business. His clientele included high military brass as well as some of the country's elected officials in key places. After all, to be successful in this business, it couldn't hurt to know the people who pull the levers in our great democracy.

Slick Willie, however, was not a procurer of military hardware, technology, or even expensive toilets. He was, at least by reputation, the best supplier of beautiful, but expensive, women in Washington D.C.

As he downed the clear amber liquid from the shot glass, he marveled at how such a small amount of liquid could warm his body so quickly. *Nothing like bourbon to help you lose your troubles.* Not that Johnson had any troubles at present. As a matter of fact, he was feeling pretty good.

Earlier, he had received a call from one of his regular clients with a proposal, which would make any businessman proud. Although he was a little concerned with the slight risks involved in the deal, he could easily handle his concern when considering the money he would earn. Fifty thousand dollars was a goodly piece of change, even to Johnson, whose gross taxable income the year before would have placed him in the highest tax bracket, if he were into paying taxes.

The doorbell chimed twice before the heavy, dark-stained, double doors swung inward exposing a warm, spacious landing open to a cavern-like great room one floor below. As Kristina ushered Senator Peter Simpson in, he couldn't help but feel the encompassing warmth exuding from the house, almost as if he was entering his mother's home in Idaho on Thanksgiving day.

Kristina led him by the arm to the stairs curving down to the great room. She talked as they proceeded, "Senators Dobson, Martinez and Eagleton are already here and senators Davies and Williams will be here shortly. Let me take your coat."

Twenty minutes later all seven senators, representing the states of Oregon, Idaho, Arizona, Utah, Nebraska, Missouri, and Tennessee, were seated around the coffee table sipping coffee and hot chocolate Kristina had prepared for them. Their conversation wandered, but mostly focused on the late March storm that laid down ten inches of water-laden snow this morning in Washington.

They were a diverse group. Five of the senators were white, one was black and one was Hispanic. They also shared a diversity of faiths including two Catholics, one Mormon, two Baptists, one Methodist, and one Jew. Four were Republicans and three were Democrats. All but one were married and most had, at least, two children.

The one common thread pulling them together was a shared loathing for the corrupt and infectious political system entrenched in Washington. Their political philosophies ranged from conservative to moderately liberal. The purpose of their collaboration, however, had nothing to do with their own particular political agenda. The purpose was to correct the process by which political agendas were advanced. All knew they were sticking their political necks out a country mile, but all were willing to take the risk. They shared a deep fear the Constitution of the country was in peril and, if indeed it could be saved, they would sacrifice their political lives, if necessary, to save it.

Rick Benson raised his voice slightly and asked for everyone's attention so the meeting could start. He began speaking, "I really appreciate all of you making the effort tonight, with such short notice, to come into our home to discuss issues of importance to our country."

His understatement drew a couple of muted laughs. Senator Colin Williams, no relation to the senator from Texas (if he was, the racist senator from Texas would probably need an adjustment to his pacemaker since this senator was black), piped, "I wonder if we're the only seven congressmen in the country who believe what we're about to discuss is of any importance?"

Benson replied, "We might be the only genuine people's representatives in the U.S. Congress."

Benson continued, "I applaud all of you for having the courage to join with me in a literal attempt to change the course of our great Republic. As I'm sure you're all aware, as mostly freshman senators, none of us have a whole lot of clout individually. Even as a group, the rules of the Senate will prevent us from having significant impact on the way the organization controls the agenda. By joining together, however, we can greatly increase our influence with the news media and, thereby, overcome some of the procedural hurdles in the Senate. The possibility of bad exposure on TV can sometimes move mountains.

"We all need to go into this with our eyes open. Once we come out publicly against some of the senators and their pork-laden bills, the pressure directed toward us by both sides of the aisle will be immense. Each of our careers will be threatened and might possibly be crushed."

Benson paused for a few seconds. The quiet in the room was suffocating as the other senators fully realized the dangerous path they were about to tread.

Finally Senator Simpson from Idaho uttered in a hushed tone, "Rick, we all realize the risks we're taking. I believe we've all made up our minds that we have a higher duty. If anyone here feels like the risks are not worth it, I suggest that person leave now."

None left.

After another four hours of discussion and gallons of coffee and hot chocolate, the group of seven made several decisions that were sure to rock the American establishment, perhaps in ways even they could not comprehend. Each, realizing secrets of past indiscretions could be used as levers against them, agreed all such secrets, if they existed, would be made public. All pertinent communications with wives, families, and other appropriate people about any such revelations would be made over the next week, prior to a tell-all news conference to be held in ten days.

Senators Dobson and Martinez were initially hesitant to embrace such a bold move, fearing the public might view such actions as those of a bunch of nuts. They all realized, however, the public, though astounded, could not dismiss seven United States senators as nutcases, and the resulting invulnerability was necessary.

The group further decided to focus initially on several of the more egregious bills in the process of making their way through the Senate. Each of the selected bills represented the worst examples of corruption, with the under-the-table-contributions, paybacks, and secret compromises that were polluting the political process in the country. It was decided Senator Benson would chair the group, and the remaining six senators would divide up into two-man teams to focus on particular bills. Each agreed to make whatever arrangements were needed to hire top-notch investigators within their allocated staff budgets. Benson suggested former FBI agents might be considered.

Finally, it was determined an additional focus should be on the policies of the current and past administrations relative to the weakening of the military and defense posture around the world. The unprecedented reductions in the country's military manpower and deployments were serious concerns. Equally as troubling, was the sale of technology and inadequate security safeguards, all in the name of good politics and profits. In the view of the senators, such policies had severely denigrated American readiness to respond to future security challenges. The seven agreed to meet in a week to prepare for the upcoming news conference.

The president's secretary was fearful of disturbing the president because he had explicitly told her not to interrupt him for two hours. She suspected President Papadakis was not engaged in any matters of state or politics. She had glimpsed an attractive twenty-four-year-old staffer entering the private study adjacent to the oval office an hour earlier, followed by the president ten minutes later. Senator Williams was on the phone, however, and was adamant the president be disturbed. He said his need to talk with the president was of national importance and could not wait.

President Papadakis justified his moral indiscretion. The blonde staffer, Meghan Singleton, after all, had approached him and suggested her willingness to service him was out of her love for the country and its president. She had maintained, and Papadakis willingly agreed, the stress on the president of the most powerful country in the world was unique and, therefore, any relief available, even if it was sexual, was more than justified. Besides, his wife, Betty, he was sure, stayed married to him only to further her own ambitions. He could not remember the last time he had made love to her.

As he was admiring the voluptuous curve of Meghan's hip as she teasingly reclined naked on the sofa, the phone's ringing shattered the mood. The president screamed in the phone, "I thought I told you no interruptions!"

A wimpy, raspy voice said, "I'm terribly sorry, but Senator Williams is on the line and insists he talk with you immediately. I tried to put him off but he said it was of national importance."

The president replied, "You'd think I could find someone with enough balls to cover for me when I need it," not considering his secretary didn't possess such accessories. "Oh, what the hell. Put him through."

Twenty minutes later the president's secretary ushered Senator Williams into the president's office, noticing the disdaining glance from the president as she shut the door. President Papadakis abruptly asked. "What the hell is so damned important I had to interrupt an important meeting?"

Senator Williams replied equally as boldly in his gruff Texas drawl, "What is so damned important is the future of this beloved country of ours. I know you and I don't see eye to eye on a lot of political issues, but we do sing the same tune when it comes to how this game is played. Sure, there's money to be made and power to be had by each of us in our own way, but you and I both know we have the people's interest at heart. Hell! They need us to keep them fat, dumb, and happy. If the public is happy, then we're doing our job."

The president interrupted, "I resent your implication Senator."

Williams, not to be dissuaded, continued, "Mr. President, you know damned well what I'm talking about here. Do I need to remind you of our conversation two months ago where you agreed to support *Williams/Hackett* if our party backed off from its investigation of the Russian chip foul-up last November?"

Papadakis wondered where Williams was leading. He knew full well he shared Williams' philosophy about the American public. He was a steadfast believer the powerful, of whom he considered himself, were ordained to run the country. The citizens were there to be tricked into voting for the right person among the elite to lead them. Although he disdained putting it in the gross, politically incorrect terms of fat, dumb, and happy, he knew in his heart that was how the system worked. The senator's reminder of the compromise Papadakis was forced to make to keep under wraps the loss of rocket guidance chip technology to Russia late last year, quickly ended the facade of innocence.

The president skewered Williams with his stare and sternly asked, "OK. What do you want?"

As the Sunday dawn slowly overtook the darkness of night, Rick Benson lay on his back staring at the little monsters and silhouettes on his textured ceiling and wondered to himself if he was crazy. Last night he had found himself in a mini-argument with his wife who now lay, snoring softly, next to him. She justifiably was petrified about the direction upon which he was embarking, wondering what the future held for her and her three children. As hard as she tried, she could not rationalize putting their family at risk in order to clean up the Washington toilet. She argued Washington had functioned in its current mode for so long, what made him think he and his band of merry men could have any effect now?

He had to admit, she had a good point. He thought to himself, *What am I doing? How can I possibly survive against these powerful old men at the controls in this stink hole?* No way could he ever jeopardize his family or his relationship with his wife. Yet, nor could he deny the overpowering urge in his gut, an almost spiritual manifestation, that his mission, his reason for being, was to lead the effort to clean up the political mess in America. *Yes,* he thought, *I truly must be losing my mind!*

Chapter 7

Early April in Moscow was generally gray, cold, and snowy. Today, however, it was sunny, bright, and warm, at least for this time of year. Even the pollution, which normally smothered the hapless Muscovites, had taken a momentary break. The weather mirrored the disposition of the President of Russia.

Anitoli Lebedov had just concluded two days of top-secret meetings with the Chinese foreign minister. The meetings could not have concluded any better. Chou, after some tough questioning, initial hesitation, and several telephone calls to the Chinese central government, had fully embraced the final elements of the Russian proposal. Chou agreed to commit substantial military forces, including half-a-million troops, to ensure a successful conclusion to the plan. In return, China was guaranteed unfettered access to cheap oil far into the future.

Several months earlier, the Chinese, after comprehending the strategic implications, had agreed to share nuclear armament technology that had been obtained from the United States over the past few years. Some of the technology had been simply purchased from American companies; the rest obtained through extremely successful espionage efforts at the Los Alamos Nuclear Laboratory.

Lebedov was surprised the Americans, through a combination of eagerness to please the Chinese, lax security at the Laboratory, and a lack of awareness of geopolitical realities, would allow the loss of such highly classified technology so easily. Chou had related to the Russian president how relatively small, covert contributions to the political campaigns of key U.S. senators and the current American president had unlocked previously locked doors.

The newly acquired technology, combined with recent technological advancements in the Russian computer industry, allowed Russian and Chinese scientists to complete engineering and construction of extremely high-yield thermonuclear devices small enough to fit comfortably into the back of a full-size sport utility vehicle.

The just concluded agreement by the Chinese to implement joint military operations, if needed in Europe, represented the final piece in Lebedov's puzzle, and it was now in place. The Russian president was convinced if *Hammer and Anvil*, the name he and the Chinese agreed to call their rapidly developing plan, actually proceeded as planned, there would be no need for any hostilities in Europe. It was, however, vital to its success to have the Chinese fully engaged and ready to do whatever became necessary.

Mustafa Mohammed had successfully channeled his grief over the loss of his family into an all-encompassing hatred of Israel and America. His devotion to the Black October organization was total, and he was largely successful in submerging his grief into his subconscious by focusing his energies totally into all-consuming training. He vowed to be ready for any mission leading to the destruction of the American Satan and its protégé, the Zionists.

It was with a good deal of curiosity and anticipation that Mohammed observed two Russians entering the base training command in the Beqa'a valley in Lebanon. He wondered what possible subject the Black October leadership would have to discuss with the Russians. Even though he was a low-level operative within the terrorist group, Mohammed knew it had been years since the Russians had provided any kind of support for their cause.

Chapter 8

Candi Christopherson slowly strolled back down the dimly lit alley leading to the back entrance of her bungalow. Located on Jefferson Street, a downscale neighborhood of townhouses and apartments on the west side of Washington D.C., Candi's apartment was surprisingly well-furnished for a person without a regular day job. She did, however, work at the world's oldest profession and, judging by the quality of the furnishings in her apartment, was successful at it. As she strolled toward home she contemplated her conversation with her pimp, William Johnson, an hour earlier. Six thousand dollars for a night's work! *That's not bad*, she thought, *about ten times my normal nightly take. Besides, it will be fun, even challenging, to score with a member of the United States Senate—who doesn't want to be scored. And, from what Slick told me, the guy is a stuffed shirt, religious freak anyway.*

Cold, slushy rain drenched the beltway in earnest. The warm morning had blown away to be replaced by an unseasonably cold, windy storm, dumping rain mixed with snow.

Senator Benson, looking out his office window at the dreary scene outside, felt the weather fit his mood perfectly. A rush of thoughts stormed through his head. Knowing in less than two hours he and six other senators were most likely going to be committing group hara-kiri, he wondered why he had ever let himself get into this situation.

Why him? Why couldn't he have just been happy with his life in the Bureau. It was exciting, good money, weekends pretty much free, with time to spend with those who mattered most to him, Kristina and the kids. Now, he was beholden to another boss—time. As the leader of the infamous (at least to some elements in Washington) group of seven, he hadn't had time to sleep, let alone spend time at home.

He was amazed how fast the capital gossip mill had spread the word about the group, after holding only one "confidential" meeting at his home ten days earlier. He was even beginning to wonder if his home was bugged. The word secret was nonexistent in D.C. He thought to himself, *The only positive thing about the news stories focusing on the group was the media had yet to take a negative spin on the group's activities. Boy, would that change tonight. Wait until CNN or the networks heard the senators publicly exposing all of their warts.*

Benson had been shocked to his core three days earlier when he was told by some of his co-conspirators about the secrets hidden in their closets. Senator Dobson, the highly respected senator from Missouri, was going to discuss with the media tonight the two-year-long affair he had with his chief of staff while serving as governor six years earlier. His wife had come within the width of a snowflake to leaving him last week when he had told her about it.

Senator Williams was arrested for drunk driving two years ago, and Senator Eagleton was going to announce to the world he was gay. At least he didn't have to confess to a wife.

The senator's gnawing fear was that the media and public might be so shocked at the candid confessions, the important message they were trying to present would be lost. He and the other members of the group were unanimous, however, in their belief the risks of not disclosing their personal imperfections outweighed all other options. Once out, the stories would quickly fade and the group would be impervious to pressure, at least from one direction.

The game plan for the news conference was to have Senator Benson introduce the group and offer a short summary of the reason for the news conference. Each senator would, thereafter, briefly speak, outlining in broad terms what he hoped to accomplish through involvement with the group, and acknowledge any personal imperfections, if any existed. All the senators were prepared to field any questions the press might throw at them afterward.

The Renaissance Mayflower Hotel was a venerable but luxurious establishment with a spacious central ballroom with gigantic medieval looking red drapes, huge crystal chandeliers, and elaborate, rich, mahogany moldings. It could easily accommodate seven hundred people for dinner. It appeared to be packed, at least from Benson's vantage point behind the podium. His heart was pounding in his chest, and he subconsciously shoved the microphone away from him lest the assembled media hear the beating.

He inhaled deeply, tilted the microphone back toward his mouth and began speaking; "Hello! My name is Rick Benson. I'm from Oregon and the fine folks in that beautiful state elected me to come to this historic city to represent them in the United States Senate. I fervently hope that will still be their desire after tonight.

"I and my fellow senators, each of whom will be speaking briefly to you tonight, are here to outline to you the reasons we feel a need to join together in what's being called the group of seven. We feel strongly the country has veered sharply from the path that was laid out over two hundred years ago by some pretty courageous men who stuck their necks out a lot further than we're sticking ours out tonight."

Benson could hear the murmuring among the members of the press as they anticipated what might be coming next in his speech. He continued, "For several years you have heard candidates for various political offices around the country, both national and local, exclaim how tired they were of politics as usual and of the negative influences of this or that special interest. Candidates of both parties have been elected on promises to clean up the mess only to become part of it.

"We seven senators don't represent those politicians as usual. As you'll see in a few minutes, we're not perfect and have our weaknesses like everybody else. You'll also discover, however, we're willing to exhibit an unprecedented openness and candor. Hopefully by doing so, you'll view us in a different light than others, realizing we truly intend to do what we say we'll do regardless of the consequences to our own political futures.

"We intend, over the next several months, to focus on a few specific areas of our government, initially with the intention of illuminating some of, what we consider, the most significant threats to our democracy. We intend to ferret out and expose the backroom deals worked out in darkness by those whom the citizens of our great land have elected to hold their trust. Our aim is to illuminate that darkness so you, who constitutionally should have the right to know what's going on in your government, will become aware of the grave danger all Americans face today to their democracy.

"We maintain many of the bills recently passed, and some currently in the process, are not what they seem. Compromise, which is advertised as an art practiced by true practitioners of democracy, has become a method of ensuring those in power stay in power. What's good for the country has become what's good for the senator or congressman or even the president."

The murmuring in the hall almost became bedlam at Benson's last utterance. Never had the Washington press corps heard anyone, other than recognized kooks, take on the power in Washington so directly. They would easily dismiss Benson as just another one except for the presence of six other senators behind him. Many wondered out loud how the poor soul at the podium ever hoped to complete his first term, let alone, have any future in American politics.

After pausing a moment for the bedlam to quiet, Benson continued, "The first step we'll take will be to oppose publicly the four most egregious bills currently under consideration in the Senate. Two of these are defense bills strongly supported by the Senate leadership on both sides of the political aisle, one is a welfare reform bill, and the fourth is a bill to raise the trade status of Russia to that of an equal trade partner with the United States. The latter two are strongly supported by the president, most Democrats, and a significant number of Republicans.

"We think all four bills contain provisions in them that pose direct threats to our Constitution, not necessarily because of the advertised intention of the bills, but because of the unseen motivations and process by which the bills are being pushed through the Senate."

Virtually all members of the media were sitting in the room in utter shock. With mouths agape, they wondered if this idiot freshman senator from Oregon was playing with all of his marbles. Then, as they again realized there were six other senators sitting behind him apparently sharing the same opinions, a feeling of unease enveloped them.

Benson finished, "I know many, if not all of you, are wondering if I've lost my bearings in this world. Let me assure you, I know exactly what I'm doing. I know my neck is out a mile, but I want to impress upon each of you the importance of what we're going to be doing. Our careers aren't worth the cost of spit and neither is yours if our great Republic continues down the current road. Ignorance is bliss but it's also our ruin, and I, and the other senators on this stand with me, will do all in our power to save this blessed country from ruin."

Senator Benson then introduced Senator Dobson as the next speaker.

Senator Dobson, and the other five senators, shocked the assembled journalists even further as they outlined their agendas and, in some cases, openly washed their dirty linen.

When the speechmaking was over, the questions posed to the senators were surprisingly few. Apparently the media hounds were too dazed to ask intelligent questions. Benson and the others knew full well, however, the lack of questions now did not, by any means, indicate they would not be in for intense scrutiny tomorrow.

But tonight they all felt intense relief to have this over with, to have finally launched their campaign to save the Constitution. Had any of them known what they had really launched and how their actions would impact their lives in unimaginable ways, perhaps most would not have done what they did. But, at the moment, the exhilaration clouded out thoughts of what might be.

One of the architects of the current state-of-the-art of compromise, Senator Williams from Texas, had just finished reading the front-page story in the *Washington Post* under the inch high heading “Group of Seven Claim Abuse of Power”. His gnarled, age-spotted hands could not stop shaking as his rage boiled just under his skin.

Those sons of bitches, he thought repeatedly in his mind. As he stewed, he slowly began forming a plan. He picked up the telephone to dial one of the several calls he intended to make. Interrupting the third ring, a raspy voice, without uttering any sort of greeting, mumbled, “Johnson, what d’ya want?”

Chapter 9

Mohammed sat in the dimly lit hut with three other Palestinians who he had never met, but who, based on the striped kaffiyehs they were wearing, were freedom-fighters like himself. It was obvious from the others' reactions, they didn't know each other either. None of them spoke, even in an attempt to make small-talk. Mohammed guessed they, like him, were too nervous to talk. Ever since he was told two hours earlier to report to the top-secret Palestinian internal affairs headquarters at the training camp, he had been sweating bullets. Although he did not know what really went on inside the complex of huts and permanent stone buildings, he had heard plenty of rumors and none of them sounded pleasant.

The first of the Palestinian freedom-fighters was ordered to stand up and was escorted by a mean-looking, older Palestinian, carrying a nine millimeter Glock automatic, into an adjacent doorway leading to one of the few stone buildings in the complex. Mohammed listened hard, trying to hear sounds of a beating, screams, or some other evidence of torture or worse. He heard nothing. His mind was racing. What had he done to deserve to be tortured or killed in some horrible manner? He racked his brain to think of something he had done to warrant such an awful fate.

After about fifteen minutes, the mean-looking guard returned alone through the same door he and the first Palestinian had exited. When he motioned for Mohammed to get up and accompany him, Mohammed had to use every bit of mind control he could muster to avoid urinating in his pants. He did his best to avoid collapsing on his shaky knees and somehow managed to lead the grizzled, old Palestinian with the menacing automatic through the door into the adjacent building. Once inside the building, the guard motioned for him to continue forward toward what looked like a steel-plated door at the far end of a long hallway. The guard reached in front of Mohammed, grabbed the round door handle, and, not too gently, pushed him into the room with the palm of his hand placed squarely in the center of Mohammed's back. He almost tripped, but was able to stagger into the room without falling.

He looked up and observed the room was furnished with some decent furniture and other decor, strikingly different than all of the other buildings or huts throughout the camp. At the back of the room was a large, heavy, wooden table with a single, out-of-place looking chair on Mohammed's side of the table.

On the other side sat three men, one he recognized as the camp commander, Colonel Hamid Sabavi, whose most distinguishing feature was the eye patch he wore over his left eye. The other two appeared to be Eastern European, probably Russian, judging from the military uniforms they were wearing. Mohammed was beginning to breathe a little easier. It was obvious no one was going to be beaten or tortured here.

The colonel gestured to Mohammed to sit down on the single chair, which he obediently did. Sabavi first pointed in the direction of the soldier to his right and said, "Please meet Colonel Ivan Litinov." He then motioned left and said, "This is Major Leonid Gorkny."

After the brief introductions, Sabavi told Mohammed he had been the object of scrutiny for the past several months, ever since his successful mission in Germany. Mohammed gulped, *Scrutiny for what?*

Sabavi continued, "You can be proud of all you've done since then. You have worked hard at the camp and have demonstrated, in spite of your grievous personal losses, a dedication to our cause that's exemplary to those with whom you train. As a result, you have been nominated to be part of a mission."

He paused and stared intently into Mohammed's eyes before continuing, "A mission that will forever change the course of history and will finally, once and for all, return our stolen lands back to us. We will be true Palestinians once again and, at the same time, rid ourselves of the Zionist whoremongers and occupiers."

The colonel went on to explain the mission would be fraught with danger, more than likely costing Mohammed his life. That prospect did not frighten Mohammed. Dying for the cause of freedom would be an honor. Many times since the bombing of his family, he had contemplated participating in a suicide mission and how glorious death would be under those circumstances.

Colonel Sabavi finished by telling Mohammed he was to continue training even harder than in the past and would be given additional training to prepare him for a yet-unidentified mission. The colonel stood up and Mohammed knew the discussion was concluded.

Chapter 10

Candi Christopherson was sitting pretty. Slick, who sometimes could be such a flaming jerk, was, today, her sugar daddy. He had just given her a down payment of one thousand dollars in cold cash and had upped the ante to ten thousand after she completed her assignment. Granted, the assignment was not without risks, but for ten thousand dollars just about any risk was okay. It seemed pretty simple. All she had to do was perform some rudimentary acting and tell a good story to the police, and she'd be ten grand to the better.

As an added bonus, her acting debut was to take place at the Washington D.C., Grand Hyatt Hotel, a pretty plush establishment, not like the places she normally frequented. She hurriedly waved down a taxi. She needed a couple of hours at her flat to fix herself properly and get emotionally prepared for her assignment tonight.

Saturdays were becoming less and less the welcome break in Rick Benson's routine than they used to be. With the pressures he was now facing, it was a rare Saturday when he could find time to be home with his family. This Saturday had been a welcome exception. So it was with extreme reluctance, he agreed, after taking the telephone call at his home just after noon, to meet the unnamed caller at the Grand Hyatt Hotel later in the evening.

The caller had told him he had information concerning the *Williams/Hackett bill*, which would nail Senator Williams' butt to the Senate wall. He claimed his information would enable Benson to prove criminal activity by the senator from Texas. He would not give any additional information over the phone but told Benson to meet him at 8:00 p.m. in room 673. Benson was to knock three—then four times to identify himself.

After hanging up the phone, Benson wondered if he was losing his mind. Was he becoming a fanatic? What was going to be the end of all of this? Even though his gut told him this was a foolish thing to do, his curiosity and urge for the kill had got the better of him, so he agreed to the meeting. Now he wondered if he should call any of the other senators or, perhaps, one of his ex FBI buddies. No! The caller said he should come alone or he wouldn't give him the information. *Besides*, Benson thought, *I've been trained to do this and have been in more risky situations before.* Benson strode back into the kitchen where his wife was fixing lunch for the family.

"Who was that?" she asked.

Benson, who normally didn't keep much from his wife, answered, "It was just a guy who said he had some information that might be helpful in a staff investigation."

He wondered why he was suddenly reluctant to share more information with her. Could it be he was more nervous about the dangers involved than he was admitting? He decided he would have to think about how much to share with her. He would have to tell her something eventually, anyway, since she would obviously wonder why he had to leave home later that night.

Kristina replied, "You and your investigations. You're going to get an ulcer! Anyway, your sandwich is ready."

Candi exited the Taxi at precisely 6:55 p.m., five minutes before the time Slick had told her to be at the hotel. She grabbed the lapels of her leather coat and pulled them tighter around her as a surprisingly cold gust of wind swirled up the street.

Her jet-black hair blew across her face momentarily hiding her Mediterranean profile. Candi, with a little bit of luck and a different set of parents, assuming she had a set, since she only knew her mother, could have been a supermodel. Her striking outward appearance, with a naturally-tanned olive complexion, long curly hair, high cheekbones, dark brown almond eyes, and full sensuous lips, could find her on the cover of *Vogue* magazine under different circumstances. With a curvy, voluptuous body to match, she was renown in the local market.

The thirty-second walk to the front entrance of the hotel seemed longer because of the cold and her nervousness. She rehearsed in her mind what she would say to the senator and the subsequent actions she would take. She tried to imagine the senator's shock when she stripped her clothes off and screamed. If he was anything like the prude Slick had described, he might have a coronary on the spot.

Actually, Candi was certain she could seduce him without having to go through the charade of being raped. She'd never met a man who wouldn't succumb to her charms, and when the police caught him in the act with her, his reputation was shot, rape or not. But, Slick had insisted she do it his way, so she figured for ten grand she would stand on her head and blow bubbles if that was what Slick wanted.

The one real worry she had was timing. What if the police did not arrive on-cue with her scream? She thought, *Boy! Would I ever have a tough time explaining my way out of that to the senator. How ironic this whole situation is. Slick, my law avoiding pimp, depending on the law to save me from a United States senator.*

Per Slick's instructions, using her real name, Candi checked into the hotel and requested suite 673. She plopped down three, hundred dollar bills, received a small amount of change and tucked it into her leather purse. As she walked toward the elevator at the opposite side of the expansive lobby, she could feel the eyeballs of the hotel clerk drilling holes in her swaying hips.

Benson wondered as he rode in the back of the Yellow cab, *What the heck am I doing?* Here he was, on the way to meet a total stranger who was going to give him what? He had no idea. His obsession was now taking over his common sense. At least he should have called a couple of his FBI friends, but they would have probably thought he was nuts to go running after such an obscure lead. He did feel good about the decision to tell his wife about the meeting. He would have felt extreme guilt had he outright lied to her, even to protect her.

He didn't tell her about the apprehension he was feeling though. Why worry her needlessly? Her reaction was one of disappointment he had to go, but didn't appear to be one of undue worry or fear. For that he was glad, at least he thought he was glad.

His thoughts were interrupted by a voice from the front of the cab. "Okay Senator, we're approaching the Grand Hyatt. I appreciate your business this evening".

The senator paid the fare, tipped the cabbie, and quickly hurried into the front lobby of the hotel to avoid the cold wind.

He glanced at his wristwatch, noting he would be a few minutes late for his appointment by the time he rode the elevator up to the sixth floor. *Oh well*, he thought, *if the guy is legitimate, he'll wait a few minutes.*

He walked briskly toward the elevators not noticing two swarthy-looking types, seated in the recessed lounge area in the middle of the lobby, following his movements with their eyes, both peering over the top edges of the *Washington Post.*

Benson located room 673 about fifty paces to the left after exiting the elevator. He took a deep breath and rapped his knuckles three times on the door, paused for a couple of seconds, and rapped four more times. He heard a deep male voice from inside say, “Come in”. He entered the room and immediately was aware of a strong, familiar, but unidentified odor.

The room was dark and the door slamming behind him made him jump. He began to ask why the lights were out when, suddenly, the room was illuminated in bright light. He immediately saw on the bed a naked, dark-haired female body covered with crimson blood. Blood was also spattered on the walls and had pooled around the body on the bed.

As he opened his mouth to utter his shock, he felt a vice-like grip on both shoulders and a cloth-draped hand cover his mouth and nose. The unidentified odor was extremely strong now as he struggled to free himself. As his consciousness ebbed away, he faintly heard the sound of police sirens.

Chapter 11

Colby Engeman was stymied. How could the Mossad have failed so miserably at identifying the target in Germany? After working so painstakingly long to plant a mole in the newly formed Black October terrorist group, the net result was over seventy dead people in Germany and several times that number of corpses in Jordan, albeit caused by his own countrymen. Engeman, a thirty-nine year old former emergency-room doctor, didn't differentiate between the two. The fact is, had his contact within the terrorist group provided timely information, none of the dead would have become dead in the first place.

Engeman never imagined being a spy. He was born in Aurora, Colorado, as the fourth child of John and Carol Engeman. John was an FBI agent, so Colby's spying instinct, perhaps, came naturally. He, however, never desired to follow in his dad's footsteps, focusing, instead, on a lifelong dream to become an emergency-room physician. He completed medical school at the Medical College of Wisconsin at Milwaukee, a four-year residency in Detroit, and was hired as a night-shift, emergency-room doctor at Presbyterian St. Lukes Medical Center in Denver, Colorado.

Six years later he was a key field officer in the Israeli Mossad, likely the best intelligence agency in the World. His circuitous route from the emergency room to the spy world could be the basis for a book itself. Suffice it to say, his Jewish heritage, coupled with a chance encounter with a high level Mossad officer, who just happened to require trauma care at St. Lukes, resulted in his current predicament. His wife, Amanda, and three children, though severely tested, initially, with the move to Israel, had now grown accustomed to the daily, tense routine of Israeli life.

Engeman longed for more time to spend with his family, but he felt—more like hoped—that Amanda understood the importance of what he was doing. Her understanding and support of his decision to give up a lucrative medical practice to move to Israel spoke volumes about their relationship.

Engeman had spent the last twelve months recruiting and training two Israeli Palestinians in a bold attempt to infiltrate the Black October organization. One of the operatives had gotten himself killed after a chance meeting with a former Arab neighbor, who recognized him as a friend of Israeli neighbors in the local community. Apparently, as a result, he could not convince the other terrorists he hated Israelis sufficiently.

The second recruit, Uday Mahmud, appeared to have been much more successful. He was actually assigned, originally, as one of the operatives for the Hamburg bombing but was replaced, early on, by a more seasoned terrorist. He had not been briefed, unfortunately, on the operation sufficiently to identify the nature of the operation and its location before it was launched. As was normally the case with terrorist organizations, information was highly segregated on a need-to-know basis.

This morning, shortly after Engeman had begun his workday at 7:00, he received a fax from Uday indicating a much bigger operation was being planned. No other details were available. Uday also stated the security surrounding this operation was extremely tight and any inquiries on his part would look suspicious. He ended with, "Hopefully, more to follow."

Engeman thought to himself, *"Hopefully, more to follow" won't cut it if we hear about the operation after the fact like the Hamburg bombing. A much bigger operation? Hell, that could be a WMD attack. And to think, I could be practicing medicine.*

Colonel Litinov waited patiently in the outer room of the office of the President of Russia. He never liked the occasional forays inside the inner walls of the Kremlin. He much preferred the association of fellow soldiers, whom he trusted almost completely, compared to civilians and ass-kissing generals in the Kremlin, with their vacillations and hidden agendas.

He knew the information he had to pass on to President Lebedov was important. He had not even had time to change his work uniform, after returning from Lebanon, before being summoned to meet with the president.

Suddenly, the heavy, double doors to the inner office opened and President Lebedov, himself, appeared with a hand on each door and welcomed the colonel to his office. Colonel Litinov, after snapping to attention, relaxed slightly and followed the president into his office. As they were walking, Lebedov said, "Colonel, it's a pleasure to welcome you to my office. I know you must be tired after your long flight back this morning. I appreciate your willingness, however, to come directly here from the airport. What we will discuss has huge implications for the future of our country. Please take a seat."

Litinov waited a few seconds for the president to sit and then relaxed into a comfortable armchair across a huge, mahogany desk from President Lebedov. The colonel was astounded at the opulence of the office. Huge bookshelves stocked with books lined the walls and thick, red-velvet drapes adorned the twelve-foot-high windows at the back. He was somewhat shocked to observe the old hammer and sickle flag of the former Soviet Union hanging limply next to the current flag of the Russian Republic.

Lebedov asked, "What did you find out in Lebanon?"

Chapter 12

Benson slowly regained consciousness. He first observed a blurry figure off to his right who appeared to be hovering over him. Other blurry figures were likewise hovering in the air further away to his left. Slowly the first apparition evolved into a more recognizable form.

Benson heard a familiar voice that appeared to be calling out to him from the distance, “Rick, Rick, wake up!”

“Where am I?”

“Rick, you’re home.”

“What happened?”

“Wait a few minutes until you’re really awake and I’ll explain.”

Benson slowly became more alert, recognizing his wife Kristina, standing next to him by the bed. He recognized Special Agent George Petrosky, an old friend and fellow agent from his Bureau days. He also saw two other dark-suited, middle-aged men whom he assumed were also FBI agents.

Kristina spoke first, “Rick, after you told me about your meeting this evening, I called George to ask him if the anxiety I was feeling was warranted, and he said he trusted my instincts, so he would recruit some help and drive over to the Grand Hyatt just to make sure things were as they should be.”

With a breaking voice, Kristina said, “Honey, you might be dead if I hadn’t called them.”

Tears streamed down her face as she tried to continue. After stammering a few other words, Special Agent Petrosky broke in and proceeded to fill in the details.

He stated, “As soon as we arrived at the Hotel, we knew something didn’t smell right. I asked the desk clerk if anyone had checked into room 673 and she replied a hooker, named Candi, had checked into the room, after paying cash, just ten minutes earlier. We immediately went up to the room, heard scuffling noises, so kicked in the door. As soon as the door flew open into the room, two hoods, who appeared to be mugging you, turned toward us with guns drawn, which was a fatal mistake on their part.

"Rick, it was a mess in the room. The prostitute was dead on the bed with her throat slit. You were unconscious on the floor, and the two thugs were both bleeding all over the floor from multiple gunshot wounds. No more than two minutes later, six members of Washington's finest arrived at the scene. They seemed to be more surprised at seeing us than all of the dead bodies strewn about the room."

Benson asked, "George, what do you think is going on?"

Petrosky grimaced, "I don't know Rick. The cops allege they had received a telephone call from the hotel claiming someone was dead in room 673. One, a Sergeant Kerry, tried to imply that, perhaps you had something to do with the death of the prostitute, in spite of the fact you were unconscious, and there were two dead goons on the floor.

"Someone doesn't like you very much. That's for damn sure. It appears the goons used ether to knock you out, and who knows what they had planned after that? It's too bad we can't ask them. At any rate, we will launch a full court press to get to the bottom of this."

With a wink, Petrosky exclaimed, "We feds don't take kindly to crimes committed against elected representatives of the people."

Senator Williams was shouting in the telephone receiver, "What the hell happened? You couldn't have screwed this up any worse! I never told you to kill anybody, and now three people are dead. What the hell were you thinking?"

On the other end of the call, Slick Willie stammered, "I, I, I don't know what happened. They weren't supposed to kill the hooker. It was just supposed to be a setup for the senator."

Senator Williams thundered, "Isn't that just great? They kill the whore and then get caught, apparently trying to mug the piss-ant from Oregon, when the FBI arrives. How in the hell did the feds get wind of this? Who did you talk to, Johnson ?"

"I didn't talk to nobody", Slick blurted out, "I promise on my mother's grave I ain't said nothin to nobody."

Williams snarled, "You'd better be telling the truth dickhead or your ass is toast. Can the hoods who screwed this up be traced to you?"

Johnson, somewhat relieved he was being asked an answerable question replied, "No, I made sure they didn't know who they were dealing with. They were only interested in the cash, and I handled that through a mail drop. Besides, they're dead."

“All right,” Williams said, “Stay out of sight, but make sure I know where I can reach you.” With that, Williams hung up the phone.

“Damn, what a shit hole of a mess,” Williams said in an exasperated whisper. *Perhaps*, he thought to himself, *this is still not totally unrecoverable. I wonder?* He again picked up the telephone and phoned the President of the United States of America.

Chapter 13

Uday Mahmud was in way over his head. He had successfully infiltrated the Black October organization. His success, however, was also his vulnerability. Ever since he had been approached by one of the cell leaders, Mustafa Mohammed, and agreed to be part of his cell, the restrictions imposed on his movements and communications had prevented him from making any contact with Engeman. It was made abundantly clear, because of the extremely important nature of the mission for which they were training, any breach of the security protocols would result in immediate termination—not just from the mission.

Uday had spent the better part of the last two years preparing for this. He had lost his mother and a sister to the insanity of the Israeli-Palestinian conflict, both blown up with ten other Palestinians and seven Israelis. They were eating lunch at a small café in Haifa, when a fanatic Palestinian suicide murderer blew herself up in the café.

He, for sure, had issues with the Israeli government, particularly the double-standard that existed in the country. But, he also realized he had more civil rights in Israel than fellow Arabs enjoyed in any other country in the Middle East, and it was very possible he could enjoy even more, if the insane conflict could be ended.

Uday realized, from the security in place, and the little tidbits of information he had gleaned from Mohammed, the operation in the works was big, dwarfing even the Al Qaeda attack on September 11, 2001. He had, however, no clues relevant to what it was, where it was, and when it was. He did have a sense of foreboding that whatever was being planned would be of such magnitude, the world would never be the same afterward.

The little, yellow dog wagged its tail at two joggers who passed him on the bike trail, one of many former railroad track beds converted to bike and jogging paths in the vicinity of Kansas City, Missouri. The dog, a Heinz 57 mutt, looked a little like a miniature yellow lab.

Nobody seemed to know his owner, yet he seemed to be well-fed. He was a regular visitor to the jogging path, and, even though it was against the law to let a dog wander off leash, none of the joggers and bikers minded his presence. He was just part of the experience.

Chapter 14

The *New York Times* headlined the story, “President Questions Presence of Oregon Senator at Murder Scene”. Similar headlines graced the front pages of other elite newspapers throughout the country. The gist of the accompanying articles was a transparent attempt by the president to smear Senator Benson, alleging his presence at the scene of a Washington homicide had sinister implications. Prior to the *Times*’ article, no newspaper had even reported the senator was present at the scene of a murder of a local prostitute—up to that point the murder had only rated back-page coverage.

Benson vainly attempted to hold the newspaper steady as he seethed with rage at the implication in the article. He came to the shocking realization, either the president knew something about the incident, or was so callous he would be willing to make political points over such a tragedy. As hard as he tried to dismiss the idea, he began formulating in his mind the possibility the president was an accomplice to murder.

Benson was certain his friend, Agent Petrosky, would have protected his identity. He wasn’t, however, confident the D.C. police were so trustworthy. Even so, how could the president have become aware of the circumstances surrounding the incident so quickly, unless he had some inside connection?

Benson decided to call Petrosky to see what the FBI had turned up on the case. He dialed the number on his cell phone and received a voice message the agent was not available but would return the call. Benson slowly hung up the phone wondering how he had got himself in such a mess. Not only was he now up against the Senate establishment, but the popular leader of the free world was now his enemy.

The Sunday talk shows were abuzz with the current Washington scandal. Senator Williams from Texas was on *Fox News Sunday* and the president’s press secretary appeared on *Meet the Press*.

Both exclaimed they had no evidence of any impropriety on the part of Senator Benson, but his presence at the scene of a brutal murder of a local prostitute in Washington earlier in the week, certainly raised troublesome questions. Both suggested Senator Benson ought to explain to the American people what business he possibly had with a prostitute, and what information he had that could help clear up the murder. Neither directly accused the senator of any wrongdoing, knowing full-well the viewing public, by implication, would assume the senator was hiding some sordid details of the incident.

Neither man anticipated the bombshell headlines Monday morning, however, when the *Washington Post* broke a story turning the brewing scandal on its head. The *Post* headline read, “FBI Reports Oregon Senator Setup”. The article quoted a reliable but unnamed source in the FBI, who said the Bureau was investigating the Washington D.C. murder of a local prostitute and possible attempted murder of a United States senator. According to the source, the FBI was working on the theory the senator was lured to the scene under false pretenses, either to embarrass and implicate him in the murder, or to set him up for murder himself. The source further alleged the focus of the investigation could lead to powerful men in the capital.

The *Post* reporter, Jack Strum went on to say no other information was furnished, but his source was impeccable. He speculated on who the powerful men might be, reminding the readers of Senator Benson’s recent press conference alleging corruption in the national government. Strum editorialized it would be hard to imagine political differences could cause anyone in government to resort to criminal activity. He acknowledged, however, he certainly did not have the information the FBI possessed.

Chapter 15

The sun was unusually merciless on this late spring day in Lebanon. Heat radiated in shimmering waves from the parched, baked, pale earth surrounding the training camp in the Beqa'a valley.

Mohammed, in spite of his zeal and dedication to the cause, found it difficult to focus on the multiple tasks at hand. He felt his brain cooking inside of his skull. He was not fully aware of the scope of the training taking place in the camp, but knew there were over a hundred freedom-fighters like himself engaged in relentless, almost nonstop training.

Mohammed, with the other three members of his cell, in addition to weapons and explosives training, were also taking a crash course in Americanism, including both American English and culture. He and his comrades had long since shaved their facial hair. They were ordered to speak English when not in class or training and concentrate on being American—not a mean feat when considering the hatred they all bore toward America.

When driving was necessary, they drove the American family station wagon, a Chevy Suburban. Several training hours were even devoted on the Suburban; how to make minor repairs, maximize gas mileage, park in tight spaces, and drive it in emergency situations. Mohammed was becoming very familiar with cornering ability, acceleration, and performance at maximum speeds.

He and his other cell members occasionally speculated where this was all headed, but only when they were alone and away from the camp, which was seldom. Mohammed had heard other freedom-fighters in other cells talking about a WMD attack on America but figured they were just speculating, like he was.

Security precautions, however, were extremely restrictive. He and his cellmates were prohibited from talking with others about ongoing training, and Mohammed had heard enough rumors of what happened to those who violated the security procedures, he didn't care to test them. All had sworn an oath to Allah, at the beginning of training, that the mission could not be compromised, even if that meant turning in or even killing a fellow team member whose actions were suspect.

All of this, the long hours, lack of sleep, no contact outside the camp, the heat, and unrelenting tension, was all worth it. Mohammed knew the payoff, whatever it was, would be decisive against the Zionists and the Satan of the earth, America. He could feel it in his soul, it was different this time. America would surely feel the righteous wrath of Allah for all of the suffering his people had endured due to the decadence and imperial pompousness of the United States. And Mustafa Mohammed was going to be an instrument in the hand of Allah to accomplish this righteous retribution.

Engeman was worried. He had not heard a word from Uday Mahmud for over a month now, and the last message that was left on his voice mail simply said, "I'm in. Something big is in the works. No time." Engeman passed on the message to his superior, Colonel Moshe Dylan, who rightly inquired, "What the hell does that mean?"

Engeman had no answers for him. He was aware Israeli intelligence had picked up increased activity in two training camps in Lebanon, but he didn't know if this had anything to do with Mahmud's message.

Inquiries with the CIA and European agencies revealed no further details. Engeman surmised they probably preferred to not know anything, or, at least, the political appointees who headed each of the agencies were of that mindset. He still had great respect for his contacts at the CIA, knowing the field officers were dedicated, hard-working individuals who still perceived the world was a perilous place, perhaps even more so now. He also highly respected CIA Director William Smith, but knew his ability to direct the agency was heavily constrained by the politicians in Washington.

He also suspected the politicians in the West had made their deals with evil, and in their best imitations of Neville Chamberlain, were convinced "peace for our time" had been achieved again. He suspected what had really been accomplished was to setup the West for terror attacks in the near future, which none of the Chamberlain imposters could remotely fathom.

The growing isolation of Israel had led to drastic increases in Israeli defense expenditures as Israel strived to become virtually security independent. The Israeli defense industry had invented, built, and installed the world's most sophisticated anti-missile/aircraft defense system. Its armaments industry was churning out the best tanks made anywhere in the world as well as aircraft second to none. And, perhaps, most ominously, Israel covertly expanded its nuclear arsenal to over five hundred warheads deliverable on a combination of aircraft and ballistic missiles.

The ER doc, turned Mossad agent, was confident in his adopted country's ability to withstand any attack from outside Israel's borders. So he wondered, *Why do I continue to feel such a sense of foreboding?*

Chapter 16

FBI Director Sydney Wilkinson, a former U.S. Attorney from Ohio, had been appointed to his current position, with unanimous Senate confirmation, by president Papadakis' predecessor. Director Wilkinson was a tall, lanky, fifty-five year-old, who, if pushed, could rip a new hole in anybody's rear end. He had a shock of gray hair that always seemed to be flying in several directions at once, and, when he was angered, observers would say his hair stood on end.

On this typically hot, muggy, summer Washington day, where cars and people seemed to shimmer when viewed out of a Washington office window, the FBI director was angry. He had received a telephone call earlier in the day from the White House appointments secretary, who had requested the director meet with the president at the White House at 2:00 p.m. His relationship with the current president was cool, at best, so he did not anticipate a pleasant conversation.

After arriving promptly at 2:00, he was directed to take a seat in the outer office where he had now been waiting for a half-hour. Finally, the secretary ushered him into the oval office where the president, sitting behind the expansive, oval-office desk, didn't say a word until Wilkinson approached the desk. Then, without bothering to stand to greet him, shake his hand, or offer the FBI director a seat, he launched into a tirade, berating Wilkinson about the FBI leak to the *Washington Post*.

Without allowing a response, the president accused Wilkinson of orchestrating the leak to embarrass him, and threatened to take action to remove the director from his position if he would not retract the information contained in the story.

The president closed his tirade by demanding, "You, Mr. Director, will discontinue this witch hunt you call an investigation immediately. Many honorable men, who have no other motive than to serve the American people, have been slandered by your FBI snitch. Any implication the murder of a drug-addicted whore, as part of a plot to setup Mr. Benson, can be traced to any officials in the government is ludicrous and will do neither you, nor your career any good!"

Finally, when the director was allowed to speak, he calmly replied the president did not appoint him and could not fire him. He didn't need to remind the president of the laws passed during the Watergate debacle that established the immunity of the FBI director from the whims of the sitting president.

Director Wilkinson then pointedly said, "Mr. President, I don't know, at this time, who contacted the *Washington Post.* It certainly wasn't something I supported or would support. As a matter of fact, I have directed the Bureau to investigate the leak, so appropriate action can be taken against the responsible persons.

"You need to know, however, the content of the report is true. The Bureau does suspect the senator was setup by someone in Washington D.C. who, in my view, is a traitor to this nation. The ability to have public discourse over political differences without fear of retribution is what has set our nation apart, and made us the beacon for the world for almost 240 years. When political power becomes the end in itself—when powerful people begin to believe their government positions are rights to be protected at all costs, forgetting they are supposed to be elected by and serve the citizens of this country, then we're on the road to oblivion as a democracy. The FBI will continue to investigate this case wherever it might lead, and that includes anybody and any office, even this one."

The president exploded, "Do you know who you are talking to? I'm probably the most popular President of the United States in recent history. If this comes down to a contest, you'll lose. Your implication I could possibly have something to do with this is asinine! You need to see a shrink to determine if you are fit to remain in your job."

Director Wilkinson bored in on the president with cold, blue eyes and, holding his emotions in check with great effort, said acidly, "Mr. President, and I say that with utter disdain, you have only steeled my conviction to pursue this investigation to its conclusion. I pray for the country my instincts are wrong, and you played no part in this mess. But, Mr. President, I will find out."

Wilkinson completed a military-like about-face and walked swiftly out of the room, leaving the president stammering something unintelligible behind his desk.

Chapter 17

President Lebedov and foreign minister Chou were seated at the huge table, finishing dinner in the spacious, dark-paneled dining room. The almost-black, mahogany table could easily seat fifty guests. The table dwarfed Lebedov and Chou and the three high-ranking military officers who were privileged to dine with them. The President of Russia, who so disdained the United States, had just finished off a distinctly American meal of prime rib and garlic-mashed potatoes and was about to consume a hot-fudge sundae. His Chinese guest was passing on the sundae, content to sip a cup of green tea.

Colonel Litinov, just returned from one of his many recent trips to Lebanon, was a guest of the president on this occasion, so he could brief the foreign minister and the generals on the status of the preparations in Lebanon.

After scooping out the last vestiges of chocolate in the bottom of the sundae dish, President Lebedov looked over at the colonel and asked with disdainful emphasis, "Well, Colonel, how are our Arab zealots doing in Lebanon?"

Colonel Litinov paused briefly before answering, caught off guard with the direct question. After collecting his thoughts he replied, "President, Prime Minister Chou, and distinguished generals, I'm pleased to report to you we're on schedule with our training. Currently, twelve four-man teams are going through extensive training in a secret location in Lebanon's Beqa'a valley. To hide their activities we have arranged for training of an additional five hundred Palestinian fighters in other locations in the valley. We feel confident Israeli intelligence has concentrated on these and is oblivious to the targeted training of the twelve teams."

The Chinese foreign minister interrupted, "What about other security measures? Any possibility of a breach could bring disaster to us all."

Litinov answered, "All security measures that are possible are in place. Each cell is independent from the others. No outside communication is permitted. We have guards watching the guards who watch the trainees. Even if, by some minute chance, a spy infiltrated the camp, there would be no way for the infiltrator to communicate. All cell phones have been confiscated and are assigned out only on a per-mission basis, if needed to complete the mission. We have state-of-the-art equipment in place to immediately triangulate any calls made in the camp. Each team member has sworn an oath to kill anybody who attempts to breach security protocols. I assure you all, no security violation is possible."

President Lebedov added, "Colonel Litinov has also assured me no mission details have been discussed with any of the Arabs. As far as they know, they will be driving explosives through building walls, similar to what happened in Hamburg, only, in this case, they know they are on suicide missions."

Minister Chou, still not convinced asked, "Will they be ready for insertion on schedule?"

Litinov replied, "We will be ready to insert all twelve teams by late September."

The discussion continued for another twenty minutes as the colonel fleshed in the details of training and logistical arrangements being put in place. Chou, appearing satisfied, indicated his weariness, and President Lebedov obliged and ended the meeting. They would have more time in the morning to discuss additional details and answer any lingering questions.

Chapter 18

"That son-of-a-bitching bureaucrat", Senator Williams snarled. "Who the hell does he think he is?"

"That's what I asked him", said President Papadakis, "but the pompous ass wasn't fazed. I'm telling you Senator, we've got a huge problem on our hands, or I should say you have a huge problem on your hands. You caused this crap-hole of a mess and you'll take care of it. I want the FBI to hit a brick wall on this. I still can't believe how badly this whole thing has been botched. What the hell where you thinking? Where did you find the clowns who screwed this up so bad?"

"Mr. President, I will take care of this. No FBI dick will ever trace this to either of us. You can count on that," Williams muttered, only half believing his own statement.

"I wish I could," said the president as he slammed the receiver down, almost cracking the cradle.

Williams was fighting the urge to vomit the lunch he had eaten a couple of hours earlier. *How could this have spiraled into such a piss-hole?* he wondered. His mind slowly coalesced around the only option that might stymie the FBI investigation. He opened his lower, right desk drawer and fumbled through a pile of loose papers and notes in the bottom of the drawer. He finally found what he was looking for, a Houston, Texas telephone number with the faded name, Vinnie, scrawled below the number. He got up from the desk, walked out into the outer office, and told his secretary he would be out for an hour or so.

He walked a couple of blocks to a small strip mall to a bank of, perhaps, the only pay phones left in Washington, clinked in sufficient coins, and dialed the Houston number.

Chapter 19

Anatoli Lebedov was having difficulty sleeping. It wasn't overly hot or muggy this particular July evening. The president was not bothered by allergies or other ailments that would get in the way of sleep; nor was his insomnia caused by any external problems or internal anxieties. His eyes were fixed in an open position because his mind was racing, contemplating the vastly complex, yet brilliant scheme he had set in motion. Various elements so necessary for his scheme to work, were coming to fruition, almost as if by divine providence, if there was such a thing.

Over the past four years, extreme, theocratic governments had seized power in virtually all Arab countries, except for Jordan. Reestablishment of the Islamic Caliphate to eventually rule the world had now become an announced goal of these governments, yet no alarm bells were ringing in America or Western Europe. Lebedov was convinced the threat posed by Islamic fundamentalism to the secular, Caucasian world, existed mainly because so much of the world's oil supply was controlled by Islamic countries. The way to control the Islamic extremists was to control the oil. Without oil wealth, the fundamentalist movement, on the march in the world, would stop in its tracks and die of famine as surely as the wretched souls in Somalia and Ethiopia.

The weak, self-serving politicians in Europe, now joined by the Americans, deluded by greed and pursuit of wealth, had become soft. They refused to see the growing Islamic threat and preferred to bury their heads in the sand of appeasement. In Lebedov's view, the populations of Europe and America were possibly duped by their leaders, but, more likely, in full agreement with them. They would, regardless, be perpetrators in their own demise.

The West was most anxious to view Russia as a honest ally and a growing consumer market. The rumors of growing nationalism and militarism in Russia were eagerly dismissed by Western capitalists as paranoia of the extreme right. The U.S. president, Papadakis, was so confident in his delusions he had withdrawn virtually all U.S. military forces from around the world and reduced the total American armed forces to less than five hundred thousand, the lowest level since the Japanese attack on Pearl Harbor.

Lebedov had, therefore, calculated he could proceed with his ambitious plans in the Middle East with little interference from the West, particularly after the twelve terrorist cells, now training in Lebanon, were set loose on an unsuspecting America.

The Chinese were willing participants in his strategy to change the course of the world, sharing the enormous risks with the Russians for a payoff of billions of barrels of oil to fuel its voracious economy. And most ironically, the Arabs, and their equally fanatical Muslim cousins in Iran, would also be willing participants, until it was too late for them.

Egypt had renounced the thirty-five year old peace treaty with Israel and led the other Arab countries in an all-consuming hatred toward Israel. Taking advantage of that hatred, Lebedov had already concluded agreements with Syria, Saudi Arabia, and Egypt, including the promise by Russia of greatly expanded military aid in return for a commitment by each of them to participate in joint military action against Israel. The Arab leaders' enthusiasm for the elements of the Russian plan of which they were aware bordered on euphoric. They most assuredly would not be so enthusiastic if they were privy to other elements of the plan they were unaware even existed.

President Lebedov had scheduled talks the following week with the president of Iran and expected similar enthusiasm and agreement. The king of Jordan was proving to be a tougher nut to crack. As of yet, the king was reluctant to enter into any arrangements with Russia.

Ayatollah Ammar Al Sadra of Iraq, the leader of the fundamentalist Iraqi Shiite faction, whose militia was on the verge of winning the brutal civil war ravaging the country, had not yet been brought into the discussions, at least to any great extent. Lebedov was confident the situation there would be resolved in plenty of time to reach an agreement with Al Sadra. He had tentatively penciled-in talks with the Iraqis in six weeks, and felt the discussions could slide an additional six weeks, if necessary, without affecting his plan's overall timetable.

Russia, slowly and methodically over the past ten years, had been modernizing its armed forces, upgrading and mass-producing more reliable and effective tanks, personnel carriers, artillery, rockets, and fighter aircraft. While not completely matching the technological capabilities of armaments in the West, the simplicity, reliability, and sheer numbers more than made up for the technology gap.

America and its NATO allies had turned a blind eye to the military buildup in Russia, refusing to believe Russia was willing, and capable, of doing such a thing. Lebedov's goal was not to fight the West, in any event. Much of the armaments were intended to supply the Muslim armies in the upcoming struggle with Israel—a struggle leading to the opportunity for Russia to gain control of much of the world's oil supply.

The summer was slowly ebbing. Uday was tired. He was worn from the unrelenting heat, training, and stress of trying to stay alive by never arousing suspicion or making even a slight mistake. He found he had to consciously remind himself more and more often why he was working for the Israelis. After hearing the sad stories of so many and feeling the palatable hatred for Israel as a result, it was almost infectious. As much as he was determined not to, he had come to personally like Mustafa Mohammed, his cell leader. He felt Mohammed's pain at the loss of his family, only too well, because he suffered a similar pain, only, as he reminded himself often, at the hands of the people whose cause he had now joined.

He had been able to make only two brief contacts with Engeman, the last one almost a month ago. He felt almost impotent since, up to now, he had so little information. Yesterday, however, Mohammed told him they were going to be moving in a couple of days, in preparation for their insertion into America. Mohammed indicated maybe one or two of the other teams were headed to another country, but the rest were going to the United States. He denied knowing what their mission was going to be. He said he had no other information to share, even if he could.

Uday had to contact Engeman, but things were moving rapidly now, and opportunities to access a phone or a fax were just about zero.

Later, in the afternoon, fate was good to Uday. He and Mohammed were assigned the task of delivering a crate of Kalashnikovs and ten thousand rounds of ammunition to an adjacent camp. The destination was approximately forty-five miles north on an unimproved dirt road. As was normal in these situations, three members of the cell would make the trip, one to drive, and two to provide security. On such occasions, the cell-leader, in this case, Mohammed, was allowed to carry a cell phone, in case help was needed. Uday wondered who would possibly attack them on the road, but, since precautions were being taken, apparently there was a threat from somewhere.

They left the camp at dusk, feeling safer from the unknown threat by traveling in the dark. Uday was nervous as they bumped along the rutted road with only the half-moon lighting the road ahead. Mohammed was driving fast for the road conditions, even in bright sunlight, and without headlights his speed bordered on suicidal.

After traveling for twenty minutes, Uday began to relax, getting used to the near-blind conditions, and trusting Mohammed apparently knew what he was doing, since they had come this far without killing themselves. Suddenly his slow return to calm was shattered. Rounding a curve, they were totally blinded by a dusty blast of wind rolling down a wadi intersecting the road. Mohammed didn't see the road curving to the west and continued driving, straight off a six-foot embankment. The Suburban landed on the front bumper causing the SUV to flip onto its top and careen twice end-over-end until it rested among a grove of wild olive trees thirty yards off the road.

The passenger in the back seat was killed instantly when he was thrown out of the vehicle upon the initial impact and then crushed when all three tons of the Suburban landed on his head on the first roll. Mohammed and Uday, who were both wearing seatbelts, were luckier. Mohammed banged his head hard on the side-window frame and was unconscious, but alive. Uday suffered a severe cut on his forehead when a shard of glass from the front window tried to lobotomize the front of his head. He was, however, conscious, though just barely.

Through a film of blood, Uday could see Mohammed's silhouette faintly outlined in moonlight. He reached over to him and felt his pulse. It was strong. He was, however, obviously unconscious. As Uday dragged his hand back along the front seat he felt a small, hard object. He picked it up and realized, even in his fading consciousness, it was the cell phone Mohammed had been given for emergencies.

He immediately recognized the opportunity and tried to remember the telephone number where, in emergencies, he could leave short messages. He fought through his dizziness and flipped open the phone and dialed the first number that came to mind. After four rings he heard a shrill, monotone voice state the number had been disconnected. He tried to focus all his remaining energy to remember the number and tried again. This time he got a recorded message in Arabic, "Akmed's Transport Company, please leave a number and we will return your call." The message sounded vaguely familiar to him, but he wasn't sure. He felt himself losing consciousness so decided to risk it all and weakly whispered into the phone, "We're leaving for America. Something big is happening. Many combat teams. In another country also. Warn everybody, Uday."

He felt himself slipping into unconsciousness and forced himself to close the cell-phone lid disconnecting the call as he lost the last vestige of awareness.

Chapter 20

George Petrosky was not the prototypical FBI agent. He was over six-feet-three-inches tall and weighed 168 pounds. Bright-red, curly hair flopped over a freckle-covered face. In other words, he was a flaming beanpole. He was, however, highly respected by both FBI management and peers alike as the cream de crème of the agency, and it was not surprising he was assigned to lead the FBI taskforce investigating the attack on Senator Benson. What *was* a surprise was the lack of progress the taskforce was making in the investigation. Months had passed, and all leads had turned cold.

The deceased hoods, who apparently killed the prostitute and attacked Benson, turned out to be two local lowlifes with long criminal records, mainly drug related. Numerous interviews with associates and other similar creeps in the community had turned up no useful information or leads. Agent Petrosky surmised they were hired by someone to setup the senator and thought they could earn some fast cash to buy drugs. The identity of their benefactor was proving to be a tough nut to crack.

Petrosky had arrived at the office early this morning, more because he couldn't sleep than for the need to follow up some hot leads. He had just finished pouring himself a cup of coffee and began reading the morning edition of the *Washington Post*, when the phone rang. He wondered who could be calling him at 7:30 a.m?

He answered, "Hello, Agent Petrosky, what can I do for you?"

A raspy female voice replied, "You can do nothing for me, it's what I can do for you, honey."

"Who is this?"

"You never mind who this is, just listen carefully. You want to know the real scoop about the incident with the senator, you need to strong-arm Candi's pimp. I promise ya, honey, you do that, and you'll be the hero."

Petrosky again asked the woman to identify herself only to hear a hollow click in the handset. He remembered the murdered prostitute's name was Candi Christopherson, and she worked for a pimp named William Johnson, also known as Slick Willie. Agents on the task force had interviewed Johnson shortly after the incident, and the consensus, at the time, was Johnson, while definitely a scumbag, had no useful information about the case.

Petrosky now was having second thoughts. It was logical there might be a connection to the pimp, since no other explanation had surfaced as to why the prostitute was at the hotel. The female caller could be another of Johnson's prostitutes with an axe to grind, or perhaps she was a friend of Candi's. At any rate, there were no other promising leads, so this one rose to the top of the list.

He decided it might be useful to shake down Johnson again, a little more forcefully this time, and see what fruit might fall from the tree. He quickly reviewed the case file, found the appropriate 302 report, and wrote down Slick Willie's last known address. He took one last gulp of coffee, grabbed the keys to a Bureau car out of the key box, and strode out of the office.

William Johnson was pleased with himself as he strolled from his Alexandria townhouse through the early morning warmth to his silver Lexus. He loved early summer in the Washington area. The temperature was in the low seventies, the humidity was low, and everything was green. *What a great day this is starting out to be*, he thought, reflecting his state-of-mind at the moment. Business was up; the springtime urges were always good for business.

He pressed the automatic lock-release on his key ring, received a wink from the Lexus in return, opened the door, and slithered into the luxurious gray-leather seat. As he inserted the key, he was thinking of Courtney, his new "business partner", actually one of his string of hookers with whom he had taken up a romantic fancy. He would be making love to her within the hour and was contemplating the pleasures he would soon be enjoying.

He turned the key and was perplexed the engine didn't turn over immediately. He was perplexed only for an instant, however, when his brain registered a bright flash before being enveloped in permanent blackness.

Special Agent Petrosky knew something wasn't right as he drove south on Washington Street, as black smoke rose into the sky in the distance. As he neared Wolfe Street, where Johnson's townhouse was located, it was obvious the smoke's origin was close to Johnson's townhouse.

He turned left on Wolfe Street, proceeded four blocks past rows of cloned townhouses, toward William Johnson's last known residence. As he approached, he observed the burning hulk of an expensive, luxury car, although he couldn't tell from the remains the make-and-model. Instinct told him, however, he would not be interrogating Johnson anytime during this lifetime.

Many weeks had passed since the Grand Hyatt scandal, as it had come to be known, broke in the national news. The immediate media fixation on Senator Benson as a possible subject had done a one-eighty. He was now viewed by all, but the most trashy scandal media, as a victim. The story was no longer front-page but did warrant a daily piece on page two. It was apparent the FBI was hitting a brick wall in its investigation, with no fresh clues to follow. Some speculation had surfaced about a possible connection between the scandal and the death of a D.C. pimp, killed in a car explosion several weeks after the scandal broke. Even that, however, appeared to be the Bureau simply grasping at straws.

Some unintended fallout from the sordid affair was the expansion from seven to ten senators in Benson's group of rebels. Apparently, at least in Benson's mind, there were a few more good men who were fed up with the corruption. The ten met regularly, at least weekly, to plan strategy.

The political establishment's strategy was to denigrate the messengers in order to deflect the message, a practice ingrained in the political process for decades. The president and congressional leaders on both sides of the aisle orchestrated venomous attacks against the ten senators, some more opaque than others, but the net purpose was the same, to destroy the reputations and credibility of each of the senators.

Papadakis, who was elected because of the vain belief of the electorate he had represented hope and change, was proving to be just another corrupt politician with a left-wing agenda. Disunity in the country had never been so severe and was being magnified by the attacks.

An unanticipated consequence of the scandal, particularly to the chagrin of the president, Senator Williams, and other congressional leaders, was the positive public response the now-expanded group of ten continued to receive. A recent *CNN/Gallup* poll demonstrated 46 percent of the public supported the group's philosophical focus. Frustration was apparently expanding among the nations citizens.

The late summer heat was stifling in the bedroom suburb of Salt Lake City. Even though humidity was almost nonexistent, the fourth day in a row of temperatures over the century mark was wearing down even the most ardent of the sun-worshipping segment of the Salt Lake population. The air conditioning whined continuously at the Sandy home of Senator Peter Simpson as it strived to offset the scorching heat with which mother nature had blessed the Salt Lake valley.

As host, Senator Simpson had just introduced the three newest members of the rebellious senators clique, John Mathews from Maine, Jack Thompson from North Carolina, and Charles McClain from Nebraska. Each expressed their enthusiasm and commitment to the group, which would be sorely tested during the course of the meeting. None of the group was prepared for the suggestions for consideration, which were about to be presented by Senator Benson.

After the introductions, Benson asked to speak and paused for a few seconds before beginning, as if mentally hesitating to say what was on his mind. After what was becoming an uncomfortable pause, he said, in a quiet but determined voice, "I'm about to suggest something to you all that, at first blush, will seem absolutely nuts. But, I want you all to ponder what I'm about to say before reacting too violently. I don't want to have Pete's beautiful carpet covered in blood."

Benson continued cautiously, "As you all know, our activities over the past few months have generated a lot of controversy and, I might add, a lot of venom being spewed in our direction. I also believe, however, it has led to a lot of public support at the grass roots level; I think a lot of people are as fed up as we are with the mess in Washington. What I'm about to propose will take advantage of that public frustration and significantly advance our ability to influence the future course of politics in our nation."

Each of the senators in the room stared intently into Benson's eyes, trying to discern what cataclysmic bombshell he was about to launch. As they all leaned forward in anticipation, it appeared if Benson suddenly stopped talking, they all would, en masse, fall off their chairs.

Benson continued, "I'm proposing we identify like-minded members of the House of Representatives and, together, announce the formation of a third political party."

The quiet in the room was deafening. No one spoke, or breathed for that matter, for what seemed minutes.

Finally, the senator continued, "I know this seems like a radical departure from good sense, but that's why we're meeting tonight, to thrash this out and come up with a plan to impact the political process in this country. Let me hear your objections and let's see if it's just a nutty idea or if it does truly make sense to consider it."

Senator Dobson spoke first, "Historically, third parties have been the kiss of death. They have never done well in national and most local elections. Why would we want to attempt to do what has never worked before?"

A few "that's right's" and nodding heads accompanied Dobson's question.

Not deterred, Benson replied, "I agree historically they haven't worked. But, the situation is totally different now. We have ten senators, 10 percent of the Senate, with probably a similar percentage of the House who will join us, and, according to the latest poll, a plurality of citizens are ready to support almost whatever we do.

"The two-party system in America has failed America. It has become a bastion of privilege—elitist organizations that merely prop up corruption. I truly believe in my heart millions of Americans are just as sick as we are with the road we're traveling. They will embrace a new party with open arms if given the opportunity to do so. I believe millions are just waiting for a realistic, functioning, plausible alternative that's not created just to further the ambitions of a kook or political extremist.

"Ask yourselves this question: Is your party prepared to give you the nomination when you are up for reelection? I don't think the establishment parties in any of our states will support us. Does our mission then just fade away? A third-party effort, at that time, won't be effective. Search your hearts. You know I'm right."

Another pregnant pause seemed interminable. Finally, Senator McClain, one of the new members of the group, broke the icy silence, "Being the newest member of this esteemed gathering, I hope nobody takes offence at my postulating, but, you know, I think Rick has made some excellent points here. I, for one, agree with his recommendation. As they say in the breadbasket of this great land. If you can't crap, then get off the pot"

Senator Dobson was next, "Do all of you know what's involved with establishment of a new party; how difficult it is to get the party on the ballots of every state? If we embark on this, we've got to be prepared to work our nails to the quick. There will be legal issues. We will need lots of money to fight the attorneys, who will surely come out of the woodwork to sue us to prevent us from becoming legitimate. Who will contact our cohorts in the House? How do we know how many of them will come along? It's going to be a lot of work. With all of that said, however, I think it's one heck of an idea. Let's do it!"

After another thirty minutes of discussion to arrive at a consensus and two hours more hammering out the next steps, the group of ten embarked on a path, which would lead to consequences that no one in the Simpson residence that hot, dry Friday in August could begin to imagine.

Chapter 21

Colby Engeman had just spent an hour hashing over the latest message he had received from Uday with Colonel Dylan. Dylan was frustrated. Engeman had been unable to contact Uday since receiving the message two days ago to get clarification. He was concerned the message seemed to have been made under duress, and he was worried for Uday's safety.

After considerable haggling, Dylan decided to pass along the message to the director of the Mossad, Ariel Levy. Levy, was an ex-general who had distinguished himself in the war in Lebanon and, later, during the expulsion of the Palestinians. He had been named as the director only last year and had, as of yet, not faced any major crisis situations.

Later the same day, Dylan and Engeman were ushered into Levy's sparsely furnished office and asked by Levy to take seats opposite from him across a beat-up, blonde-colored desk. Levy, who still appeared fit, even as he neared his sixty-seventh birthday, was a man of few words. After bringing his right hand up to about neck level as a gesture of hello, the only word out of his mouth was a question, "So?"

Colonel Dylan cleared his throat and proceeded to tell the director of the latest message from Uday.

Levy asked, "Well, what do you think we should do with this loaded piece of garbage? It doesn't tell us anything, yet could be indicating a nuclear bomb is going to be set off in America and other places."

Dylan gestured toward Engeman and said, "Colby knows the source well and I think it would be beneficial to hear what he has to say."

Engeman swallowed hard, cleared his throat, and said, "Sir, I trust Uday explicitly, and if he says something big is about to happen, something big will happen. I also think he might have been hurt or worse, based on the shortness of the message and the weakness of his voice. My understanding of how he and the other cell members have been managed, precludes him from knowing many details of the operation for which he is being trained. I don't think he knows more than he stated. I do believe, however, something big is in the works, and I feel strongly we need to pass on a warning to America.

"What shall we warn them?" bellowed Levy, interrupting Engeman. "Something big is going to be attacked! We need more, boys. You need to dig deeper."

Colonel Dylan, sensing the conversation was about to end, decided to risk his future career out of a gut feeling they might not get much more until it was too late. He abruptly blurted out, "Sir begging your pardon, but, as Colby said, Uday might be dead and we most probably won't get more actionable intelligence. It's your choice whether or not to sit on this information. Personally, I think we should warn the Americans of the real possibility of an attack of unknown dimensions. Let them make the decision how credible the message is. At least, they could watch for cells infiltrating their country. I believe Colby is correct in his assessment."

The director eyed Dylan icily and then slowly stood up from his chair. Both Colonel Dylan and Engeman jumped up from their chairs.

Levy looked from Dylan to Engeman and back to Dylan and then spoke, "Colonel, not many soldiers have the balls to tell me when I'm wrong. I salute you for standing your ground. I also agree we must warn the Americans, but I also believe we desperately need more information. I will do my job. You two need to do yours."

With that, he brought his hand up to his forehead in a salute that was his method of saying goodbye. Dylan and Engeman returned the salute, twirled around in a smart about-face, and marched in lockstep out of the director's office.

The next morning, FBI Director Sydney Wilkinson received an encrypted international telephone call from the director of the Israeli Mossad. Wilkinson had welcomed Director Levy as the new head of Israel's vaunted intelligence organization, having previously acquainted himself in detail with Levy's military history and personal life. He felt Levy was an Israeli patriot who would be honest and forthright with non-Israelis but would never allow such forthrightness to compromise his country. He knew when Levy telephoned it would be for only critically-important reasons.

Levy related to Wilkinson the brief message the Israelis had received from their Arab source. He tried to impress on Wilkinson that, even though the message was brief and short on details, his agency was certain it was accurate. He also, honestly, expressed his distrust of President Papadakis; an opinion Wilkinson shared.

The Mossad director stressed the sensitivity of the source, admonishing Wilkinson if the president, for political reasons, identified the source of this information as an Israeli informant, the information stream would dry up, and people would die. He said, therefore, he was furnishing the information only to the FBI director and not through Israeli governmental channels to the president. The Israeli prime minister was in full agreement with this approach.

He would leave it up to Wilkinson to choose the most effective way to act on the information without jeopardizing the source. Levy apologized to Wilkinson for having no corroborating or additional intelligence, but the Israeli government felt he should share the minimal information he possessed. The United States government could respond to the threat, of course, in whatever manner it deemed appropriate. Wilkinson thanked him and the conversation ended.

Chapter 22

Ivan Litinov was troubled. As long as he could remember, as a youthful member of the Komsomol, an overzealous cadet in the Taskent/Uzbekistan Joint Arms High Command Military Academy, the Soviet Union's equivalent to West Point, and a fast track young army officer in the Soviet Army, he reveled in the glory and power of the Soviet Union. His world came crushing down around him when the USSR collapsed in the late 1980s. Almost overnight, all of his assumptions and aspirations were dashed.

With the election of President Lebedov, he felt a spark of hope. He knew the new president shared his feelings that Russia had been betrayed, not only by Gorbachev and Yeltsin, but by the Russian people themselves. With Lebedov, Russia now had a leader who was not afraid to assert strong leadership, even raw power, to restore Russian glory.

As a result of his newfound optimism in his country and, particularly, its new leader, Colonel Litinov was eager to serve when given the opportunity. The colonel's proven ability to analyze and think on his feet had led to his appointment as the president's chief troubleshooter and director of special operations.

Serving the president, initially, had been exhilarating. As he became aware, however, of the full scope of the planned terrorist attacks on America, he was beginning to have attacks of conscience. He had no problems with the collateral deaths of civilians, accepting that as just part of war. The deliberate bombing of civilians in World War II, by both sides, illustrated the point.

Detonating nuclear weapons on an unsuspecting civilian population, not at war, was difficult for Litinov to justify under any circumstances he could contemplate. Those millions of deaths, most certainly, would not be considered collateral damage. In spite of his misgivings, he was committed to carrying out the plans as they unfolded. Ivan Litinov, first and foremost, was a Russian soldier. Duty required he complete his mission.

After nearly crushing the colonel's ribs in a overly exuberant bear hug, the President of Russia exclaimed, "It's great to see you after such a long time."

It had really only been a couple of months since he had talked face-to-face with Lebedov and had participated in numerous telephone calls in the meantime. Colonel Litinov realized the Russian leader was probably overly keyed-up, anticipating a positive, comprehensive update from Litinov. A few too many vodkas earlier in the evening likely added to his exuberance.

Lebedov motioned with his hand and said, "Have a seat. We have a lot of ground to cover this evening, don't we? Now, let's see. Where do we start?"

President Lebedov actually had the agenda for the meeting outlined in explicit detail. He was subconsciously overly condescending to the colonel to mask his genuine excitement at how well the plan *Hammer and Anvil* had progressed.

"First, tell me how the training has progressed?"

The colonel replied, "The training has progressed almost without problems. One thing you can count on with the Palestinian martyrs is dedication. If our own recruits were equally motivated, we would be controlling the world by now. The only incident marring the past couple of months was a car accident injuring one of our team leaders and killing one of his team. Another team member was injured, but both he and the team leader have recovered nicely. It appears they were driving too fast in the dark on a mission to deliver automatic weapons and ammunition and, in their zeal to complete the mission, ran off the road. As I said, these people are a dedicated bunch.

"Each team has been trained to function totally independently, and every team member has been cross-trained in every specialty. All have been instructed in detail on how detonate the explosives, although none has any idea what kind of explosives we're talking about.

"We have gone to great lengths to ensure knowledge is insulated from level to level. Each team will be advised of their target destinations only when in the United States and, then, only when we're about to launch the operations. No team will know another team's target. None of the terrorists will ever know the lethality of the bombs they are carrying until they trigger them, and then, only for a flash of a second. I'm confident the only person who has any idea of what will be delivered in the Suburbans is Al Zouri himself, and he hasn't a clue how powerful the bombs really are."

“I’m rambling on”, Litinov apologized. “Do you have any direct questions or should I proceed?”

“Proceed”, directed the president with a wave of his hand, “I like what you’re saying.”

“Next week, we begin the infiltration process. Twelve teams will travel to Mexico. Entering the United States will be a little problematic but should be doable within acceptable risks. Al Zouri has successfully negotiated with the Salazar cartel in Mexico to smuggle our zealots across the porous border of America for several million American dollars. Salazar has no clue where the money originated. I guess he suspects it’s Saudi money. At any rate, I’m confident all twelve teams will be set up in appropriately-located safe houses by the end of September. As I said before, at that point, no team will know where any of the other teams are housed.”

The colonel continued, “Getting the Arabs in place is relatively easy, when compared to the logistics of smuggling twelve thermonuclear weapons into America. Even though the technology gained from the Americans has enabled us to create extremely powerful bombs in small, lightweight packages, the lead shielding and packaging we’ve had to employ to prevent discovery, has caused a serious weight problem. I think we’ve solved the dilemma, however, by dividing the devices into four separate shipments on Chinese registered vessels sailing to America in October. In each case, the ships will be carrying heavy industrial equipment, and we will be able to hide our precious cargo among the crates. Security at United State’s ports is lax. The Americans never really implemented many of the port security improvements recommended after *nine-eleven*, and, since each device will be completely shielded, I’m sure we can pull this off without a glitch.”

Litinov detailed other aspects of the operation to the president’s satisfaction and finished with a question, “When do we pull the trigger?”

Lebedov paused before answering the question. Finally he said, “Let me just say, our purpose in doing what we’ve planned is to cause such a cataclysmic event in the United States, they will not be able to respond to events in other places in the world with any meaningful impact. With that in mind, we will want to maximize our ability to castrate the government. Timing will be determined by that overriding goal.

“One other item, Colonel,” Lebedov said quietly as he paused and stared into Litinov’s eyes. “We also need to detonate a bomb in Tel Aviv.”

The colonel gasped, “What are you saying? Trying to smuggle a team, let alone a nuclear device, into Israel compounds the risk of this whole operation immeasurably.”

The president raised both hands in a gesture meant to stop Litinov’s objections. “Colonel”, he said, “figure out how we can do it. Al Zouri is insistent on it and his cooperation is key to this whole thing.”

“But, I don’t …”

“Enough”, shouted Lebedov. “I give the orders; you follow them.”

Colonel Savabi had been talking for over an hour, extolling the virtues of the great leader, Al Zouri, the glory of the cause, and the wonderful blessings awaiting the martyrs for Allah. Uday’s mind wandered as he tried to look interested. He wondered if Savabi, the master of pontification, would be willing to discover, firsthand, the blessings awaiting those who die for Allah. He also wondered how he was ever going to get out of this insanity alive.

It was early September, and he had fully recovered from the accident, with only a purple scar on his forehead to remind him how close he came to not having to worry about how he was going to get out alive. The miracle of his and Mohammed’s survival from the accident was overshadowed by a greater miracle. No negative ramifications had occurred as a result of his use of Mohammed’s cell phone in the wrecked suburban. Uday was certain a record of his call to the Israeli telephone number would be discovered. Apparently even the Black October security apparatus could make a mistake. For whatever reason, the call record was never discovered, or was ignored. Either way, Uday felt his inevitable death was just delayed for a few months. He was part of a suicide squad and could see no realistic way to escape his fate.

All of the terrorist cells were scheduled to leave the camp tomorrow for various destinations. He knew Mohammed’s cell was headed for Mexico along with other cells, although he did not know how many; nor did he know his ultimate destination. He didn’t even know where in Mexico they were headed and was quite sure Mohammed didn’t know either. He figured more information would be forthcoming tomorrow, since they would be receiving fake passports and identity papers then. It was probably not such a bad thing he couldn’t contact Engeman. Why risk it when he had so little information to pass along?

Chapter 23

The FBI director entered the tastefully furnished office of CIA Director William A. Smith. Smith, who had been appointed by the previous president and had managed to keep the job ever since, was a balding, pudgy man, who looked more at home in a D.C. bar watching the Washington Redskins get beat again, than running America's premier spy agency. His appearance belied his capabilities, however. He was a hard-bitten spymaster, having come up through the ranks over the past thirty-two years. Smith and Wilkinson had a mutual respect for each other but little personal affection. They both were extremely competent in what they did and, thus, realized the importance of cooperating and sharing information. Smith was also aware of the notoriously poor relationship the FBI director had with the president.

"It is nice to see you Sydney", said Smith as the FBI director took a seat in a comfortable, somewhat-worn, tan, leather chair. "What can I do for you?"

Wilkinson waited a few seconds before answering, appearing to make sure he said what he wanted to say exactly the way he wanted to say it. "As you know, Bill, the president and I do not see eye-to-eye on a number of issues. As a result, it has created an almost intolerable situation. I find it's difficult to communicate with him, even in cases where he vitally needs information. It's virtually impossible to schedule a face-to-face meeting with him to discuss critical national security issues. Everything is funneled through George Lukavitz, his attorney general, who, frankly, sees every bit of information only in terms of the political impact on the president."

Wilkinson continued, "Bill, yesterday, I received a call from Ariel Levy, who passed on some incomplete but, I believe, extremely important information indicating we're going to be attacked again."

Smith's eyebrows furled into a scowl. "Attacked again, you mean like the World Trade Center?"

"Worse. According to the information, whatever is coming is going to be big, much bigger than *nine-eleven*."

"How good is their information?"

Wilkinson replied, "Apparently they feel their source is unimpeachable. My dilemma is how to pass this along to the president and national security people and have them take it seriously. The administration has pretty much taken the European position relative to terrorism, refusing to believe there is still a threat, preferring to buy-off would-be attackers. They also view Israel as the number one stumbling block to establishing peace throughout the Middle East and, perhaps, the whole world. The president would, no doubt, dismiss any information coming from the Israelis as Jewish paranoia, regardless of the authenticity of the information. Levy, himself, perceived the president couldn't be trusted with this information, entrusting me to do something with it without jeopardizing the Israeli source."

Sounding exasperated, Wilkinson continued, "I need your help Bill. I'm convinced something is afoot here, which will likely result in a catastrophic attack against our country. The president is not concerned, however, and combining his disinterest with a seriously weakened *Patriot Act*, we're hamstrung in our ability to respond. I have already sent out a classified order to our field offices to increase informant contacts and take other appropriate steps, but, as you know, our ability to dig up critical information in this area is almost nonexistent because of the administration's actions last year.

"I need the president to issue an executive order to temporarily restore the ability to issue FBI administrative subpoenas and obtain "sneak and peak" warrants. Without those provisions we'll be trying to stop this attack with one arm tied behind our back. I'm convinced he won't act on the basis of what I've told him because of the negative political impact such an order would have both domestically and in Europe."

Smith rubbed his chin as he contemplated Wilkinson's dilemma. Finally, he replied, "Sydney, it's truly unfortunate your relationship with the president is so sour. It's hard to imagine how the government can function in times of crisis when political correctness and personal animosity takes precedence over clear thinking and pertinent discussion.

"I do agree, however, we've got to take action, in spite of the president's "p.c." mindset. I will do what I can within the agency to try to dig up more info, but, as you well know, the CIA has pretty much been gutted relative to human intelligence on the ground. Perhaps we need to go around the president. I understand you're on pretty good terms with Senator Rick Benson, am I not correct?" Wilkinson nodded. The chief spy paused with a sly smile creasing his face, "Well, here's what I think might work …"

Chapter 24

As President Lebedov peered down on the landscape slowly passing under the wing of the huge two engine Tupolev TU-204, he wondered what the world would look like twelve months from now. *Where will I be? Will I be the most powerful man in the world or will I be a few ashes scattering in the wind?* Normally not one to second-guess himself, he couldn't help but wonder if he could control the events he was about to unleash.

As he continued his eastward journey to meet with Chou En Lo and the Chinese premier, Zhu Jiaboa in Beijing, he was sobered, upon reflection, that he and the Chinese leaders would be making irrevocable decisions tomorrow morning, which could result in magnificent glory for Russia on one hand, or, the possible destruction of the world, on the other. Comprehending no world leader has ever had the power, as he had now, to utterly change the face of the earth, the Russian president was left with conflicted emotions. He was confident in his course, but had enough innate common sense to understand the unimaginable consequences of failure.

Chapter 25

Senator Benson continued staring at the barely visible ceiling illuminated only by the faint, green glow given off by the smoke detector and filtered light sneaking in through the wood-shuttered window. He hadn't been able to fall asleep for the last two hours, not due to his wife's soft snoring, but because of the million, or so, thoughts racing through his mind.

In the two weeks since he and his co-conspirators had made the fateful decision to launch the third-party effort, they had met with mixed success. At least thirty House members had initially indicated possible support for the effort, but nine of those subsequently declined to join. The news had leaked to the press, and the senators were being vilified by the mainstream media, even being accused of tarnishing the fine traditions of America. Commentators were going to great lengths to remind America of the historical failures of past efforts to establish viable third parties.

The president had also used several opportunities to add his opinion of the idea, besmirching specifically Senator Benson. He accused the senator of "denigrating the cherished two-party system that has served the country well for over two hundred years only to sooth his own inflated ego." Adding to the clamoring chorus were equally damning pronouncements from leaders in the Senate and House from both parties.

One extremely promising bit of information was the result of a *Fox Dynamic Opinion* poll of twenty-two hundred citizens taken two days after the news had leaked, demonstrating a 51 percent positive reaction to the possibility. That so many people would react positively to the idea of a new party with hardly any information, indicated a remarkable dissatisfaction with the current state of affairs.

Another concern was the telephone call he had received earlier in the evening from the FBI director who requested an urgent meeting the next day. Director Wilkinson would not be specific on the phone but indicated the matter was urgent. Benson agreed to meet with him at his Bureau office at 10:00 a.m., which was even more unusual since tomorrow was Sunday. Benson couldn't imagine what was so urgent and of such a nature the director would request a meeting with him, rather than members of the executive branch. He was sure it had nothing to do with the events earlier in the year at the Grand Hyatt. That case was dead as far as Benson knew, and he couldn't imagine the director would set up an urgent meeting on Sunday morning to discuss a new lead.

Yes, the senator thought, *there certainly is a lot to think about, but why now? I need to sleep.* But, no matter how hard he tried, sleep wouldn't come.

At precisely 10:00 a.m., Senator Benson was ushered into the FBI director's office by a young FBI agent who had the weekend duty assignment. During normal business hours, Director Wilkinson's administrative assistant would handle the ushering task. But since today was Sunday, the rookie agent had the assignment.

The director walked around from behind his desk and greeted Benson with a vice-like, heartfelt handshake. Then, with one arm around Benson's shoulder, he guided him to a plush, brown-leather chair that, while appearing oiled and well-taken-care of, was obviously well-used.

"Would you like a cup of coffee?"

Benson, replied, "No thanks, I'm fine."

Wilkinson then took a seat in a second brown-leather chair facing the senator. "You're probably wondering what the heck could be so important I'd call you out of your home on a Sunday morning to come down here and meet me?"

Benson replied, "Yes sir, you're right about that. I can't imagine what could be so urgent."

The FBI director grinned broadly, "Well, I think when I'm finished talking with you, you'll agree we needed to talk this morning. I have recently come into possession of some pretty frightening intelligence information indicating a potential terrorist attack on the United States dwarfing the attack on the World Trade Center in 2001."

Benson's expression sobered as he felt a chill buzz down his spine.

Wilkinson continued, "Senator, I haven't known you for very long, but I've come to trust you explicitly. Therefore, I need to have your word that key parts of this information I'm about to share with you will remain confidential."

Benson paused for a few seconds, wondering what Wilkinson had to say, and why to *him*, and then nodded his head, "You've got my word."

"Senator, this information I received two days ago was furnished to me under extreme confidentiality by the director of the Israeli Mossad. The information didn't contain a lot of detail, but Director Levy assured me of its veracity. It was specific in one respect; the attack on the United States and other countries was going to be big and was to be carried out by several terrorist cells."

The director's tone hushed to emphasize the secrecy of his next statement, "Levy was also adamant this information not be passed on to the president in its entirety, since he was afraid the president would use it as an opportunity to slam Israel, regardless that the informant and others might die. As you know Senator, both you and I have had our issues with the current administration. I'm convinced the information would not be acted upon, at best, and, at worst, the president would use it for political purposes."

Benson asked, "How I can I help?"

The director continued, "Before I get to that, let me tell you what I believe we need to do to respond adequately to this threat. Last year the president gutted the *Patriot Act* by deleting from it the ability we so desperately need to react quickly to any intelligence leads and infiltrate suspected terrorist support groups and sympathizers. The terrorist scumbags do most, if not all, of their clandestine work in a relatively few mosques and Islamic charitable organizations in the United States. The bad apples, unfortunately damage the reputations of legitimate mosques and charities. The administration has made it virtually impossible to infiltrate such organizations or to respond to actionable intelligence information fast enough to stop an attack. Today terrorist cells, once inside our country, can disappear from view, and we will have no way to locate them.

"Furthermore, the country's borders with Canada and Mexico are woefully unprotected, so identifying potential terrorists coming into the United States is almost impossible.

"Senator, I'm convinced you and your compatriots, who apparently are on the verge of launching a third political party, are the only force with enough clout to have a chance to force a change in our current thinking. The latest polls show increasingly strong support for your group. I think that represents a considerable amount of grass-roots power. The president is an ostrich with his head buried in the sand. I hope to God it doesn't take a nuclear explosion to pull his head out."

Benson was awash in thought. *How could this great country have gotten to this point, where even those tasked with developing intelligence information to protect the very existence of the country, can't trust that information with the elected leader?* He did not comment for a few seconds, appearing to stare right through the FBI director, prompting the director to ask, "Senator, are you all right?"

Benson, slightly startled, replied, "I'm sorry, I just got a little caught up with this for a second. What have we come to when you, the director of the FBI, can't share critical information with the executive head of our country?"

Before Wilkinson could reply, Benson continued, "Director Wilkinson, I will do what I can. I've got to think through this a bit. I certainly don't want to compromise the Israeli source, either. Let me work on this for a few days. I will call you back once I have figured out an approach that will accomplish our goals."

They both stood up together and shook each other's hands. Wilkinson thanked Benson profusely for listening and for whatever help he could provide in the future, and added ominously, "Don't think about this too long. I'm not sure how much time we have."

Benson just nodded and soberly exited the director's office, passing by the duty agent without so much as a glance.

Chapter 26

Largely unknown, or perhaps ignored, by the security apparatus in the West, things were in motion in China, which in earlier times would have created anxiety throughout the democracies in Europe and North America. Huge quantities of war material were on the move, including trainload after trainload of tanks, artillery, rockets, ammunition, and troops all headed north and west toward Russia. Russia and China had announced a week earlier they would be conducting war games with each other in far-eastern Russia, as a cover story, which was accepted without question by the United States.

Even as satellite surveillance observed trains continuing westward, the West was mollified into acquiescence by explanations the movements were all part of the war games and training exchanges between the two countries. Leaders in the democracies appeared more than willing to accept explanations, which were, at the very least, questionable. They refused to believe a more ominous explanation was a possibility, even though, some intelligence experts were sounding alarms.

Pablo Salazar was an extremely successful businessman, at least in his own mind. The fact his business consisted of causing misery to millions and deaths to thousands didn't alter his inflated opinion of his importance. Having achieved his lofty status from humble beginnings as a street orphan in Sao Paulo, only added to his feeling of superiority.

When contacted a few months ago by Alawai Al Zouri, the infamous head of Black October, Salazar was more than accommodating to meet with him. After all, they were both successful businessmen, though their focus was a bit different. Any opportunity to make more money was welcome.

The deal he and Al Zouri had agreed upon was to smuggle forty-eight individuals into America for one hundred grand per head, totaling just under five million dollars for doing what he had been doing successfully for the past decade for much less money.

It made no difference to Salazar what Al Zouri's ultimate intentions were. Although not informed of those intentions, he hated America and would not mind at all if a few Americans met the same fate of those on September 11, 2001. The Saudis, whom he assumed were footing the bill, had money oozing out of all their body orifices, so why shouldn't they share some of it with him?

The hot late September day was waning when Salazar, sitting behind an enormous desk impatiently ushered into his study one of his key lieutenants, Juan Escobar. Salazar was anxious to hear Escobar's report on the status of the deal with Al Zouri.

Escobar, who had been given the assignment to coordinate the arrangement with the terrorists, was, as usual, astounded by the opulence of Salazar's study. Cherry-wood stained bookshelves lined the entire length of one wall and were full of books, arranged as an art form by themselves. On the walls were hung exquisite, priceless paintings, most likely from several European masters. The windows were framed by lush, maroon, floor-length satin and velvet draperies illuminated by the light from sparkling, crystal chandeliers.

He was abruptly startled from his wonderment when Salazar bellowed, "What the hell is wrong with you? You act like a little brat at Disneyland. I want to know what's happening with our Arab friends—now!"

Escobar stuttered, "Sorry boss, this place is gorgeous." He continued with his report, "All forty-eight Arabs landed over the past four days in Mexico City and Guadalajara without any problems. They were met at the airports and transported to six safe houses."

Salazar interrupted, "Are you sure nobody's been burned?"

"Yeah, boss, I'm sure."

"When do we take them north?"

"We will begin in a week, and by the end of next week they will all be ready for insertion. One group will be in Hermosillo, a second in Ciudad Juarez and the third group in Nuevo Laredo."

Salazar warned, "Juan, no screw-ups will be acceptable here. There's a lot of money riding on this, and your ass is on the line if any part of this fails. Are you certain you can insert all forty-eight without any getting stopped?"

"I'm sure", Escobar replied in as convincing tone as he could muster. "We're using our best 'coyotes' and the most protected routes into the States through Arizona and Texas. Besides, the American's heads are so far up their asses, smuggling has become as easy as walking your dog in the park."

"Don't get overconfident Escobar", warned Salazar ominously, "or I'll be burying you in the park."

"It'll be done boss. Don't you worry."

"All right. Get the hell out of here," spitted Salazar, miffed at Escobar's overconfidence.

Chapter 27

"Well Rick", exclaimed Richard Dobson, "we certainly have a conundrum here, don't we? We've got to protect the source of this information, which means we can't mention the Israelis. By not identifying them, however, there is no basis to claim validity. It's almost as if we're stuck with saying, 'I heard this rumor the other day'. We'll get laughed off the air."

For the past two hours, Senators Benson and Dobson had been considering the information Benson had received the day before from Director Wilkinson without making much progress toward any sort of coherent action plan. Every time an option was considered, they slammed into the secrecy wall; how to sound credible without compromising the source.

Dobson's wife, Camilla, entered the den where the two had been struggling for the past two hours, carrying a tray loaded with crackers, cheese, and hot chocolate.

She asked, "Why don't you two take a break for a minute? You both look like you've been wrestling an alligator".

"Camilla honey," Dobson sighed, "this alligator, unfortunately, is about to rip a chunk out of our country's hide if we don't come up with a plan to stop it, so we just don't have time to take a break. We sure do appreciate the goodies, though. Thanks sweetheart."

Recognizing the concern in her husband's voice underneath his attempt to sound calm, Camilla replied, "You're most welcome. Let me know if you two need anything else." She turned and exited the den as gracefully as she had entered.

Senator Benson spread cheese on a Wheat Thin, took a bite, and glanced across the books lining the east wall of the study. As he sighted one of Tom Clancey's earliest novels, *The Hunt for Red October*, he thought for a moment, then turned to Dobson and said, "Richard, I have an idea—subterfuge."

"What do you mean, subterfuge?"

"Do you remember reading *The Hunt for Red October*? The Americans secreted one of Russia's most powerful subs across the

Atlantic ocean to a safe port in America by using subterfuge. We can do the same."

Dobson looked puzzled, "I don't know where you are going with this."

"Listen to me," chortled Benson in an audibly excited voice. "Our problem is we cannot claim the Israelis as our source nor can we be too specific about what we know, but we can get the message out anyway by subterfuge. Let's just make something up, at least in regard to the source of the information and the specifics. We can even spruce up the specifics, since we don't know much to begin with, and make it a real believable story, while protecting the truth. Our ultimate goal, anyway, is stop what might be a catastrophic attack, so, in this case, maybe the end justifies the means."

Dobson's eyes brightened. "Ya know, I think you've hit on something here. Keep in mind though, if it ever comes out we have fabricated something this big we're finished. What do we do about the other eight senators?"

"We tell them of course, what we plan to do," Benson sighed. "If we sink, we might as well sink together."

Chapter 28

The Russian colonel was satisfied with the arrangements. Litinov had spent the second week of October in the Chinese port city of Tianjin, on China's Gold Coast. His stay there was all business, even though the city provided much to see. Other than trying the city's unique cuisine on one occasion, when he savored the city's famous braised, creamed cabbage, Litinov enjoyed little the city had to offer. His week was spent breathing in the rancid, fish-laced air of the docks and adjacent warehouses.

Now, however, he was finished, having seen the last of four heavily-laden, Chinese-registered freighters sail this morning. He calculated the last ship, "The Morning Star", would steam through the Yellow Sea by tomorrow tonight and would be well past the southern tip of Japan twenty-four hours later.

Spread among the cargo of heavy manufacturing equipment, meant to satisfy an ever-increasing Mexican and Central American appetite, were twelve crates containing a heavy cargo of a different kind. Litinov contemplated the nuclear monsters secreted in those crates and wondered if he, or anyone else on the earth, could imagine the world to emerge after they were unleashed. He had become somewhat of an expert on nuclear weapons, at least of this type.

Each of the bombs packed 475 kilotons of explosive power, almost forty times that of "little boy" and "fat man", the two fission bombs that obliterated the cities of Hiroshima and Nagasaki in 1945. Remarkably, each was small enough to fit in the back of a Suburban, albeit a specially altered Suburban. The bombs were lithium-fueled, fusion bombs, each weighing about eight hundred pounds, very similar to the American W-88 warhead still used on the Trident II missile submarines.

Each warhead was capable of leveling a city the size of San Francisco, and Litinov shuddered when contemplating the casualties from the blasts and resulting fallout. The economic disruptions would be equally severe.

He couldn't eliminate from his mind the haunting fear America, in spite of all the safeguards in place in Lebedov's plan, would find out who was behind this horror and would retaliate with devastating force. The colonel could only hope Lebedov was right, and the four ships he had just sent steaming toward America were not the four horsemen of the apocalypse, leading Russia and the world to annihilation.

Uday Mahmud, Mohammed, and their two teammates, had spent the last three days traveling over choking, dusty, dirt roads as they made their way northward in Mexico. Actually, twelve terrorists were traveling in the three-car convoy, each team in a separate car. Their driver, a swarthy, pocked-marked Mexican who went by the name of Chico, had uttered virtually no sounds other than a series of grunts during their time together. They assumed he couldn't speak English, and they certainly couldn't speak Spanish.

Uday had not had any time alone, other than to pee on the side of the road, and, therefore, had no opportunities to contact Engeman. Mohammed had told him they were going to arrive tonight at a Mexican city, Nuevo Laredo, located just south of the Texas border. Sometime during the next two or three days they would enter the United States.

Uday was tired of breathing dust continually and would welcome a break tonight. He could sense Mohammed and the others were keyed up and excited, in spite of the grime, knowing they were soon to be martyrs for Allah. Uday tried to portray the same emotion outwardly, but inwardly was filled with dread. He knew his fate was sealed with his fanatical friends, in spite of anything he could do.

Chapter 29

Benson and Dobson met with the other eight senators a day after their initial discussion about their plan. A couple of the senators expressed concern with what was being proposed, but a consensus was reached eventually when all realized the danger facing the nation.

Benson was now waiting in his Capitol Building office for the FBI director who had cleared his calendar upon receiving Benson's call. Three days had passed since their previous conversation and both men sensed the urgency of meeting again. Director Wilkinson arrived shortly after 3:00 p.m. and was immediately ushered into the senator's office by Benson's administrative assistant.

"Welcome Director Wilkinson, it's good to see you again," Benson proffered without a lot of enthusiasm. "It's just too bad the circumstances of our meeting are so disconcerting."

Wilkinson responded, "I agree. It's not pleasant to consider what we have here on the table is it? So, what did you and your fellow conspirators come up with?"

Benson smiled at Wilkinson's lame attempt at humor and replied, "You know what is really funny Director? What we came up with might actually be a crime."

Wilkinson responded incredulously, "What are you talking about?"

Benson continued, "Well, you see, we don't have a lot of specific information to pass on or present to anybody, nor can we divulge the source of our information, so what we have decided to do is a subterfuge."

"A what?"

"You know, a trick or an attempt to persuade without divulging the whole truth. We came to the conclusion we won't get anywhere with the president unless he feels there really is a threat, and the public perceives the same, and makes it politically uncomfortable for him not to respond."

Wilkinson's curiosity was aroused and he asked, "How do you propose this subterfuge be accomplished?"

"That's where we need your help," replied the Senator.

Wilkinson shifted uncomfortably in his chair and mumbled, "I'm probably going to regret this immensely, but in view of the circumstances, what can I do?"

Benson paused for a couple of seconds and then said, "Well, I'll tell you. As soon as possible, we would like you to attempt to schedule a meeting with the president. If you absolutely cannot get past Attorney General Lucavitz, then discuss this with him. Either way will serve our purpose."

"And what would you have me tell them?" the director asked, with a faint but growing smile on his face.

A week had passed and Washington was in turmoil. The third-party conspirators had again scheduled the grand ballroom at the Renaissance Mayflower Hotel to announce to the nation their intentions, and, judging from the previous press conference held in the spring, it was sure to be unique, if not explosive.

Poll after political poll reported an increasing level of public support for what the senators were about to do. No matter how the Washington and New York media tried to spin it, it was evident a large segment of the country's population was behind the establishment of a third party. The most negative poll numbers were at 49 percent support, with one poll, the *Fox Dynamic Opinion Poll*, as high as 56 percent. Other polls had indicated a majority of America would be tuning in to watch the announcement, since it promised to be such a historically unique event.

Senator Benson, again, would be the spokesman for the group and was spending his last few minutes in a nearby guest room primping and rehearsing parts of his speech. He realized before the evening was over, the Washington press corps and the public would be shocked to their cores.

"Senator, it's time," reminded June Thompson, Benson's administrative assistant.

Benson responded a bit timidly, "Okay, I guess there's no time like the present."

Benson entered the ballroom and was astounded at the huge crowd gathered to hear the historic announcement. It was obvious there were more than just news correspondents in attendance. Benson glanced around the crowd and noticed many Washington politicians, including Senator Williams. A fleeting thought went through his head for a horrifying moment. *What if one of them has a gun?* He quickly brought his paranoia under control.

He took a drink from the glass on the podium, made sure the teleprompter was working, although he would not need it, made one last sweeping glance over the crowd, and began to speak. "My fellow Americans, as I stand before you today, I'm humbled by the great honor it is to do so. America is a wonderful country with a history of a democratic tradition that others in this world can only envy. To be part of that great tradition as a United States senator is truly humbling and yet exhilarating. I believe in my heart service in the United States Senate, the House of Representatives, the Executive branch, and even the Supreme Court is, and should be viewed as just that—service. All government employees, and we all are government employees, either elected or hired by our citizens, should serve at the pleasure of the public.

"Somehow, we have lost sight of that principle. Government has become, in many ways, our master, whose purpose is to control our lives, to make us feel good, believing we still choose the politicians who lead us. The reality is different. Elected government's mission now is to fool the public, keep them blissfully happy, while actually coddling and maintaining in power the self-appointed elites in our country."

The assembled throng was dead silent. If there were any gasps, none made it any further than the gasper's throat.

Benson continued, "Who are the power elites? They are the people with money, with power, who run many of our global corporations. They are the internationalists whose loyalty is not to America but to the global company and global economy.

"Now I'm not condemning American corporations generally. I know many corporate leaders who do not, in my view, fall into this category. They are honest, ethical executives who are American patriots. However, there are too many, way too many, who are not patriots, who exert maximum influence on the American political process.

"What has this done to us? It has turned our society into a gratification society. For many Americans, all that's important is what can make you happy today; tomorrow be damned. Take no risks, don't rock the boat, ignore it, and maybe any problems will just disappear. We, who are embarking on this new course, feel strongly our country is in an unfortunate downward spiral; not fatal yet, but it will become so if our course stays the same.

"This mindset has led our elected officials to refuse to recognize the dangers facing our country. We enter into agreements with terrorists who continue preaching the destruction of the United States, blindly believing that, just because we want it so badly, peace will flourish without cost. We have so quickly forgotten the lessons of the attack on September 11, 2001. We ignore the plight of the Palestinians and the loss of innocent Israeli lives, preferring to let the sore in the Middle East continually fester. Our government pays lip service to world problems but does nothing, unless it has a positive impact on the global, industrial bottom line.

"To reverse this greed-induced slide toward our own demise, my colleagues and I, including ten senators and twenty-one members of the House of Representatives, are announcing today the birth of a new national political party, the American Freedom Party. This new party will be a party of the people, beholden to them and only them. We will develop a platform over the next few weeks and intend on selecting a candidate for the presidency, as well as candidates in congressional races in all fifty states.

"One of our first priorities will be the restoration of the American military and the reemphasis of the primary job of the national government, to protect the country and its people. Our government's preparedness to confront terrorism today is dismal. We're unprepared to deal with even a minor terrorist attack, and our highest leadership refuses to take any steps to deal with potential threats. It seems short-term political considerations and cozy relations with our European friends are more important than stopping an attack on our country."

This time, there was an audible gasp in the ballroom. Someone in the back of the hall shouted something, indecipherable to Benson.

The senator paused before continuing, thinking, *Oh boy, here it goes!* "Earlier this week the director of the FBI, Sydney Wilkinson, attempted to report to the president some extremely disturbing intelligence information indicating a massive terrorist attack on the United States was planned and was in early stages of execution. The information was from an extremely reliable source in Pakistan, reporting the planning and resources for the attack were being supplied by elements of the Al Qaeda terrorist network.

"The president refused to meet with Director Wilkinson, instead referred him to the attorney general, George Lukavitz. The director provided the intelligence information to Lukavitz, who summarily dismissed it as bogus. He reminded the director that, so-called, faulty intelligence given to the second President Bush led to the Iraq war, and he wasn't about to try to persuade the president to respond to unsubstantiated information from an obscure source in Pakistan."

Seven hundred people sat in stunned silence.

Benson slowly surveyed the silent audience before continuing, "I'm not telling you this to smear Attorney General Lukavitz or the president. I'm telling you this to force the issue. We're vulnerable and intelligence from a reliable, proven source points to a massive terrorist attack on the United States of America, while this administration chooses to do nothing."

The crowd exploded, five or six hundred people shouted questions at the same time. Benson observed several politicians from both parties get up and leave the room. He raised both hands and motioned for quiet. As the noise subsided he asked, "Will you hold on for just a few more minutes? I'm almost finished.

"We as Americans, must demand our government do what's necessary now to protect us. Our national and local police agencies are hamstrung, blinded by the politically correct actions of our government. Key provisions of the *Patriot Act*, deleted from the law last year, have made it virtually impossible for the FBI to develop any meaningful intelligence information relative to potential extremist attacks. They are now faced with only the option of investigating the case after the bombs have exploded. I pray those bombs are not nuclear.

"Our total lack of concern for border protection, particularly the Mexican border, gives terrorists virtually an open door into our country to carry out whatever nefarious plans they have. My colleagues and I demand the president take immediate action in these two areas. Failure to act now, in view of the intelligence information we have received, is, at best, a dereliction of duty and, at worst, treason."

Then pausing again, he continued. "I remember reading a quote several years ago attributed to the eighteenth century political writer, Edmund Burke, 'All that is necessary for evil to triumph is for good men to do nothing.' I think that's where we are at the moment. Millions of good Americans need to make the conscious decision that evil will not triumph. We need to take back our democracy and be willing to make those necessary sacrifices, sometimes even including our lives, to restore the grand tradition born on this earth in 1776. May God bless this country."

With that, the senator strode off the podium to his left and exited the ballroom. Surprisingly there was some applause. Apparently even in this bastion of political correctness and expediency, there were some who shared Benson's fears and desires to right the American ship.

Within ten minutes of the conclusion of Benson's speech, Sydney Wilkinson received an urgent telephone call at his suburban Washington home. The FBI director, at first, didn't recognize the caller, since the first words uttered on the other end of the phone were, "What the hell have you done?"

Wilkinson asked, "Who is this?"

"Who do you think it is?" the CIA director indignantly replied.

"Oh", muttered Wilkinson, thinking of the negative ramifications, which could occur should Director William Smith not buy into his and Benson's scheme, "Let me explain …"

Chapter 30

The next morning, both presidents of the world's nuclear super powers were livid.

President Papadakis had spent the first two hours of his morning sitting at his desk in the Oval Office stewing over Benson's speech. He even cleared his morning calendar to allow for more stewing time. *How could that arrogant pipsqueak from Oregon impugn the integrity, the honor, and the tradition of the political process that had served this country, or at least the leadership of this country, so well for so many years? Where in the hell did he get the audacity to say what he did?*

Finally, after thinking about what options he had, he settled on one that, upon reflection, made the most sense. Fully aware of the public support for the new political party, he needed allies in this war. He grabbed the phone, dialed his secretary's two-digit number, and instructed her to arrange to have Senate and House leaders of both Parties at a meeting in his office first thing in the morning.

Halfway across the world, President Lebedov was also stewing. Upon hearing the accusations made by the American senator in his speech the night before, Lebedov was sure that, somehow, security had been breached, threatening the successful launch of *Hammer and Anvil*. He was expecting Colonel Litinov at any moment, having summoned him early in the morning after hearing the senator's speech.

The double doors swung open and before the colonel could walk through them, the Russian president stood up from behind his desk and exploded, "What the hell have you done, Litinov?"

Litinov, not knowing yet why the president was so angry, replied in a stunned tone, "I don't know what you're talking about."

"Colonel, our operation has been compromised! That's what I'm talking about."

Litinov sunk involuntarily into a chair in front of Lebedov and muttered, "What has happened?"

Lebedov also sat back into his high-backed chair and proceeded to inform the colonel of the American senator's speech the previous night. He calmed somewhat as he talked.

When he was finished, Litinov tentatively asked, "Mr. President, can I speak frankly?"

The president nodded and Litinov, staring the president directly in the eyes said, "Mr. President, I don't think our mission has been compromised."

Lebedov nodded again while raising his eyebrows indicating for Litinov to continue.

"The Americans really don't know anything. Just look at what they are saying. They couldn't have a source from Pakistan who would know anything about *Hammer and Anvil*, plus Al Qaeda has nothing to do with this. I think they might have received some information about something else but not our operation. And, even if they did, it's obvious they don't have enough information to threaten it.

"The senator is, in my view, posturing to gain public political support. There's no way the American president will take any meaningful action anytime soon and then it will be too late. We have taken every precaution to ensure the operation will remain secret until we pull the trigger."

Lebedov rocked back in his chair and said nothing for a few seconds, appearing to contemplate what Litinov had just said. Finally, in a much calmer tone, he responded, "Colonel Litinov, I've trusted your judgment from the beginning and am inclined to trust it again now. You, however, have got to redouble your efforts to control security. None, I repeat, *none* of the cell members in the United States can be left alone, even to pee. Under no circumstances, can any of the teams be seen out in public. I know we have instructed them well in English and American culture, but, regardless, the only exposure that will be risked is when they drive the SUVs to their targets. You must make Al Zouri understand the importance of my directions. Is that clear?"

"Yes sir," replied Litinov.

"Now, Colonel, what's the status of the Israeli phase of this project?"

Chapter 31

Larry Fuller prided himself in his ability to sell cars. He bragged to his wife, his brother-in-law, and anybody else who would listen that he could sell a Suburban to an old lady with a cane. He considered himself a professional automobile specialist. He had worked at the Martinez Chevrolet dealership in San Jose, California for the past three years and had been salesman of the month on more than a few occasions.

Today had been a slow day. Only three people had been in to look at cars, and none of them were seriously interested, and it was already approaching noon. Perhaps, it was the wet, drizzly weather the area had been experiencing the last three days. That's when a well-dressed, Middle Eastern looking man entered the dealership and began perusing the loaded, forest-green Suburban displayed in the showroom.

"Isn't she a beauty?" offered Fuller as he strode up behind the potential car buyer. "Can I help you figure out a way to drive her off the lot today?"

The Middle Eastern man turned slowly toward Fuller, smiled, and said in near-perfect English, "Probably not this one. If you've got one that has what I want, however, you'll make yourself some money."

Dollar signs registered in Fuller's eyes. "I'm sure I got just what you want."

The Middle Eastern man smiled faintly and explained, "What I'm looking for is a black Suburban, automatic, with tinted windows. It has to have a big-block V8 engine."

Fuller replied, "Let me go check our inventory log, and I'll be right back."

Fuller left and returned five minutes later and enthusiastically exclaimed, "You're in luck. We've got one out on the lot, which just arrived yesterday. Let's walk out there for a look."

Fuller and the Middle Easterner walked out to the east side of the lot where a row of shiny, new Suburbans were parked. The fifth vehicle in the line was a black Suburban with heavily-tinted glass. It almost looked evil, if such an epithet could be attributed to a SUV.

The Arab, whom Fuller assumed the man to be, opened the door, glanced at the interior for a few seconds, stood up, and said to Fuller, "I'll take it."

Fuller, caught by surprise, stuttered, "I…I…I'm sure we can make you a deal you'll like."

"How much is it?"

"It's $52,999 as she sits."

The Arab stared into Fuller's eyes and said, "I'll pay you fifty thousand in cash, if you can close this deal in the next thirty minutes."

Fuller shrunk inwardly as he met the man's stare. The Middle Easterner's eyes were black and chilling, exhibiting no emotion. The all-star car salesman adverted his eyes and replied, "I think we can do that. Follow me."

Similar conversations were taking place in twelve Chevrolet dealerships in several other cities, and, within the space of forty-eight hours, twelve thermonuclear-transport vehicles were en route to four rendezvous locations in the United States.

Mohammed was surprised how cold it was in northern Mexico's desert in October. He and eleven other freedom-fighters had been hiking for the past two hours toward the Rio Grande River, separating Mexico from America. He knew they would shortly be climbing aboard several rubber rafts for the twenty-yard float across the greatly diminished river. One of the two Mexican guides responsible for Mohammed's team directed them, en route, by hand gestures and said nothing to them, although he did speak in Spanish to the other Mexican.

It had to be past 2:00 a.m. as they approached the river. There was no moon as the weather was overcast, but Mohammed could still ascertain they were approaching the river. He could dimly see the earth descending down toward the riverbank.

As they got closer, he could make out four dark blobs protruding from the exposed, dry river bottom that, he assumed, were rafts. Off to the southeast, the lights of Laredo, Texas cast a greenish hue on the cloud deck. Mohammed estimated they were, at least, twenty kilometers from the city.

No lights of any kind were visible up or down the river. If there were border patrols in the vicinity, they were walking in the dark. The

Mexicans did not wait. The moment the entourage arrived, the rubber rafts were dragged into the water and the Palestinians were directed to climb into the rafts. Oars were handed to two men in each raft, and it was obvious what the Mexicans needed them to do. Uday was one of the rowers in Mohammed's raft.

The trip across the river took just over a minute and was completed without incident. Once on the opposite bank, the men hurriedly exited the rafts and climbed up the embankment where they were confronted by a ten foot, chain-link fence topped with concertina wire. The obstacle was quickly neutralized by a pair of wire cutters. Mohammed was amazed a simple, non-electrified fence was all that protected the United States' border.

Two other men, who also appeared to be Mexicans, materialized out of the dark and motioned Mohammed and his companions to accompany them. After another three hours of walking they approached a multilane highway. Mohammed knew from maps he had memorized it was Interstate 35, leading north from Laredo to Dallas and on into Oklahoma. They appeared to be at some sort of rest stop. Three cars were parked in a parking area adjacent to restroom facilities. No other cars were at the stop.

A couple of members of one of the other teams needed to use the restroom. The three teams, thereafter, loaded the cars and proceeded northward well under the speed limit on the Interstate. Each car was driven by an English-speaking Caucasian American, none of whom Mohammed had seen before. Very little conversation took place. Mohammed figured they were all too physically spent. He didn't know where they were headed, but felt more relaxed now they were in America. After a few minutes he dozed off into a fitful sleep.

Chapter 32

At no time in recent political memory was the country as polarized as it was now. The sharply divided electorate in the 2008 presidential election paled in comparison. Some commentators at the extremes were even making references to possible civil war, though more rational voices on both sides of the political spectrum scoffed at such notions.

Senator Benson's speech at the Renaissance Mayflower Hotel was viewed by over one hundred million Americans, and the reactions were generally either very supportive or vehemently opposed. The polling organizations went to work the week after the speech. The results were remarkably consistent: 50 percent supported Benson's views about the direction of the country and the need for a new political party, and 48 percent were opposed. Only 2 percent had no opinion either way.

When the question being asked focused specifically on a possible terrorist attack and the need to take overt actions to counter it, the public seemed more concerned, albeit only slightly so. An average of 55 percent of those polled believed we were unprepared and emergency action was warranted to address the possible threat.

Editorial commentators from all sides of the political spectrum continued to focus on the speech and congressional and presidential reaction to it. The Sunday talk show circuit served as a venue to express two opposing opinions. Benson was either held up as the greatest patriot since Washington or a Benedict Arnold traitor with not much room in between.

Chapter 33

Nicholas Papadakis had always viewed himself as being an extraordinary political operative, with the uncanny ability to always land on the right side politically of any issue. His political skills, after all, had allowed him to pass sweeping social bills through Congress, which, prior to his presidency, would have been unthinkable. He was able to save billions by cutting the defense budget in half and incur the admiration of the world by bringing the troops home. The American people loved him, or at least they once did, until his omniscience began to be challenged by the upstart from Oregon and his lackeys. He was determined to live up to his self-defined reputation in the current political crisis and restore his diminished luster, regardless of the cost to the Republic.

He was hosting a meeting that had begun forty minutes earlier in the Oval Office with the Senate and House majority and minority leaders, and four other key congressional leaders, including Senator Jack Williams from Texas.

The president had launched the discussions with brutal candor, which had immediately raised the defenses of the elected representatives of the people. It had taken about forty minutes to get over the posturing and exclaimed positions of innocence. Everybody finally reached somewhat of a consensus. As a group, they were truly facing a crisis, which, if not countered effectively, could easily result in, not only their defeats in the next elections, but a fundamental change in how politics worked in the United States. Though none would admit it in such simple terms, if they couldn't stop the American Freedom Party snowball now, the American people in the future might actually be able to choose the political leaders they eventually elect.

President Papadakis, who had manipulated the others effectively into acceptance of his remarkably candid point of view, continued to address the group. "Since we're all in agreement we face a grave political crisis, I'd propose we adopt an equally grave plan of attack to counter this. First of all, I'm convinced the rise in support for Benson's party is only temporary and can be reversed by attacking Benson personally. I think we can paint him into the old McCarthyism corner, and most Americans, who don't even know who Joe McCarthy was, just know it's bad to be associated with him. I'm sure we can marginalize Benson and the other misguided fools who've jumped on his bandwagon.

"Between all of us present we can just about monopolize the TV news talk shows, particularly the major networks, and all we need to do is have the same consistent message. I'm sure the major newspaper and wire service outlets will also print everything we say. The key to marginalizing this incipient movement is to keep up the talk, don't let it die, until the American public is sick of hearing about it.

"All of us need to keep up the pressure on our fellow Senate and House members. One thing we can't tolerate are more defections. They all need to know this threatens them as much as us."

The Speaker of the House, Tom Randall, interrupted the president, "All right, Mr. President, we hear you. We know what we have to do. But what about the information concerning the terrorist attack? If an attack takes place and we've done nothing, we'll get defeated at the polls anyway."

The president eyed Randall coldly, "Speaker Randall, there is not going to be a terrorist attack. That was sheer political postulation on Benson's part. I've talked with the CIA director, and he told me the CIA has no information that corroborates the FBI's allegations, even remotely. Don't you think the CIA would know if something was up? I'll be damned if I'll act on questionable intelligence. We did this several years ago and got ourselves into a war. Furthermore I will never reinstitute the provisions of the *Patriot Act* I fought so hard to eliminate last year just because of the paranoia of our FBI director. I'm not willing to pay the political price with my base of support to do such a stupid thing, even if I thought we faced an attack."

More than one of the politicians present wondered to themselves, *Why wouldn't we want to expand our intelligence gathering capabilities if an attack was imminent?* Since none, however, was willing to believe the president was wrong in his assessment of the risk, they kept silent.

The president continued, "The same is true of our borders. Where do you think all of our Latino support will go if we close down our southern border? I'm not going to commit political suicide, and I highly suggest none of you contemplate it either.

"Furthermore, I'm going to demand the resignation of Wilkinson on grounds he is mentally unstable. He publicized an extremely-serious, unfounded allegation that directly threatens the public's emotional well-being, simply to salve his irrational fears."

All nodded and murmured their approval to the president's plan to demand Wilkinson's resignation.

After the murmuring faded, Senator Williams noisily cleared his throat, as if announcing he was about to speak, and in an authoritative tone directed his comments to the president. "Mr. President, you, as usual, speak eloquently and confidently about how we will defeat these rebel congressmen. But, what if you're wrong? What's our option B?"

Papadakis quickly responded, "Senator Williams, that's a reasonable question, and what I propose will not be option B but will be the capstone, if you would, to this whole plan. As you know, I will be giving the State of the Union speech on January 30 next year. During that speech, I will recommend the Senate initiate proceedings to censure Senator Benson and the other senators and expel them from the Senate."

The assembled politicians looked aghast. Speaker Randall expressed their combined concern when he asked, "How can you do that? For what reason?"

Papadakis paused briefly and his mouth turned up at the corners into a slight smile. "Gentlemen, you forget, we together form a huge majority in both the House and Senate and can vote for anything we want. Believe me, I'll make the case for censure in my speech. All you have to do is ensure your compatriots are incensed sufficiently, as a result, to vote appropriately when the time comes."

The "enemy", at approximately the same time, was holding a caucus twenty-five miles to the southwest of the Oval Office. Their goals were similar, albeit from the opposite direction. In addition to ensuring survival, they were planning how to increase the support for the party and position the party to participate fully in the electoral process next year.

Ten senators and twenty-one members of the House were meeting in a conference room in an office complex in Arlington, Virginia, which had been rented the previous week as the new party headquarters for the American Freedom Party.

They had already laid out plans to open party offices in each of the fifty states and identify candidates for party chairpersons. Plans were also formulated for holding major fund raising events over the next few months.

Senator Eagleton was addressing the caucus, "I can't stress how important it is to get our organizations on the ground up and running. To be successful, it's imperative we get this done as soon as possible. We need money immediately, so we can hire staffers and other professional help here in Arlington and in our state offices. We need good people who know state laws and what's necessary to gain recognition of our party across the country. I'm truly excited about what we're up to here, and I'm convinced we can change the direction of our country and literally save our struggling democracy. Thanks for listening."

Benson, as the nominal host of the gathering, stood up to offer some concluding remarks, "As you know, a couple of weeks ago, I announced to the nation we were under a terrorist threat, and it was imperative the country take action to counter the threat. Well up to now, the administration has done nothing other than try to denigrate the messengers. As a matter of fact, the president is now demanding the resignation of Director Wilkinson. He hasn't demanded my resignation yet."

Laughter erupted from several of the caucus participants.

Benson continued, "I think we need to keep public pressure on the president to take action against the terror threat. I'm convinced it's a genuine threat. Over the next several weeks I, and others in the room, will be guests on a variety of news programs and will keep up the pressure. I just hope the public will be concerned enough to keep the political heat on the administration, so Papadakis will do something before it's too late to do so.

"I would also propose we consider offering Director Wilkinson a position within our party as security advisor, which might be most appropriate at this time, since he's under a lot of pressure to resign from the FBI. Any comments?"

Nobody raised any objections.

Benson closed the caucus meeting, "I appreciate your hard work tonight. We've got a lot of work ahead of us, but I'm sure, with your commitments as expressed tonight, we'll be successful. May God bless."

Benson strolled around the conference room shaking hands with his fellow caucus members. As he said his goodbyes, he thought to himself, *We've got a good start, but I worry what's ahead of us.* The senators concerns were not unfounded, in ways he hadn't imagined.

The yellow mongrel trotted up the path leading to the park. He was proud of himself since he had just successfully stalked and grabbed an unwary starling and was now carrying it in his mouth. He was going to present it to his master, a jogger and frequent park user, who had befriended the dog and routinely brought food for the mutt to eat. Today, the yellow dog was going to return the favor.

Chapter 34

Joe Johnson was a long-haul driver and was proud of it. He had driven the roads of America for the past twenty-two years. He missed the old twenty-four gear, stick-shift, dog-nosed Kenworth he had driven for most of those years. He had to admit, though, he was getting used to driving his current rig, a new, fully-automatic, teal-green Freightliner Coronado.

He had spent the past two years driving for Monarch Distributing, an American company headquartered in San Francisco. Monarch imported heavy industrial equipment from China for customers in America, Mexico, and Central America.

What Johnson didn't know was Monarch was not American-owned, at all, but was a distributing arm of a huge Chinese government-owned conglomerate to which billions of American dollars flowed monthly. Corporate accountants for all sorts of American corporations, inebriated on the liquor of cost saving, directed billions of dollars worth of purchase orders to China, who could manufacture quality equipment for a fraction of the cost of similar equipment made in America.

Johnson wouldn't be concerned, regardless, about who actually owned Monarch, even if he was privy to that knowledge. He was just interested in driving his rig to Dallas, Texas, a route he had driven many times over the two years he had worked for Monarch.

It was early in the afternoon on a unusually-warm November day, especially surprising considering how cool it usually was on the San Francisco docks. Joe was pleased the loading of his trailer was nearly completed. He couldn't wait to get started. He loved the growl of the 625 horsepower, Caterpillar diesel engine as he tooled down the freeways of California, Nevada, and states beyond en route to Dallas. Contemplating the awesome power he was sitting on when driving his rig was almost a spiritual experience for Joe. He had no way to comprehend the even more awesome power hidden in the trailer he was tasked with delivering to the warehouse in Dallas.

Johnson took a last look at the crates to make sure they were packed securely, closed, then sealed the rear doors of the trailer. He made a cursory check of the trailer brakes and other safety equipment on his rig and climbed up into the cab of the Freightliner. After a couple of tromps on the accelerator, causing black smoke to erupt from the two stacks, Johnson eased the eighteen-wheeled monster out from the dock toward the open gate in the chain-link fence surrounding the docks.

Fifteen minutes later, Johnson was motoring across the Oakland Bay Bridge, eventually to connect with Interstate 80, headed toward Nevada and Utah. He was on his way and he was in heaven.

Joe Johnson was driving the last of four trucks to leave the San Francisco dock over the previous two days. Three others were headed toward Monarch Distributing Company warehouses in San Jose, Minneapolis, and Pittsburgh. All were carrying heavy industrial equipment—and twelve thermonuclear weapons.

"What the hell am I supposed to tell the Americans?" bellowed the leader of Israel's premier intelligence organization. Engeman was wishing Colonel Dylan had not insisted he accompany him to Director Levy's office this blustery December day. His fear Levy was not in his finest form was being borne out excruciatingly clear.

"What do you mean you haven't had any contact with your source for almost three months? Hell, he's probably dead as a rat in a trap. What else have you got to add to this story? Without something else, it's going to fall on its face with major repercussions with our American friends. Is there anything you're getting that could be remotely tied into this operation in America?"

The colonel spoke hesitantly at first, but then gained confidence as he spoke, "Director, our intelligence assets in Kyrgyzstan, Chechnya, and Armenia are all reporting large movements of Russian military hardware headed south toward the Iranian and Iraqi borders. It appears these shipments are huge, consisting of the latest Russian T94 and "Black Eagle" tanks, motorized troop carriers, artillery, and lots and lots of SAMs, both AS 12s Gladiators and SA-X-20 Triumphs, Russia's latest surface to air missiles. We're also getting reports of equipment-laden ships sailing from Black Sea ports, through the Bosporus, apparently headed toward Egypt."

Levy, curtly asked, "What does that have to do with a terrorism operation in America?"

Dylan just as curtly replied, "Hear me out. You need to couple all of this with the recent war games between Russia and China and the apparent movement of hundreds of thousands of Chinese troops to central Russia. Director, those troops have not returned, and the war games ended weeks ago. Something big, maybe unprecedented, is up, and my gut is telling me this is all related, including the planned terrorist strike in the United States."

Levy stroked his chin, looked up over his wire-rimmed reading glasses, and in a muted tone said, "My gut agrees with your gut, but we can't pass on our best gut opinions to the Americans. We need some actionable intelligence." He shifted his gaze to Engeman. "What do you think?"

Engeman cleared his throat and postulated, "Director, I suspect the Russians are behind everything that's going on, even the terrorist activities in the States. I don't know enough to be certain about anything, but, to be honest with you, I'm scared to death the Russians might have armed the terrorists with nukes. Perhaps they feel a terrorist attack will give them cover to do something elsewhere. My gut is telling me Israel is also in grave danger."

Levy nodded and soberly replied, "My instincts are telling me you're right, but we just don't have enough information."

Staring with vacant eyes from Engeman to Dylan and back, the director solemnly, almost in a whisper, addressed them, "The future of our country, and perhaps the world as we know it, is in your hands. You have got to dig up more. I can't discuss this with the Americans until we have some concrete evidence to present. We can't just postulate possibilities with them. You know how the current U.S. administration views Israel. We might as well claim aliens from space have landed in Jerusalem."

In a rare display of respect, even affection, Levy encouraged the two Israeli master sleuths. "I have ultimate confidence in your ability to do what has to be done to corroborate what's little more than theory at this point. But if you're right, and I unfortunately believe you are, time is of the essence." With that, the director stood up and saluted both men smartly and stated, "May God be with you."

Chapter 35

The CIA director was in a quandary. He had been summoned to talk with the president shortly after Senator Benson announced the formation of a new political party. He had answered the president's questions about a possible terrorist attack as forthrightly as possible. The president, however, had taken Smith's answer that the CIA did not yet have evidence to corroborate the information from the Pakistani source, as an outright denial such an attack was even being contemplated.

Although he was highly skeptical of the eventual success of FBI Director Wilkinson and Senator Benson's scheme, he could not see any other practical alternatives. Without any hard evidence to support the existence of a terrorist plot to attack the United States, Smith's hands were tied. And try as they might, the agency's best had not been able to turn up anything even hinting of a terrorist attack on America.

Smith was savvy enough, however, to know lack of information didn't mean something sinister wasn't underway. He trusted the Israeli Mossad director and believed the Israeli wouldn't have passed on the intelligence information had he not been convinced of its veracity.

Current unexplained events occurring in Europe and the Middle East were adding to the director's anxiety, even though he could see no outward connection to a possible attack in the United States. Recent photographic intelligence from two KH-13 EIS satellites confirmed hundreds of thousands of Chinese troops, allegedly in Russia for the long-ago completed war games, remained in Russia and had moved westward toward eastern Europe. Other satellite surveillance indicated unusual movement of military equipment on roads leading south toward the Iranian and Iraqi borders and via ships, loaded in ports on the Black Sea, and heading through the Bosporus toward Egypt.

With severely limited assets on the ground in Iraq, Syria, and Iran, it was difficult to ascertain the destinations of the military hardware. Smith had working contacts with Israel, however, and knew the Mossad had excellent intelligence assets throughout the Middle East. Yesterday morning, the Israelis reported large quantities of military equipment and supplies were beginning to arrive in Iran and the Arab states surrounding Israel, with the exception of Jordan.

This morning at the weekly national security council briefing, Smith brought up the latest intelligence information only to have both the national security advisor and the president tell him he was paranoid and not to worry. The president assured him the Russian leader, Lebedov, was a man of peace and was certainly not going create problems in the Middle East that could erupt into a conflagration. "The Israelis are habitual exaggerators," claimed the president, "and have their own hidden agenda."

Smith attempted to argue the evidence was beginning to point to the contrary, at which point the president reminded him it was misinterpreted evidence, which got the United States into the Iraq war in 2003. Smith almost replied with an even more loaded question, *What evidence are you looking for, a mushroom cloud?,* but realized a similar question was also posed before the Iraq war. Being politically astute and knowing when an argument was not winnable, Smith declined to argue further and said virtually nothing else during the meeting.

Two hours later, sitting at his desk, he sipped on a cup of black coffee and contemplated this morning's conversation. The administration's refusal to even consider the possibility of trouble in the Middle East, coupled with the presidents cavalier dismissal of a possible terrorist attack, was extremely disconcerting. He felt a foreboding that evil was preparing to launch itself again upon the unsuspecting world, and he had very few options do anything about it.

"What the hell is going on?" muttered Smith out loud to nobody in particular, since nobody else was in his office.

Christmas in America has become a holiday of extremes. Most retail stores can claim business success or failure for the year depending on Christmas. It has become a holiday where commercialization is rampant with media of all stripes promoting overindulgence. Santa Claus is no longer the wonderful old man with a pot belly bringing gifts to all the world's children. He is now the chief marketing tool for giant department store chains, convincing kids their particular store's products are better than a competitor's. Christmas has even become a politically incorrect word. In many places in America, it's now called winter break or, simply, the Holidays. Being PC hip means you wouldn't want to offend someone by calling the holiday after the original intent—to celebrate the birth of Christ.

Regardless of commercialization and political correctness, most Americans still considered Christmas a special time of the year. Families and friends still gathered together, sometimes only once each year at Christmastime. Whether the purpose was to "party on" or to remember Christ's birth, the Christmas holidays were still a welcome break from the stresses of the world.

This was no exception for the Benson family. While carrying on the fun tradition of Santa Claus for the youngest son, Tyler, who at age six was beginning to ask pointed questions about Santa, the Bensons also celebrated Christmas for what it was traditionally intended. An abiding faith in God formed the foundation for Senator Benson's basic values and provided the fuel, which kept him from giving up the fight upon which he had embarked.

The week-long break from the stresses of the battle with the Washington establishment was welcome and reinvigorating.

The continuing fight being waged in the print and television media between the two sides was unrelenting and vicious. Things had been said by surrogates representing both sides that were brutal and, specifically from the president's side, outright lies. As the State of the Union speech approached, it seemed the president, who could read the polls better than most, had begun to run scared. While big-city newspaper and network news coverage was slanted toward the establishment, coverage from cable news and smaller influential newspapers mostly offset the bias.

The latest polls showed support for the new third party growing steadily. In mock elections, should Senator Benson be the party's choice for president, Benson trailed the once-popular president by only two or three percentage points.

Just before the Christmas Holidays, the *New York Times* broke a story on its front page, citing an anonymous but reliable administration source, that President Papadakis intended to call for a Senate censure of Senator Benson and the other nine senators. The story quoted the source as claiming their actions over the past few months constituted a treasonous breach of trust with the American people. The article claimed the president fully intended to call for their expulsion from the Senate.

The *Times* article set off a firestorm on the TV talk shows. Constitutional experts were almost unanimous in agreement there were no grounds for censure, and, if it occurred, would create a constitutional crisis of historic proportions. Other political pros were convinced the president had the votes in the Senate to push through a censure. What the diametrically opposed factions of the citizenry would do was an open question. Civilian unrest, even violent conflict, was being discussed as a remote possibility. Just the fact possibilities were being discussed sent chills down Benson's spine.

In an attempt to dampen down the growing anger, Benson had scheduled a news conference in mid January to address the issues and hopefully calm the public. What he planned on doing, however, would be another shock to the Washington elite. It appeared the political dispute was about to boil over into a full blown crisis.

Chapter 36

The Monarch Distributing company warehouse in Minneapolis was a large, old, red-brick building with a rusty-steel roof. Most of the windows on the exterior of the building were broken, which didn't matter since they were boarded up anyway. It looked similar to just about every other rundown building in this particular section of the Minneapolis warehouse district. Its nondescript appearance was purposeful, as was everything else associated with the operation of the company. The key to Monarch's success was its blandness. A passerby might even think the warehouse was abandoned.

Inside it was a hive of activity. Crates of Chinese-manufactured industrial equipment were stacked three-pallets high in long rows. Heavy-duty yellow and orange forklifts, as well as robot transporters, appeared to be in constant but random motion as orders were picked and prepared for shipment to a Central or South American manufacturing plant.

Hidden in the bowels of the warehouse was a second, more recently constructed, enclosure, heavily protected by a state-of-the-art security system. IP closed circuit TV cameras and motion sensing alarms protected all entrances to the newer structure. The walls and ceiling were steel-reinforced concrete and could withstand virtually all types of explosive charges except for a direct hit by a bunker-buster bomb. It would be an unusual event, to say the least, for one of those to drop on a building located in Minneapolis, Minnesota.

Inside of the concrete enclosure, actually a warehouse inside of a warehouse, several mechanics and auto body technicians were working on three brand-new, black Suburbans parked adjacent to the east wall. Two hydraulic lifts were located in the same area and were used, as needed, by the mechanics and technicians as they continued to make modifications to the frame, bottom sheet metal, and suspension systems of the SUVs. None of the mechanics or technicians were told why they were modifying perfectly good, brand-new vehicles, but they were all being paid enough to not care to ask questions. They simply had to follow written instructions and diagrams and complete their work by January 15.

Occasionally the workers would observe foreign-looking individuals surveying their work, people from the Middle East and Eastern Europe. None of the observers ever spoke to the mechanics, so their nationality was just a guess.

Located on the far west side of the inner warehouse were three large crates enclosed in heavy-gauge, floor-to-ceiling chain-link. Motion and infra-red detection alarms protected every square inch of the chain-link enclosure, and a series of four closed-circuit TV cameras were trained on the crates. Monitoring devices were attached to each crate. None of the men working on the vehicles had any idea what was being monitored. Several other smaller crates were stacked three-high at the far south end of the warehouse. These did not appear to be protected with any type of electronic security system.

The mechanics and technicians couldn't help but wonder what was in the crates, and some shared guesses with each other while downing Michelobs at a nearby bar after work. None of them were even remotely close with their guesses.

With less than two weeks to go before the State of the Union speech, the country was abuzz with speculation. Last night, during a prime time news conference, the president launched another bombshell, asking for the resignation of FBI Director Wilkinson. This morning, Senator Benson announced the former FBI director had accepted a position with the new party as its homeland-security advisor.

The citizenry was more aware and more involved in the political drama playing out than any time in the history of the Republic. Millions of Americans were planning on tuning in to Senator Benson's press conference scheduled in two days. Rumors were rampant throughout the country. Many speculated the senator was going to submit his resignation. Others were sure he was going to announce his candidacy for the presidency, even though the election would not be held for two years.

Under everybody's radar screen, buried on the back pages of most major newspapers and seldom mentioned in the electronic media, were ominous developments in other corners of the globe. An unprecedented buildup of military power was occurring in Arab countries surrounding Israel. Tons of top-of-the-line Russian equipment was pouring into Syria, Iraq, Saudi Arabia, and Egypt, as well as non-Arab Iran. Mobilization of troops was occurring in each of the countries and stores of supplies and thousands of troops were deploying at or near the Israeli borders.

Israel for its part, had reacted with restraint, partially mobilizing certain headquarters and key defense units, but not yet a full mobilization. Israel's righteous demands to the UN for a halt to the military moves of its neighbors were landing on deaf ears. Certain European members, particularly France, even blamed Israel for the growing crisis, faulting Israel for the unresolved Palestinian/Israeli conflict.

The red flag which appeared to be missing, was the lack of any trigger for the current crisis. Nothing had happened to cause the Arab states to threaten war. No incident had sparked the buildup. It just began to happen. Even now there were no unusual belligerent statements coming out of the government mouthpieces of the Arab dictatorships. They were acting as if nothing was unusual, and the military moves were routine.

Equally little attention was being paid to military moves occurring in western Russia. Though on a smaller scale than what was occurring in the Middle East, tens of thousands of troops and supporting equipment were moving westward and southward toward the Ukraine, Georgia and Azerbaijan borders. Even more ominous were troop movements through Belarus toward Poland, a NATO member. Large elements of the troop formations were Chinese, which, at any other period of time in the last hundred years, would have set the alarm bells ringing. Not today. Hardly a ripple of concern was being expressed in the capitals of Western Europe and America. The possibility of war in Europe was not even worth contemplation. The civilized world had left such thoughts back in the twentieth century. In this new millennium the global economy ruled. Nobody would be stupid enough to threaten that.

Chapter 37

Ariel Levy was in one of those "damned if you do and damned if you don't" situations. All of the intelligence flooding his office, consistently pointed to a real threat to Israel. The military buildup on his country's borders was massive and indicated an attack was imminent. Nothing was being said, however, from Israel's neighbors indicating any critical issues were fomenting a crisis. It was as if the Arab governments were oblivious to what their own armed forces were doing.

The international pressure on Israel to act with restraint was enormous. Apparently Europe felt, with logic stood on its head, if Israel mobilized or made any defensive military moves, then the Arab buildup would be justified.

Absolutely zero information had been developed to illuminate the alleged imminent terror attack on America. Levy explicitly trusted the judgment of Colonel Dylan. If the colonel was convinced Engeman's source inside Black October had furnished accurate intelligence about the attack, then Levy was prone to believe it. He was also afraid the reason for silence from the source was he was probably dead.

The director of Israel's supreme spy agency knew in his gut there was a connection with all that was happening, but he could not connect enough dots to know exactly what that connection was.

He had reluctantly come to the conclusion, in spite of serious misgivings, to recommend to the Israeli prime minister the country prepare herself for war and immediately order full mobilization. Israel could not find herself unprepared again as happened in the Yom Kippur war in 1973, which nearly led to a catastrophe.

Levy would be meeting with the prime minister, and cabinet, in a special emergency session early tomorrow morning to discuss the deteriorating situation and make critical decisions. It was sure to be a most sobering meeting.

Mohammed was restless. For the past two months he, and his team, had been cramped in two upstairs bedrooms of a small, white, shake-shingled house, which appeared to be cloned from every other house in the neighborhood. The few trips outside the house to buy groceries, served as the only respite to the numbing boredom. Never alone, even on the quick trips to the grocery store, Mohammed was growing weary of the constant companionship.

This morning was going to be different. Even the weather seemed to portend change. The past several days had been typical gray, overcast, January days, exacerbated by the smoky discharges from the still-functioning, Minneapolis manufacturing industry. Today Mohammed woke up to a clear, crisp, sunny, but extremely cold morning. Although he didn't particularly like the raw air, it, at least, was a welcome change from the drab setting of the last several days.

Mohammed and his three comrades had been contacted the previous day and told they would be picked up this morning and delivered to a warehouse located in the Minneapolis warehouse district for comprehensive instructions related to their mission. They were told to pack all of their belongings, which didn't amount to much. Finally, it appeared all the training and waiting were now going to result in decisive action.

Mohammed and the others shared the excitement as well as the apprehension of what might be ahead. While all of the terrorists knew this was going to be a suicide mission, the knowledge they were now going to be briefed on the particulars of the mission, itself, was sobering. More than one of the Palestinians struggled with doubts.

One particularly had doubts, but not because his dedication and courage was faltering. Uday Mahmud was dedicated, no doubt, but not to committing suicide for the glory and blessing of Allah. He was dedicated to stopping the insane violence that was destroying the Middle East and now threatened to destroy the world. He was also desperate, since he had been unable to contact anyone on the outside to warn them of the coming attacks.

A little after 9:00 a.m., a five-year old, somewhat-dinged, blue Chevy Blazer pulled up; its white exhaust swirling lazily into the cold, clear, morning air as it idled in front of the house. Uday and his three terrorist comrades filed out the front door for the last time. Three climbed in the back seat and Mohammed slid into the shotgun seat. Mohammed recognized the driver from his time in the training camps in the Beq'a valley.

Little was said during the forty-five minute drive through the Minneapolis suburbs, passing initially by neat little shake-shingle or maroon-brick homes, and then innumerable row houses as they approached downtown. Turning east before reaching the downtown high-rises, they approached the old warehouse district. As they continued deeper into the district, Mohammed was amazed at the endless dirty, red bricked warehouses they drove by as they traveled toward their destination. None of the four were the least bit familiar with the areas they passed through, and it would have been virtually impossible for any of them to describe the location of the Monarch Company warehouse once they arrived.

The Blazer had barely rolled to a stop, when two unknown, clean-shaven, dark-haired men, obviously Middle Eastern, opened the car doors on the side closest to the warehouse and ardently directed the team out of the car into an open side door of the warehouse.

Once inside, they were ushered to the southeast corner of the warehouse where a dozen folding chairs had been arranged. An eight-by-four-foot, folding table was set up ten feet in front of the chairs. Three folding chairs were tucked in behind the table. Two naked, glaring, light bulbs hung about ten feet above their heads providing barely adequate light. The light reflected dimly off what appeared to be a much newer concrete structure built inside the warehouse, obviously not visible from outside the old building.

The rest of the warehouse was illuminated by florescent lights hanging over endless aisles of crated machinery stacked three-crates high. None of the several orange forklifts, which were visible from the darkened corner where Mohammed and the others were sitting were moving. As a matter of fact, it did not appear anybody else was in the warehouse.

A few minutes later, the same side door through which Mohammed and his team had entered the warehouse, squeaked open again, and eight other Palestinians entered and were lead to the remaining seats. Other than nods and grunts to acknowledge each other's presence, no words were exchanged between the twelve men. All of them realized the deadly seriousness of what they were about to do, and conversation at this point was superfluous.

Uday did not recognize the speaker. He appeared to be in his sixties, with a long, scraggily, graying beard and thick spectacles at the end of a bulbous, pocked nose. He was wearing a black and white checkered kaffiyeh that marked him a Palestinian, but, for some reason, Uday doubted his lineage was from Palestine. Uday and the others listened to him rave about the glorious sacrifice each of them was going to make to deal a death blow to the American Satan and its Jewish swine lackeys.

After a twenty minute diatribe, the speaker introduced a second individual seated to his left behind the table who didn't appear to be Arab. He was introduced as an ally in the battle against the great Satan and would be providing specific details about each mission. He appeared to be Eastern European but, as was the case with the first speaker, was not introduced by name, nor did he identify himself.

The Eastern European stranger paused for several seconds as he scanned the room. After slowly eyeballing each of the twelve terrorists in an obviously ominous manner, he said in heavily-accented Arabic, "What I'm about to tell you is top-secret and cannot be discussed anywhere but here in this corner of the warehouse. I'll be presenting the operational plans each of the three teams will follow to ensure the ultimate success of our mission. After I've addressed you all as a group, I will hold separate meetings with each team to furnish specific information relative to each team's individual mission. Any discussion of the instructions each team receives with any other team or team member is prohibited. Any breach of this protocol will result in the violator's termination from the mission and premature exit from this earth life. Do I make myself clear?"

The speaker scanned the faces of each of the twelve to solicit individual nods from each person. Uday nodded when his turn came. The realization was taking form slowly in his mind. He was going to have to pay with his life to have even a remote chance of warning the unsuspecting world.

The emergency session of the Israeli cabinet droned on well into the afternoon. The cold wind blowing in from the Mediterranean reflected the cold news emanating from the meeting. While there was unanimity the threat facing the country was grave, there was spirited discussion on the best course of action to meet the threat. In the end, even though some of the more moderate members expressed concern about world reaction, the decision was unanimous to order a full mobilization of Israel's military reserves. None wanted to be on record of favoring a course of restraint, should an attack catch Israel unprepared.

Later that night, the prime minister of the Jewish state, Ravid Ben Gurion, would announce to his countrymen over national television the country's very existence was being threatened. During the prime-time speech the people of the small, but determined, country would learn their sons and daughters would again be called upon to sacrifice their blood in its defense.

Chapter 38

As Senator Benson prepared for the news conference scheduled at 9:00 p.m., he reflected on the news that had come over the *AP* wire. Israel was ordering full mobilization of its military. He wondered what on earth was happening? War appeared to be imminent in the Middle East for no apparent reason.

The news had hardly made the wires, when France and Germany vehemently condemned Israel for taking such a provocative step. Their condemnation was immediately followed by an equally strident denunciation of Israel by the White House.

Benson wondered what they expected Israel to do. Under the circumstances the mobilization appeared to be the only prudent course. He reminded himself almost automatic condemnation was now the politically correct thing to do by the West, regardless of the circumstances.

Benson's unease was growing as a gnawing feeling in his gut was telling him events were in motion that would have huge consequences for the world. Looking at seemingly unrelated events in Russia, the Middle East, and America, he feared the events were not random but were related in some macabre manner.

He had decided to add a few comments in his news conference opening speech about the world situation. The politicians, press, and media might think the world developments were back-page filler, but he didn't. Knowing the audience tonight would be huge, it was a great opportunity to raise some alarms with the citizenry.

Tom Randall hesitated before responding to the president's latest suggestion. Papadakis had just proposed the unification of the Republican and Democratic Parties into a single entity. According to the president, together, they could more effectively confront the surging momentum of Senator Benson's new Party. Randall was a popular, eight-term congressman from Connecticut who had developed a carefully cultivated reputation for integrity and telling it like it is. He was not yet ready to take the huge step the president was suggesting.

The thought that immediately entered his mind was that his constituents would see through such a move. They would recognize the merger of the two Parties was strictly political maneuvering in order to confront the new grass-roots challenge posed by the American Freedom Party. He could imagine the headlines, *The Entrenched Beltway Power Elite Unite to Stifle the People's Dissent.*

Randall exclaimed, "Mr. President, I think we'd better be pretty careful before embarking on such a course. We don't need to do that to win the vote to expel Benson and the others. You have enough support on both sides in the Senate to make such a move appear bipartisan and in the best interests of the country. "

Papadakis eyed the Speaker icily, "You're getting squishy on me Randall. We all know what's at stake here, your future and mine, and I'll be damned if I'm going to be cautious in this fight. Winning at all costs can be the only outcome."

"I agree we must win", said Randall meekly. "I just think the timing of what you're suggesting is critical. With the terrorist scare and everything else going on, we don't need more controversy. We'll know a lot more about if, and when, such a move is necessary after your State of the Union address on the thirtieth."

After several seconds of contemplating, the president again drilled into the Speaker's eyes and said forcefully, "Okay, we'll address this question again after my speech. I want your commitment, however, you'll do what's best for all of us, regardless of your own personal agenda. When decision time comes Randall, will you be on board or not?"

Tom Randall, always cautious of the impact of any decisions on his carefully manicured reputation replied, "I agree, let's look at it again early next month, after we have had time to measure the impact of your speech."

The president, abruptly changing moods, smirked, "Randall, I have never thought you had much backbone, just kind of meandered wherever the political winds blew you. I think we're at a crossroads here, and it's time you belly up to the bar and join the team. This terrorism talk is just another way for the malcontents to stir up the masses."

Randall, taking offence at Papadakis' disrespectful directness, shot back, "You know if you are wrong, your political legacy won't be worth the toilet paper to wipe your ass."

With that, Randall twirled on his heel and left the Oval Office without so much as a nod goodbye to the shocked president.

All major newspaper, television, and internet news outlets had gathered at the Doubletree Hotel Crystal City in Arlington for Benson's news conference. Anticipation was swirling that the senator was going to announce his candidacy for the presidency.

All knew the current occupant of the White House was going to trash Benson during his State of the Union speech next week and announce his goal of having him and the other rebel senators expelled from the Senate. Few of the assembled journalists believed the president's aim was strictly legal, but equally few believed he did not have the votes to do what he was proposing. Yes, anticipation was running exceptionally high this particular evening.

Promptly at 9:00 p.m., late enough to ensure all-four time zones would be able to tune in, Senator Benson strode purposefully up to the podium at the head of the Crystal Ballroom.

After pausing to survey the audience and take a few deep breaths, the senator from Oregon began speaking, "I greatly appreciate all of you attending this news conference this evening. I have only a few comments to make before we begin with your questions, so I'd ask for your forbearance for a minute or two.

"I have a few issues to address briefly. It's anticipated during the State of the Union speech next week, the president intends to ask the Senate to consider my, and my colleagues, activities over the past several months as censurable, with the eventual aim of having us expelled from the Senate. I consider even the fact he would contemplate such an action as more evidence of just how far down the slippery slope we've slid toward outright refutation of the United States Constitution.

"Rather than sit in the vaunted halls of our country's Capitol only to be vilified by our president on national TV, I, and my congressional colleagues will be holding our own caucus elsewhere."

There were audible moans heard from a few of the assembled journalists.

Benson continued, "We have reserved a convention hall in Senator Mathews' home town of Bangor, Maine and will gather there with our families to listen to the president and subsequently respond with our own State of the Union message. Of course, any of you who want to attend with us are more than welcome."

A clamor of murmuring voices rose throughout the crowd as journalists from all venues attempted to figure out, at that moment, who would represent their various agencies at the alternative State of the Union speech to take place in Bangor, Maine. All knew such a newsworthy event would have to be covered.

The senator waited a few minutes for the clamor to die down and then spoke again. "The second issue I want to mention tonight regards something of equal concern to our nation. As most of you are aware, military buildups are continuing in both the Middle East and on the western borders of Russia. Additionally, our country has received credible reports of a planned massive terrorist strike on our country in the near future. In view of potential threats to our interests, all of these seemingly-unrelated events pose, it's imperative the United States government respond in appropriate fashion. To date, the administration has been silent.

"Even you journalists, for the most part, have relegated stories about these events to the second page, when, in times past, they would be headlines. The biggest story to hit the front page this morning was Israel's mobilization, not the massive Arab build-up, which preceded it.

"The American Freedom Party urges the administration to discontinue political posturing and demand explanations from the governments behind these unwarranted military moves. We further urge the administration take whatever steps are necessary to protect us from something even worse than *nine-eleven*. Emergency legislation is needed immediately to allow the FBI to fully do its job in collaboration with the CIA. Failure to act now could lead to a catastrophe of unimaginable proportions."

"I will now take your questions."

It seemed like a million hands shot into the air at once. Benson looked over the crowd briefly and pointed to Jed Grobin, White House correspondent for CNN.

"Senator!" yelled Grobin. "In view of the president's reference to possible treason, don't you think holding a second State of the Union speech will just play into his hands?"

"No," replied Benson. "In spite of what he thinks, I'm not aware anywhere in the Constitution where it says formation of a third political party is treasonous or prohibits that party from holding its own caucus to present its own view of the current state of our country."

Benson glanced from Grobin to the left side of the room and, pointing to Mary Lancaster, a reporter from the *Washington Post*, said, "Mary, what's your question?"

Lancaster asked bluntly, "Senator Benson, are you going to run for President of the United States?"

Benson, equally blunt but with emphasis framing his answer so there would be no wiggle room. "Absolutely not. Not under any circumstances."

The questions and answers continued for the better part of an hour. Some of the questions were obviously adversarial in nature but Benson answered all directly without equivocation, which led to begrudging approval by the journalists present. They were not accustomed to so many direct answers by a politician, and the approving nods and whispers, which were apparent as the evening wore on, were also observed by the national viewing audience.

Chapter 39

Uday slept fitfully. The bunk provided for him in the warehouse was comfortable enough, and the temperature was maintained at a reasonable level. Viewing the same pale-blue walls, same fire-suppression water pipes, same orange forklifts, and the same rows of stacked pallets would probably drive anybody nuts over time. He and his fellow bombers, however, were not destined to be in the warehouse for an extended amount of time. No. It wasn't the surroundings, which were causing Uday insomnia. It was what he and the others were about to do.

A few days earlier, the Eastern European stranger had explained all of the remaining rules to be followed and identified their target. The setup was foolproof, at this point, in Uday's mind. He could not envision an opportunity to communicate any warning messages.

His and the other two teams were to be sequestered in the warehouse and could not leave until it was time to implement the final mission, which would begin in less than a week. It was stressed over and over by both the Eastern European stranger and Mohammed that, under no circumstances, was the target destination to be discussed with any member of the other teams.

Uday was told their target was the forty-two story One Kansas City Place Building in downtown Kansas City, Missouri, and the team was to arrive at the target destination no more than thirty minutes before it was time to detonate the explosives carried in the belly of the black Suburban.

They were instructed to park in the garage under the building and detonate the bomb at exactly 8:15 p.m. on January 30. The timing was critical. If for some reason they were delayed and couldn't reach the target, they were told to detonate the explosives at exactly 8:15 p.m. regardless where they were at the time.

The only exception was if they were chased and stopped by the police and were unable to talk or shoot their way out of being apprehended. In that case, they were instructed to detonate the explosives before they were captured. Before resorting to use of weapons, if stopped, the driver of the SUV would first attempt to talk his way out of trouble. If ordered out of the car, the other three would open up with their previously hidden mini Uzi machine pistols. How ironic, thought Uday. *The team was issued mini Uzis manufactured by Israel. AK-47's were just too big to hide.*

The team was to leave the Minneapolis warehouse at noon on Monday, January 30, and drive the 460 miles to Kansas City, arriving at the target no earlier than 7:45 p.m. The only authorized stops were for gasoline and bathroom breaks. On those occasions, nobody was to be alone. Uday would have to pee with a partner. The schedule allotted the team enough time for the trip with about sixty minutes of fudge time, while at all times staying within posted speed limits. The police did not need a reason to stop them.

The type of explosive they would be triggering was never discussed, and questions about it were deferred with the admonition not to ask again. Uday suspected the explosives were not the typical plastic or nitrogen based explosives previously used. He had convinced himself, reluctantly, the explosives were nuclear, at the least, a dirty bomb of some type.

The instructions to detonate the explosives were exquisitely simple. A hidden panel at the rear of the SUV's center console opened to reveal two switches. The switch on the left armed the bomb, and the switch on the right triggered it. All members of the team were instructed how to arm and trigger the bombs, and each practiced repeatedly on a dummy constructed exactly like the real thing. The switches looked and felt like toggle switches on a piece of manufacturing machinery.

They were instructed to arm the bomb once they were within twenty miles of the target, or if it appeared they were going to be stopped by the police. Triggering the bomb, thereafter, was a simple flip of a switch. The Eastern European instructor emphasized, a little too strongly, there was no automatic timer to trigger the bomb in case the team got cold feet. Uday suspected there probably was an automatic timing device, just in case, although, knowing full well the fanaticism of his comrades, a back-up timing device would never be needed.

The explosive itself was hidden from view and was not accessible to any of the team members. All they were permitted to see was the triggering panel. Other than the panel, the interior of the SUV was unremarkable, and a casual observer would never suspect what was lurking under the rear seats.

Uday had to find a way to communicate to Engeman, otherwise the world was headed for a most uncertain future.

Another sleep insomnia sufferer was the President of Russia. Even though the briefing the day before by Colonel Litinov assured President Lebedov all the pieces were in place, and the plan was virtually foolproof, the Russian leader, nevertheless, was suffering an extreme case of nerves. A plan this complex, with such broad strategic goals, would never come off without some mistakes somewhere. Lebedov's hope was any mistakes would be covered up eventually by a successful outcome.

His biggest concern, without doubt, was the comparatively risky action being taken against Israel. The risks associated with the venture in America were enormous, to be sure, but, for the most part, were behind them now. Israel, however, was a different story. The plan called for the bomb to be detonated in Tel Aviv, driven there by a team leaving early on January 31 from Lebanon. The Israelis were not fools and were obviously on guard for a terrorist attack as well as conventional military attack. Damn the Arab sensitivities, which necessitated what Lebedov considered an unnecessary diversion from the real mission.

At this point, the only option that would normally be available to soothe one's soul was to pray for success, and even that option was not available to the soulless Lebedov.

Chapter 40

The Speaker of the House is second in line to the presidency, immediately after the vice president. It is a bit of an oddity how the line of succession works since, as often as not, the Speaker is of a different Party. It wasn't always that way. In 1792 the first elected Congress passed the *Presidential Succession Act* listing the President pro tempore of the Senate (usually the senior member of the majority party) as next in line after the vice president followed by the Speaker of the House. In 1886, Congress, in all of its wisdom, decided the country would need someone with executive experience to run the country, so replaced the President pro tempore of the Senate and the Speaker of the House with the president's cabinet members, led by the Secretary of State. Then, in 1947, President Harry Truman signed a bill changing the presidential succession to what it is today, bringing the Speaker of the House and President pro tempore of the Senate back on the succession first team.

The second man in line to the presidency was miffed. His recent conversation with the president still rankled him. Tom Randall was a politician from the marrow in his bones to the hair on his skin, but he still felt a great deal of respect to the institution he led. The president's plan to request that the Senate censure and expel senators, whose only crime was the founding a new political party, was, in Randall's view, a gross abuse of power. Corruption of this magnitude, could cause irreparable damage to the supports underpinning the Constitution.

Randall was convinced the president, even if successful with the vote in the Senate, stood a good chance of ending up on the losing side of the burgeoning movement taking hold across the country. Randall, under no circumstances, wanted to be on the losing side. As a result, he purposefully dialed a set of numbers into his cell phone to offer his help to the alleged enemy.

"Hello, Senator Benson speaking"

"Hi Senator, this is Tom Randall. You're probably wondering why I'd be calling you a day before the president's State of the Union?"

Benson, caught totally off guard, stammered, “You might say that. What can I do for you?”

“Well”, Randall paused for a second or two, “I think the answer is what I can do for you.”

PART TWO

ATTACK

Chapter 41

11:55 a.m., January 30—Minneapolis

Two brand new, though somewhat dusty, black, three-quarter ton Chevy Suburbans were parked side-by-side in front of the rusty-steel paneled warehouse rollup doors. Mohammed and his three-man team were in the lead SUV, Mohammed driving and Uday occupying the shotgun seat. The driver's side window was down, and the Eastern European stranger was again giving last minute instructions. He re-emphasized the importance of obeying all traffic laws and blending in as much as possible so their journey could proceed without interruption. Uday's faint hope was four, Middle Eastern men in a new, black Suburban might just not blend in enough to cause someone to ask questions.

All twelve martyrs had been awakened early this morning for prayers and devotions prior to the first SUV leaving at about 4:00 a.m. Uday could only guess its destination.

At precisely noon, the rollup door screeched open as the rusty pulleys and rollers objected to movement of any kind. A flash of bright, winter sunlight, exacerbated from reflection off of six inches of snow, temporarily blinded all near the door. Mohammed gained his vision back after a moment of squinting, put on his wire-rimmed Oakley sun glasses, and keyed the ignition, starting the 325 horsepower Vortec, big-block V8. Without looking at any of the remaining people in the warehouse, Mohammed eased the black bearer of ultimate mass destruction through the rollup door, turned left, and began his journey to rendezvous with Allah.

8:00 p.m., January 30—Jerusalem

The Israeli prime minister was shaken. The extent of the military might arrayed against his country as just described by the head of his country's intelligence arm, Ariel Levy, was staggering. The Israeli cabinet had just been briefed about the most current situation preparatory to choosing between limited options to meet the threat.

None of the cabinet members spoke for several minutes, each wrestling with self-doubt and worry over what they had just heard. Over half-a-million Arab troops were massed on the Syrian and Egyptian borders armed to the teeth with the latest Russian military technology.

Finally, George Meier, the former general, current defense minister, and venerable senior member of the Labor Party broke the silence. “We have to strike first. We have to hit them hard with every tool at our disposal, maybe even nuclear.”

The reference to nuclear caused bedlam as all seven cabinet members began talking at once. Prime Minister Ben Gurion held up his hands in an attempt to bring silence to the deliberations with limited success. Finally he bellowed, “Shut up, all of you!” That did it.

“Let General Meier continue.”

Meier hesitated, and then said, “I’m not saying we should attack with nuclear weapons as a first resort, but I’m saying our preemptive strike must be successful, at all costs. Literally thousands of planes are massed behind the Arab armies, and I’m doubtful we can knock them down in sufficient numbers to avoid a catastrophe if we wait for them to attack first. What I’m suggesting is we launch a massive air and rocket attack on the enemy’s air forces and follow with coordinated land attacks against their massed armies. If we can achieve a degree of surprise and bloody their noses before they attack us, we can dampen their enthusiasm and level the playing field. I have had plans already drawn up to do this and can launch within twenty-four hours.”

Paul Fleischmann, the minister of finance and the nominal dove in the Israeli cabinet raised the only objection, albeit, a mild one. “Can you be sure of success by attacking their massed armies?”

Meier looked at Fleischmann with a condescending smile and replied, “Paul the only successful outcome I can guarantee is my death some day. Truthfully, the odds of success are reasonable. We’ve discovered some chinks in their armor that will give us the openings we need to do some real damage. I’m confident the IDF will force them into a defensive posture right from the get go. The key, as I said before, is to use maximum force early and be prepared, as a last resort, to go nuclear should our gamble not work. We’re facing a critical situation here and there are huge risks involved no matter what we do.”

Fleischmann, while agreeing with Meier in principle, felt the need to offer one more nuanced opinion. “World opinion will crucify us.”

The prime minister responded. “Paul, what would you have us do, prostrate ourselves in front of Egyptian or Syrian tanks, so world opinion will be on our side?”

Fleischmann remained silent.

Ben Gurion stood up from the table and asked, “Okay, are there any objections to what the defense minister proposes?”

The prime minister slowly surveyed each face in the room. All, even Fleischmann, nodded their determined though grim assent to the plan. Within twenty-four hours Israel would be at war, a war of survival.

Chapter 42

1:00 p.m., January 30—Bangor, Maine

The Bangor Civic Center and Auditorium, while not providing the historically rich setting of the Washington D.C. Capitol Building, was more than adequate to accommodate the new Party's history making alternative to the president's annual speech. The auditorium capacitated six thousand people. Probably one-third that many were expected to attend tonight to hear Senator Benson's contrasting message.

Benson, the nominal but reluctant leader of the fledgling party, Kristina, and children had arrived the night before and were occupying a suite in the Hampton Inn on Bangor Mall Boulevard. The suite was nice and clean and, most importantly for the kids, had a heated, indoor pool.

The children were swimming and the senator and his wife had a few moments to themselves. "You know honey," Benson mused out loud, "if the public, or even my fellow conspirators, knew the doubts I have about tonight, this whole fiasco would probably die a painful death overnight. I have not sought, nor do I want to be the leader of this thing, but it's as if I'm cursed with an ever-tightening noose around my neck.

"Oh Rick," she sighed. "What have you got yourself into? The old adage, 'it is what it is' applies here, I believe. You're the leader because history and the good Lord have put you here at this time and at this place. Who else can do it? I pray every night for you honey, asking someone else be given this burden, and, you know, the only answer I get is there is nobody else. You're it Rick, like it or not."

Benson eyed his wife with caring eyes, and replied, "Well I hope God helps me avoid stepping on my tongue tonight. There will be millions of folks to watch me do that."

"What does the schedule look like tonight?" inquired Kristina.

"The president is scheduled to begin his speech at 9:00. The senators, representatives, and their families will gather in the auditorium anytime after 8:30. After listening and watching the president on the big screen for probably the better part of an hour, it will then be my turn."

She asked, "Who else will be there?"

He answered, "With the huge press contingent plus interested citizens, I'd guess we'll have upward of two thousand people in the audience. You need to be prepared Kristina. I'm anticipating the president's speech is going to be pretty harsh and personal, against me particularly"

She looked at her husband with mock alarm, "You're not serious are you? I thought the President of the United States would never do something like that. After all, he is the president!"

Benson was about to reply when he realized his wife was good-naturedly mocking him. Instead his face broke into a big grin as he pulled her face to his and kissed her."

At about the same time, six hundred miles to the south, another speechmaker was penciling in last-minute changes to the State of the Union speech. The president had been holed up in the Oval Office for the past three hours reading and rewriting portions of the speech. He did not have the doubts plaguing the senator from Oregon about his leadership. He was the leader of the free world and deserved to be so. His task tonight, as he saw it, was to present such a convincing case to the masses that few would disagree with his opinion.

Papadakis was a good enough politician to realize he could not come on too strong tonight, or the public would begin to view Benson as a victim rather than a troublemaker. Yet he needed to make the point the future of the Republic was at stake, if the public embraced the radical ideas emanating from this upstart political movement.

He felt confident he just about had the text where it needed to be. It would show him as strong and decisive, yet with appropriate aplomb and empathy to his political enemies.

Yes, thought Papadakis, *tonight will be the beginning of the end for those reprobates.*

How that last thought would be turned on its end before the evening was over was beyond the president's remotest imagination.

Chapter 43

9:00 p.m., January 30—Moscow

Moscow was in the midst of a bitter, winter blizzard. Colonel Litinov had been trying to warm up since arriving at the Kremlin two hours earlier. He was just finishing a final briefing to the Russian president.

"Forty-eight hours after the detonations in America and Israel, a full-out, three-pronged attack will commence on Israel by the armies of Egypt, Syria, Iraq, Saudi Arabia, and Iran. Fully five hundred thousand troops will be involved in the initial assault with more held in reserve ostensibly to exploit any breakthroughs achieved."

The president interrupted, "How sure are you there will be a breakthrough?"

Litinov replied matter-of-factly, "There won't be a large scale breakthrough. I'd anticipate the opposite. The Arab reserves will end up being thrown into the grinder fairly quickly to stop Israeli counterattacks, probably on both fronts. The Muslim armies will be hard-pressed to hold back the Israelis for more than a couple of weeks. I believe Israeli losses will be severe but, in the end, they will destroy most of the attacking forces, without resorting to nuclear weapons."

Lebedov, suddenly alarmed, asked, "What would prevent the Israelis from occupying Saudi Arabia or Iraq and taking over the oil fields?"

The colonel confidently replied, "They would have to totally defeat the massive Arab armies first, before considering pushing on to the oil fields. I could visualize the possibility they would enter Syria and, perhaps Egypt, but going further would overextend their lines significantly. By then, they will have suffered huge losses and I don't believe the Israeli public would support an extended war. Besides, before that could happen, Russian troops would be entering Iraq and Iran and heading toward Saudi Arabia. Keep in mind, Israel will have already suffered a nuclear blow in Tel Aviv."

The Russian president seemed satisfied but said almost in passing, "The Israelis have surprised us before. I hope your confidence is warranted. Now tell me how the planned attack on Tel Aviv is progressing?"

The colonel paused for a couple of seconds, taking a breath before proceeding, "You have known my reservations with this part of the plan from the start, Mr. President. I'm confident, however, our plan will work. In about four hours an official United Nations van, with three fully accredited diplomats on board, will enter Israeli territory through Lebanon. It will head toward Tel Aviv. The van will be carrying one of our warheads. The diplomats are really three of our Palestinian martyrs. They will detonate the bomb at precisely 5:15 a.m. tomorrow morning in downtown Tel Aviv. The early detonation will not cause the casualties a later explosion might cause, but it's important it occur at precisely the same time as the other detonations in America."

The president suddenly stood up, extended his hand to the colonel and exclaimed, "Well done, Colonel. Get some rest. It will be a busy day tomorrow."

Colonel Litinov smartly saluted, did an about face and walked out of the office, wondering how Lebedov could be so nonchalant about the horror he was launching on the world. Tomorrow, more civilians will be killed in one night than were killed in four years of World War II. Litinov shuddered as he contemplated his role in this nightmare. *What have I become, a monster more evil than the worst of the Nazis?*

3:45 p.m., January 30—Osceola, Iowa

Uday and his traveling companions had made good time even though snow had fallen the night before. Minnesota and Iowa transportation-department road crews were efficient masters of the highways, and the road surfaces were, for the most part, dry. As they approached the Osceola, Iowa, exit, Mohammed indicated they were going to pull off the Interstate for a fuel and bathroom break. He figured stopping for fuel in an obscure town like Osceola would raise less attention.

After exiting, Mohammed drove the SUV east on U.S. Highway 34 about three miles to a rundown, Shell gas station on the south side of the highway. It looked almost deserted. After stopping at one of two pumps, he directed the two Palestinians in the back seat to use the bathroom first, while he gassed up the Suburban.

Uday knew this would be his last chance to figure out a way to get a message to Engeman. He had actually contemplated surprising the other three in an attempt to kill all of them with his Uzi before they could react, but decided the odds were too small of him surviving the exchange. There had to be a viable opportunity at this gas station. He just had to find it.

After five minutes the other two returned, and he, and Mohammed, walked into the store to pay and use the restrooms. As Mohammed used a credit card to pay for the gas, Uday looked around the small store, stocked sparingly with chips, cookies, and sundries as well as an assortment of drinks. As he surveyed the interior, his eyes, at first, passed and then returned to something in the shadows adjacent to the hall leading to the restrooms. As he squinted to focus better, his brain recognized he was staring at a payphone on the wall next to the restrooms.

He knew Mohammed had to use a stall in the restroom, since he had been constantly passing gas over the past seventy miles and had commented he needed to find a restroom soon. A plan formed in Uday's mind. Even though the rules were explicit that nobody was ever to be alone, Mohammed would not expect Uday to be in the stall with him while he took a crap.

They entered the rest room and Mohammed immediately entered the nearest of two stalls. He surprisingly closed and locked the stall door. Uday emptied his bladder as quickly as he could and slipped out of the restroom to the pay phone. He prayed it was still in service. Uday had long ago memorized a number to be used only in emergencies that would ring directly to a cell phone carried by Engeman. He could only hope Engeman would pick it up, since it was almost 1:00 a.m. in Israel.

Uday dialed a long string of numbers and after what seemed to be ten rings the phone was answered. A monotone, metallic voice droned, "please deposit ten dollars." Uday very deliberately, trying to control his rising panic, deposited the money into the dollar bill receptacle. Miraculously, the receptacle accepted each dollar with no rejects. The voice droned, "Thank you for using AT and T. I will connect you."

After a series of clicks, silence, and more clicks, he, finally, heard a ring.

Mohammed, battling with constipation, was taking longer than he wanted to, but knew wishing it done didn't' get it done. He called out to Uday to tell him he might as well go back to the Suburban and wait with the others. When he didn't get a response, he called out again—louder. Still, there was no response. A surge of anger, then panic crossed his mind. Where was Uday? He knew the rules.

Mohammed stood up, suddenly oblivious to his constipation, jerked his pants up, latched his belt, and kicked the stall door open.

After an interminable period of time, a slurred voice on the other end answered, "Hello."

Uday breathlessly stammered, "This is Uday."

After a pause, as Engeman tried to force his sleepy brain to work on all cylinders, he blurted, "Yes! Yes! Uday, where are you? Are you all right?"

Uday yelled, "Shut up and listen! I don't have any time. I'm with three others in a black Suburban headed for Kansas City, Missouri. I'm calling from a small town south of Des Moines, Iowa. The car is carrying a bomb, I believe it might be nuclear. There are other cities …"

Suddenly the restroom door banged open, and Mohammed rushed out and immediately spotted Uday. "What are you doing?" screamed Mohammed.

Uday, knowing he was out of time, started to speak again into the mouthpiece but was cut short when an explosion rocked the small store. Uday felt only a moment of pain before his world went dark. The nine-millimeter slug entered just behind his left ear and exited through his right temple spraying brain matter and bubbly, crimson blood over the pay phone, adjacent wall, and soda pop dispenser.

Mohammed grabbed the phone and jerked it out of the wall. He then looked around the store and saw the shocked clerk staring at him with huge, saucer eyes. He calmly walked up to the counter and shot her in the forehead causing her to ricochet off of the cigarette display and fall, with a thump, amidst a cascade of Lucky Strikes and Marlboros. He quickly glanced around to ensure there was nobody else in the store and walked briskly to the waiting Suburban.

The two other bombers had exited the Suburban upon hearing the shots with their Uzis at the ready. Mohammed screamed at them to get back into the SUV, cussing them for displaying their weapons.

He slid behind the wheel, keyed the engine, and squealed out onto the highway almost leaving one of the terrorists behind as he scrambled to jump into the back seat with the door swinging wildly.

Mohammed, with eyes wide with anger and stoked with adrenaline, shouted in the rear-view mirror, “That spawn of Satan sold us out! We have got to move now and reach our target at all costs. Be ready to shoot it out if stopped by the police. We cannot be stopped.”

After a silence of sixty, or so, seconds, as his two fellow martyrs sat dumbfounded in the back seat, Mohammed briefly turned his head to look at them and said, “Arm the bomb now.”

Engeman stared at the telephone, temporarily paralyzed. He couldn’t believe what his ears were telling him had just occurred. He slowly realized he didn’t have the luxury of sitting there and contemplating Uday’s message. He pressed down on the disconnect button to get a dial tone and immediately dialed the home number of Colonel Dylan.

Three minutes later he and Dylan were on a conference call with Ariel Levy. Dylan didn’t try to paraphrase what Engeman had told him, he simply said, “Colby, tell the director what just happened.”

Engeman began, “Well sir, I’m not completely sure what to make of the call I just received. I’m sure it was Uday Mamud, our source with the Black October terrorist organization, but he was cut off by what sounded like a gunshot. The information I was able to get was ominous but not in any detail.”

The director impatiently asked, “Well what did he say?”

Engeman replied, “He said he and three others were in a black Suburban en route to Kansas City, Missouri, and the Suburban was carrying a bomb, possibly nuclear. They were supposed to arrive sometime tonight. He also indicated other cities might be involved, and then he was cut off by the gunshot.”

“Is that all he said?”

“The only other thing was he was calling from a small town south of Des Moines, Iowa.”

“Do you believe he is dead?” asked the director.

Engeman somberly answered, “Unfortunately, yes. I’m just about positive.”

The director slowly rubbed his forehead with his right hand as his head bowed. Finally he muttered, “Well what now?” Then answering his own question he said, “First thing we’d better do is pass on this information, as little as we have, immediately to the American government. I don’t trust any of the self-absorbed pinheads in the current administration, other than the CIA chief. I’m not even sure he can convince the administration this is serious, but we have to try. I will call him and then the prime minister.

"If bombs are going to be exploding in America, what are the odds of them trying to detonate one here?"

Engeman and Dylan stared at each other, both coming to the realization the odds were indeed high the terrorists would consider Israel a target, particularly when considering the Arab armies massed at the borders. Dylan turned back to the director and slowly nodded his head, saying, "I'm afraid we have to consider the odds high, maybe extremely high."

Without being asked, Engeman volunteered, "I'll make some calls and see what's going on at the Lebanese border. It's the only border still open, and only to restricted-diplomatic traffic."

The director stared directly into his eyes, "Make it fast. We have so very little time. I just hope there isn't an atomic bomb already sitting in one of our cities."

Chapter 44

5:15 p.m., January 30—Washington D.C.

After five interminably-long rings, the administrative assistant to the director of the CIA picked up the phone. “This is Fran Richardson, administrative assistant to Director Smith. How can I help you?”

A somewhat gruff-sounding, heavily-accented, older voice on the other end of the line impatiently demanded, “This is Ariel Levy, I need to speak immediately to Director Smith.”

“I’m sorry sir, he is currently unavailable. May I leave a message for him?”

“An audible sigh in Richardson’s earpiece preceded a somewhat calmer voice that stated, “Ms. Richardson, perhaps you do not recognize me. I’m the director of the Israeli security service, and it’s imperative I speak with Director Smith. This is a matter of extreme urgency, perhaps a life and death situation for millions of your citizens. No matter where he is, I must talk with him now!”

Richardson’s heart suddenly began pounding in her chest, as she comprehended the message and heard the genuine urgency in the caller’s voice. Not knowing exactly how to respond to the director, she stammered, “Director Levy, I believe he is in a staff meeting with his directorate heads and left instructions to not be interrupted under …”

Levy interrupted her, “Ms. Richardson, we have no time here. You must interrupt him. It’s urgent you do so. Do I make myself clear?”

“Yes sir, I will find him, please hold.”

Two minutes later, Director Smith hurriedly strode into the outer office of his executive office complex. He glanced at his pale administrative assistant, wobbly standing next to her desk, and, as he walked by, directed her, “Ring it in to my office.”

Smith entered his office and hadn’t yet reached his desk when the phone started ringing. He picked up the phone, as he swung around to the back of the desk and settled into his leather chair.

"What's going on, Director Levy?"

The Mossad director sounded grim, "I'm afraid I've got some very ominous information to pass on to you. I only hope you can react in time. About thirty minutes ago, one of my field agents received a brief telephone call from our informant placed inside the Black October organization. We had feared the source was already dead, so the information came as a surprise."

Smith inquired, "Was this the same source of the information we received last year regarding a terrorist attack on America?"

Levy replied, "Yes. As I said, we thought he was dead, since we had not heard from him for so long. His message was brief and was cut short by what sounded like a gunshot. He stated he, and three other terrorists, were en route from Minneapolis to Kansas City, Missouri in a black Suburban, carrying a bomb to detonate in Kansas City. Our source believed the bomb might be nuclear."

Smith's ability to hear shut down for a few seconds, as he tried to comprehend what Levy had just said. He interrupted Levy, "You said what? It might be nuclear?"

Levy enunciated clearly, "That's what the source said. He also stated there were other targeted American cities."

"When was this supposed to happen?" asked an incredulous Smith.

The Mossad director replied, "He said it would happen tonight. He said they were en route, and he was calling from a small town just south of Des Moines, Iowa. That's all of the information we received. My agent heard a gunshot and the phone went dead."

Smith took a deep breath, as he felt sudden dizziness, and said to the Israeli, "I'm grateful for the information, and I'll call you back again as soon as I can get a handle on what's happening."

As he was setting down the phone into the receiver he vaguely heard the Mossad director say, "Good luck."

The immensity of the crisis confronting the director was overwhelming. The head of America's premier spy agency was at a total loss how to respond. He buried his head in his hands hoping to discern something Levy had said that did not ring true. It all rang true.

He sat back in his chair, grabbed a notepad, and began writing a list of priorities to do now, thinking, if he could pause for a few minutes and write down what had to happen next, he would not forget some crucial detail.

After a minute of writing, he slammed the notebook on the table top and thought to himself, *You idiot. Get a hold on yourself. You know who to call.*

Knowing full well how difficult it would be to convince the president and his appointed lapdog heads of the NSA, the FBI, and the Department of Defense of the severity of the situation, Smith decided to take some tactical steps first and call the Iowa State Highway Patrol chief directly. He picked up the phone, rang the outer office, and asked Fran to get him the number, which, in spite of her emotionally devastated state, she promptly did.

The chief of the Iowa State Highway Patrol, Ed Robinson, was a career police officer. He spent twenty years in the Des Moines Police Department, rising to the rank of captain, before being appointed to his current position. As a professional, he was not prone to making hasty judgments on any information he might receive relative to potential crimes occurring in his jurisdiction.

After answering the telephone, which rang into his office at the Iowa State Capitol Building, he was shocked when he became aware the caller was the director of the CIA. That was, to say the least, an unusual event. Robinson asked, "What can I do for the CIA?"

Smith got right to the point, " Chief, I've just got off the phone with the director of the Israeli Mossad who informed me a source, imbedded deep in the Black October terrorist organization, had, within the hour, paid with his life to give them vital information relative to a terrorist attack on America."

Smith continued briefing the chief, telling him all the information the CIA leader possessed. After concluding the briefing, Smith asked if any reports had been broadcast over the state police radio, or any other source, indicating someone had been shot south of Des Moines. The chief was unaware of any reports but paused briefly to direct a subordinate to check on it.

After a short discussion, the chief and CIA director agreed to a two-pronged approach. First, the state police would coordinate with the sheriff departments of five Iowa south-central counties and quickly canvas the small towns south of Des Moines, focusing on gasoline service stations to determine if a shooting had occurred. Second, the chief would send out an all-points-bulletin and set up road blocks on I-35 and other highways south of Des Moines to locate a black Suburban carrying three men.

The chief pointed out almost an hour had passed since the call from the informant had been received, so it was possible the Suburban had already crossed into Missouri. He advised he knew his equivalent with the Missouri State Police and would make contact with him to broaden the APB and set up roadblocks there.

The CIA director thanked Chief Robinson for his help and asked him to call back the moment they could verify a shooting had occurred. He explained how critical that information would be to corroborate the veracity of the rest of the information.

Smith hung up the phone and thought, *Now for the difficult part, convincing the administration there is indeed a threat.*

About twenty-five minutes prior to the conversation between the CIA director and the chief, Jeb Hincappe, a northbound sales-rep for Drexhall Pharmaceuticals, exited Interstate 35, at the intersection with U.S. Highway 34, and headed east toward Osceola, Iowa. He had no business reason to drive to Osceola, only personal ones. His bladder was about to burst, he needed some caffeine to keep him from falling asleep, and his car was low on fuel.

He drove his blue Ford Taurus, in the darkening dusk, for another ten minutes and noticed a Shell gas station on the right side of the road a few hundred yards ahead. As he approached, he observed it appeared pretty rundown, maybe not even open. He just about drove by but noticed an "open" sign hanging inside the front door to the store. He swerved, skidding on the loose gravel as he made a hard right turn into the station. He pulled up to the left of the first set of pumps, punched the gas-cap button on his door, and slowly straightened his stiff legs as he rose from the car seat.

Hincappe was surprised the old pump would work with a credit card. He swiped the card, waited for authorization, and began pumping gas. With that done, he purposefully strode toward the store door, aching to relieve his bladder.

As he entered the store he was surprised to see nobody behind the counter or anywhere else in the store. He spotted the restroom sign near the back and proceeded in that direction, hoping he didn't need a key. As he rounded the last set of food racks he noticed the pay phone was missing the receiver; it appeared to have been ripped off the wall. Then he saw dark-red, lumpy liquid splattered on the phone, wall, and soda pop dispensing machine to the right. He froze. Slowly he glanced down and recoiled in sudden fear. A body was slumped grotesquely on the floor with a silver-dollar-size ragged hole on one side of the head.

The salesman gasped for air at the same time his bladder released in his pants. Oblivious, he turned to run back out the front door and noticed a pair of female legs extending at an odd angle out from behind the front counter. Cigarette boxes were scattered around the legs. He opened his mouth to scream, but no sound escaped.

He rushed through the front door directly to his car, fumbled with the car door, and bumped his head as he slid behind the steering wheel. He tried three times before successfully inserting his keys in the ignition, started the engine, and accelerated, tires squealing, out onto the highway.

After driving in panic for about a mile, common sense caught up to him. He realized he needed to call the police and report what he'd just seen. He quickly grabbed his cell phone from the drink holder embedded in the consul and dialed 911.

The national security advisor, Charles Plimpton, had just listened patiently as CIA Director Smith briefed him on his conversation with the Israeli intelligence chief. When Smith was obviously finished, Plimpton, with more than a little sarcasm, asked, "Is that it?"

Smith, taken aback somewhat with the response, replied, "That's it Charles. I'm, however, waiting for information I should receive shortly, which would verify a shooting took place. If it did, then I believe we have to take this information at face value and act accordingly. How can we afford not to?"

Plimpton smirked, "Well, Director Smith, I agree if the information is accurate, we certainly need to find the bombers and stop them before they can do anything nasty. But, I, to be honest with you, think this is just Israeli bullshit, trying to deflect us from concerns over their preparations for attacking their Arab neighbors."

Smith's eyes opened wide in disbelief. What did he just hear? He incredulously asked, "You really believe Israel is behind this military crisis in the Middle East? You're beginning to believe your own political propaganda."

Plimpton shot back, "Who in the hell do you think you're talking to? I'm the national security advisor to the president, and, as such, deserve your respect."

Smith countered, "You deserve nothing if you're willing to put political calculations ahead of national security. After all, isn't this what you're supposed to do, advise the president on national security matters? I'm just asking you to advise the president on a matter of extreme urgency."

Plimpton replied, "I'll tell you what, Mr. Smith. You find something that will corroborate this cock and bull story, and then, maybe, I'll pass this on to the president. Now I've got some pressing matters of more importance to take care of. You do realize the president is speaking to the nation tonight don't you?"

Smith could hardly keep his mouth from dropping open. This horse's ass was so totally incompetent and blinded politically, he wouldn't even accept the possibility of a nuclear catastrophe, even with actionable intelligence staring him in the face.

Smith disgustedly turned around and marched out of Plimpton's office, not bothering to shut the door as he left.

5:45 p.m., January 30—Des Moines, Iowa

The phone was just half-way through its third ring when Ed Robinson picked up the receiver from his desk top. The Clarke County sheriff was on the other end and breathlessly exclaimed, "Chief, we got em!"

"You mean you stopped the Suburban?"

The sheriff sheepishly replied, "Well, no, I didn't mean that. Our deputies responded to a 911 call and discovered two bodies at a Shell service station in Osceola. One was a female, probably the clerk, and the second was a dead Arab. They both had been shot in the head."

Robinson, trying to calm the excited sheriff down a bit, asked deliberately, "How do you know the man is an Arab?"

The sheriff replied, "Well, Chief, he just looks like one."

Robinson, knowing the importance to the future investigation of the crime scene, directed the sheriff to make sure the crime scene was secured and to not process the scene until help arrived. The sheriff agreed.

Robinson pressed the disconnect button on the receiver cradle, got a dial tone, and dialed Smith's cell phone number.

After two rings, Smith answered, "Hello?"

The chief stated, "Hi, this is Chief Robinson. We just received confirmation a shooting had occurred in Osceola, Iowa. According to the sheriff, one of the deceased is an Arab."

Smith felt a sudden fatigue come over him. His stomach became queasy. He had hoped and prayed a shooting did not occur, that this whole thing was an elaborate terrorist scare tactic. He even imagined Plimpton was right, and the Israelis made up the story. Now, however, America was facing its worst nightmare.

"Chief", Smith stated solemnly, "we've got to find that Suburban."

Robinson, fully comprehending the gravity of the situation even without observing Smith's contorted face, replied, "Director we're doing everything possible. The Missouri State Police and all local law-enforcement agencies are looking for the vehicle. I've even dispatched a hundred, Iowa troopers to Missouri, at their request, to help. We'll find it and stop these sons of bitches!"

Chapter 45

The target of all this frenzied activity was still on Interstate 35, having crossed the state line into Missouri thirty minutes earlier. Mohammed was no longer driving, having traded places in order to think more clearly and put together an emergency action plan if needed. He figured it would be just a matter of time before the authorities discovered the bodies at the Shell station in Osceola. He didn't know how much information Uday had spilled to whomever he was talking with on the phone but he calculated their mission was compromised to one degree or another.

His goal was still to reach the Kansas City target. If that was no longer possible he would get as close as he could, shooting it out with any police who tried to stop them. No matter what, he would ensure the bomb was detonated.

As he sat in the shotgun seat, staring absently out the side window, and contemplating the next few hours, he felt the SUV brake suddenly. He looked forward and could see brake lights on cars ahead of them. As they rounded a gradual curve and crested a small hill, a double column of red tail lights stretched ahead of them, topped in the distance by a panorama of blinking red and blue lights. *A road block!*

"Take the next exit," screamed Mohammed to the driver.

Fortunately, they were approaching an exit on the right leading to U.S. Highway 136, eastbound. Mohammed hurriedly opened the Missouri Roadmap he retrieved from the side door pouch and calculated a route, using state and county roads, which would drop them onto Interstate 70, east of Kansas City. He figured the smaller roads would also be blocked but with fewer cops, so they had a better chance to shoot their way through any roadblocks they might encounter.

The black beast swerved to the right, almost missing the exit, the driver obviously panicked. Mohammed swore at him and slapped him on the back of the head. "Pull yourself together!"

They ran the stop sign, turned left, and proceeded east at eighty miles-per-hour. There was no longer a need to obey the speed limit.

Five miles farther east they ran into a second roadblock. This time, however, only two patrol cars were blocking the highway. The road was narrow and forested on both sides. There was no other traffic stopped at the road block. Mohammed figured they could ram the Suburban through the middle of the two cars but would risk immobilizing their vehicle in the collision. A better option was to slow down before arriving at the road block and take the police by surprise. Hopefully they could kill them all before they could react effectively.

As they approached the police cruisers, Mohammed was amazed to see one trooper waving his arms at them, standing on the approach side of the two cars. Two other troopers were positioned behind each of the cars, but none of the officers had any weapons pointed at the approaching car. Mohammed realized in the dark the SUV's lights were preventing the troopers from identifying the vehicle as a black Suburban.

He instructed the driver to click on the high beams when they were within twenty meters of the road block. The troopers would be blinded by the beams, and Mohammed figured it would be fairly easy to kill all three within a few seconds at that close range. He discussed his planned attack with his team, directing the driver to kill the officer in front of the cars, while he and the other terrorist would take down the two officers behind the cars.

The plan went off like clockwork. Within ten seconds after the driver clicked on the high beams, all three officers were dead.

The keys were in the patrol-car ignitions, and it took them only a few seconds to back the cars off the side of the road. They piled back into the SUV and proceeded down the road to their fate. Mohammed relaxed a bit. *Perhaps*, he thought, *we might make this happen yet.*

Chapter 46

Smith had decided to take another risky action. He doubted the newly appointed FBI director, a generous contributor to the president's past election campaign with no other credentials, would be receptive to his entreaties for action. He decided to bypass the head of the Bureau and contact the Special Agent in Charge (SAC) of the Kansas City Field Office directly. He hoped the SAC was as disappointed and frustrated with what the president had done to his agency as Smith was.

His hopes were not dashed. SAC Reynolds a, twenty-two year veteran of the FBI, after some perfunctory objections, agreed the situation was too critical to deal with the political "bullshit" he would have to face if the FBI director had to be involved. After being fully briefed on the situation, he agreed to contact the head of the Missouri State Police and coordinate efforts with him. His field office could put three fully-equipped SWAT teams in the field within thirty minutes and mobilize a force of over one hundred agents within an hour.

Next Smith telephoned the national security advisor to the president to update him. Plimpton's first response was, "Now what?"

After Smith informed him a dead Arab had been discovered shot to death south of Des Moines, he suddenly sobered, finally realizing there just might be a crisis in the works.

"I think I better inform the president," said Plimpton belatedly.

Smith thought to himself, *Duh, you stupid son of a bitch,* but merely said, "Make that as soon as possible. Time is of the essence."

Plimpton contritely asked, "What else do you think we need to do?"

Smith curtly answered, "I suggest you inform the military. This could be a lot bigger than can be handled by local law enforcement. I'd also suggest you consider postponing the State of the Union message tonight."

"What, are you out of your mind?" bridled Plimpton. "I thought this was focused on Kansas City, not Washington. The president will never agree to do that."

Smith, again shocked at how partisan, political thinking could cloud good judgment to such an extent, replied, "That's my advice. What the president does is his choice."

"That's right Mr. Smith, we can't let the fear of a terrorist attack on Kansas City disrupt the government's business can we?"

Smith, matter-of-factly ended the conversation, "I'll keep you updated."

He set the receiver down slowly into its cradle and muttered to nobody in particular, "If I live through this tonight, I'm resigning tomorrow."

Missouri State Police Captain Tom Finlayson had been trying for ten minutes to make radio contact with any of the three officers manning a roadblock five miles east on U.S. Highway 136. Finlayson, the area commander, dispatched a police cruiser to check out why there was no response.

Ten minutes later the captain received a radio transmission all three officers were dead, having been shot with automatic weapons. Finlayson was devastated. He was personal friends with two of the troopers, and knew, between them, they left behind two great ladies and five children.

He immediately radioed the state police command center, set up in Independence, Missouri, to pass on the awful news. The crisis was boiling over.

7:20 p.m., January 30—White House Oval Office

"Mr. President, I appreciate you making the time to see me with such little time left before your speech" offered Plimpton meekly.

The president half shouted, "Cut the crap Plimpton. You told George here," motioning to his attorney general, "this was a national emergency. Now what's so damned important you had to interrupt my preparations for the most important speech of my tenure as president?"

"Well …well," stammered Plimpton, "the CIA director has received intelligence information from the Israelis that…"

"The Israelis," exploded Papadakis, "Don't you know they would say anything to garner sympathy? They are about to enter a war with the Arabs and…"

"Sir!" interrupted Plimpton, "the information he received has been corroborated. The Israelis had a source who called them from

Iowa and told them he, and three others, were on their way to Kansas City to explode a bomb. The Israelis heard a gunshot and believe the informant was shot. Earlier this evening the police in Iowa found an Arab who had been shot to death south of Des Moines, Iowa."

Plimpton talked as fast as he could to get the information out before the president interrupted him again. He need not have worried. The president was at a loss for words for the moment. Finally, he asked, "What kind of bomb?"

Plimpton replied, "They don't know for sure but the informant indicated it could be nuclear."

The president interrupted, "You mean like an atomic bomb or a dirty bomb?"

Plimpton continued, "I don't know sir, and apparently the informant wasn't sure either."

The president's eyes widened as he looked up at the ceiling. He then looked at Lukavitz for a few seconds, took a deep breath and mumbled, "Here we go again, another nuclear bomb threat. What does CIA Director Smith think?"

Plimpton replied, "He thinks we ought to alert the military just in case, and, also, you should postpone your speech tonight."

The president bristled. "Now that's the stupidest idea I have ever heard from Smith. I think he's losing his nerve. I will not postpone the most important speech of my presidency because of a possible terrorist threat on Kansas City, Missouri. I do think, however, a military alert is in order; not any type of mobilization of Guard troops, or anything like that, but just pass on the information. I'm convinced what we have here is a home-grown plot, of which the Israelis are more than willing to take advantage."

Lukavitz finally offered an opinion. "Mr. President, don't you think it might be prudent to brief the Senate and House leaders on this, just in case it gets out of control?"

"George," replied the president, "all we need is one of the leaders to get weak-kneed on us, and we could panic the whole Congress. No, I think we should keep this our little secret tonight." He pointedly stared into Plimpton's eyes. "Don't you agree Charles?"

Plimpton, ever willing to oblige, eagerly answered, "You're totally correct Mr. President. No need to have anyone panic."

Chapter 47

3:30 a.m., January 31—Jerusalem

Engeman, Dylan, Levy, Prime Minister Ben Gurion, and Defense Minister Meier were meeting in Ben Gurion's government office, having arrived five minutes earlier.

Engeman informed the small, worried, but determined group, that, approximately thirty minutes earlier, a United Nations white, Ford Econoline van, with all of the appropriate UN markings on the side doors, had entered Israel from Lebanon. It contained three credentialed UN employees who stated their destination was Tel Aviv. The need to enter Israel at such an ungodly-early hour was not ascertained. Apparently the border guard, upon inspecting the diplomatic credentials, felt they had their reasons, and it was none of his business to check further.

"So we don't know if this van is legitimate or is carrying a bomb do we?" inquired the prime minister.

"No." replied Dylan, "There has not been any other traffic through the border this evening. It's got to be our van."

The Prime Minister asked, "What do we do?"

Defense Minister, Meier, spoke, "We don't have time to check with the UN to determine if the occupants of the van are truly diplomats."

"Where are you going with this?" asked the prime minister.

Meier replied, "I think we just bite the bullet, assume the van is hostile, and take it out with a missile strike."

Ben Gurion asked incredulously, "Won't that set off the bomb?"

The defense minister answered, "Not necessarily. We have at our disposal some high tech warheads developed to kill Hamas leaders, over the past decade, that create a lot of initial heat but relatively little concussion. I believe if we use one of those we can kill the occupants but avoid detonating the bomb. I'm afraid if we try to stop the van, the terrorists will set off the bomb before we could kill them all. "

"Are you *sure* it won't set off a nuclear explosion?" asked Ben Gurion again.

Meier hesitated and then responded soberly, "I can't guarantee anything at this point, except it would be better if an atomic bomb detonated in the desert north of Tel Aviv than in the city center."

"There will be hell to pay if it turns out to really be a UN van with UN diplomats on board," offered Director Levy.

"There's going to be hell to pay no matter what happens tonight," answered the prime minister. "George, make it happen."

6:30 p.m., January 30—U.S. Highway 65

Mohammed was praising Allah. Surely He was watching over the three martyrs so they could fulfill their destiny. They had been traveling almost an hour since shooting their way through the roadblock and had not encountered any more roadblocks or police.

Mohammed had plotted a route he hoped would get them close to their target destination without being stopped, dropping them onto I-70, no more than twenty miles east of their target.

He figured they could still reach their target by 8:00 unless they met overpowering resistance. In that case, he would ensure the bomb was detonated.

Same time – Police Command Post, Independence, Missouri

SAC Reynolds and Missouri State Police Director Robert Ratcliff were both scratching their heads trying to second-guess the terrorists. Knowing now the firepower the extremists possessed, both knew they could not afford to spread law enforcement personnel too thin. As a result, they had made the decision to establish fewer, but more heavily-manned, road blocks in a tighter circle around Kansas City. The concentration was on all highways and county roads leading into the city from the north and east.

They had determined the Suburban had sufficient time to have traveled almost to I-70, but the odds were the terrorists would not be so brazen to travel on I-70 for any appreciable distance. The thinking, therefore, was the Suburban would approach I-70 not too far east from Kansas City.

Reynolds had also dispatched scores of agents in Bureau cars, traveling in pairs, to many of the county and state roads north and east of Kansas City. The goal was not to try to stop the bombers, but to locate the Suburban, hopefully without being seen themselves.

The CIA director had telephoned Reynolds earlier in the hour to report the president was now aware of the situation but was not willing to authorize military involvement. That would have been futile at this juncture anyway, since whatever was going to happen would happen long before troops could arrive on the scene.

Smith stated the president was convinced this was just a home-grown cell of disgruntled extremists and really just a law-enforcement matter. The president also refused to postpone the State of the Union speech tonight. Both the state police director and SAC prayed the president was right, but deep in their souls feared he was wrong, maybe dead wrong.

It was a waiting game now. Reynolds and Ratcliff could only hope they had covered all the bases, knowing failure to block a certain road could lead to a catastrophe.

4:00 a.m., January 31— Coastal Highway, *Michimoret*, Israel

Even before meeting with the prime minister, Levy, and the others, the Israeli defense minister had issued the necessary orders to carry out the only option available to save Tel Aviv. Meier knew full well the prime minister would approve his plan, since there really were no other options.

The plan Meier had ordered was not without risk. If a nuclear explosion occurred, all participants in the strike would be killed, as well as, several hundred Israelis living in small coastal towns in the vicinity. As tragic as it might be, this was preferable to a detonation occurring in Tel Aviv, where tens of thousands would be incinerated.

An Apache helicopter, carrying rockets fitted with incendiary, low-explosive warheads, would conduct the attack. It would take place on the Coastal highway, between the towns of *Hadera* and *Netanya*, near a hamlet called *Michimoret*. Three fire trucks, equipped with fire suppressant foam, would be waiting nearby the attack location to rush to the scene to suppress any resulting fire, hopefully in time to prevent an explosion. Additionally a team of six commandos would rush the van immediately after the strike to ensure all van occupants were dead.

The plan was not foolproof but was the best that could be thrown together at such short notice. Meier had ultimate faith in his soldiers. All participants had volunteered and knew the risks. If it could be done, they would do it.

Chapter 48

7:15 p.m., January 30—Missouri County Road

The Federal Bureau of Investigation has a storied history and over the years thousands of Americans have dreamed of becoming an FBI agent. One successful dreamer was Special Agent Tyrell White, an FBI veteran of ten years. White had qualified to be a special agent by completing law school at the University of Texas in Austin. Friends and family often ribbed White about getting a law degree to become an agent, when there were so many easier ways to qualify. They also felt, as an African American, he could get further ahead in the world as an attorney. White didn't care. He was fulfilling his dream.

One might wonder how the law degree was benefiting him in the current situation. He was driving a Bureau car, followed by a second car about five hundred yards behind, on a dark, lonely, Missouri state road northwest of Kansas City. He felt their task qualified as trying to find the old needle in the haystack. They were looking for a black suburban, on a black road, on an almost black winter night, in the middle of nowhere. He had seen exactly two other vehicles headed in the opposite direction during the last thirty minutes, one which appeared in his headlights to be a farmer's beat-up Dodge pickup, and the other a full size, light-colored sedan of unknown make and model.

He and his partner in the car behind had worked out a scheme they hoped would help them if, by some small chance, the Suburban headed their way. If it passed White, and he believed it might be their quarry, he would radio the trailing agent who would provide a second opinion. If they both agreed it was a black Suburban, then they would follow it at a discreet distance and radio their position ahead, so an effective road block could be established. The trick was to make as positive an identification as possible and not be identified themselves in the process. White was fully aware of the firepower contained in the Suburban.

4:20 a.m., January 31— Over *Michimoret*, Israel

Jimmy Solo had always dreamed of being a fighter pilot. As a six-year-old boy standing next his mother in a field near their Kibbutz in northern Israel, he marveled at the jets flying overhead. He was never quite able to achieve his dream but had settled for being an Apache helicopter pilot. In retrospect, it was a good result because Jimmy had become one of the most decorated helicopter pilots in the Israeli defense forces.

He knew it was because of his reputation, he was selected for the current assignment. He also knew it would likely be his last assignment. The odds were stacked, and not in his favor. What he was tasked with doing was the last hope for thousands of innocent Israelis, so he was committed to completing the mission regardless of the personal cost. He knew if he did not live through it, his young wife Sophia, and his twin girls, would be taken care of. He had General Meier's assurance of that.

As he approached the Coastal Highway he could see a few lights from *Michimoret* shining underneath him. He thought, *If those poor souls only knew what the next five or ten minutes might bring them.* He pitied them.

Two minutes later, peering through Aselsan M930 night vision goggles, he could see his target ahead, crossing in front of him driving south on the highway. The United Nations decals were dimly visible on the side of the van. He settled the helicopter about five hundred feet up and a half mile behind the Econoline. He flipped on his fire-control switch, arming the rockets, lined up the rear of the van in his helmet visor sighting device, offered a short silent prayer, and pressed the launch button.

A single rocket screamed from under the Apache and curved in a downward arc toward the van. About ten seconds later the van erupted into a fireball. Solo grimaced and closed his eyes expecting to be vaporized by an onrushing wall of heat. Nothing happened. He opened his eyes, looked down at the burning van, and could see flashes from automatic weapons, as Israeli commandos ensured the make-believe UN diplomats were too dead to detonate the bomb. He noticed three trucks rushing to the location and, upon arriving at the scene, opening up with fire suppressant foam. The fire was out almost immediately.

There was no explosion. He had done his duty and survived. He ached for his wife and girls. He turned the helicopter around and headed back to base. A thought briefly popped into his mind. *I sure as hell hope they really weren't UN diplomats.*

FBI Agent White first noticed a growing halo of light over the crest of the road about a half mile ahead. After a few moments, two high-beamed headlights popped into view. When the oncoming vehicle didn't click off the high beams, White clicked his on briefly. It worked. The oncoming vehicle's beams dimmed.

White was traveling at about thirty-five miles-per-hour. It appeared the onrushing vehicle was traveling considerably faster. White would have only a moment, as the vehicle passed, to try to identify it.

As the vehicle flashed by his car, the glare from the headlights diminished suddenly, and, as he glanced out his driver's side window, his brain instantly computed what his eyes saw. It was a dark colored Suburban.

He immediately clicked the button on the radio speaker in his right hand and hollered, "It's our baby."

Five seconds later a voice on the radio simply said, "Confirmed."

White and his partner waited a minute until the Suburban had disappeared over the crest of the hill to their rear. Then, they both made quick U-turns and headed after the SUV, intending to close just enough to keep the tail lights in sight.

7:30 p.m., January 30—Command Post, Independence, Missouri

Director Ratcliff and SAC Reynolds had few options. They had just received the radio message from Agent White and, based on his identification of the County Road, it was apparent terrorists were going to be entering onto I-70 only ten miles east of Independence. They had barely enough time to assemble sufficient resources to establish a roadblock on the Interstate, within the city limits of Independence itself.

Ratcliff immediately radioed to three police vehicles, which were already located east of the terrorist's vehicle, to set up an initial roadblock a mile east of the location where the Suburban would be entering I-70. By doing so, they could reduce civilian traffic on the freeway and avoid civilian casualties should a violent outcome occur.

He took similar action to block east bound lanes a mile to the west of the main Independence roadblock.

With no other real options, Ratcliff issued the orders and police cruisers and FBI vehicles headed toward the designated location on I-70 in Independence. Three FBI and two state police SWAT teams were to provide the heavy weaponry at the road block, which would be manned by at least fifty additional state and federal law-enforcement personnel. This was it. The terrorists would go no farther. The orders were to shoot to kill.

Ratcliff sincerely hoped the Suburban identified by White was the right Suburban. If not, some innocent people were surely going to be shot to death.

7:40 p.m., January 30—Independence, Missouri

Mohammed casually noticed the headlights in his rear-view mirror, which had been following them for the past fifteen minutes. He was not overly worried about them, since they were far back and had not closed the distance. It was a little strange they had not noticed a car behind them before. He was convinced Allah would bless them and see them through to the end of their mission. There was no longer any reason to worry.

Mohammed had been driving for the last sixty miles. As the leader of the mission, he felt strongly he should be driving the vehicle as they neared the target.

They crested a hill and immediately below them was the I-70 intersection. Mohammed slowed, made a right turn, and headed up the onramp to the freeway. He noticed the traffic was exceptionally light for early in the evening but didn't think much about it, other than it would enable them to make good time on the freeway. He passed a mileage sign on the right indicating Independence was nine miles ahead. He knew Independence was just east of Kansas City.

Chapter 49

8:40 p.m., January 30—Bangor Civic Center and Auditorium

The crowd, though larger than Benson expected, was still dwarfed by the cavernous auditorium. It included the families of the senators and representatives, a huge press and media contingent, and at least two thousand supporters of the new party.

A large projection screen was set up at the front of the room, more than large enough for all members of the audience to see and hear the president comfortably. They would also be able to see Senator Benson on the same screen, when he followed the president, even though he would be speaking live from a podium to the left.

There was a loud buzz throughout the auditorium as people offered opinions of what the president would say and what might happen next in the country. Currently being projected on the screen was one of the major network anchors, teamed up with three other network correspondents, discussing their "informed" opinions on the same subjects. The noise in the auditorium precluded anybody from hearing what they were saying, but few in the crowd cared.

Chapter 50

7:45 p.m., January 30—Roadblock at mile-marker 16, Interstate 70

The rapidly organized roadblock was not perfect but, in view of the less than thirty minutes available to them, would have to do. Basically a dozen or so police vehicles plus two semi-trailers were set to roll into a blocking position when the Suburban was within one mile of the location. Prior to that time, they parked on both shoulders of the freeway to let the civilians still on the highway pass without hindering traffic.

Several teams of law-enforcement personnel, armed with M16's, were deployed five hundred yards east of the roadblock on bluffs overlooking both sides of the freeway, in case the terrorists attempted to turn back east.

FBI Agent White, trailing a few hundred yards behind the Suburban, continued to read off the freeway mileage markers into the radio mike, each time he passed one.

7:50 p.m., January 30—Mile-marker 17, Interstate 70

Agent White thought to himself, *Here we go*, as he passed mile-marker seventeen and radioed ahead to alert the roadblock. He felt confident sufficient force was in place to end this nightmare but was worried, nevertheless. He personally doubted the terrorists had a nuclear device hidden in the Suburban they were driving, not believing their organization, whatever it was, had the wherewithal to obtain such weapons. He believed they could possess a dirty bomb, which would be bad enough by itself.

The yellow Labrador mix had found a home with his human jogging buddy. Life was indeed grand for the dog, free to run along the jogging and biking paths running north of the Interstate in Independence, yet able to return at night to a warm doghouse, albeit in the human's garage. The dog didn't care. He had all the food he needed and a place to call home.

Tonight he was making his last round of potty breaks along the trail when a rumbling noise caught his attention and caused him to look southward and down to thc highway below him. His eyes caught the sudden flashing of bright lights and movement as two semi-trailer trucks and a dozen police cars moved into place on the freeway. He, of course, could not fathom what was going on. After all, to a canine brain, a semi-trailer truck would resemble a huge, growling animal of some sort.

Mohammed was lost in thought, reflecting on his life of a year ago. He missed his wife and children profoundly, but hadn't let his mind dwell on them much until now. Perhaps because he knew he would shortly be seeing them, he allowed his mind to remember them, his daughter's smiling face, Anwar's mischievousness, and his wife's understanding caresses.

Cresting the hill, he was jolted out of his nostalgic thoughts by the sight confronting him five hundred yards ahead. A massive phalanx of cars and trucks were spread across both sides of the freeway with lights flashing. The whole area was lit up with bright spotlights already illuminating the Suburban Mohammed was driving.

At the speed they were approaching they would not be able to stop much before reaching the roadblock, even if that were their plan. Mohammed told the others, "Get ready, this is our time to meet Allah."

He floored the throttle and began accelerating toward the soldiers of Satan confronting them. Both Mohammed and the terrorist in the front, passenger seat rolled down their windows, stuck their Uzis out, and opened fire wildly in the direction of the road block.

The martyr in the back seat rested his thumb on the detonation switch ready to flip it just before crashing into the blockade of trucks and cars ahead.

The Labrador mix had lost interest in the huge, growling animals on the freeway below and was about to turn and trot back to his new home. A new sound caused him to stop and view the scene once again. He could hear a staccato-popping sound and noticed repeating flashes of light emanating from the sides of a smaller growling animal approaching the larger ones. Then a much louder sound erupted from where the larger animals were, almost a roar, accompanied by multiple flashes of light all around the larger animals.

It appeared the smaller animal was about to attack the larger animal when suddenly, for just a moment, the dog's brain registered an extremely white, blinding flash, before the world before him went black.

Chapter 51

9:00 p.m., January 30—Bangor Civic Center and Auditorium

"Mr. Speaker, the President of the United States," echoed the resonant bass voice of the sergeant-at-arms as he introduced President Papadakis to the Speaker of the House, Tom Randall. As is the custom, after several minutes of hand shaking while the president made his way to the podium, Randall stood and introduced the president to the assembled senators, representatives, and other government officials and invited guests.

The president, of course, wouldn't begin his speech for a few minutes, as the traditional standing ovation would take about that long to subside. Nobody at the Bangor Civic Center joined in the ovation. As a matter of fact, they continued talking with each other as they had done for the past half hour. The crowd finally quieted down when the president actually began to speak.

"My fellow Americans," began the president, his face filling a good portion of the screen at the front of the auditorium, "I deem it a special honor to be able to address you tonight to discuss the state of the union."

The latest leaked information, according to press sources, was the president would not get into the highly anticipated portion of his speech, dealing with the senators and representatives listening to the speech in Bangor, until the second half-hour of the speech. The first portion would concentrate on the administration's domestic and foreign policy accomplishments during his second year in office, emphasizing the peaceful, terror-free world he had helped promote.

Papadakis was just getting into his speech, when there was some sort of commotion. The TV viewers across the nation and in the Bangor auditorium could see the perturbed look on the president's face as his eyes briefly looked to the right. He suddenly stopped speaking and actually turned to stare at something occurring at that location.

The network cameramen, almost in unison, swept their television cameras in the direction of the president's stare, where a small knot of men were holding an intense discussion. Finally two of the men, who looked like Secret Service agents judging by their earpieces, broke away from the group and approached the president from the side, briskly walking up the stairs toward the podium.

The president drilled a hole in the leading man's head with his eyes. That didn't deter him as he continued toward the president. Viewers could see the president mouth the words, "What the hell is going on?"

The first Secret Service agent reached the podium, leaned toward the president, and whispered something in his ear.

The president's mouth dropped, and his face went sickly pale. Papadakis then, without a word, accompanied the agent to the president's right, down the stairs, and immediately out of the House chamber. The second agent then stood behind the podium to make an announcement.

"Ladies and gentlemen, please listen carefully."

The noise in the chamber, which had risen significantly from an initial murmuring, immediately died.

"There has been a significant terrorist attack at Independence, Missouri, just outside of Kansas City." He continued with a purposeful lie, "We don't know, at this time, the nature of the attack or if other cities might be targeted but feel strongly it would be prudent to evacuate the Capitol Building, as soon as possible. Please don't panic. We need to evacuate by rows."

No one in the chamber heard his final statement as pandemonium erupted. The rush to the doors was instantaneous as infectious panic spread throughout the crowd.

Those watching in the Bangor auditorium stared at the screen in shock as they watched hundreds congressmen and government officials, people who minutes before were dignified representatives of the United States government, scramble over one another in their rush to exit the building. Nobody watching was blaming those in the House chamber for their behavior. They were more likely thanking God they weren't there to panic with them.

8:14 p.m., January 30—Presidential limousine

The Secret Service agents had forcefully deposited a disheveled president into the back seat of the armored presidential limousine. The driver was ordered to proceed immediately, at utmost speed, to a secret bunker, located about a mile west of their current location. Nobody in the limo knew what was going on, only that the Kansas City area had been devastated by a nuclear explosion. It was imperative the president be safely secured into the secret bunker, constructed shortly after the terror attacks on September 11, 2001.

As the limo began accelerating away from the Capitol Building, the agents were oblivious to a black Suburban parked on a Washington D.C. side street less than four blocks from them in the direction they were headed.

As the horrific scene continued to unfold on the big screen at the Bangor Civic Center, Senator Benson sat and stared like the other twenty-eight hundred people in the audience. It was as if he was watching some sort of political-terror, action movie, churned out of the sordid imagination of a Hollywood screenwriter, only this was real. As he and the others continued to watch, there was, suddenly, an extremely-bright flash on the screen followed by instant static.

An immediate deathly silence fell over the distraught audience. After several seconds, at the realization of what might have just happened, a few women in the crowd began to weep. Then whispers, and a few people were shouting out, "What happened?"

Finally realizing something catastrophic had just befallen the nation, Benson intuitively recognized the need to say something to those assembled in Bangor, as well as whatever American audience would be able to listen and see him speak.

He rose and made his way over to the podium.

As more and more people in the audience became aware he was at the podium, the crescendo of noise died as fast as it began.

Benson surveyed the crowd, pausing to gather his thoughts, not knowing what to say, only that he needed to say something. Finally he began, "All of us gathered here, as well as my fellow countrymen who can see or hear my voice, know something extremely serious has befallen our country tonight. At this point, I can only conjecture what has happened in our nation's capital. I do know, as do you, a terrorist attack has occurred in the Kansas City, Missouri area, although any details about that attack are unknown at this time."

He continued, "If an attack has occurred in Washington D.C. it's possible the leadership of our federal government has been impacted, possible severely. I and my fellow congressmen here will make every effort possible to ascertain what has happened and will report what we find to you as soon as we can obtain reliable information.

"I realize those of us here represent just a fraction of our national government, and none of us were elected to any nation-wide office. Until we can determine, however, if the president, or any other national leaders identified in the presidential succession plan, are able to function, we will continue to do our best to serve, in the interim, as the federal branch of our government.

"In the meantime, I'd ask state and local governments to initiate whatever actions they deem necessary throughout the United States to preserve the peace in their respective localities and to provide help of whatever kind is needed tonight and tomorrow."

Benson's eyes began to tear and he bowed his head briefly as he fought to gain control of his emotions. He looked back up into the TV cameras. His eyes had become steel. "I would ask our military leaders, who are listening, who have not been impacted immediately by the attacks, to place our military assets around the world on maximum alert to be prepared to meet any exigency. Whoever was behind what has happened today will find they have not cowed America, they have, instead, awakened her. May God bless this great country and each of you. Thank you."

Benson turned to his right and descended the few stairs to the floor level. Initially dead silence greeted him. Then suddenly, as if on cue, the audience stood and the auditorium erupted into applause.

Chapter 52

9:15 p.m., January 30—New York City

Times Square, located where Broadway cuts across the intersection of Seventh Avenue and 42nd Street, famous for its New Year's Eve bashes, had once again become a favorite haunt of the Big Apple's city dwellers. While falling into disrepute before the turn of the century with a mélange of porn houses and peep shows, it was revitalized recently with the restoration of some of the old grand theatres including the New Amsterdam, famous for the *Ziegfeld Follies*. A recently-constructed, fifty-seven story skyscraper had become its newest landmark.

In spite of the cold night, a sizable crowd of about fifteen hundred brave souls had gathered at Times Square to watch the electronic bulletin board project the president's State of the Union speech. Many thousands more were dining in the restaurants or enjoying the latest theatrical productions on Broadway.

Sitting ominously in the sparsely illuminated Madison Square Garden parking garage about a mile south of Times Square was a black Suburban with tinted windows and four, barely-visible occupants inside. One of the occupants in the back seat leaned forward briefly and reached toward the center console for something.

The first thing the lovers, the January tourists, the New Yorkers out for an evening of party-making, and the ever-present homeless beggars noticed was the sudden brightness of a noon-day sun. For a moment it even felt like a hot, summer day at noon. For a few hapless souls who happened to be crossing the intersection and were not shielded by a building, it was considerably hotter than the noonday sun. Their exposed skin instantly fried into third-degree burns as the thermal radiation from the nuclear blast slammed into them.

No more than a second or two later, the lucky ones, shielded by the tall buildings, were no longer lucky. The blast's ten pounds-per-square-inch pressure wave and accompanying four hundred miles-per-hour wind, turned buildings, cars and humans into so much flying debris. From the epicenter of the explosion, outwards for a mile in every direction, virtually everything was destroyed. The beating heart of New York City, in a matter of a few seconds, had been silenced forever.

9:15 p.m., January 30—Atlanta, Georgia

CNN Headquarters was bustling, as was the case for all major news organizations. The president's State of the Union message this year was particularly newsworthy—what with the almost explosive political atmosphere in the country. CNN's production, leading up to the speech, was pretty typical, with its anchor and leading correspondents in a constant give-and-take dialog about the speech and its ramifications to the country. The big cable network also planned on covering Senator Benson's speech, scheduled to follow the president. In years past they had always broadcast the out-of-power party's rebuttal to the State of the Union, and this year was not so different. The out-of-power party just happened to be truly out of power, at least in the view of CNN.

As the producers and news correspondents anxiously waited for the president to get to the real meat of his speech, they were shocked at the interruption by the Secret Service and aghast when the evacuation of the Capitol Building was announced.

For a few moments they were utterly dumbfounded when their television monitors registered a flash and then blackness. Their confusion was only for a moment, however, because, suddenly, their own studio lit up as if a gigantic spot light had been turned on directly over CNN Headquarters. A distant rumble quickly grew into a terrifying roar, and the exterior walls seemed to come together like a pair of hands trying to trap a fly. Downtown Atlanta was extinguished in little more than an eye blink.

9:15 p.m., January 30—Miami, Florida

Jesse and Raylene Nygaard loved retirement. Jesse, a former computer programmer, had retired from his lucrative job with American Pharmaceutical about ten years earlier. When Raylene retired from her school teaching job two years later, they relocated to Miami. They were both tired of cold weather, so the move from Chicago was heaven sent. They loved sitting out on the redwood deck of their tenth floor condo, as they were doing this particular evening. They purchased the condominium with the equity from the Chicago home after living in it for thirty-four years.

The Nygaards had been blessed with three children who were now all married with kids of their own. Grandpa and grandma loved to see the grandkids but loved to see them leave as well. Today had been one of those days. Jim, their oldest son, his wife and two children, a four-year-old boy and an eighteen-month-old girl, had visited for most of the day. They had left an hour earlier, and Jesse and Raylene were now just starting to unwind as they viewed the Miami skyline from their ten-story perch.

They had known the president was speaking this evening, but, at their age, figured he couldn't say anything, which would change their lives, so what would be point of watching him rant on the television.

Their condo was situated on a small rise about five miles east of downtown Miami, and they had a marvelous view of the downtown skyline.

As they sat daydreaming, suddenly an extremely bright flash lit up the skyline almost instantly engulfing it. The Nygaards immediately felt a searing heat blistering their faces, arms, and exposed legs.

They squinted and watched horrified as a boiling mushroom cloud rose over the city. They could see a rippling, accelerating wall of dust and debris rushing outward from the fireball toward them. They sat paralyzed, unable to look away or take any action to save their lives.

Miami, the city which had withstood Andrew and other monster storms the Atlantic had conjured up against her, was no more.

8:15 p.m., January 30—Chicago, Illinois

The Bulls were having their best season, since Michael Jordan slam-dunked the team into the NBA championship game two decades earlier. The game tonight against the Utah Jazz was reminiscent of the Bulls/Jazz series in the mid nineties, when a flu-ridden MJ led the Bulls from behind to one of the more memorable victories in NBA playoff history. The fourth quarter was underway with the score knotted at seventy-eight.

Billy Jackson was a Bulls fan from his toes to his ears. Ever since he was old enough to crawl he had been a Bulls fan. He had saved enough money earned at two jobs over three years to pay for season tickets for himself and his eleven year-old son. They sat on the team side fourteen rows up and yelled, clapped, and booed. He loved every second.

Billy, and the rest of the boisterous crowd, knew nothing of the catastrophe befalling their country tonight. The State of the Union speech could not begin to compare in importance to what was taking place on the beautiful wood floor of the cavernous United Center. Seating nearly twenty-three thousand, it was one of the biggest professional basketball arenas in the United States.

A relatively few of the packed crowd noticed the sudden bright light flashing in the skylights high overhead. More noticed the rumbling sound that could be felt, more than heard, in the vibration of the seats. After several seconds, the increasing roar overpowered the din of the crowd causing even the professionals on the court to stop playing and look up toward the source of the sound.

A sharp crack was heard as the east wall of the United Center seemed to surge forward along with thousands of fans seated on that side. Huge chunks of the wall, along with chairs and human bodies, were propelled across the arena's open space landing on the court and opposite fan seating area.

The pressure wave continued through the building blowing holes in the west wall but not destroying it completely. The wave had lost enough of its energy over two miles from the blast epicenter, that it was not capable of destroying the entire building. Half of the roof structure collapsed as the east wall was blasted inward.

Most of those not killed instantly by the pressure wave were entombed by tons of debris. Billy Jackson and his son were two of the very few lucky ones. A huge girder had come down and wedged at an angle, providing a few feet of space between it and the floor in front of a row of seats where Billy and his son had been thrown. Though in shock, Billy called out to his son who responded weakly.

Both would be able to crawl through the pitch blackness and debris to safety. Hundreds of thousands of other souls who had called Chicago their home were not so fortunate.

8:15 p.m., January 30—Detroit, Michigan

The seventy-three story Marriott Hotel, the center tower of the Renaissance Center, a complex of six, high-rise office buildings, is the tallest hotel in the United States. It was the capstone of the

Renaissance Renovation project begun in the 1970s as only a partially successful attempt to rejuvenate downtown Detroit.

The spacious parking garage underneath the building was the current hangout of a wannabe terrorist named Abdalluh Abu Azzam. He had immigrated legally to the United States six years earlier from Saudi Arabia. Azzam had quickly been absorbed into a small group of extremist Muslims who met regularly at the neighborhood Wahabi Mosque. Anti-American propaganda was routinely spewed by the Imam.

Azzam and his extremist friends had been planning a perverse, overly-ambitious project. They intended to bomb the Renaissance Center. Azzam's current assignment, and the reason he was skulking around the underground garage, was to scope it out and determine where the optimal locations were to set explosives. As he rounded the back corner of the garage and began slowly driving his ten year old Mazda forward toward the exit, he noticed a new, black Suburban parked on his left, five stalls in from the exit. He thought he saw movement in the back seat of the Suburban, though he couldn't be sure, since the windows were tinted, and the garage was not well illuminated.

If Azzam only knew what was about to happen to him, he might have smiled at the irony of the situation. But he would never know and certainly didn't have time to smile as the black Suburban and Azzam were both suddenly vaporized as he was about to drive by.

The Renaissance Center ceased its existence, becoming little more than a two hundred-foot-deep crater in the center of the city. There would no longer be a need for renovation projects in downtown Detroit.

8:15 p.m., January 30—Houston, Texas

Robert and Kathy Rodino loved politics. Since their marriage twelve years earlier, both had demonstrated their passion through active involvement in the Houston area Democratic Party. Robert served on the Harris County Democratic Party Board, and Kathy entertained serious thoughts about running for the Texas legislature, although she and her husband considered that a long shot at best.

Tonight, snuggled together on the plush sofa in front of the TV, they were anxious to listen to the president's State of the Union speech. Their growing anticipation over the past several weeks was about to end as they listened to the president begin speaking.

The abrupt end to the president's speech, his exit from the Capitol Building, and subsequent sudden ending of the broadcast was matched in shock value, when an extremely bright flash lit up Rodino's family room. Both looked to the northeast toward downtown, Houston, where the source of the light seemed to be. Over the distant treetops, they could see a rising mushroom fireball illuminating the nighttime sky, as if the devil himself was unleashing his demons.

Robert, realizing almost instantly what was happening, grabbed Kathy by her arm and dragged her with him to the master bathroom at the opposite corner of the house. Once inside the bathroom, he slammed the door shut and embraced his wife tightly as they both lay in the porcelain tub.

Several seconds later the home shook as if in the midst of an earthquake. After a few moments, the shaking stopped. Robert tentatively opened the bathroom door, expecting his house to be gone. It stood just as it did when they first entered the bathroom. Other than a few dishes shattered on the hard, ceramic-tile floor in the kitchen, everything appeared to be okay.

The same could not be said for downtown Houston, ten miles to the northeast. The once-beautiful, modern skyline now appeared to be nothing but blazing skeletal hulks, standing as mute testimony to the technological triumph and moral decadence of mankind.

6:15 p.m., January 30—Las Vegas, Nevada

The State of the Union message might as well be broadcast to the far side of the moon as far as Buck Hansen was concerned. His overriding goal at the moment was to win back the fifty-five grand he had dropped playing Texas hold-em poker for the past four hours in the Bellagio casino. He, his wife, and four kids under eight, living in Phoenix, Arizona, were about to lose their home to the uncaring, greedy bank. Buck had come to Vegas, one last time, to win enough money to stave off the foreclosure. The fact his gambling habit had led to his family's current desperate situation, didn't seem to register in his addicted brain.

Buck loved the sights and sounds of Las Vegas, particularly those emanating inside the casinos. The continuous ding, ding, ding, and tinkling sounds were music to Bucks ears as slot machines announced winners all over the casino floor. Buck knew he was going to be a winner, too. It was just a matter of time before his luck turned, and he would rake in the cash.

As he slowly peered at his three hold cards, his heart nearly exploded in his chest. He was holding three kings, and the dealer had just dealt a fourth king down on the table. Nobody was going to beat four kings. His fortunes were suddenly looking really good.

As he reached for a stack of blue chips, the interior of the casino suddenly brightened as if a lightning bolt had discharged in the middle of the room. A second later, thunder, much louder than generated by a lightning bolt, shattered Buck's short-lived anticipation of winning a big hand. As Buck, and his gambling cohorts, turned toward the apparent origin of the sound, they registered, for just a moment, an apocalyptic vision of the elaborately decorated walls, roulette and black jack tables, slot machines, chandeliers, bodies, and indescribable debris all hurtling toward them at four hundred miles-per-hour as a nuclear-blast wave scoured the building.

The city of neon lights, the place where marriages are done and undone all in a day, where "what happens here stays here", the famous Las Vegas strip was now a crematorium. All that was left of the once-magnificent tribute to mankind's worship of wealth, greed, and carnality were a few burning skeletons amidst a landscape of carnage and devastation.

6:15 p.m., January 30—Los Angeles, California

The commute home always rankled Ashley Jurgens. She lived only twenty miles from downtown Los Angles, yet the commute routinely took her two hours. She worked on the thirty-fourth floor in the sixty-two story Aon Center tower and lived in Long Beach. Tonight, the commute was even worse than normal, and it didn't help she was unable to leave work until almost 6:00 because her curmudgeon boss left her to clean up his mistakes.

Jurgens was a marketing rep for Andrews Biomedical, a medical software company, headquartered in Los Angeles. She had moved to Long Beach two years earlier from Boise, Idaho. After earning her MBA at Boise State University, she thought moving to L.A. would be an adventure. She never imagined how different living in the smog-infested, congested Southern California environment would be from the open spaces of Boise.

Working for her fifty-three-year-old, five-foot-six inch, micro-managing boss, whose management style was a casebook study of the little-man complex, only increased her dislike of the current situation.

Her mind wandered, as she vaguely listened to the radio, as the President of the United States was introduced and began his State of the Union speech. As she contemplated a whole series of unrelated subjects, she became instantly alert as the radio newscaster's voice suddenly took on an excited, almost panicked tone. She wondered what was happening. The newscaster was describing the panic he was witnessing at the Capitol Building, when the transmission abruptly stopped and was replaced with static. A sudden queasiness in her stomach told Jurgens something awful was happening in America.

Her foreboding was instantly prophetic. A sudden, intensely-brilliant light behind her caused her to glance into the rear-view mirror. The vision horrified her. Her mirror was filled with a boiling fireball expanding upward and outward from the center of the city. Jurgens had driven her two-year-old Toyota Corolla only about five miles since leaving her office, not nearly far enough away from the exploding, nuclear conflagration behind her.

The Toyota was suddenly hit by a monstrous sledge hammer causing Jurgens to lose control of her car. The freeway became a demolition derby as vehicles of all sizes careened and bounced off each other. The Corolla's airbag deployed, and her seatbelts held her upright as the car slammed into three other vehicles before sliding sideways into the center median.

Miraculously the location where the Toyota came to rest was in a recessed gully and provided a degree of protection from the massive winds generated by the detonation five miles distant. Jurgens, bleeding profusely but still conscious, watched, in horror as cars slammed into eighteen-wheelers and exploded. Other vehicles seemed to be flying as the blast wave tossed them like fluttering leaves.

As she slowly lost consciousness, she realized she would no longer have to worry about her commute. She only hoped her home in Boise was still there. Ashley Jurgens would live to return to her family in Boise. Thousands of other families in the greater Los Angeles area would grieve for loved ones who would never be found, let alone return to them.

6:15 p.m., January 30—San Francisco, California

The beautiful city by the bay was a great place to live, at least in the mind of Johnny Desmond. He and his partner of a little over a year, Jake Broussard, rented a quaint, pale-green, shake-shingled townhouse on twenty-fourth street in the Castro District.

He and Jake had mildly anticipated President Papadakis' speech tonight, not because of the controversy regarding the American Freedom Party, but because of their interest in the president's stance on gay rights. The president's support of same-sex marriage had garnered the support of the gay community in the country, and Johnny and Jake were no exceptions. They had serious doubts about what would happen to the progress their movement had made over the past several years if the American Freedom Party was able to gain power, even though one of the founding senators of the party was openly gay. They had barely settled in on the old, billowy sofa in their small, but adequate, living room, when the scene at the Capitol unraveled. They, like millions of other Americans, were profoundly distressed by the unsettling events witnessed on the TV screen.

The black suburban was parked innocently on Sproule Lane, a small side street off of Clay Street, near the top of Nob Hill, a little less than three miles distance from Johnny's townhouse. Because of the SUV's lofty location, a flip of the switch would set off a detonation mimicking an air-burst explosion. The San Francisco downtown to the north, east, and south of the epicenter would be totally destroyed.

Johnny looked over at Jake whose eyes were registering the same agitated emotions he was feeling. "What's going on?", Jake blurted out.

Before Johnny could respond, the room was eerily illuminated by a bright light filtering in through the closed shutters. The temperature in the room increased immediately causing both to struggle to breathe.

Johnny staggered to the north-facing window and peered out between two wood shutters to be greeted by a broiling inferno. A few seconds later the blast wave, exerting a pressure of over five psi accompanied by 160 miles-per-hour winds, slammed into the north side of the townhouse and swept the walls and contents, including its human inhabitants, to the south.

6:15 p.m., January 30—Seattle, Washington

Perhaps no other landmark identifies the Seattle area better than the Space Needle, built in 1962 as a futuristic symbol of the Seattle World's Fair. The 605 foot structure remains a marvel of design and construction. Resembling a flying saucer sitting on top of a spindly-legged tower, it was anchored to a 120 square-foot, underground foundation. Enough concrete to fill 467 cement trucks was dumped into the foundation. The completed Space Needle was built to withstand severe earthquakes as well as two hundred miles-per-hour winds.

The Sky City Restaurant, located in the bottom portion of the saucer-like top of the Space Needle, was one of Seattle's premier eating spots. By rotating continuously, it was designed to give the diners a 360-degree view, regardless of the seating location. At 520 feet, the view was spectacular.

Seated at an exterior table and enjoying the exhilarating experience, as the Seattle panorama slowly rotated by them, was a newly-married couple from Newport Beach, North Carolina. Jose and Rosa Martinez were relishing the last evening of their five-day honeymoon. They were scheduled for a late-morning flight out of Sea-Tac International the next day. The Martinez's had chosen Seattle for their honeymoon mainly due to a *Discovery Channel* program, six months earlier, about the construction of the Space Needle. It just seemed an intriguing place to go. They were not disappointed.

Jose sipped his coke as he eagerly awaited the rib-eye filet he had ordered fifteen minutes earlier. Rosa, who had ordered braised, poached salmon, was aimlessly staring toward the city skyline thinking what a beautiful city Seattle was.

Below, and about a half mile to the east, a blinding white light suddenly exploded in Rosa's face. Jose started to turn toward the light, when the windows shattered, and the interior of the restaurant erupted into flame. The searing heat enveloped the young couple causing instant death. A few seconds later a tremendous force impacted the Space Needle far in excess of the two hundred miles-per-hour winds it was built to withstand. The saucer, unhinged from its supporting tower, flew out into Puget Sound, disintegrating as it went, almost like the flying saucer it was built to resemble.

PART THREE

RECOVERY

Chapter 53

One of the smaller conference rooms, at the Bangor Civic Center, was serving as the temporary seat of government for the United States. The congressmen had spent the last ten hours trying to determine what had befallen the country and what immediate actions should be implemented now.

They had learned, through military sources, a total of twelve cities had been attacked with nuclear devices, but they knew little else. No contact with Washington D.C. had been possible, and Benson and the others were assuming the worst; the president, cabinet, and all members of Congress that were present during the speech were dead. Past practice had always ensured one person in the line of succession was secreted elsewhere. Benson had tried to determine, to no avail, who was absent and if that person was still alive. In view of the wide-spread destruction incurred in the capital, it was doubtful anybody was left in the line of succession.

Within two hours after the attacks on America's cities, Benson had phoned General Douglas Taylor, commander of the United States Central Command, at McDill Air Force Base in Tampa, Florida. General Taylor acknowledged none of the Joint Chiefs or nationally elected officials who were in Washington could be located, so until the situation clarified, he would consider the congressmen at Bangor as the functioning national government. The military chain-of-command would, therefore, look to them for strategic direction.

Taylor agreed to contact the commanders of the other eight unified commands, to ensure all nine commanders were in agreement with the chain-of-command he proposed. He and Benson both agreed any single general attempting to take charge of the government would compound the catastrophe immeasurably. He candidly told Benson he was worried about one of the unified command generals, joint-forces commander General Theodore Cooke. He felt Cooke, who was the most conservative of the nine commanders, had a tendency to shoot first and ask questions later and was sure to blame Russia for the attacks, even in the absence of hard evidence.

Benson stressed the importance of keeping Cooke under control. Destroying the world because of an unsubstantiated suspicion was an extremely bad solution to the unprecedented problems faced by the country now. Taylor agreed and would solicit the help of the other commanders to ensure such a scenario did not occur.

The general also confirmed he had heard Benson's speech on TV and had taken immediate steps to raise the military alert level to DEFCON two, the highest level short of all out nuclear war. He had very little additional information to add, but indicated he would call Benson back as soon as more was available.

Three hours later, General Taylor called back and assured Benson eight of the Unified Commands were on board. General Cooke had reluctantly agreed to wait and see for now. Taylor was confident Cooke would not do anything without consulting the others first, and he considered the situation manageable in the short-term. He warned Benson, however, Cooke could be a big problem in the future and might have to be removed before the problem became uncontrollable.

Taylor, in a solemn tone, asked, "Is anybody else in the room with you now?"

Benson, wondering why the sudden secrecy, answered, "No, I'm alone. Why does it matter at this point?"

The general responded, "Senator, I'm sure you haven't thought thoroughly through what's happened yet—none of us have. But, as you know, the president was always accompanied by a military attaché carrying the codes to launch a nuclear strike if, God forbid, that ever became necessary.

Benson replied, "Yes, I'm aware of that." Then, realizing the implications of where the general was heading, added, "How does that concern me?"

The general continued, "The attack on Washington D.C. put us in an almost untenable position for a short period of time. There is nobody in a position to order a counter attack if nuclear-tipped missiles were launched in our direction from Russia or any other country. That's possibly one reason to suspect Russia wasn't behind this, otherwise they would have followed up immediately with a full scale attack against our nuclear facilities and subs." Almost as if he was thinking out loud, the general followed with a muted, barely perceptible, "Unless, of course, there was a different motive."

"What do you mean?" queried Benson, startled at Taylor's insinuation.

General Taylor replied, "It's probably best to ignore that last comment for now, Senator. Let's let the facts, as they develop, speak for themselves. In the meantime, it's imperative we fix this gap in our nuclear chain-of-command. We feel our only viable option, at this point, is to ask you to assume that liability. Without civilian control, the decision to trigger what could be the end of modern civilization, is left solely to the military, which, in view of what we've already discussed, is not in the best interests of our democracy."

Benson was momentarily stunned, never for a moment contemplating assuming this ultimate responsibility. Finally, he gathered his emotions sufficiently to respond, "General, why me?"

"Who else Senator?"

Benson, smart enough to realize there wasn't anybody else, but agonized nevertheless, simply uttered, "Okay, do what you need to do."

General Taylor explained a marine colonel was already en route with a briefcase containing the appropriate codes with instructions on the process to be followed should it ever be necessary. He would arrive at the Bangor airport as a passenger on an F-16 jet within the hour.

Taylor continued for a few minutes, explaining the military had ascertained a total of twelve cities had been devastated, but little additional data was available. He stated information was coming in slowly, but steadily, and he would have a much better handle on the situation in a few hours.

It was agreed the general would travel to Bangor within twelve hours to brief those present on all available information and determine what the next steps would be militarily.

The general expressed his concern about the safety of the congressmen in Bangor. Benson informed him a large police contingent was at the Center, but they would all feel safer if military assets could be deployed. Taylor advised he would contact the Maine governor and order available National Guard troops to immediately deploy to enhance security at the Civic Center.

For the past several hours, senators and representatives had been taking turns manning an impromptu phone bank, attempting to contact the governors of each state, including those attacked, to get a feel for the situation in the country and attempt to head off any potential civil unrest. By 2:00 p.m., January 31, all but three governors had been contacted. It was not known if the remaining three were still alive, since they were from the states of Georgia, California and Washington.

A consensus was reached to take a four-hour break to get some food and much needed sleep and reconvene later in the evening at 7:00. Few, if any, of the congressmen expected to get more than a few minutes of fitful sleep considering the gravity of the events shaking the nation. The break, nevertheless, was needed to allow each of the participants time to think and coalesce their thoughts into solid recommendations.

Chapter 54

Halfway across the world, *Al Jazeera*, the Qatar based independent Arabic television and radio news station, had just broken into its regularly scheduled news programming to broadcast a "special news bulletin". The *Al Jazeera* anchor, recognized throughout the Arab, world began speaking in Arabic into the TV camera, "We have just received a communication from an unidentified spokesman for the Black October organization. We cannot, at this time, verify its authenticity but believe it does come from the highest levels of the Black October leadership. The communiqué is as follows: 'All Arabs rejoice. Last night glorious freedom-fighters struck a death blow against the great Satan and its lackey, the Zionist state of Israel. Many of America's decadent cities now lay in ruin, and millions of its infidels have paid for their smug arrogance with their lives. We call on all Arab and non-Arab Muslims to join us now, on this dawn of triumph, to finish our holy Jihad and destroy the Zionists forever. Allah is great."

Colby Engeman and Colonel Dylan soberly discussed the events of the last twenty-four hours, while seated in a small, sparsely-furnished alcove adjacent to the main office in Prime Minister Ben Gurion's residence. Both had arrived five minutes before the scheduled time of a briefing by the Israeli defense minister but had now been waiting for thirty minutes. Neither took particular offence at having to wait, realizing the events of the past evening were of such momentous gravity, the delay was more than understandable.

Finally, the simple, single, wood door opened, leading to the prime minister's scaled-down equivalent of the Oval Office. Ben Gurion, himself, leaned through the door to welcome Engeman and Dylan. He warmly, but soberly, shook each of their hands as they entered through the door, gesturing with his arm toward two empty seats, at the back of the massive circular mahogany table, obviously reserved for them.

Already seated at the table were the minister of defense, George Meier, the Mossad director, Ariel Levy, and the Israeli chief of staff,

General David Wiseman. Another individual in civilian dress, unknown to both Engeman and Dylan, was seated next to Levy. No other cabinet members were present. Engeman assumed they had already been briefed by Meier and had left, probably the reason he and Dylan had to wait in the outer office.

Once Engeman and Dylan were seated, the prime minister circled the table briefly with his gaze and then began speaking. "Gentlemen, I fear recent events, culminating with the horrific nuclear attacks on America, have set the world on a course with an outcome, at best uncertain, and, at worst, catastrophic to civilization as we know it.

"As you all know, our country is encircled by enemies whose armies, as we speak, are ready to invade from every direction with the intent, not merely to conquer, but to exterminate us, our wives, and our children from the face of the earth. I'm convinced the events in America are intrinsically connected with the threats facing us; exactly how, I don't know.

"Nor do I know, with certainty, how the terrorist group Black October obtained the nuclear weapons, which they used to devastate our American ally and attempted to detonate in Israel, itself. I suspect those weapons are of Russian origin and are tied, somehow, into the military moves occurring in eastern Europe and the recent vast shipment of Russian arms to our enemies.

"I'm totally committed to finding the answers to these questions and taking whatever measures are necessary to preserve our small country. Secondly, I'm equally committed to do what we can to help our friends in America, who have, through much blood and sacrifice over the years, preserved freedom for millions in this world."

Staring directly at Engeman and Dylan, the prime minister gestured with his right arm toward the unidentified civilian and continued, "This evening, I have asked Joshua Bergmann, chief nuclear scientist with the Israel Atomic Energy Commission (IAEC), to take a few minutes and brief us on what has been discovered, so far, about the unexploded nuclear device we recovered near *Michimoret* early this morning." He shifted his gaze to Bergmann and nodded.

Bergmann, a grand nephew of Ernst David Bergmann, the founder of the Israeli nuclear program, worked twelve-hour days at the top-secret nuclear research complex in the Negev desert at *Dimona*. He was the architect behind Israel's startling expansion, both qualitatively and quantitatively, of its nuclear arsenal. He looked every bit the mad scientist with black, horned-rim glasses and jet-black, curly hair planted, in a sloppy mess, on top of his head.

When he began speaking, however, a deep, resonant, bass voice belied his, otherwise, scant, bony frame. "While we have only just begun our analysis of the nuclear device, I must say it didn't come from any Muslim country. It's much too sophisticated. We have not found any identifiable marking on the device, but our preliminary best guess, at this point, is it looks an awful lot like an American Trident warhead. I believe the Americans call it a W-88."

All five mouths dropped in unison around the table.

"How the hell did the fanatics get a hold of American warheads?" blurted the Israeli defense minister.

"I didn't say it was American," replied Bergmann in his calm, bass voice. "It *resembles* an American warhead. We don't know where it's from, at this point. It could be a copy manufactured elsewhere, probably in Russia or China. We can't do much more with it without some help from the Americans. I'd suggest we ask them for some technical help. In view of what happened there last night, I'd expect them to send the best they've got to help us resolve this issue."

"Thank you Joshua," interjected Ben Gurion. "I will attempt to make contact with whatever government is left in the United States as soon as this meeting is over and expedite your request. In the meantime, we will excuse you to return to your extremely important work to find the answers we so desperately need."

Bergmann rose quickly from the table, nodded slightly to those still seated, and briskly strode from the room.

The prime minister waited until the door closed and then, nodding toward Defense Minister Meier, asked, "OK George, what happens in the morning?"

Chapter 55

Exhausted as he was, sleep pretty much evaded Benson. Way too much information was crowding the circuits of his brain. Finally after two hours of trying, he slipped into a fitful sleep only to be awakened a half-hour later by Kristina who, against her womanly, compassionate objections, gently shook Benson awake to take an urgent telephone call from Israel.

At first, through the fog of exhaustion, Benson had a tough time registering who was on the other end of the phone, particularly considering the heavy, chopped accent. Finally after repeated questioning, he realized the Israeli prime minister, Ravid Ben Gurion, was trying to talk to him.

"I apologize Mr. prime minister," Benson offered, "I haven't had a whole lot of sleep and am doing my best to clear my mind. I think I'm okay now. Please, how can I help you?"

The prime minister replied, "Senator Benson, I can't begin to imagine the agony you and your countrymen are suffering. You have no need to apologize to me. I can somewhat relate to lack of sleep, since I have been suffering the same fate recently. What I want to discuss with you is of such importance that, in spite of your obviously loving and wonderful wife's objections, I insisted on waking you up. You need to hear what I have to say before you take irretrievable, crucial steps in the next few hours and days."

Benson's curiosity was heightened at Ben Gurion's choice of words. It appeared Ben Gurion was assuming Benson was now leading the country, which was certainly far from fact, at least in Benson's mind.

Ben Gurion continued, "Senator, what I'm about to tell you is of utmost importance and is critical to the survival of my country, as well, perhaps, to the continuation of civilization as we know it. I hope I'm overstating the situation but am afraid I'm not."

Benson interrupted, "Mr. Prime Minister, before you go on, you need to know I do not lead our government and am probably not the person you should be discussing this matter with now."

Ben Gurion interrupted Benson's interruption, "Senator, unfortunately, you know as well as I do, your country no longer has any national leadership, at least in Washington, so you, Senator Benson, are the closest thing remaining."

Benson blushed at the prime minister's implication he was the national leader by default, even though he was slowly realizing that was probably the case. He noticed the black attaché case sitting on the dresser and was reminded that a few hours earlier another person had also made the same determination.

Ben Gurion continued, "I can't afford to wait until your country sorts this all out and chooses a new president. That could take weeks or months. I've got to trust your judgment with the information I'm about to share with you. Can I trust you Senator?"

Benson took a deep breath, accepting the fact that events had thrust upon him the heavy mantle of leadership for the country, at least over the short-term. After what seemed like an interminable pause, he answered the Israeli, "I don't see any other options at this point. I think under the circumstances, our two countries will have an ongoing need to trust each other explicitly."

The prime minister continued as if the conversation had never been interrupted. "In less than four hours the Israeli defense forces will launch preemptive air strikes against the Islamic forces arrayed against us in Egypt, Syria, and Lebanon. Our goal is to destroy as many anti-aircraft missile sites and aircraft as possible and gain air superiority over both theatres within forty-eight hours. We also intend to launch almost-simultaneous ground assaults with the goal of eliminating the threat from Egypt first before doing the same in the other direction."

Perhaps anticipating Benson questioning why he was providing the American with Israeli war plans, Ben Gurion explained, "Our country is launching these attacks, because we're convinced we have no other options. To wait for the vast armies surrounding us to attack first would be to commit national suicide. We anticipate the world reaction to our attack will be immediate condemnation of Israel and, to be honest with you Senator, we don't care. Our tiny country is sick to death of always having to defend everything we do to the United Nations, when we're the only country in the Middle East that practices democratic principles and values life and freedom.

"We would hope, under the current circumstances, America will understand and support our decision. I'm confident, when you consider additional information I'm about to give you, there will be no hesitation to do so."

Benson was shocked with the information the Israeli was imparting to him, probably more due to the blunt delivery than content, but his curiosity of what might come next tempered his shock. All he could muster over the phone was a limp, "Please continue."

The prime minister shocked Benson further with his next statement, "Early this morning, just before your country experienced the surprise nuclear attack with such catastrophic results, Israeli Defense Forces were able to stop a similar attack from occurring in Tel Aviv and were able to recover an unexploded nuclear warhead."

Benson interrupted again with an explosion of questions. "What are you saying? How did you know? Do you know the origin of the warhead? Did you ..."

The Israeli adroitly cut off Benson's questions. "I will provide you with all of the information I can. You need to understand, however, we have many unanswered questions ourselves. As a matter of fact, some of those questions can be answered only by Americans."

Benson, taken aback at the implications of what Ben Gurion was saying, replied cautiously, "What do you mean, prime minister? Are you implying the attack on our country was home grown, carried out by some sort of American conspiracy?"

The Israeli replied, "No, I don't believe that for a second. You need to know, however, our preliminary analysis indicates the device we recovered looks a lot like the warhead the United States has used for several years on the Trident ICBM. We can't be sure without some assistance from your country's nuclear experts, which leads me to the second reason I'm calling you. We would like to formally request your assistance to help us determine the origin of the bomb."

Benson paused for a moment, trying to comprehend the import of what the prime minister had just told him, as well as absorbing the idea he was being asked to make critical decisions normally reserved for the leader of the free world.

He cleared his throat and replied, "Most certainly, Prime Minister Ben Gurion. I will take the necessary steps to identify our best nuclear experts and make them available to you as soon as possible. It's imperative we determine who is behind these attacks. Do you have any theories at this point?"

The prime minister cautiously responded, "We don't have any hard evidence to support any theories yet. Our intelligence analysts, however, are working on a theory, and I repeat, at this point it's just a theory. The attacks on America, the attempted attack on Israel, the buildup of Russian-armed Arab armies on our borders, and the military moves taking place in eastern Europe and southern Russia are all related. Our best guess is Russia, perhaps with Chinese help, is behind all of this in some sort of grandiose plan to become the primary power in this part of the world. If Russia controls Middle Eastern oil, they become the world's new superpower. Western Europe has already pretty much acquiesced to Russian hegemony. I presume that's why they were not attacked.

"I feel that Black October, the terrorist organization claiming responsibility for the attacks, is just a dupe of the Russians, probably blinded to the long-term risks to themselves. Furthermore, I …"

Benson stopped Ben Gurion in mid-sentence. "If what you are theorizing is true, it will mean World War III. Should we ascertain, without reasonable doubt, Russia was behind the slaughter of several million Americans, I don't see any choice but to respond in kind. The American public will demand such a response."

Ben Gurion continued, "I don't know whether we'll ever be able to prove Russia's involvement beyond a reasonable doubt, but I'm convinced sufficiently in my own mind of their involvement. I think the only prudent course of action for us is to take steps now to counter Russia militarily. I hope America will agree. That means, first of all, total defeat of the Muslim armies poised to attack the state of Israel.

"Secondly, the oil fields in Saudi Arabia, Iraq, Kuwait, and the smaller states on the Gulf cannot be allowed to come under Russian control, or Russia will surely have won its primary objective.

"Third, Israel can never allow Iran to possess usable nuclear weapons, which, according to reliable intelligence assets in place today, is extremely close to reality. Iran would never hesitate to launch such weapons, once they possessed them, particularly if Israel is defeating them militarily.

"Senator Benson, the final reason for my call is to solicit your commitment to enter this battle with us. I believe Israel has the wherewithal to accomplish the first goal without American military involvement, other than establishment of an effective re-supply chain. We would anticipate the defeat of the Arab and Iranian armies arrayed against us will exhaust some of our higher-tech military assets rather quickly and would request your urgent help to preclude critical shortages.

"After an initial victory over the Arab armies, I'm fearful of what we might face once Russian troops enter the battle. Israel most certainly cannot defeat the Russians alone. Therefore, Senator Benson, it's critical for America to be committed militarily at that point.

"Finally, I'm requesting the United States covertly loan Israel a dozen B2 Stealth bombers to facilitate a successful attack on key Iranian nuclear sites within the next two weeks."

In spite of the gravity of the situation, Benson could not refrain from asking the prime minister in a slightly sarcastic tone, "Is there anything else you would like?"

There was no laughter on the other end.

Benson attempted a weak explanation. "I'm sorry to sound flippant, but this whole conversation has caught me so off guard, I'm reeling. We have just suffered a horrendous attack that killed millions of innocents. You're now asking me to think rationally and commit our country to possibly the opening shots of World War III, leading to unimaginable consequences."

Benson waited a few seconds to compose his thoughts. "Prime Minister, I find your logic hard to dispute, and I see very few alternatives to what you're suggesting. I'm not the leader of our country, however, and cannot commit it to any course of action. I do understand the gravity of the events, which are quickly unfolding, and the need for a prompt response.

"I'll make this promise to you. In less than two hours, I'm meeting with all the senators and representatives who remain alive, as well as the general in command of the United States Central Command. General Taylor has been authorized to represent all other American military commands. We will review your analysis of the situation and your requests and will have an answer for you before the end of the day. That, sir, is the best I can do."

Benson heard Ben Gurion take a deep breath before he replied, "I sympathize with you fully, Senator. Please keep in mind the extreme confidentiality of the information I shared with you. Under the circumstances we're currently facing, I also understand why you'll have to discuss this with other people. I trust explicitly you'll do what's right and look forward to your call in a few hours. May God bless us."

Benson continued staring at the telephone receiver in his hand for almost a minute, after he heard the hollow click on the other end. The need to exercise real leadership, with the ability to make critical decisive decisions now thrust upon him, was a crushing, overwhelming responsibility. His mind was rushing through a hollow tunnel into an ever-darkening black hole. In the next few hours he could be responsible for extinguishing all human life on the planet. He slowly put the receiver in its cradle, looked up toward the ceiling of the motel bedroom and uttered in a plaintive tone, “God, please help me!”

Chapter 56

The sound of wailing sirens punctuated the cold, dreary day as weary medical responders, and other volunteers of all stripes, attempted to cope with the disaster that had befallen Kansas City. As was the case with all the stricken cities, the task seemed hopeless.

The Overland Park Regional Hospital, located about seventeen miles, as the crow flies, southwest from ground zero, was typical of the hospitals not destroyed by the blast in the Kansas City area in terms of coping with the onslaught of injured and dying patients. Patients being brought to the hospital were suffering from severe burns, broken bones, hemorrhaging, and internal trauma, compounded in many cases by radiation exposure.

Thousands of injured victims soon overwhelmed the 224-bed medical center. After the injured lined every hallway and filled every waiting and office area, the hospital began turning them away, directing ambulances and private cars to nearby schools and churches where hardwood, gym floors and pews became beds.

The Overland Park hospital, built in 1978, was Johnson County's only trauma center, and, as such, had the wherewithal to handle trauma cases but not to the degree required now. The hospital quickly ran out of necessary medical supplies. Bed sheets were torn up for bandages. Surgeries were performed without anesthetic in hallways and waiting areas. Surgeons wore the same scrubs while operating on patient after patient. The tile floors in hallways soon became slick with blood. At times, the chaos in the surgical suites, corridors, and waiting areas reminded onlookers of old photographs of battle-field hospital conditions during the Civil War.

The situation in the schools and churches was dire. In some locations, no medical help was available, and hundreds were dying, in spite of the best efforts of untrained volunteers and the less injured to help them.

The bomb that detonated in Independence killed virtually every living thing within a one-mile radius from the epicenter of the explosion. A blast force of twelve pounds per square inch, accompanied by a wind of close to five hundred miles-per-hour, obliterated all buildings within a half mile from ground zero, leaving at most, partially destroyed foundations. At one mile out, a few of the strongest buildings constructed of reinforced, poured concrete were still standing, though on fire. Thermal radiation from the blast caused instantaneous flash fires throughout this area of desolation.

One to two miles out, structural skeletons of buildings remained, thrusting up into the sky like relics from centuries before. Single family dwellings were blasted to rubble. Fifty percent of the population was killed. Almost all of those still alive had been injured.

Further out to about three miles, single family dwellings were heavily damaged if not destroyed, office buildings no longer had windows, and some were heavily damaged. Many upper floors had been scoured out, and the contents, including people, had been strewn on the streets below. Five percent of the population was dead with thousands injured.

Beyond three miles, residences were moderately damaged. Most injuries were sustained due to flying glass and debris and thermal radiation.

Because the detonation was at ground level, a huge amount of radioactive earth and debris was blasted high into the atmosphere. Any human being within a two-mile circle from the center of the detonation, who survived the initial blast, was almost assured of a subsequent death due to radiation exposure. A fifteen miles-per-hour, easterly wind carried near-certain death to Missourians living east of Independence. Fallout, measured at near three thousand REM, rained down on anyone unlucky enough to be unprotected. A person, thus exposed, would likely die within a few hours. Over the next two days, thousands more, up to seventy miles east, would be exposed to smaller but still lethal doses of radiation. The Independence blast immediately killed upwards of fifty thousand people and injured at least five times that amount. Within a week, another forty thousand injured would die.

As bad as the devastation was in Independence, had the detonation occurred in Kansas City, as originally planned, tens of thousands more would have died due to radiation poisoning. The mushroom cloud would have dumped its lethal fallout onto populated areas east of Kansas City, including Raytown and Independence. Independence's fate appeared to have been sealed, regardless. The city simply vanished from the landscape. The fallout on the relatively sparsely populated areas east of Independence kept casualties there to a minimum.

Similar scenarios were being played out in the eleven other destroyed cities. Since most of the detonations occurred in city centers, where the initial blast energy was absorbed by multiple, high-rise buildings, the areas of extreme destruction were somewhat smaller. The initial blasts and subsequent downwind radiation poisoning, however, caused extremely high mortality counts due to the dense populations around the downtown areas and surrounding suburbs.

The country had suffered a devastating blow. It was certain to change the course of the world in a direction schemers in Moscow, terror mongers in Lebanon, appeasers in Europe, and patriots in Bangor could not begin to fathom.

Chapter 57

Molly's Tavern in Coeur d'Alene, Idaho served three different brands of ice-cold beer on tap. This evening, not quite twenty-four hours after the devastating attacks on America's cities, Jack Thornton was gulping down his fourth mug of Michelob, his favorite of the three. At the table with him were four other members of the white-supremacy organization, which Jack led.

The Liberty Militia, a relatively obscure, far-right organization, unknown to the American public but better known to the FBI and the citizenry of Coeur d'Alene, boasted about eight hundred, card-carrying members. The organization's creed pretty much blamed all of the nation's problems on Jews, nonwhite minorities, and the liberal politicians in Washington.

Thornton, a former Navy Seal commander who had commanded a company of Seals in Operation Desert Storm, was, most recently, an out-of-work, security consultant and divorced father of three. He was referred to as General Thornton by the eight hundred militia members, including the four at the table. Unknown to the FBI, was the degree and quality of training, which had taken place over the past two years, and the sophistication of the weaponry possessed by the organization. By all measurable standards, the Liberty Militia was roughly equal in weaponry and training to a light infantry battalion in the United States Army.

Latest FBI intelligence considered the militia simply another right-wing hate-group that was more bluster than risk to anybody.

Thornton, enjoying a buzz from the Michelob, was discussing matters of importance in a subdued voice to his subordinates around the table. "Gentlemen, our time is now. The Jews and colored faggots have really done it to us this time. Our country has let them lead us down the primrose path to where we're helpless to confront our godless enemies. Well, no more! It's God's divine will we confront these perverts now and put an end to our nation's downward spiral."

The four subordinates nodded enthusiastically as they looked back and forth trying to out-nod each other.

Thornton continued, "This tragedy that has befallen our nation provides us now with the opportunity we have been waiting for. The government, if there is any remaining, will be overwhelmed just trying to save their own skins. The task of coping with the millions of American citizens killed by the godless perverts who attacked us, will divert the attention of the military and give us the time we need to consolidate our leadership over the new America."

More animated nods around the table.

"I believe with all my heart God is calling upon us to establish a new America, first in northern Idaho, but, subsequently, all over the west. This will happen once the white race in the west catches our vision and joins us in our crusade to separate us from the colored immigrants, Jews, and homosexuals wrecking our country."

Thornton paused for a few seconds to soak in the adulation of the four patriots, whose wide eyes were moist with emotion, then continued, "My order for each of you is to mobilize your companies over the next three days and be prepared to assemble the troops next Saturday at oh-eight-hundred at our Priest River training facility. We'll prepare to march, thereafter, on Coeur d'Alene and establish a new America."

About twenty-three hundred miles to the southeast of Molly's Tavern, in Norfolk, Virginia, another right-wing zealot was sitting behind his desk contemplating how best to ensure the closet-commie bastards who attacked America last night would be brought to justice. Perhaps a more appropriate description of the direction of his thinking would be how justice could be brought to them. Lieutenant General Theodore Cooke, had no intention of mollycoddling the Russians, who, he was sure, were responsible for the attacks. If it was up to him, rockets would already be on their way to destroy the Russian hordes, once and for all.

He couldn't believe the other unified commanders had thrown their support behind the remnant of congress hiding up in Maine. The only way this country could survive now was for the military to take control of the government. Now was a prime opportunity to eliminate the influence of the left-wingers running the press and television media, and the liberal educators ruining the colleges in America. The civilians in Bangor were no better. In his view, they were products of the left-wing culture.

The general was sure many, if not a majority, of Americans shared his disgust of how low the country had descended. He was equally sure a majority would be clamoring for revenge, once over the grief of losing so many fellow citizens. His duty was to channel that desire for revenge to support for him. Once he had the citizenry behind him, it wouldn't matter what the liberals in Bangor said or did.

Chapter 58

An early February blizzard of unprecedented ferocity pounded Moscow. The howling, sixty-miles-per-hour winds combined with heavy snow made moving around in the city a virtual nightmare. The conditions did not interfere with ongoing intelligence review and planning by the Russian military. All of the players in the apocalyptic theatre, being directed by President Lebedov, were already in the Kremlin, having been secured there for the past forty-eight hours.

Colonel Litinov and General Dimitry Yeremenko, chief of the Russian general staff, and a few other key military commanders, were seated around the mahogany table in the president's office. Lebedov was expected to join them at any moment to discuss the latest intelligence and military preparations for the next phase of *Hammer and Anvil.*

Forty minutes later, an obviously agitated president strolled into the office from his private residence entrance. As those at the table stood, as was the custom, waiting for Lebedov to sit down and command them to be seated, the atmosphere in the room darkened considerably. Lebedov sat down at the end of the table but did not direct the others to sit. He surveyed each face in the room as the men stood at attention, stared directly at Litinov, and finally exclaimed, "The Israelis recovered an unexploded bomb! How in the hell could you have let that happen?"

General Taylor arrived at the Bangor Conference Center at about 6:15 p.m., having been flown into the Bangor Airport as a passenger on an Air Force F-16. His choice of aircraft significantly reduced the travel time from Florida. Upon his arrival, he immediately sought out Senator Benson who had given up trying to grab some sleep.

In the thirty minutes left before the scheduled meeting with the other congressmen, as the general sipped a lukewarm cup of coffee, Benson briefed him on the conversation he had just had with the Israeli prime minister. Taylor's demeanor remained calm, almost as if he had already suspected the information Benson relayed to him.

After Benson had concluded the briefing, the general looked deeply into Benson's eyes. Benson felt Taylor was staring directly into the interior of his head. The general calmly stated, "Senator, I think it's imperative this country have a leader, a person the citizens can rally around and the military can trust and follow. You are that person."

Benson began to object, "General, I can't just assume ..."

The general cut Benson off in mid sentence, "We're way beyond having to follow a political process. We don't have the luxury of time to do that. Maybe six months from now we'll be able to engineer some sort of election, but, by then, the world could be nothing but a smoking cinder. After all, yesterday, you agreed to assume liability for the nuclear trigger.

"I'm going to propose to the congressmen that they throw their support behind you as the interim President of the United States. I have already discussed this with the other military commands, except for Cooke, and they were unanimous in their support for you to assume this role. Senator, it's imperative our country have a strong leader now, this evening, not tomorrow or the next day. Then, it might be too late."

Benson stared absently into the general's eyes. "I ... I ... appreciate your confidence in me, but what you are asking is—well, unprecedented to say the least. I fully understand the immediate need for leadership on the national level, but I'm not sure I'm the person for that role."

General Taylor waited without saying a word as Benson wrestled with his thoughts.

Finally, Benson said, "General, I'll agree to abide by the decision of the folks we'll be meeting with momentarily." For a second time in less than an hour he said, "That's the best I can do."

The general smiled faintly. "I can take that risk."

Litinov was incensed. It was all he could do to avoid bursting into a suicidal tirade against the President of Russia. He thought to himself, *That arrogant asshole has the audacity to dress me down for failure of an operation I warned him, from the beginning, we shouldn't do.*

Instead, he meekly responded, "President, we knew from the beginning this part of the operation posed the biggest risk. There's no way we could've anticipated the Israelis would be able to uncover the plans in time. Perhaps they had a spy buried within the Black October organization. That would have been beyond my control."

"It was your duty as a soldier of mother Russia to prevent that," countered Lebedov.

Litinov disregarded the whisperings in his mind to shut up and responded more forthrightly, "Mr. President, you forget the recruiting and control of the Arab suicide bombers was in the hands of Black October, not under my direct influence. Their mistakes led to the breach of security, not any failure on my part."

Lebedov rose quickly out of his chair and glowered ominously at Litinov. Then as the realization Litinov was correct slowly encompassed his mind, he calmed and said to all others around the table, "Be seated."

He addressed Litinov again this time in a more cordial tone. "So, Colonel, we agree the weak link in this operation was always the Arabs. What's done is done. The question now is what do we do to minimize any fallout?"

The colonel relaxed and replied, "The warhead the Israelis recovered closely resembles the American W-88 warhead, one of the multiple warheads on the tip of the Trident II ICBM. That alone should confuse them. Why would American warheads be used to blow up American cities? Eventually with American help, I'd guess they will suspect the warheads were supplied to the terrorists by us or China, but they will have no proof, at least not sufficient to warrant a nuclear response. By that time our operation in the Middle East will be a fait accompli."

The president, expecting a positive answer, asked, "Colonel, do you feel the devastating blow suffered by America yesterday will be sufficient to cripple any military response?"

Litinov, anticipating the president's expectations, nevertheless answered forthrightly, as he briefly scanned the faces of the others sitting around the table. "I hope so Mr. President. The Americans are sometimes hard to understand. After the attack on Pearl Harbor Admiral Yamamoto was reputed to have said, 'I feel all we have done is awaken a sleeping giant and fill him with a terrible resolve."

The president's face visibly paled.

The colonel continued, "A new generation of American leaders, much more concerned with temporal success, wealth, and personal power, have controlled America during the past twenty years. Will they be as equally enraged as the World War II generation? Who's to say? They might not be in control anymore, anyway. Our intelligence sources tell us the American government was destroyed in Washington, which of course was our intent. That raises the question now, however, of whom will replace them, particularly over the short-term. Let's hope we haven't shot the dog only to face a lion."

The faces around the table were sober as each of the schemers tried to mentally justify the risks, which now confronted them. There was obviously no turning back, but none had, before this moment, truly acknowledged the slippery slope upon which they had embarked.

After a lengthy silence, President Lebedov turned toward General Yeremenko and said, "Please General, brief us on the state of our preparations for the next phase of the operation."

Chapter 59

Nine senators and twenty-one representatives sat stunned upon hearing Senator Benson's recapitulation of his conversation with Prime Minister Ben Gurion.

Benson followed the briefing with a suggestion that a discussion of a response to the Israeli prime minister be put off until later in the meeting, after all present had an opportunity to be briefed by General Taylor on the extent and effects of the attacks on America's cities. They agreed. Benson then nodded toward the general.

General Taylor cleared his throat and began, "It's hard to know where to begin to describe this tragedy that has been inflicted on our country. We know a lot of generalities at this point but need some time to be able to report more accurate information. We do know twelve cites were attacked with devastating results.

"It appears only one attack was partially thwarted, an attack on Kansas City, Missouri. Due to the heroic efforts of local law enforcement and the FBI, Kansas City wasn't bombed. Unfortunately, however, a suburb to the east, Independence, Missouri was obliterated. Because the population in areas east of Independence was relatively sparse, radiation-related deaths were minimized. Even so we estimate, when all the casualty numbers are known, over one hundred thousand people will have died in the area with ten times that many injured."

The mood in the room had turned hopelessly bleak as the Congress members considered how bad the casualties must be in the other cites, since the general considered the Independence attack as being partially thwarted.

The general continued, "The other destroyed cities are Washington D.C., New York, Miami, Atlanta, Chicago, Detroit, Houston, Las Vegas, Los Angeles, San Francisco, and Seattle. Since the detonations took place in the downtown areas, there was total destruction of the infrastructures and economic engines of each city. Radioactive fallout over the densely populated areas adjacent to the downtown areas has been intense, and casualty figures for these cities will be in the millions, possibly as many as twenty million."

The silence in the room was deafening. Tears were running freely down many of the shaken legislators' faces, staring blankly ahead. Then a female member of the House started to sob uncontrollably and was soon joined by another female and a few men. The general recognized the need for a short break and uttered nothing as tears filled his eyes as well.

After several minutes, Senator Dobson looked up at the general and asked, "Is there more to come? I mean, are there going to be more attacks?"

General Taylor replied as honestly as he could, "Senator, I cannot guarantee anything at this point. The evil scum who did this, however, made a critical mistake. Our military assets are completely intact, no damage whatsoever. Our defense posture is at DEFCON 2. We have taken steps to secure our ports and critical infrastructure. As I speak, troops are on the move in our country to reduce the odds of another successful attack. Twenty thousand troops have been deployed to secure the Mexican border. Several thousand Maine National Guardsmen have been deployed in Bangor, forming a tight defensive barrier around you all here at the Civic Center."

The general continued, "As most of you know, our military resources worldwide have been severely depleted over the past three years as the former administration implemented its policy of slashing defense spending to fund its new social programs. While I'm not trying to make any political statement for, or against, the programs, the fact is, our defense posture in the world has greatly suffered. I'd request urgent consideration, in view of the unfolding events, to nationalizing the National Guard. We should also significantly increase our recruiting efforts to expand our force levels. By doing so, I believe we will have sufficient troop numbers to achieve our immediate goals. If things really get out of hand, we might have to even consider starting up the selective service system.

"As a prudent step, I have ordered four carrier strike-groups to sail immediately for the Mediterranean and Indian Oceans, just in case events call for such a power projection. In view of what the Israeli prime minister has reported, it seems those moves were providential. I assume you are all in agreement. If not, the orders can certainly be rescinded.

"Now I know you all have a tremendous burden on your shoulders, just to figure out how to keep the country's critical machinery moving. I need to sit down and let you all do your work. Before I do, however, I desire to make a recommendation.

"The country is at a crossroads. It can pull itself back up by its bootstraps, or it can fall apart with disastrous consequences for the rest of the world. America has a critical need right now. It needs a leader it can follow, who can inspire it to unite to recover from this horrible atrocity and fight the enemy, whoever that might be. I and the other unified command generals have all agreed the person the country needs tonight is Senator Rick Benson. That would be my recommendation to you all. The country cannot wait a day longer. Yesterday, anticipating your agreement, the military turned over the nuclear trigger to Senator Benson."

Benson opened his mouth to offer some objections, or at least other options to be considered, but before he could utter a word the room broke into almost-rhythmic, subdued applause as each member stood and indicated approval to the general's suggestion.

The meeting at the Bangor Convention Center lasted well into the early morning hours of the next day. To meet the almost inconceivable medical and social needs of the millions of injured and displaced citizens across the country, a cabinet level position was created to direct and coordinate the country's response. Senator Charles McClain of Nebraska, was unanimously picked to take on that responsibility.

Former FBI director, Sydney Wilkinson, was reappointed to head the FBI and was given the urgent task, along with the CIA, of investigating the attacks to identify the perpetrators. William Smith had earlier telephoned Benson and agreed to continue leading the CIA. During the previous evening, the events occurring around Kansas City necessitated Smith be working at his office in McLean, Virginia when the explosion detonated in the capital. As a result, his life was spared.

Other senators and representatives were appointed to head up critical agencies based on expertise each possessed. The huge federal bureaucracy, with all its resources, was headless. It was imperative new heads be appointed with a mandate to eliminate malcontents and red tape and utilize critical resources quickly and effectively.

Senator Dobson agreed to take on the role of Treasury Secretary and to immediately focus on the chaos the attacks created in the American banking system.

After some discussion, mostly to clarify military options available, a consensus was achieved to respond positively to the Israeli prime minister's requests. Until evidence could be uncovered to the contrary, it was deemed prudent to accept Ben Gurion's theory and take necessary steps to counter Russia's ambitions. A few wanted to strike back at Russia now with nuclear weapons but reason prevailed. Exterminating humanity was not an effective method of retribution, particularly when the evidence against Russia was only circumstantial.

All of General Taylor's recommendations were unanimously approved with the exception of the immediate nationalization of the National Guard. Based on continuing consultations with the state governors, a decision on that issue would be made in the near future. An overriding concern was the fear of uncontrolled looting and other civil unrest in the areas near the detonations. Looters would most likely be committing radiation suicide if they entered the areas of destruction, but people prone to looting aren't known for their intelligence or foresight.

A team of experts in nuclear weapons technology would be assembled and quickly flown to Israel to assist in evaluating the warhead the Israelis had recovered. It was deemed the highest priority to identify the origin of the weapon, especially, in view of the military moves being contemplated.

General Taylor accepted responsibility as the interim chairman of the unified commands of the United States military, which would function as the Joint Chiefs until a replacement organization could be created. He was tasked with formulating several military contingencies depending on the evolving world situation. At the least, at this point, the United States would support Israel as requested. Twelve B2 Spirit stealth bombers would be on their way to Israel within forty-eight hours.

The general also committed to working with the CIA and Israeli intelligence to locate Black October's headquarters and bases of support and develop a plan to destroy its leadership and capability once and for all.

Senator Peter Simpson, from Utah, accepted the role of interim United Nations ambassador with instructions to represent U.S. interests in the world body. Nobody in the room thought the UN would do anything to prevent the imminent conflict in the Middle East or help restrain the resurgent terrorist activity in the world. The United Nations had been duped into virtually become an arm of Russian and Chinese foreign policy.

Network and cable TV reporters, who had remained at Bangor, eagerly accepted the assignment of reestablishing nation-wide broadcasting capability. The network and cable organizations' headquarters had been destroyed in the blasts, but technicians in unaffected areas were busy rerouting signals off multiple communications satellites circling the globe. Interim President Benson was assured country-wide communications would be restored totally within a few more hours.

Benson would telephone Prime Minister Ben Gurion as soon as the meeting adjourned. He would address the nation the following evening.

Chapter 60

White, curly contrails crisscrossed the early-dawn sky miles ahead, and high to the right of Solo's sight line as he piloted his Apache, at one hundred feet, toward a column of smoke rising in the distance. He felt some satisfaction knowing the dozens of contrails were evidence the Air Force jet jockeys were ensuring Egyptian jets wouldn't be taking pot shots at his bird.

Solo led a squadron of seven other AH-64 Apaches approaching Abu-Ageila with the aim of destroying as many Russian-made tanks as they could. The pre-mission briefing indicated the Egyptians had concentrated one infantry and two armored divisions near Abu-Ageila, and the column of smoke indicated the jet jockeys had found some of those tanks.

As the helicopters closed the distance to the town, Solo could see smoke columns rising from several different locations, mostly from destroyed tanks and other vehicles, but also from adjacent buildings. He could just make out through the smoky haze a column of armored vehicles leaving the area, headed west. It appeared the column contained about forty vehicles, included lorries, armored troop transports, and at least twenty-five T94 Russian tanks.

Solo keyed his radio and calmly said, "Let's go get 'em."

With that, five choppers lined up in a gradual downward curve to the left as they approached the rear of the column. Solo led the formation with the intent of destroying the lead tank to create a road block for the rest of the column.

Two remaining Apaches maintained altitude and hovered over the battlefield. Their role was to provide cover for the attacking force and were armed with sixteen AIM-7 Sidewinder air-to-air missiles and eight Hellfire missiles. Combined with a twelve hundred round, thirty-millimeter chain gun, the choppers had more than enough firepower to protect the force from an Egyptian counterattack. The assumption was a potential counterattack would be from Russian made Hind helicopters.

The six attack choppers were configured with 16 Hellfire missiles each, plenty of firepower to destroy the Egyptian column.

Solo raced at over 150 miles-per-hour approaching the column from the rear and slightly to the right. When the Apache was about six thousand yards from the lead tank, Solo's gunner located it in the target acquisition sensor, using Direct Viewing Optics (DVO), locked on the magnified image of the tank, and launched a Hellfire missile. The laser guided missile arched downward toward the tank trailing a white rope of smoke.

A few seconds later the T-94 evaporated in a huge fireball.

The other five choppers duplicated Solo's actions, ripping into the stalled column like airborne praying mantises. Smoke from exploding tanks and vehicles was blotting out the sun. Several of the vehicles in the column swerved right or left off of the road, attempting to evade the carnage, only to find themselves bogged down in the sand.

Five minutes into the attack, Solo heard one of the covering Apache pilots issue an alarm, "Bogies coming in from the south."

Solo glanced in that direction and saw three Russian-made Hind attack helicopters approaching fast from the southwest. A second later he observed four contrails headed in the direction of the Hinds as the two covering Apaches did their job. He nonchalantly put the oncoming threat out of his mind and continued with the task at hand.

Two distant fireballs confirmed his confidence as two of the Hinds were hit. The third abruptly turned tail and attempted to retreat as fast as it could. Unfortunately for the Egyptians inside, a Sidewinder was closing on it much faster than it was retreating.

The six Apaches were finishing the attack with their chain guns strafing any remaining signs of life. The entire column was destroyed within fifteen minutes. Solo, feeling briefly remorseful, silently justified the killing, thinking, *It didn't have to happen. These people left us no choice.*

All eight helicopters turned to the east and headed home, looking for targets of opportunity on the way.

After a day of fighting with chaotic reports of success and failure flooding the prime minister's office, Ben Gurion was anxious to hear the first official briefing by his military commanders. Defense Minister Meier and chief of staff, General David Wiseman entered Ben Gurion's office together. After the requisite handshakes, greetings, and offers of coffee, Ben Gurion didn't hesitate, looking directly at Meier and simply asked, "Well?"

Meier, in turn, looked across the table at Wiseman and requested the chief of staff brief them both.

Wiseman took a sip from his cup of coffee, cleared his throat and began, "Mr. Prime Minister, George, our forces have fought valiantly against extreme odds, but I'm gratified to be able to say, at this point, after a day of hard fighting, we're accomplishing our plan. As you know we faced over two hundred fifty thousand troops with over nine hundred tanks in the Sinai poised to attack us from the west. Additionally, the Egyptians had over six hundred aircraft in the theatre including top-of-the-line Russian Mig 29s and Su 30 fighters.

"Our initial launch before dawn against the Egyptian anti-aircraft missile defenses and airfields consisted of 350 fighters and fighter/bombers. We anticipated large losses, mainly in our attempt to destroy the Russian built AS 12s and SA-X-20 Triumphs missile systems the Egyptians had deployed in large numbers to protect their airfields. We did lose aircraft, at least thirty-five have been reported downed, but the missile defense system is virtually nonfunctional and over 250 Egyptian aircraft have been destroyed. Many of the remaining aircraft that were able to take off have fled westward to bases over the Suez. I'm confident that, by mid-day tomorrow, we will have complete air superiority over the Sinai battlefield.

"General Goren's two divisions of six armored brigades, supported by two mobile infantry brigades, has encountered only sporadic resistance on the coastal road through El Arish. He anticipates lead elements of his force will be at the canal by the end of the day tomorrow.

"Two divisions, led by General Perez, attacked Abu-Ageila two hours after the initial air attack and, with sustained support from the Air Force, chiefly Apaches and Cobras, have been able to rout the Egyptian armor, destroying much of it in the process.

"Another force of similar size was launched at dawn from the Negev and is driving west through El Thamed and Nekhl toward the Mitla Pass.

"Through unrelenting air attacks, using our attack helicopters and pressure from Perez, we have been successful in herding the Egyptian forces toward the main road from Ismailia to Bir Hasanah. The more we can concentrate them there the easier it becomes to destroy them.

"Within forty-eight hours I'm confident we will have forces of sufficient size at Mitla and Gidi passes, as well as the Suez, to block virtually all Arab forces in the Sinai from retreating. Then I believe we can force them to surrender and end the conflict in the Sinai.

"Our campaign against the Syrians, Iraqis and their allies to the north is mainly a holding action at this point except for our attempt to gain air-superiority. That seems to be going equally well as our Sinai effort. By the time we launch ground assaults in a couple of days, we should have complete air superiority over those theatres as well.

"Two Syrian armored divisions, along with an Iraqi infantry division and a Saudi armored regiment, did launch an attack in the Golan, but it was repelled with heavy losses with only moderate losses on our side.

The Jordanians have not launched any offensive operations, which does surprise me. They have apparently honored the peace treaty between our countries. Perhaps we should consider making some confidential diplomatic entreaties to them to see if we can keep them out of the ground war. It would certainly speed things up if we didn't have to worry about fighting them. We have already taken a bit of a gamble with Jordan. We didn't send any aircraft into Jordan to attack airfields or missile sites. Perhaps they will respond to our restraint.

"One interesting item has surfaced. There has been no contact, whatsoever, with Iranian troops, even though we had reports they had sent two divisions to Syria. Perhaps they are being held back in reserve.

"We started this campaign with much trepidation. I feel much better this evening. We have suffered, and I don't mean to minimize that, but, so far, our plan is proceeding better than we ever could have anticipated. Our Israeli youth have performed magnificently again. We should honor them."

The prime minister thanked the general for the good news, agreeing the Israeli military was again performing superbly against great odds. He stated, "Before you both leave to continue leading our country in this vital battle, I wanted to pass on some more good news. I received a call from the new American president this morning and he has committed America's full support in our struggle, including replacement supplies now and troops and air support later, if and when we need them.

"Additionally a flight of twelve B-2 Stealth bombers will be landing at Ramon Air Base in the Negev tomorrow evening. General

Wiseman, it's time to fine tune our contingency plans for Iran. We have got to eliminate that threat for good."

Honoring Israeli troops was the farthest thing from the Russian president's mind as he demanded an urgent meeting of the United Nations Security Council to discuss Israel's attack on its "peaceful" neighbors.

Holding an emergency meeting would be a logistical nightmare since UN headquarters was a casualty of the nuclear attack on New York. The Russian president, regardless, had telephoned the leaders of each Security Council member, except, oddly, the United States, and demanded they send a representative to an emergency meeting to be held tomorrow in Moscow.

Even more odd was the complete absence of any calls for the UN to meet to consider the attacks on America, even from the new American government. Perhaps a real world realization had set in, the UN was pitifully weak when it came to arbitrating potential conflicts involving veto-wielding members. Or, perhaps, America now realized the UN was not its friend but served only as a forum for most of the rest of the world to oppose U.S. interests.

Moscow was Lebedov's recommendation for an interim headquarters. He calculated correctly the Western European countries would not object, out of fear of offending Russia, and the other members of the Security Council could be cowed into line. Having the United Nations headquartered in his capital would provide him with the leverage he needed to ensure it didn't get in the way of his ongoing plans for the future of the world.

The Israeli advances in the first day of the war, though part of Lebedov's predictions, were more extensive than expected. He was still confident, however, the Israeli Army would bog down somewhat as they turned eastward toward Syria and Iraq, giving Russia time to move troops and equipment into place to save the Arabs from destruction. Once the troops were in place, the oil fields would become a permanent Russian resource to fuel its new superpower role in the world. What happened to Israel, at that point, made no difference to the Russian president.

Using the United Nations now as a sounding board and a way of applying pressure on Israel, would provide cover in the future when he launched military operations to the south.

The Council meeting was set for early the next evening.

Chapter 61

Benson launched into his first real meal since dinner thirty-six hours earlier. He, Kristina, and his children surrounded a table in the Village Inn Restaurant adjacent to their motel. The new President of the United States woofed down a three-egg-and-sausage, western omelet full of saturated fat and cholesterol. Normally an oatmeal fan in the morning, Benson succumbed to his cravings and injected his body with a dose of artery sludge in spite of the questioning look from his wife. He even ordered a side of bacon.

Following his example, his children were also working feverishly on plates of eggs, bacon, sausage, and pancakes.

The unrelenting tension of the previous day was relieved, somewhat, by the meal and the welcome companionship of his family. He knew only too well, in a few moments the tension would ratchet up again. He looked at his wife and asked, "Honey, do you think a United States president ever sat with his family at the Village Inn in Bangor, Maine and ate a western omelet?"

Kristina, flustered a bit with the unexpected question, finally allowed a smile and replied, "Mr. President, I seriously doubt this has ever occurred before. But then, these are rather unique circumstances aren't they?"

The question, unfortunately, brought Benson back to reality. "You are right, these are unique circumstances. Did I mention to you we have decided to establish a new location for the capital, at least temporarily?"

Kristina raised her eyebrows, "Where will that be?"

"Denver, Colorado. It has been relatively free from fallout, is centrally located, has an excellent international airport, and, if it should ever come to this, can be readily defended."

A frown appeared on Kristina's face. She did not reply right away as she tried to understand the implications of her husband's last comment.

Sensing her dismay, Benson put a hand on her arm and added, "Honey, it won't come to that, I'm certain. It's just planning for a worst case scenario. I shouldn't have said anything."

Kristina looked into Benson's eyes and said, "I love you Rick. Don't ever feel like you can't share your concerns and problems with me, no matter how awful they might be."

Realizing he didn't particularly want his children to overhear this conversation, he glanced quickly around the table and was relieved to see all of them totally engaged in reducing the piles of food on their plates.

Reminiscent of scenes throughout the ravaged cities in the United States, the horror of downtown Manhattan was an apocalyptic nightmare. In a circle extending outward from Madison Square Garden to Bryant Park to the north, Washington Square Park to the south, and bordered by the Hudson River and the East River, the devastation was catastrophic.

Because of the hundreds of energy absorbing, high-rise buildings in the vicinity, the actual zone of total destruction, where virtually nothing stood, was relatively small, perhaps a thousand yards in any direction from the epicenter. Madison Square Garden was now nothing but a crater one hundred-feet deep and five hundred feet in diameter. The Empire State Building, the most famous New York landmark, only two blocks from Madison Square Garden, was a crooked spine sticking grotesquely four hundred feet into the grimy soot-filled atmosphere.

United Nations Headquarters located on the East River, about a mile and a half from ground zero, was still standing but was merely a shell, the insides scoured out as if by a monstrous sandblaster.

The beacon to so many thousands over the years, the Statue of Liberty, stood magnificent, but forlorn, in the Upper Bay, watching over the dead docks and wharves lining the lower East River.

Further out from the center of the explosion, the destruction was not as catastrophic, but the loss of life was staggering. Chinatown to the south and Central Park to the north were little more than morgues. Downtown Newark suffered greatly.

Perhaps the greatest loss of life, however, occurred on Long Island. The amount of debris thrown up into the atmosphere was magnified significantly by the tons of destroyed building material. The winds, blowing briskly that night, blew the radioactive fallout directly over Long Island bringing horrible, lingering death to hundreds of thousands of New Yorkers living on the Island. Many thousands, who lived through the first night, would die within one to two weeks as cells, particularly in the upper digestive track and bone marrow, were slowly destroyed causing massive diarrhea and internal hemorrhaging.

The picture was not totally bleak, however. Heeding the need for help, thousands of volunteers were streaming into eastern New Jersey and the unaffected regions north of New York City to help man the hospitals and temporary care centers being set up in churches, schools, and private homes. Hundreds of volunteer doctors and other medical practitioners were beginning to fill the critical gaps at the makeshift hospitals and refugee centers.

The governors of New York and New Jersey activated thousands of National Guard troops, who were setting up road blocks and barriers, so distraught family members, curious onlookers, and looters could not enter hot zones where near-certain death awaited.

The staggering, long-term problems created by the attacks on America were a long way from even beginning to be addressed. As had been the case in the past, however, Americans all over the country were stepping up to aid their fellow citizens in need.

Chapter 62

The newly appointed U.S. ambassador to the United Nations was livid. Ambassador Simpson had found out an hour earlier, from a telephone call from his British counterpart, the Russians had demanded an emergency meeting of the Security Council, and it was scheduled to be held in Moscow in less than fourteen hours. The British ambassador was dumbfounded that Simpson knew nothing about the meeting. After hearing an explanation of the purpose, Simpson told the ambassador he needed to make arrangements for a diplomatic visa as well as emergency travel plans and would call him back.

Simpson had not yet called him back, since he was being stonewalled by the Russians and had not been able to obtain a visa. Granted, the Russian embassy had been destroyed, as well as consul offices in Los Angeles and San Francisco. Regardless, the Russians had no business hindering a country's UN ambassador from attending an emergency Security Council meeting—unless, of course, there was an ulterior motive.

Frustrated at not being able to solve the dilemma, he picked up the phone and dialed Benson's temporary phone number in an office that had been set up for the president at the convention center.

After two rings, the president answered the phone, "Hello, this is Rick."

"You mean the president," replied Simpson good naturedly.

"Oh yeah, I'm having a real struggle with that part of this job," said Benson modestly.

"Rick, err, I mean Mr. President, I think the Russians are trying to cut us out from any influence in the United Nations."

"What do you mean?"

Simpson explained his conversation with the British UN ambassador and his failed efforts at obtaining a diplomatic visa.

Benson replied, "Peter, why don't you call the British ambassador back and see if the British will be willing to represent our position at the meeting. I'm sure Lebedov will try to get a unanimous condemnation of Israel, and we owe it to the Israelis to prevent that if we can. The Brits can still veto such a resolution, if they will."

Fifteen minutes later, Simpson was again on the line with his British counterpart. He explained the position of the American government to the ambassador and, unfortunately, only got a tepid, "I'll see what I can do," in response.

Simpson wondered to himself, *What's happening to this world of ours?*

For the last time, technicians and other workers were sprucing up the Bangor Civic Center in preparation for a primetime speech by the country's new president. The speech was less than an hour away, and the electronics technicians were making final tests on the speaker system to ensure it would work flawlessly. Other technicians from all three networks and major cable news outlets were also making last minute adjustments to their television cameras and associated electronics.

Plans had been announced earlier in the day for the president and other government officials at Bangor to leave the next morning for Denver, the new site of the nation's capital.

Ever since the major TV outlets had re-established nation-wide broadcasting capabilities, newly-appointed network anchors had been broadcasting to the nation the events of the past two days. All outlets cancelled normal programming and offered only nonstop news coverage.

To their credit, none of the pundits had uttered negative comments about the appointment of Senator Benson to the presidency. They had sufficiently witnessed his charisma and leadership ability over the past several months to realize, at such a critical time in the nation's history, he was probably the only man capable of uniting the country.

They and the rest of the nation's citizens, were hurting badly and were petrified of what tomorrow might bring. The new president's message to the American people would have to be powerful, yet humble. It would have to give the people hope in the continuing values of the country, which had been so badly tarnished over the past several months. And perhaps most importantly, the message would have to reassure America the country was still strong; that it could determine responsibility for the merciless attacks, and have the will to hold the perpetrators, regardless of whom they were, accountable. It was, indeed, a tall order for the former freshman senator from Oregon.

As he slowly rocked back and forth on the thread-bare recliner, Jack Thornton stared at the TV screen waiting for the new president to appear. He turned his head briefly toward the back of the doublewide that served as his and his children's home and yelled, "Shut your damn traps, or I'll come back there and shut em for you." His children were acting like children and making noise.

Thornton contemplated what the next few days would bring as his divinely appointed mission was about to come to fruition. *Two more days are all I have left to live in this heap of a trailer,* he thought to himself, naturally assuming, as president of his new America, he would be treated to accommodations befitting a person of such stature.

His thoughts were interrupted when the television anchor announced the president had entered the civic center auditorium. Thirty seconds later, President Benson stood behind the podium gripping both sides tightly, with a stern, determined look on his face. There was no applause to greet him. Thornton thought to himself, *What has this retread liberal got to say?*

Benson was nervous yet determined. He knew the country desperately needed reassurance life would return to normal. Benson was not sure he could reassure them it would. He felt what was most important was that the people know what had happened and be willing to accept the hard choices staring at them in the near future. He had already committed to never mislead the American public, regardless of the consequences. He was convinced such deception had created the conditions that led to the attacks two days earlier.

He began, "My fellow citizens, it's with sorrow and great trepidation I stand before you this evening. Our country has suffered a grievous blow perpetrated by the vilest of cowards. Their purpose is to destroy freedom throughout the world, knowing if America can be defeated then the world is ripe for conquest.

"I will not try to sugarcoat what has happened to us. Twelve great American cities have been destroyed causing the death of millions of citizens. I don't know yet how many millions have died, but I fear it could be as many as twenty million, innocent Americans.

"Our national government, including the president, vice president, the cabinet, most of the Senate and House of

Representatives, the Joint Chiefs, and most agency heads perished in Washington D.C.

"As many of you know, ten senators, including myself, and twenty-one members of the House of Representatives, were in Bangor, Maine when the attack occurred, and our lives were spared. As the only elected national leaders remaining, we have worked unceasingly over the past two days to organize an interim national government to lead our country during the next few perilous months. It is anticipated that elections to choose permanent leaders can be organized within six months.

"After some discussion concerning the process, I was nominated to serve as interim-President of the United States, and the body of congressmen at Bangor voiced their unanimous support for the nomination. I didn't seek this position but will accept it with my solemn commitment to work, to the extent of my ability, to lead this country out of the tragic circumstances in which we find ourselves.

"Many of these American patriots, who are with me in Bangor, have accepted temporary assignments to lead the critical agencies that have been so disrupted by the attacks on our cities. They have been contacting your state and local governments to see how state and federal responses to the disaster can be coordinated. Bureaucratic red-tape, which has traditionally slowed responses to past emergencies, will not be tolerated. Each new agency head has the authority to fire anyone, on the spot, who places roadblocks in the way of our ability to assist those in need.

"I have had numerous consultations with the United States military leadership and have established a constant communication link. The historic subordinate relationship the military has always had with the country's political leadership, remains as strong today as it was a week ago. Our military assets were not harmed by the attacks on our country and continue to remain on the highest level of alert.

"Security at our borders, docks, airports, and critical infrastructure has been strengthened immeasurably, and I'm confident we're doing all that can be done to protect us from further attacks. The FBI, CIA, and other intelligence agencies, are working together, day and night, to uncover any additional plots and identify any individuals who have a connection with the attacks or plans for future attacks.

"I cannot guarantee we will be able to prevent terrorist activity in the future. I can guarantee we will do as much as is humanly possible, with the vast assets we can bring to bear, to stop future attacks. To help us in this critical task, I have issued an executive order implementing all of the former provisions of the *Patriot Act* that were dropped by the Papadakis administration. While I know some will be bothered considerably by my action, I give my solemn pledge; those who abuse this act will be disciplined and prosecuted, if warranted.

"I also pledge that those evildoers who directed these terrible acts of violence against so many innocent people will be identified and will be held accountable. Let there be no misunderstanding by any nation who is listening to me tonight or who reads a written version of this speech tomorrow. America will not be shaken! We will not be cowed! If you thought these barbaric acts would bring us to our knees, you are sadly mistaken.

"We're working day and night to determine the origin of the nuclear devices that were supplied to the Islamic extremist cowards who have no value for human life. We will succeed in that task and will—mark my words—we *will* hold you accountable."

Benson paused for a moment, obviously fighting to maintain his emotions, and then concluded. "The path we must follow over the next few days, weeks, and months is not clear at this point. We know, obviously, there is evil in this world that will stop at nothing to see our defeat. The sacrifices we will be called on to offer in this battle could be of the ultimate kind. If that be the case, I'm confident we have the blessings of God with us in our struggle. Free agency, the ability to choose our way of life, where we live, and what we do is a divine gift, and the struggle we face to save that gift is worth any sacrifice.

"My prayers are with all of you who are suffering, who have lost loved ones and friends. My heartfelt gratitude goes out to all of you volunteers who have sacrificed so much to help your neighbors. Without you, our country could not survive. But my fellow Americans; we will survive, not just today but through the turbulent times ahead. I'm most grateful for the opportunity to serve you. I ask for your support as we face the uncertain future together. May God bless America. Thank you."

Chapter 63

Three hours after President Benson's speech, a translated transcript of the speech was being read by Ivan Litinov. The colonel had read and reread one phrase in the speech. "We will succeed in that task and will—mark my words—we will hold you accountable!"

Litinov knew in his heart those words were not just postulating by a greedy politician looking for votes. He knew instinctively the new American president was out of a different mold. He wondered to himself, *What have we started?*

Apparently his boss was having the same anxieties, because ten minutes earlier Lebedov had telephoned the colonel and ordered him to come up with a plan to destroy the unexploded bomb in Israeli hands within the next twenty-four hours. The president maintained the bomb was the only link that could lead directly to Russia. Litinov smiled slightly as he contemplated the fear he heard in Lebedov's voice during the phone discussion. *Yes*, he thought, *the old bastard is having second thoughts about what he has done. Destroying the whole world wasn't part of his plans.*

Ambassadors representing thirteen of the fifteen countries currently on the Security Council had been arriving in Moscow for most of the afternoon. The last delegation from Venezuela arrived on a chartered United, Boeing 747, which touched down barely an hour and a half before the scheduled start of the Council meeting.

Each of the delegations were driven in Russian black Volga's over the treacherous, ice-covered roads from Moscow's Sheremtevo International Airport. It was a harrowing eighteen mile journey to the Ararat Park Hyatt Moscow Hotel, which had been designated as tonight's Security Council meeting location.

The ambassadors filed into the hotel's main ballroom, the last delegate seated at the oblong, oak table five minutes before the hour. The seat normally reserved for the American ambassador was conspicuously empty.

The ballroom was nicely furnished with green, ceiling-high brocade draperies pulled back from the frosted windows. Three crystal chandeliers hung from the coved, gold-accented ceiling and illuminated the room brightly. The large, oblong, oak-stained table sat on a dark-green plush carpet. The surroundings contrasted sharply with the normal setting in New York, which was now a smoking ruin.

Precisely at 6:00 p.m. the Russian UN ambassador stood and, to the surprise of the other delegates around the table, announced the Russian president, Anitoli Lebedov, had requested a few minutes to address the Security Council. Before any of the delegates could raise objections to the breech of normal protocol, the president, himself, entered the room through the large, double doors at the front of the room.

The president strode forcefully up to the podium, raised both hands to quiet the murmuring rustling through the throng, and began speaking in heavily accented English. "I know many of you are wondering why I have chosen to begin this meeting in such an unorthodox manner, bypassing customary diplomatic protocol. Let me assure you, my friends, I would never have done this, if the importance of my message wasn't so urgent."

He paused, looked around the table, and continued, "I notice my American friends are absent from their accustomed spot. That's truly unfortunate, but, in view of the tragedy that has befallen their nation, I can understand their absence."

The British ambassador almost choked out loud upon hearing such hypocritical duplicity issue from Lebedov's mouth. It was apparent, however, from the nods and facial expressions, the others seated around the table swallowed his comments without any pain whatsoever.

Lebedov continued, "I, as well as you, grieve with our American friends at the terrible losses they have suffered once again at the hand of cowardly terrorists. My country, individually, as well as a caring United Nations, offers all the assistance to the Americans, which they feel they need from us.

"Many might now think we must unite together militarily to destroy the terrorist groups once and for all. I think that's not only an impossible task, but isn't the right course to take. The Americans are, unfortunately, partly to blame for the tragedy that has overtaken them."

Audible gasps were heard by some at the table. A few members actually uttered exclamations of protest.

The Russian president raised his hand above his head to quiet the group and said, "Let me explain. I'm convinced the main reason terrorism plagues our world is continued occupation and military aggression by the state of Israel. The United States, as Israel's historic and continuing sponsor, has become the prime target of the terrorist groups fighting against the Zionists. Without American support, Israel could not continue its aggressive policies against the Palestinians and other bordering Arab states."

Several delegation heads nodded, apparently sharing Lebedov's analysis.

Levbedov continued, "While, I personally, in no way, condone what was done to America, I do fully understand the motives behind the attack. Such actions, as horrific as they are, are the only means these repressed people have to strike out against Israel.

"Now, we're witnessing Israeli aggression all over again, on perhaps the grandest scale of all."

Making no reference to the fact hundreds of thousands of Arab troops had massed on Israel's borders, armed to the hilt and primed to attack the small country, Lebedov continued to rail on Israel. "I'm demanding the Security Council unanimously pass a resolution that Israel stop all military activity at once and withdraw from all captured territory. Furthermore the resolution must state, failure to do so, within forty-eight hours, will result in additional action by the Security Council, including a military response.

"If Israel does not head the Council's demand within forty-eight hours, then I'd additionally propose the Security Council authorize Russia to take military action to destroy the Israeli Army and impose a final solution to the Israel problem, to end this ongoing cancer once at for all."

A few of the European ambassadors were aghast at Lebedov's choice of words. They were all too aware what the words, final solution, meant seventy years ago. Other delegates, from third-world countries, particularly from the two Muslim countries on the Council, were nodding and whispering to each other enthusiastically, apparently thinking Lebedov's choice of words was just fine.

The Russian president concluded, "I will now leave you to your deliberations, but please recognize the urgency of this matter. The Israeli aggression must be stopped now. Millions of peaceful, innocent Arab women and children are at extreme risk and urgently need your resolve to stop a new holocaust from occurring."

The British ambassador was again horrified at the Russian's extremely tasteless reference to another holocaust. He was the only person in the room distressed apparently, as the other delegates enthusiastically applauded the president.

Lebedov turned from the podium without taking any questions and strode toward the same double doors through which he had entered earlier. As he walked, he couldn't control a tiny smile from appearing on his face. He knew his speech hit a lot of positive chords and felt assured the Council would pass the resolution he wanted. He was a little worried about the British ambassador but didn't believe the British had the political balls to buck the rest of the Council. At worst, they might abstain, which would be okay.

He had set it up brilliantly. He knew the Israelis would not stop within forty-eight hours. He would, thereafter, have UN authorization to take military action, the best cover possible to carry out the final elements of *Hammer and Anvil.*

Chapter 64

The flight of twelve B-2 bombers to Israel provided an opportunity for six American nuclear weapons experts from the National Nuclear Security Administration (NNSA) to enter Israel undetected. The six, including four nuclear physicists and two engineers, represented the highest level of expertise at NNSA. They were charged with working with the Israeli scientists to identify the country of origin of the bomb recovered at *Michimoret*.

After arriving at Ramon Air Force Base, a convoy of Israeli military vehicles transported the visitors under extremely tight security on a restricted paved road to the *Dimona* Research complex, a short distance away from the base.

As they approached the complex, the six scientists marveled at the extensive security systems in place around the facility. What looked like upward-turned crates on wheels, enclosing a series of hollow tubes, caught their attention while still several miles from the complex. The scientists, all knowledgeable on the latest military hardware, recognized the crates as Israel's state-of-the-art, Arrow anti-ballistic missile systems. Closer in, they recognized more familiar Patriot missile configurations. Interspersed were American made Hawk/AMRAAM surface-to-air missile batteries.

An air attack on *Dimona* would be suicide. Only a stealth bomber might be able to survive, and, with the latest target acquisition radar available to the Israelis, even that would be doubtful.

Reinforced, heavily-manned bunkers circled the facility in two massive rings, one about a thousand yards out and the second about half that distance.

The scientists instinctively knew, with this much security on display, the actual lethality of what wasn't seen was probably extraordinary.

The convoy stopped briefly at the first of three security gates before being allowed to enter. Three, ten-foot, chain-link fences, with concertina wire lining the tops, encircled the complex. The waiting was longer at gates two and three.

Finally the line of vehicles stopped in front of a nondescript, windowless, rectangular-shaped building. One of the Israeli soldiers referred to the building as Machon two. The scientists would later learn Machon two was one of ten separate structures at the complex labeled Machon one through ten.

Each of the Americans was escorted by two Israeli soldiers to a solid-steel, single door at one end of the building. As they approached, the door was opened, and a slight man with a black, curly mop of hair, wearing black, horned-rimmed glasses greeted them in a surprising booming bass voice. "Welcome my friends to *Dimona*, Israel's worst kept secret. My name is Joshua Bergmann, chief nuclear scientist with the Israel Atomic Energy Commission. I'm very glad to see you all."

The top-of-the-line Mikoyan Multiple Function Fighter 1.42, known in the West as the Mig-35, was in super cruise, at forty thousand feet, heading southwest at over eight hundred miles-per-hour. The pilot of one of the best, if not the best, multi-role fighters in the world had led his squadron of twelve Mig-35s over the northwest corner of Iran, across the middle of Iraq, and they were now passing through Jordanian airspace.

The target of this powerful force was the *Dimona* Nuclear facility in the Negev desert in Israel. When briefed on the mission earlier this morning, the Russian pilot experienced serious misgivings about the mission, although, he had the presence of mind to keep them to himself. He had heard from reliable sources of the formidable air defenses covering all of the approaches to the *Dimona* facility and felt this mission was suicidal.

As was explained by a Colonel Litinov, who apparently had some sort of direct line to the President of Russia, the Mig-35s were chosen for the mission because of their stealth capabilities, which provided the attackers the best chance of success against such a formidable target. He further explained the mission was top-secret and vital to the critical interests of mother Russia, and failure could have very serious consequences for the country.

Because of the top-secret nature of the mission, each of the planes had been painted to look like Iraqi fighter jets with the appropriate Iraqi insignias.

Since the *Dimona* complex was only thirty-five miles from the Jordanian border, once the jets left Jordanian airspace, it would only be a matter of minutes before the jets reached their target. While the planes' stealth capabilities were significant, they didn't match the American F-

117 stealth fighter. As a result, the Russian pilot was deeply concerned about what might happen when they crossed over the border.

His worry was not unfounded. While still fifty miles from the border, his onboard radar picked up blips of close to a dozen bogies closing on an intercept course from the northwest. He wasn't particularly concerned about fighting it out with the Israeli fighters. The Migs, configured as they were with the latest Russian air-to-air AA12 Adder missiles and fifth generation pulse-Doppler radar guidance systems, were more than a match for any jets in the Israeli Air Force. He was concerned, however, that they had already been spotted on Israeli radar.

Using preplanned cockpit to cockpit hand signals, he directed six of the Migs, heavily armed with air-to-air missiles, to break off and confront the Israeli planes. Hopefully that action would provide a sufficient time cushion for the remaining six jets to reach *Dimona*. He then put his Mig into a steep, power dive followed by the other five. They leveled out only two hundred feet above the scrub-bush and sand desert, which raced by below them.

In contrast to the six planes on their way to intercept the Israelis, the strike aircraft were each carrying four Russian, KAB-500, satellite-guided, bunker-buster bombs designed to explode only after deep penetration.

The Russian commander knew, in his heart, his flight was strictly a one-way affair. He only hoped one or two of the Migs could successfully launch its payload before being blasted out of the sky.

Deep in the bowels of Machon two, six American nuclear scientists were being introduced to the object of their affections, a dark, shiny-metallic, cone shaped, 475 kiloton nuclear warhead. Joshua Bergmann was just beginning to brief the six Americans about what the Israelis had already discovered during their preliminary examination of the unexploded bomb, when the air raid sirens began wailing.

Bergmann reacted to the startled expressions on the American's faces with a slight smile. "No need for concern my American friends. We're six stories, fully sixty feet underground, and surrounded by two feet of steel' reinforced concrete. We could not be in a safer location on this whole complex if there actually was an air attack."

One of the physicists, not totally convinced they were out of danger asked, "Have you ever been attacked here before?"

"No," replied Bergmann, "at least nothing was ever able to get close enough to drop any ordinance."

Bergmann waited a few seconds to ensure all the Americans were feeling at least secure enough he could continue his briefing without too much distraction. Once assured, he began talking again.

The Russian jets continued screaming westward over the desert. The pilot of the lead plane could make out the outline of the *Dimona* reactor dome on the horizon. It would only be a few more seconds and his squadron would be in range to launch the bunker busters.

From the front of the plane it appeared New Year's Eve spaghetti streamers had been thrown into the sky by scores of revelers all at one time. He recognized immediately the streamers were smoky contrails from multiple missiles headed his way. He knew from intelligence briefings, evading the latest generation of American Hawk anti-aircraft missiles was virtually impossible, once they locked on the target, and he knew the Israeli complex was protected by Hawk SAMs.

The Russian commander also knew the aircraft would have to gain altitude to ensure the guided bombs they were carrying would have enough altitude to slam straight down into the target. That would expose them completely to the oncoming missiles. He could only hope his squadron could release the bombs before the missiles destroyed the Migs.

The jets were now in range and, almost like a flock of starlings, all six jets accelerated upward together to gain necessary altitude. Suddenly two fireballs erupted as two of the Hawks found their targets. Two seconds later a third Mig exploded. The Russian commander desperately watched his altimeter, needing a little more. Two more fireballs flashed in his peripheral vision. He was the only one left.

As two smoking snakes approached him head on, he acquired the target, a long rectangular building, and zeroed in on location of the elevator shaft. He released all four of the eleven hundred-pound bombs a second before both Hawks slammed into his plane.

Bergmann was midway through his briefing when a muffled bang, accompanied by a shudder in the building itself, caused him and the Americans to quickly glance upward toward the concrete ceiling. A moment later, the ceiling, itself, seemed to part as a massive explosion obliterated everything in the room, human and nonhuman. Within a second, the indestructible six-story, Machon 2, top-secret facility exploded into a massive underground fireball.

Chapter 65

Dawn was breaking over the heavily-forested, snow-covered landscape north of Coeur d'Alene. The winding Priest River was hidden under a cold blanket of gray fog, which swirled in and out of the stands of Douglas fir and bare aspens. Intruding unceremoniously upon this surreal scene were convoys of rundown Jeep Cherokees, RJ7's, Chevy Suburbans, and a multitude of broken-down wrecks of every kind as the soldiers of the Liberty Militia descended on Camp Liberty.

In stark contrast to this motley assemblage, were lines of military vehicles parked in neat rows on a plowed staging area north of the complex of buildings functioning as headquarters for the camp. They included a score of Humvees, forty deuce-and-a-half troop carriers, five APCs, assorted half tracks, one Huey helicopter, and one fully operational medium tank, a Vietnam era M-48 Patton. Unknown to the rank and file members of the militia and the FBI was the source of funding for the fleet of military vehicles. Even General Thornton only knew his benefactors as a shadowy cartel of southern businessmen who shared Thornton's vision of American democracy.

The phantom financiers also provided sufficient monies to equip up to nine hundred soldiers with M16s, M-60 Machine guns, anti-tank rockets, grenades, two hundred thousand rounds of ammunition, and state-of-the-art communication equipment along with uniforms, back packs, belts, and all of the other accouterments required by an operational battalion.

At precisely 0800 hours, 803 members of the Liberty Militia fell into company-size formations on the windswept parade field to be inspected and addressed by their commander. Each was dressed in full winter gear with packs, rations, rifles, and one hundred rounds of ammunition. They were ready, both physically and mentally, for the upcoming mission and waited patiently for the final orders. Two years of rigorous, nonstop training had prepared them for today. The anticipation was palpable.

Thornton exited the headquarters building and walked between companies' two and three. Immediately, 803 militiamen straightened to attention. Thornton strode confidently to the front-center of the battalion, came to attention, and waited for a couple of seconds for his staff officer to order the battalion to stand at ease.

Using a loud speaker, and cognizant of the cold, the general made his remarks brief and to the point. "My fellow Americans, today is our day. We have trained long and hard for this chance, and the evil, godless cowards who attacked our cities have given us a golden opportunity to create a new America. All I ask from each of you is what I'd expect of myself, total commitment to restoring this Republic back to the original, magnificent experiment our founding fathers envisioned.

"A country free from Jews, Negroes, Latinos, Orientals, Muslims and the purveyors of filth, the homosexuals, is a most worthy goal. We will begin that process today, when the world will hear us declare northern Idaho as the seat of our new America.

"Your company commanders have their orders and will brief each company and individual platoons on their mission. We will roll at oh-nine-hundred. May God be with you."

The 803 troops erupted in cheers yelling Thornton's name repeatedly in unison. The general couldn't hide a broad smile as he entered the headquarters' building through the same door he had exited a few minutes earlier.

He was certain millions of Americans were equally fed up with the leftward direction of the country, particularly now the government's weakness had been so graphically demonstrated. Once he secured his objectives by sunset tonight, they would flock to his support and choose him to become the new president of the restored America. That sounded extremely nice thought the ex Navy Seal, *President Thornton instead of General Thornton.*

Chapter 66

Enraged was probably not strong enough to describe the new American president. The new UN ambassador, Senator Simpson, had just notified Benson the Russians were still stonewalling him on obtaining a visa, and he would not be able to attend a second Security Council meeting in Moscow at noon the following day.

Two days earlier the Security Council by a near unanimous vote, with only Great Britain abstaining, had passed a resolution condemning the Israeli attack on the Arabs, demanding an immediate cease fire and withdrawal from occupied territory. Since then, the Israelis had not only failed to heed the Security Council demand, but had surrounded and cut off one hundred seventy-five thousand Egyptian troops in the Sinai and were preparing to launch ground operations against Lebanon and Syria.

At Russia's bidding, the Council was convening tomorrow to authorize punitive measures against Israel, possibly including military action. Without an American presence, such a resolution would assuredly pass, and Russia would gain the justification it needed to inject troops into the Middle East for the first time in history.

Benson was becoming more convinced the Israeli prime minister's assessment of Russian intentions was true. No other interpretation could adequately explain Lebedov's actions of the past three days.

As he was contemplating the cascading events and trying to determine what was the appropriate course to follow, a telephone call from the Israeli prime minister forced his hand. His administrative assistant stuck her head through the office door and said, "Mr. President, the Israeli prime minister is on the phone and says he has urgent information for you."

"Thanks June," replied Benson as he thought to himself, *What now? It can't get much worse*.

It, indeed, got much worse. Ben Gurion advised the president of the attack on *Dimona* and the complete destruction of the building that housed the bomb recovered by the Israelis. Even worse, in addition to the bomb being destroyed, twenty-five, top nuclear scientists, including all of the American experts, were killed in the explosion.

"Who did it?" was the only question that came to Benson's distraught mind.

"Well, president," replied the prime minister deliberately, "I'm convinced it was the Russians, but again we don't have proof beyond doubt."

"Couldn't you identify the planes that attacked you?"

Ben Gurion responded, "They were Mig 35s, but had Iraqi paint and markings. Our intelligence assets, however, never reported the Russians supplying the Iraqis with such jets. I think the Russians simply painted them."

Benson collected his thoughts, "Did you shoot any of them down?"

"Yes, replied Ben Gurion, "we shot them all down, but one of them was able to launch its payload of guided munitions before it was destroyed."

"Did any pilots survive?"

"No, it appears the Russians wanted to ensure nobody would be captured, so none of the three pilots who ejected had parachutes attached to their ejections seats. The poor hapless wretches were not much more than stew meat after falling from thousands of feet. One pilot, however, was partly recognizable, and he had blond hair and blue eyes. I've never met a blond, blue-eyed Iraqi."

The conversation continued for another ten minutes as the Israeli leader outlined Israeli military plans over the next week. It was clear Israel had made the irrevocable decision to destroy the Arab armies and bring down the governments of Syria, Lebanon, Iraq, Saudi Arabia, and possibly Iran. At the least, it was Ben Gurion's aim to destroy the potential nuclear capability of Iran, which, according to U.S. and Israeli intelligence, could produce three or four nuclear weapons within a couple of months.

It was obvious Israel was on a collision course with Russia since accomplishing its goals would thwart Russia's. Neither the prime minister nor Benson had any illusions about where that confrontation would lead.

Benson knew it was now decision time. He had committed, earlier, that the United States would not let Israel face down Russia alone, and the Israeli was now calling on him to honor that commitment.

The new president weighed his words before speaking. Finally, he slowly uttered fateful words that would set the world on a course of unimaginable consequences. "Prime Minister Ben Gurion, I have already asked General Taylor to prepare a plan to insert American troops and air power into the Middle East to support your country. I will issue the order today to initiate that process on an emergency basis. I fear we're making a decision that could end civilization as we know it, but twenty million Americans are crying out from the grave to stop Russian tyranny from succeeding. I fear that success even more."

Bob and Ruth Ginsburg loved farming, which was a good thing since they had been doing it for the past thirty-five years. Bob and Ruth had inherited a 230-acre, potato farm near Rathdrum, Idaho from his dad, and, even though they were both getting long-in-the-tooth, they were still running the farm at a profit. Wintertime was a bit of a break for farmers like the Ginsburgs. No planting, plowing, weeding, and spraying; just occasional forays into the cold to patch up a broken water pipe or repair some overused farm equipment.

On this early Saturday morning they were headed north on State Highway 41, in Bob's '96 Ford F-250, en route to Spirit Lake, where their twenty-eight-year-old son, John, and wife, Linda, ran a bed-and-breakfast.

While the wind was howling at a good clip, the sun was out, and the road was dry in most places. Windblown snow, however, made for occasional poor visibility. The Ginsburg's were making good time, in spite of the conditions. After cresting the crown of a hill they observed ahead that the bottom of a thousand-yard-long dip in the road was obscured due to blowing snow.

Slowly, as if appearing out of nothing, an ominous ghostly apparition took shape at the edge of the whiteout. Mr. Ginsburg squinted in an effort to understand the vision in front of him. He instinctively braked the blue pickup. As the distance narrowed, to the Ginsburg's shock and dismay, they recognized the approaching apparition as a huge battle tank, followed by a string of military vehicles trailing back into the white mist.

The grizzled, potato farmer locked the wheels of the old pickup as it skated to a stop on the right shoulder in six inches of snow. The military convoy closed the distance quickly. The Ginsburg's stared in amazement as the tank passed by them, stirring up swirls of snow, followed by scores of khaki-green-colored trucks filled with troops, trailed by several half-tracks, and Humvees. A few of the soldiers stared back at them but most paid no attention.

After what seemed like forever, the last vehicle in the string passed by them. A soldier sitting in the drivers-side, back seat briefly looked and smiled and, to their surprise, smartly saluted the old couple through the open side window.

As they watched the convoy disappear over the crest of the hill Bob looked at Ruth, shook his head and said, “Honey, I’ll be darned if I know what that was. There’s no military base around here, and besides, the military no longer paints their vehicles that poop green color. I’d bet …”

Suddenly a deafening “whoop-whoop-whoop-whoop” stopped him in mid-sentence. A dark shadow passed overhead, and, as he looked back through the rear window, the retreating silhouette of a Huey helicopter was framed in the window. All he could say was, “I’ll be damned!”

Chapter 67

America's collective grieving was slowly evolving into rage and an understandable lust for revenge. Media-discovered experts, crawling from under rocks everywhere, were postulating theories, hourly, as to who was behind the attacks on America's cities. More and more people were coalescing behind the theory Russia was behind the attacks. Exorable momentum was building to take action. Strident calls by some for a nuclear strike on Russia failed to rationalize the consequences.

Faced with increasing pressure to take action, President Benson wrestled with his own gut desire for revenge against the more logical realization that an order to unleash the missiles would condemn the country, and probably the world, to mass extermination. Yet he knew once the evidence was strong enough, he had to be willing to take whatever action was necessary, otherwise he would condemn the world, not to mass extermination, but to twenty-first century slavery.

Taking advantage of the rising momentum for revenge, General Cooke had appeared several times on network talk shows openly criticizing President Benson's inaction, growing bolder with each appearance. His latest appearance, on an hour-long Sunday news special, pushed the treason envelope. It included a call for Benson to resign the presidency and allow the military to take over the function of governing the country until those responsible for the attacks were brought to justice. A relatively small, but growing, vocal minority of citizens appeared to be supporting the general's viewpoint.

Benson knew he had to do something quickly to quiet the rising chorus or risk a rupture of 225 years of democratic civilian rule in America. He had two critically important calls to make. He made the first one to General Taylor. After a ten-minute discussion, he made the second call.

The British prime minister had been in office a little over two years. The Tories had finally been successful in sweeping the elections after a long run by Labor. Left-over resentment of England's involvement in the Iraq war had been Labor's undoing.

The prime minister was young and resembled his predecessor, only shorter. His politics historically were fairly conservative by European standards but mainline in terms of reaching accommodations with militant Islam. He was, however, deeply shocked and saddened by the events of the past week in America and was in the process of reevaluating the British viewpoint on dealing with terrorism.

Since it was Saturday, he finished his work early and had just settled into the old, deep-brown, leather recliner in his study to do some reading, when the phone rang. The maid answered it in the kitchen and, a few seconds later, knocked on the study door.

"What is it?" asked the prime minister.

The maid answered in an obviously excited voice, "Mr. Prime Minister, it's the President of the United States."

Ten minutes later, the prime minister slowly placed the phone earpiece into the cradle mumbling to nobody particular, "Sometimes I wonder if our special relationship is worth it."

He had just promised the new American president to do whatever it took to delay and, if necessary, veto consideration of a military response by the UN Security Council to Israeli actions. He contemplated the just completed conversation. *If half of what the American just told me about Russian intentions is true, then the world is in for some very troubled times.*

Chapter 68

"Virtually all organized resistance has stopped," replied General Wiseman to the Israeli defense minister's question about the status of the campaign in the Sinai. "Some pockets are still resisting, but, by the end of the day, any organized resistance should end. We have captured over 120 fully operational Russian tanks and large quantities of other military hardware we can convert to our use against our enemies to the north."

"How extensive have our losses been?" asked General Meier.

Wiseman replied, "We've lost a little more than fifty fighter jets, a score of helicopters and about seventy-five tanks. We have suffered about thirty-five hundred casualties including 565 battle deaths."

"That's 565 too many," replied the defense minister. "Are you prepared to launch the ground assault against Syria and Lebanon tomorrow general?"

Wiseman answered, "Yes George, we have over eighty thousand troops and eight hundred tanks ready to cross the line at dawn tomorrow. For the past week the Air Force has pounded Lebanese, Syrian, Iraqi, and Saudi positions and I'd anticipate a breakthrough within hours after the initial assault. Once that happens, the road to Damascus is wide open."

General Meier asked, "How big a threat does the Syrian Air Force pose?"

"It has been nonexistent since the end of the second day," replied Wiseman, rather smugly.

"Assuming your optimism is correct, and we reach Damascus within three days, what's your longer-term strategic plan?" inquired Meier.

Wiseman paused before replying and, looking Meier square in his eyes, hedged his answer, "Well, George, I know what I'd like to do. It's dependent, however, on two events out of the IDF's control. If the Americans can engineer a delay in the UN Security Council of at least a week or more, and the prime minister is successful with the current negotiations with the king of Jordan, then I'd say we should swing our forces east from Damascus into Iraq, continuing to Baghdad. A second force could enter Saudi Arabia from the south through Jordan, cut to the Gulf coast through Riyadh to Qatar and move north to Basra. Then the two forces could come together along the Tigris River, and we would either control, or be able to prevent Russia from controlling, almost all of the Middle East's oil with the exception of Iran."

The defense minister's eyebrows shot upward. "Why don't we just conquer the rest of the world while we're at it?"

Wiseman smiled. "George, I know you've been thinking along the same lines. After we have defeated the Arab armies arrayed against us on the Golan and in Syria, there will really be very little to stop us from doing what I just outlined. The keys to the whole thing are America's ability to delay the Russians from early intervention and, subsequently, their response militarily when the Russians do act. I have no illusions about our ability to hold off a full-scale Russian attack on our own."

Meier, somewhat coyly, cracked a little smile, leaned forward in his chair toward Wiseman and said, "David, I have some good news for you relative to all your concerns. Ben Gurion informed me less than an hour ago the Jordanians have agreed to let us move two armored divisions and three armored infantry brigades through their territory to the Saudi border.

"The king candidly admitted the Russians had put enormous pressure on him, and the other Arab leaders, to attack Israel, but the king smelled something funny, and the prime minister merely confirmed his suspicions. He is sticking his neck way out to do this, so I cannot stress enough the importance of staging our forces at the border, as quickly as possible, with no interaction with Jordanian civilians.

"He has also granted us permission for unlimited military over-flights of his territory for at least two weeks. Apparently the king recognizes, in contrast to the blinded leaders of the other Middle East countries, Russia poses more of a long-term threat to their continued existence than anything we would do temporarily."

"What other good news do you have for me?" asked the now smiling Wiseman.

Meier paused and stared at Wiseman with a little smirk on his face. He then said, "Even though the Americans have apparently been blackballed at the Security Council meeting in Moscow later today, the new American president, I think his name is Benson, informed Ben

Gurion the British have agreed to act as their surrogate and will delay, or veto if necessary, any authorization for military action against us."

"What if the Russians come in without UN authorization?"

"Well, David, I believe they probably will, but only when they realize they are not going to have any international protection to do so. That leads me to the third piece of good news I have. The Americans, as we speak, are moving four more carrier strike groups into the Middle East, three in the eastern Mediterranean and another one in the Gulf. The USS Eisenhower is already in the Gulf, and all five carrier groups will be on station within the week.

"They are also flying into Israel over the next four days three hundred, front-line fighter jets, including F16s, F22 Raptors, and two squadrons of F35 Joint Strike Force Lightnings, all with American pilots. Additionally twelve ships will be arriving at Tel Aviv over the next five days with 350 crated replacement jets and more than enough parts to repair all of our damaged aircraft still flying. Also included are 150 Abrams M1A2 main battle tanks and an equal number of Bradleys.

"Over the next two days, the entire American 82nd Airborne Division will arrive in Israel. Longer term, within three weeks, the Americans will have deployed two heavy armored divisions and four mobile infantry divisions to Israel with at least that much more in the pipeline.

"David, the best scenario will be if the Russians realize their bold plan has been countered, and starting World War III is not worth the huge risks of their own destruction."

Wiseman, though immensely gratified at Meier's good news, nevertheless was sobered when contemplating how risky this whole game had become. He reluctantly asked, "What's the worst case scenario?"

General Meier somberly replied, "The Russians don't wait and come in sooner with force. If the Americans respond with force, it could escalate very quickly to a nuclear exchange, particularly since the Americans already suspect Russia was behind the terror attacks last week."

Wiseman bowed his head briefly, almost as if the weight of events forced it down, and then emotionally replied, "General, how did our little fragile democracy get in the middle of this?"

Chapter 69

The adrenaline rush pulsating through Thornton's circulatory system had not been experienced since he led a team of Seals on a covert, reconnaissance mission in Kirkuk, Iraq, just before the United States invaded over a decade ago. Now, as he rode shotgun in the Huey, he observed two squads peel off of the convoy below, deploying at one of five roadblocks being established on the perimeter of Coeur D'Alene. He was as proud now as he ever was leading Seals into combat.

Thornton also deployed two platoons at the Coeur D'Alene airport, located five miles north of city center off of U.S. 95. Their assignment was to prevent any airborne attempt to reinforce the local police and sheriff departments by state law-enforcement agencies or the Idaho National Guard.

Another company had the mission of assaulting, if necessary, the Coeur D'Alene Police Department on Schreiber Way on the north end of town. Thornton himself would lead the remaining three hundred soldiers, backed by the M-48 tank, against potentially the toughest target, the Kootenai County Sheriff's Department. It was located near Coeur D'Alene Lake on Garden Avenue, adjacent to the Kootenai County courthouse, which housed the county government and court offices.

The sheriff's department could field nearly two hundred deputies, but Thornton knew, on a late Saturday morning in February, only a portion of the force would be working, and most of those would be on patrol.

Once all of the targets were secured, he intended to launch the second phase of his plan. To do that, his forces would have to liberate the local radio station from the liberal homo-lovers who ran the station. Then he would be able to broadcast his appeal to a waiting America to come and join his revolution.

Unknown to Thornton, Sheriff Jack Tomlinson had scheduled annual terrorism response training for his department, and half the department was present in the courthouse for the training. Even more ironic, the topic being discussed, as Thornton landed in the chopper, and his troopers arrived on Garden Avenue, was how the department would respond if the facility, itself, was attacked by terrorists.

When the alarm siren sounded, many of those attending the training thought it was a drill, part of the training they were receiving. A couple of bursts from an automatic weapon, however, from the other end of the building, dispelled that thought. The deputies in the large training room scrambled, quickly strapping on their department-issued, .40 caliber Glock, semi-automatic pistols.

As the deputies hurried down the hall leading to the main foyer at the center of the building, Sheriff Tomlinson was standing in a recessed office door and motioned for ten of the deputies to come over to him. He instructed them to exit through a rear utility door without being seen, rush next door to the public-safety building, and gather up the department's arsenal of twenty M-16s, several shotguns, and all the ammo they could carry and bring it all back to the courthouse. The sheriff felt the three-story courthouse could be more easily defended than the one-story, public-safety building.

As the first deputy approached the end of the hall, where a set of doors on the right opened into the foyer, he crouched down in order to peek around the corner and see what was happening.

Five uniformed military types were standing over four prostrate men, including one deputy, lying on their stomachs. The three civilians had their hands interlocked on the back of their heads. The deputy was flopped haphazardly, with one arm under his body and the other extended sideways. A pool of crimson was slowly expanding under his head. All five of the soldiers had M-16 assault rifles aimed at the far-north end of the room where two other deputies were crouched down behind two overturned desks with their pistols drawn. One of the soldiers, who appeared to be in charge, was yelling and gesturing toward the two cornered deputies.

Suddenly one of the soldiers glanced over at the deputy peering around the corner and whipped his automatic rifle in that direction. He wasn't fast enough. The deputy had already drawn a bead on the soldier and dropped him with a single shot to the neck. The other four soldiers wrenched their heads in the direction of the shot allowing the two deputies crouched behind the desks to open up on them, creating a deadly cross fire. Three Liberty Militia members were down before any of them could return fire. The remaining two rushed the exit door and dove through it as a .40 caliber slug caught the trailing soldier in the butt.

The United Nations Security Council meeting was not going well, at least in the eyes of the Russian hosts. It began cordially enough as the Russian ambassador spoke first and, in a rambling thirty-minute speech, painted the Israeli military aggression as the greatest threat to civilized countries of the world since the Third Reich. He expected his call for immediate authorization for military force to counter the Zionist threat would be pro-forma. He was wrong.

The British ambassador had yet to speak, when the ambassador from South Africa stood to raise objections to military action before sanctions were given a chance to work. It was a great segue for Sir Thomas Stanwick, Great Britain's UN representative, to second the objection.

After five hours of rhetoric, both supporting and objecting to the Russian demand for authorization to use force, the Council adjourned with no resolution, not even one addressing the application of sanctions. The next council meeting was scheduled for the following Wednesday, four days later. It was hoped by the members of the Council that private discussions and negotiations, in the meantime, might improve the environment for the next meeting.

The environment surrounding Anitoli Lebedov had deteriorated markedly over the past two hours and waiting four days for another Security Council meeting could not possibly improve it. His carefully groomed plans to lead the United Nations in defense of the helpless, peace-loving, Arab countries had hit a major roadblock. He had not even contemplated the possibility of a delay, let alone failure, to pass a force resolution.

He desperately wanted a United Nations sanction to carry out his plan to control the oil fields of the Middle East until it was too late for anybody to do anything about it. Taking unilateral military action, without UN legitimization, might make it too easy to connect the dots back to Russia for the terrorist attacks on America.

As Lebedov sat in his plush office chair, nervously chain-smoking a pack of Russian cigarettes, he mentally cursed the Israelis. *Those damned Jews. Why are they so brutally efficient militarily? In World War II they quietly allowed Hitler to nearly exterminate them. Why in hell do they have to be so aggravating now?*

Snow had begun falling at about 3:30 a.m. and about two inches was on the ground by dawn on Sunday morning. General Thornton, not wanting his first day as the president of the new America to be born in a bloodbath, had been negotiating all night long with Sheriff Tomlinson, to no avail. As luck would have it, the sheriff had nearly a hundred, well-armed deputies barricaded in the Kootenai County courthouse facility, and they were more than willing to fight it out with Thornton's soldiers. Thornton suspected the sheriff had made radio contact with the state police, and they would react with force as the awareness of the situation expanded. He was confident his forces could deal with any state response.

For his long-term plan to work, however, he was counting on any federal response to be delayed as federal politicians wrung their hands over taking any action that could have negative political ramifications. In Thornton's view, initiating a blood bath, using federal troops against fellow Americans, would certainly have negative implications, particularly with the liberal media and politicians that ran the country.

It was imperative the Liberty Militia begin broadcasting, as soon as possible, to recruit the thousands of real Americans Thornton would need to create the new America. He was sure the rump United States government in Denver would follow the lead of its predecessors and negotiate for an extended period before contemplating any sort of violent response. He needed that time to generate sympathy and support.

Phase two, however, could occur only after all of the initial targets had been secured. His plan had been implemented successfully elsewhere but not here.

Time was short. As reluctant as the general was to shed blood, at least at this stage of his plan, he knew the sheriff and deputies must either surrender or be destroyed within the next few hours, or Thornton's new America could die before it was born. After a few more moments of mentally searching for more options, Thornton picked up his Motorola hand-held and belched orders to move up the M48 into attack position. Perhaps he could force the sheriff to surrender with a few shots from the tank.

Twelve shiny, black, white-topped, Crown Victoria Interceptors, with Idaho State Police emblazoned on each of the front doors, were moving as fast as the snow-covered road would allow, headed north on U.S. 95 approaching the Spokane River Bridge. Each car contained four, heavily-armed, state troopers grimly committed to helping fellow officers in need. None knew what to expect, since the information filtering out of Coeur D'Alene was sketchy at best. They instinctively knew what they were facing was unlike anything they had ever dealt with before.

Sergeant Ben Pollock of the Liberty Militia was in command of the platoon's third and fourth squads, consisting of twenty-two men, protecting the north side of the Spokane River Bridge. They had relieved the first and second squads just fifteen minutes earlier.

Squinting to see more clearly through the falling snow, Pollock, a body shop technician by trade, could barely make out a string of flashing red and blue lights approaching his position from the other side of the bridge. He hollered, "Here they come. Get ready!"

The sergeant, not sharing his commander's hesitancy to shed blood, looked around until he found one of his two corporals. "Corporal," he ordered, "Zero in on those bastards with the M72 and take out the first one as soon as he is within a hundred yards. Once the first cruiser is destroyed, it will be a turkey shoot on the rest."

Forty seconds passed until the leading Ford was in range. The corporal shouldered the M72 Light Anti-tank Weapon (LAW) and targeted the first police vehicle. The LAW belched fire as a rocket screamed from the tube. Trailing white smoke, the rocket bee-lined toward the first vehicle until the warhead found its target. An erupting fireball filled both lanes of the bridge as debris blasted skyward. A second Interceptor slammed into the exploding inferno and skidded sideways through the bridge side barrier, plummeting toward the frigid Spokane River below.

Pollock bellowed, "Fire!" The squad opened up with their automatic weapons.

Four police cars in the rear of the state police convoy successfully backed away from the inferno. The remaining eight vehicles were quickly disabled, and many of the troopers were cut down trying to exit the cars.

It was all over in less than five minutes. Twenty-five Idaho state troopers lay dead or dying on the snow-covered asphalt or in the icy waters below. Seven managed to crawl away from the carnage and escape through the snowy murk.

Chapter 70

General Wiseman's optimistic estimate of breaking through the Syrian and Iraqi lines within three days proved to be wrong. After twenty-four hours there were no lines left. The road to Damascus was wide open. The only obstacle to reaching the city itself was the logistics nightmare such unexpected success had created.

The Israeli Defense Force, never hesitant to exploit every opportunity, pushed armored columns forward with breakneck speed up two routes; one through Baniyas and Qatana, Syria, and the other further east on the main road from Al Qunaytirah, at the northern edge of the Golan, to Damascus. The intent was to form a lid to the north to bottle up two hundred twenty thousand soldiers, the bulk of the Syrian and Iraqi armies. Once that was accomplished, the IDF anticipated wholesale surrender and the capture of hundreds of top-of-the-line Russian T-90S tanks, BMP-3 Infantry Fighting vehicles, mobile artillery, and tons of ammunition and other military hardware. Much equipment was already abandoned by terrified soldiers, more afraid of being attacked from above by Apaches than of becoming lost in the desert.

Ironically, a rising concern was the lack of trained troops to operate all of the captured equipment. Nobody had anticipated the bonanza of weapons being blended into Israel's armed forces.

Meanwhile, two armored divisions and three armored infantry brigades had managed to slip through Jordanian territory and deploy on the Saudi border without raising the concern of anybody other than a few nomadic Bedouins. The nomads initially thought Jordan was being invaded by Saudi Arabia. When they realized they were looking at Israeli tanks, they were too shocked to react and didn't have the means or desire to take any action, anyway. Bedouins, historically, didn't really care who headed the governments in the Middle East, since they didn't bother with borders. As long as they were left alone, the King of Jordan could be an alien from Mars.

It looked like the highly mobile, but extremely lethal, force would be in action sooner than anticipated if reports from the north were true. It appeared the Damascus plum was about to be picked, and, once that happened, the entire orchard was ready to be harvested.

Chapter 71

Accurate news of the chaotic situation around Coeur D'Alene was slow to reach the new White House in Denver. By early Monday morning, it was clear a substantial, well-armed, paramilitary force, representing an extreme far-right agenda, had attacked the law enforcement installations in Coeur D'Alene and had sealed off the city of thirty thousand.

Reliable, but sketchy, information indicated at least forty-two police officers had been killed in three separate incidents; two at roadblocks leading into the city, and the other at the Kootenai County courthouse where a siege was still continuing. Reports from the courthouse indicated the attackers had fired several tank rounds into the courthouse causing several casualties there, but approximately eighty-five deputies were still putting up a determined fight.

The president had already participated in two lengthy telephone conversations this morning, and it was only 5:45 a.m. One was with General Taylor, who awakened the president an hour earlier to update him on the Israeli moves into Syria and Saudi Arabia, the worsening situation in Idaho, and plans to resolve the growing confrontation with General Cooke. The second call was with the governor of Idaho who desperately needed federal troops to help restore order in northern Idaho. His situation was critical, mainly because the bulk of Idaho National Guard troops, who might normally be available to respond, were already deployed near Seattle in the recovery efforts underway there.

The president informed the governor he would take all steps necessary to stop the bloodshed and put an end to the insurrection in Coeur D'Alene. An emergency cabinet meeting was being scheduled later in the morning at 9:00 to give General Taylor time to fly into Denver. Benson did his best to sooth the governor's concerns and told him he would call him at the conclusion of the meeting.

At about the same time, the "wanabe" president of America, General Jack Thornton, was drilling holes in the dark ceiling as he lay awake on the king bed in a $420 per night suite at the Coeur D'Alene Marriott.

He had decided the previous night that his forces would launch an all-out assault on the Kootenai courthouse at noon on Monday to put an end to the bad publicity the Militia action was generating. He knew word had leaked out that scores of police officers had been killed and was afraid he would lose any chance of support if the public viewed his actions as simply a bloodthirsty attempt to take power. The siege at the courthouse had to end to stop the hemorrhage of information.

Broadcasting from the city's only TV station, KCDT TV 26, an affiliate of PBS, would be useless while the national press concentrated on the siege at the courthouse. He thought, *Damn the bad luck. Why did the whole sheriff's department have to be scheduled for training on the one day I set for liberating America? So far this shit has cost me eight good men dead and twice that many wounded.*

In the morning he would augment the forces for the assault, adding an additional two hundred troops skimmed from the forces guarding the airport and the police station on Schreiber Way. He thought to himself, *This has got to work tomorrow, no matter what it takes.*

Chapter 72

President Benson showered in cold water to awaken his mind for the trying day ahead. After dressing in tan khakis and a striped, button-down shirt, he sat down at the make-shift kitchen table and poured himself a bowl of mini-shredded wheat, sprinkled a tablespoon of sugar on the already sugared cereal, and drowned it with 1 percent milk. He figured the low-fat milk would offset the excess sugar.

A half-hour later he entered the ornate ballroom decorated with old, oak-stained, exposed beams and century-old, crystal chandeliers. The main ballroom of the old Parkside Mansion on York Street, which served as the Denver White House, had been converted into the primary conference room where cabinet level meetings were held. Benson considered the old, but grand, mansion sufficient as the temporary seat of government until elections could be held in six months and a permanent location decided upon by the new government.

All members of his minimal cabinet were present along with the heads of the FBI and CIA. General Taylor had not yet arrived, but word had just been received he was en route from Denver International Airport and would be arriving in about fifteen minutes.

Benson began the meeting anyway, welcoming his cabinet and agency heads. He then asked Senator McClain to update the group on the status of the recovery effort going on in the country.

"Thank you, Mr. President," McClain began. "I would be glad to furnish the latest information I have.

"First, some positive news. Our latest official estimate on the casualties our country suffered has been drastically reduced, based on actual numbers counted and analysis of information pouring in from survivors. As you recall, our early estimates were up to twenty million people had perished. We're now confident the number is half that, still a horrible blow, but at least on the positive side of our initial fears.

"A second positive development, perhaps, depending on how one looks at it, is the almost total lack of looting or lawbreaking in the affected areas. I believe there are two factors in play here. The quick deployment of National Guard troops to the perimeters of all impacted locations has greatly enhanced the security situation. Possibly more significant is the sobering fact most of the would-be looters lived in the inner cities that were destroyed and perished in the detonations.

"The progress toward recovery differs somewhat depending on the city. New York, for example, has more problems than most, mainly because of the extreme casualty levels, high amounts of debris, and continuing problems with deadly radioactivity. That said, I still want to express my admiration for the response of thousands of Americans. In virtually all cases, the millions of injured and, unfortunately, dying Americans are receiving at least adequate medical care and housing. Literally thousands of doctors and other medical practitioners are volunteering at makeshift hospitals in churches, schools, warehouses, and even homes. Surgery centers have been set up, and severely injured people are being cared for.

"We still have a long road to tread, however. We feel we have a handle on the short-term needs, but long-term is another question. Whole cities are going to have to be rebuilt in different locations. None of the city centers will be inhabitable for years. What do we do with the millions of displaced citizens?

"The federal government, still with substantial resources, is working closely with the governors to come up with workable plans for the long-term. Virtually all bureaucratic red-tape hamstringing previous massive recovery efforts has been eliminated to get this done. We've actually fired three agency heads who failed to grasp the new reality.

"We would anticipate we'll have a long-term plan ready for your review and the president's approval in four weeks. I realize that represents unheard-of speed. But like I said, this is a new reality. Do any of you have any questions I can answer in the few minutes before the general arrives?"

Senator/Secretary of the Treasury Dobson raised his hand and asked, "Charles, any early estimates on the cost?"

McClain smiled faintly. "You might have a better estimate than I. Let me say this, however. The cost will obviously be in the billions, perhaps even a trillion dollars. We all need to realize, though, it will take decades to rebuild what has been destroyed, and the money spent on reconstruction will actually be a boost to the economy.

"The massive expenditures of both federal and private funds, in the long run, will be offset by the expansion of jobs and industries related to the reconstruction effort. I'd anticipate a short-term need to raise taxes, at least temporarily."

Another senator/cabinet member bluntly asked, "Do we know for sure who's behind the attacks?"

McClain, nodded toward the FBI director, Wilkinson, and said, "The FBI director might be in a better position to answer that question."

The FBI director turned his head toward the president with an expectant look on his face.

Benson, taking the cue, answered the question. "Let me take that question. We know the terrorist group Black October has taken credit for the attacks, and we're confident they indeed were responsible. At this point, though, we don't know for sure who furnished them with the nuclear warheads other than the suspicions about the Russians we discussed earlier in the week.

"What we'll discuss in a few minutes with General Taylor will shed some light on what we suspect, and what actions we're contemplating to take against both Black October and the nation, or nations, we suspect furnished the weapons. Let's wait a few minutes for the general to join us, before I go into much more detail about this. I'd like to recommend, however, even before the general arrives, we go ahead and authorize the nationalization and general mobilization of our National Guard. As Senator McClain reported, looting is not an issue, and the active armed forces badly need the infusion of men a general mobilization will offer. Are there any objections to this course of action?"

There were none.

Dobson looked directly at the president and offered a recommendation. "Mr. President, I think it would be a balm for the Republic if you could find time in your schedule to visit, at least, some of the devastated cities over the next few days."

Several heads bobbed in agreement.

Benson's face was creased with a broad smile. "Mr. Dobson, I think that's a wonderful idea. It's so good, in fact, I already asked June, yesterday, to make arrangements next week to do just that."

Sheriff Tomlinson and his deputies were in dire straits. Ten deputies had already been killed in yesterday's assault, mainly due to tank fire initiated by the militia. Thirteen were wounded, six severely, and there was very little in the way of medical help available. One paramedic, who happened to be in the courthouse when it was first assaulted two days earlier, had run out of bandages and had reverted to using undershirts to stop bleeding and cover gaping wounds. The county commissioner's offices were being used as a makeshift hospital.

Ammunition for the M-16s, shotguns, and personal weapons was adequate for now but would run out if a sustained assault took place. The sheriff suspected such an assault would occur today.

Throughout the crisis, Tomlinson had been able to maintain both radio and cell-phone contact with the outside, communicating mainly with the state police in Lewiston. His only hope was the governor would be successful in expediting a strong federal response before it was too late.

A column of militiamen, riding deuce-and-a-half's, just arrived from the Coeur D'Alene police station, increasing Thornton's assault troops by a hundred men. Another column was headed south from the airport, which would further augment his force. Eventually he would have over five hundred troops for the assault on the courthouse. Thornton was sure that would be sufficient, combined with sustained tank fire and support from the Huey, to end the siege quickly.

Chapter 73

The five Apaches were in a loose formation headed north above Damascus looking for targets. It appeared the Syrians and their allies had disappeared leaving perfectly functional equipment abandoned along the roads to the south. None of the helicopters had so much as fired a rocket in anger for the past hour.

The pathetic scene unfolding below them even softened the hearts of the hardened chopper pilots. Literally hundreds of thousands of refugees were crowding all highways leading north out of Damascus. The wretched citizens of Syria apparently believed their government's anti-Israeli propaganda.

Solo and the other pilots knew the columns of refugees hid thousands of Syrian troops also trying to escape the Israeli onslaught, but they figured, so what? The soldiers had become refugees and posed no immediate threat to Israeli soldiers pushing up from the south.

Solo barked into the radio and ordered the squadron to peel off to the east to continue the search for any enemy vehicles, which might potentially pose a threat to the upcoming assault eastward toward Baghdad. He knew that would occur soon, within the next couple of days, as soon as the Israelis could consolidate their positions around Damascus.

"I will not allow those damned Jews to torpedo Russia's destiny," bellowed Lebedov, jabbing an index finger toward his director of special operations, as if the colonel were to blame.

"They will pay an ultimate price for their aggression if they don't back down, and Litinov, you'll ensure that happens."

Litinov was stunned at the president's insinuation. He responded in an inquiring tone as he peered into the president's eyes hoping to see a different message than he feared. "I'm not sure I understand what you mean sir."

Lebedov replied sneeringly, "Colonel, let me make it clear to you. I will give the Jews forty-eight hours to withdraw from all of the

Arab territory, or else I will destroy their country with a massive nuclear strike. You, Colonel, will make the necessary arrangements with our strategic nuclear forces to ensure we can carry out the threat."

Litinov replied, "Mr. President, I probably don't need to point out to you the Israelis have their own nuclear arsenal. What's to prevent them from retaliating against us?"

Lebedov rose from his chair, veins bulging in his neck, leaned over the mahogany table, spilling a half-full cup of coffee, and stared menacingly at the colonel. "Do you think I'm a fool Litinov, who knows nothing? Of course I know the Jews have a few bombs. They can't simply retarget them in a day or so, nor would they dare target Russia. I'm confident the arrogant, little, Jewish bastards will believe I'm bluffing and won't withdraw. That's why you'll ensure it will be the last time they call anyone's bluff."

Litinov tried to hide his obvious shock at what the leader of Russia was planning. He tried one last attempt at reason. "Mr. President, I mean absolutely no disrespect, but I'm just trying to weigh all the possible consequences. What about the American reaction?"

The president postulated, "The Americans are done. They don't even have a legitimate government anymore. The new, self-appointed president is a nonelected, temporary fill-in and would not dare push his country into a war with us to save the Jews. I'm right Colonel, you can count on that."

Litinov, resigned to the fact the president's mind was made up, simply asked, "When?"

Lebedov sat back down and paused before answering, causing Litinov to wonder if this whole plan was just a spur-of-the-moment, angry outburst, which could lead to a second holocaust.

"The United Nations has become nothing more than a pathetic bureaucratic hindrance to our plans," muttered Lebedov, "and I anticipate they will not authorize the use of force when they meet Wednesday, or anytime soon thereafter. We must proceed, therefore, without authorization. I will give the Israeli's an ultimatum two days after the Security Council meets, so the attack should be ready to go by next Monday."

Litinov was now sure the president was improvising as he went. The thought the whole world could be destroyed by a plan hatched during an angry outburst, sobered the colonel. He knew his duty as a soldier was to his country but not, necessarily, to the insane ravings of a leader poisoned by his own ambitions.

He stood to attention, saluted the president smartly, executed a military about face, and walked briskly out the heavy, double doors. As he exited the president's office, his mind started formulating options.

Chapter 74

"General Taylor, we appreciate your willingness to fly up here in the middle of the night. It's truly unfortunate the situation both at home and in the world is so disturbing that we're all becoming insomniacs."

The president continued, "I believe it's imperative we make the necessary decisions and move very quickly if we're to save the lives of many brave, law-enforcement officers in Coeur D'Alene this afternoon.

"We also need to discuss the growing crisis in the Middle East and would ask you to brief us on the latest Israeli and Russian military movements in the area and what our response has been, and will be over the next few weeks. The need to make quick decisions and respond to the insurrection in Idaho, however, is paramount and urgent. Without further delay, I will turn the time over to you to brief us on the current situation and what plans are in motion to rectify it."

The general scanned the assembled cabinet members, briefly making eye contact with each before beginning. "Gentlemen and ladies, I too feel the tension to which the president has alluded. It's imperative we have as much information as possible and make reasoned, though tough, decisions based on that information.

"Fifteen minutes ago, I received a fax from our intelligence sources monitoring a KH-12 satellite that just passed over the Coeur D'Alene area. They report there has been significant movement of vehicles from the north toward the courthouse. It appears the militia is bringing in reinforcements, probably to launch an assault on the courthouse later today. It's also reported the crazies have at least one tank, likely a Vietnam era Patton, and a Huey helicopter.

"The state police in Lewiston received a cell-phone call from the Kootenai County sheriff, who is in the courthouse with about eighty deputies, indicating eight tank shells were fired into the building yesterday causing a score of casualties, including several dead.

"The militia has roadblocks manned in five locations and have participated in at least two violent actions at those roadblocks leading to the death of several more Idaho police officers. They also control the airport, about ten miles north of the courthouse, but have reduced the number of gunmen at that location, probably to participate in the assault on the courthouse.

"The situation is critical, and, to avoid a bloodbath at the courthouse, immediate military action is required. This has gone way beyond a law-enforcement problem, in my view.

"I have, on my own initiative, ordered elements of the 101st airborne to attack and control the airport and land two battalions of paratroopers there. Additionally I have dispatched a squadron of Apache helicopters from Mountain Home airbase with orders to destroy the tank and Huey threatening the courthouse and provide air support for the deputies.

"All of these orders can be rescinded, if need be, since it will be noon, Idaho time, before the attacks can be launched. I'd urge you to authorize me to proceed, but the decision is, of course, yours to make. Thank you."

Benson, trying to comprehend the dimensions of what the general had just outlined, rose from his chair and looked around the table. "I feel like Abraham Lincoln must have felt when he ordered U.S. troops to war against fellow Americans. I think we need to take just a few minutes to discuss this, but the discussion must be brief if we're to save lives. Anybody have comments?"

A few of the cabinet members whispered to their neighbors around the table, but no one indicated a desire to offer an opinion. Finally Senator Simpson spoke, "Mr. President, General Taylor, I think I can speak for the rest. There is a new reality in this country. Delay, negotiation in a hopeless cause, appeasement; we have all tragically seen where that can lead.

"I think it's imperative we do whatever it takes to end this insurrection in Idaho, for that's what it is, an insurrection. If our nation is to survive the catastrophe that occurred last week, it has to be united to go forward. For a right-wing, racist group to take advantage of a tragic situation and threaten that unity is unconscionable and must be stopped, before it can infect other parts of the Republic."

The president nodded his head at Senator Simpson and said, "Thank you. If there are no more comments, I agree with the general and authorize him to carry out the plan he has just presented.

The Kootenai County complex, including the courthouse, public safety, and justice buildings, was situated in a triangle bordered to the north by Garden Avenue, on the east by North Government Way, and on the west by Northwest Boulevard.

Thornton's plan was fairly simple. He intended to use his tank to demoralize the deputies in the courthouse, forcing them to keep their heads down, while five hundred, assault troops advanced on the three-story building. The troops would move forward quickly from the buildings about a 150 yards in front of the courthouse across North Government Way. They would have to advance through an open park and parking lots, but the tank shelling and .50 caliber machine-gun fire from the Huey would provide adequate screening cover for his troops. He planned on leading the assault from the shotgun seat in the helicopter.

The morning had been uneventful for the tired, hungry deputies barricaded on the second and third floors of the courthouse. That was about to change drastically.

Just before noon, the tank, which had been so deadly the day before, clanked into plain view from behind a small office building. It was positioned a little over two hundred yards away across North Government Way. It turned so it was facing directly toward the front of the courthouse.

Just as the barrel of the 105 mm gun started to lower, Sheriff Tomlinson yelled, "Everybody down!" anticipating an imminent shot from the tank. A couple of seconds later a sharp bang was heard, followed, in a second or so, by an eardrum-busting explosion at the far west-end of the courthouse. The sheriff heard a pained scream that died into silence.

Tomlinson knew it would take a few seconds for the tank to reload so he stole a quick look at the scene in front of the courthouse. Swarms of troops were pouring from the back of two office buildings across North Government Way and were quickly advancing between the buildings toward the courthouse. Movement at the roofline of one of the buildings caused him to glance in that direction, and a Huey helicopter slowly appeared, like an apparition, above the building.

Suddenly in his left peripheral vision, a white streak angled downward, and, as he turned his head to the left, the tank erupted into a fireball, launching the turret fifty feet into the air.

A couple of seconds later, the Huey helicopter that had been flying directly toward the courthouse, veered drastically to the right as another white smoky streak flashed just to the left of the chopper. Three seconds later the Huey's luck ran out as a second rocket slammed into the cowling covering the engine. The magnificent fireball radiated heat on the faces of the deputies staring at the fireworks demonstration in the sky in front of them.

It took a few moments before the understanding of what had just happened registered in the sheriff's mind. Finally, realizing he and his deputies were no longer alone, he yelled, "Open fire!"

Five hundred Liberty militiamen, who moments before were yelling and screaming as they advanced toward sure victory, were now thrown into a state of shock and panic. In a few seconds they had lost both the tank and helicopter that were to provide decisive firepower and cover for them. More devastatingly, they had lost their beloved leader, the president of the new America.

As they hesitated, a devastating volley of automatic and small-arms weapons fire erupted from the courthouse. At the same time, four AH-64A Apache helicopters, two coming from each side of the open area before the courthouse, opened up with AWS 30 mm automatic chain guns. Men were falling like bowling pins.

In reaction to the carnage, the remaining troopers of the Liberty Militia threw down their rifles and raised their hands high over their heads. Several still lost their lives before the wholesale surrender registered with the deputies and chopper pilots.

Only 135 insurrectionists remained standing as Sheriff Tomlinson and seventy-five deputies exited through the front courthouse doors to accept their surrender. A military crisis of extreme concern had now become a law-enforcement activity, at least at the Kootenai County courthouse.

Word of the death of Thornton and the surrender at the courthouse spread quickly to the sixty militiamen barricaded at the airport and Coeur D'Alene Police Department. Rather than face certain death for a lost cause, the militiamen gave up to soldiers of the 101st Airborne without firing a shot.

Militiamen manning the roadblocks did not get the word about the events at the courthouse and offered tough, bloody resistance before surrendering to paratroopers who had parachuted in behind each of the roadblocks. Escape for them was hopeless, as armored roadblocks were set up a few hundred yards outside each of the five militia positions.

When it was all over, the first significant armed insurrection in the United States since the Civil War had cost the lives of fifty-two law-enforcement officers, three soldiers from the 101st Airborne, and 365 members of the Liberty Militia. In comparison to the carnage caused by the terrorist attack two weeks earlier, the casualties were minimal. The emotional impact to the country, however, of the federal government's quick, decisive response, was immense. A new reality now existed in America.

The Russian Bear's failure to heed Admiral Yamamoto's fateful warning, first uttered seven decades earlier, would bring the world to the brink of catastrophe. The sleeping giant had again awakened!

PART FOUR

RESOLUTION

Chapter 75

The Joint Forces commander, responsible for one of America's most powerful unified commands, had been sitting for ten minutes in the outer office waiting to see the President of the United States. General Cooke initially contemplated simply ignoring Benson's order to report at the Denver White House, which he received yesterday morning, but then thought better of it. He wasn't ready to declare a coup quite yet and knew ignoring a presidential order would have amounted to just that.

Moreover, perhaps now would be as good a time as any to confront the naïve senator and force his resignation from the office to which he had appointed himself. Cooke's conviction of the righteousness of his course was rock solid, and he was confident he could intimidate Benson.

Cooke noticed a red light flash on the phone sitting on the corner of a desk behind which sat an attractive, gray-haired woman. The woman glanced up and said, "You can go in now," nodding toward the solid, double doors leading to the president's office. Without a word or glance, the general stood up, grabbed the door handles, and forcefully opened both doors, as he pompously entered the office.

President Benson looked up from behind his desk, as the general entered the office with a flourish. Cooke strode directly to the desk and stood at attention, towering over the sitting president, who did not stand to greet him.

After a moment, Benson stood up, calmly walked around the desk, passing by Cooke without a word, and walked to the doors the general had not bothered to close and closed them. He then returned and took a seat in his leather chair behind the desk.

After fixating on the general's eyes for a few seconds, Benson said matter-of-factly, "Please take a seat," nodding toward a comfortable-looking, tan-leather chair to the left front of the desk.

Cooke replied, "I'd rather stand. You ordered me here. What can I do for you Senator?" consciously addressing Benson by his former title.

Benson, knowing what was about to happen, couldn't prevent a slight smile forming on his face. "General Cooke, the reason I summoned you here this afternoon is to ask for your resignation."

Cooke, taken off-guard by Benson's directness, shot back, "You're the one who should resign. Nobody elected you. You're just like all the other liberal, money-sucking appeasers who lost their miserable, useless lives in Washington. The commies did us all a favor. It's just too bad the rest of you weren't there."

The president was amazed at Cooke's venom. He thought to himself, *Just imagine if this guy really did have his finger on the trigger!* Knowing any additional conversation would be pointless, Benson interrupted Cooke's tirade and said, in a voice raised just enough for Cooke to hear, "Then, you're fired."

The general, staring with blind fury into Benson's eyes, yelled back, "You can't fire me you pipsqueak son-of-a-bitch. I command enough military power to take over this government on a whim. What makes you think you have any power to fire me?"

Before Benson could answer his question, Cooke was startled by the sound of the double doors leading from the outer office unlatching behind him. He turned quickly, and his jaw dropped as he recognized General Taylor, accompanied by two armed, military-police officers. The MPs stood at attention on either side of Cooke.

"What is going on here?" General Cooke demanded, staring coldly at Taylor.

General Taylor answered Cooke's question directly. "As the President just said, you've been relieved of your duty. Furthermore, the three highest-ranking officers on your staff have either resigned or have also been relieved. You, General Cooke, no longer command anything."

"You can't do this to me!" hissed Cooke.

General Taylor calmly replied, "That's not all General. Your verbal attack and threats to our Commander in Chief amount to treason. As a result, I'm ordering you be placed under arrest."

The MPs quickly grabbed Cooke's arms before he could protest. He was handcuffed and quickly escorted, almost carried, out while yelling unintelligible obscenities back over his shoulder as he left.

The noise of the general's ranting slowly subsided as he was led down the hall and outside to a waiting military police vehicle. June, the president's administrative assistant, had left the outer office in anticipation of what was going to occur and, fortunately, was not subjected to Cooke's rage.

General Taylor grinned slightly and raised his eyebrows as he looked at the president. “Well, what will be the political fallout from this?”

Benson thought for a moment and replied soberly, “General, handling any political ramifications will be a piece of cake compared to the problems we would’ve faced had we let this continue. The country and I will be in your debt for helping resolve this.”

Taylor stood to attention, smartly saluted the Commander in Chief, and replied, “You’re most welcome sir.”

Chapter 76

The spy business is a whole other world. Intelligence officers are routinely assigned to work at various embassies throughout the world and are given important sounding titles like Consular Affairs Officer. In reality, they are spies.

Tyler McNabb was one of those, having been assigned by the CIA to the United States Embassy in Moscow for the past two years. McNabb didn't start out his professional career as an employee of the CIA. After graduating from Indiana University Law School in Bloomington, he took a position with a medium-size law firm in Evansville, Indiana and was a successful attorney for a few years. As an avid follower of world affairs, however, he could not resist a good CIA recruiter's entreaties to join the agency.

His wife threatened to eliminate his ability to procreate, when initially approached with the idea. She, and their four children, ranging in age from four to thirteen, gradually grew into the new life and now considered living in Russia as something of an adventure.

McNabb knew his title of Consular Affairs Officer fooled nobody. His Russian counterparts knew full well what he did. It was a game they all played. He knew he was always going to be the one kicked out of the country first, should there ever be a diplomatic tit-for-tat required. He had long ago accepted that risk as part of the job.

This evening he was hurriedly walking toward his Russian Volga, trying to get out of the numbing cold as fast as possible. His only hope was the heater would work tonight. The underground garage was not heated, and the few light bulbs, poorly illuminating the parking area, provided no heat whatsoever.

As he approached his car, he noticed out of the corner of his eye a large figure wearing a heavy, woolen coat and Russian-bear, fur cap pulled down around his ears. As he turned reflexively toward the man, his world suddenly went black as someone from behind encased his head in some sort of black sack.

McNabb instinctively grabbed at the bottom of the sack to pull it off but suddenly found his arms pinned to his sides by two immensely strong arms. A second set of arms, probably from the first man with the fur cap, grabbed both his legs, and he found himself being carried away from his car.

A moment later, he was roughly thrown into the back seat of another vehicle and, in spite of his struggles, soon found his wrists handcuffed in front of him and his arms secured to the sides of his body by what appeared to be duct tape.

He heard the car engine start up and felt the car moving. As it exited the garage, he thought it turned left. McNabb's heart was pounding in his chest as adrenaline flooded his body. He couldn't imagine the Russian government sanctioned his kidnapping, so he was fearful that, whatever this was, it would definitely not have a positive outcome.

All of the best-trained, motivated intelligence operatives, with access to the most-high-tech equipment, sometimes are successful only through blind, dumb luck. Such was the case with the information that had just been received by Colby Engeman at his small Tel Aviv office.

A remotely piloted mini-drone, called the Mosquito, was conducting a nighttime, photographic-intelligence sweep over Lebanon's Beq'a Valley on this unusually-warm, February evening. It just happened to photograph a man, who looked a lot like Alawai Al Zouri, reclining in a patio chair next to three other Arabs at the back of a rundown hostel. The hostel was located in an area long suspected of harboring Black October terrorists leaders. It was apparent from the photographs Engeman was viewing, Al Zouri was oblivious to the presence of the drone.

In the past when such a lucky break presented itself, the Israeli Air Force would immediately be dispatched to destroy the target without any additional verification of the accuracy of the information. Sometimes innocent people were killed. Enough bad guys were eliminated, however, to offset the mistakes.

Today was different. A United States Seal team was in Israel for the express purpose of exploiting such a break. The United States wanted to capture Al Zouri alive, if possible, to identify who supplied the warheads for the attack on America. Engeman agreed a live Al Zouri could be squeezed sufficiently to provide a considerable amount of information. Engeman wished he could do the squeezing. He doubted America had the squeezing expertise possessed by the Israelis.

He picked up the telephone and made a quick call to Colonel Dylan who would set the operation in motion. Within twenty minutes five Blackhawk helicopters, supported by an equal number of Apaches, had crossed the Lebanese border headed north.

The nominal Consular Affairs Officer estimated they had been traveling about thirty minutes when the car made a sharp left turn and came to a stop. He heard a garage door closing. A couple of seconds later the left door of the car opened, and a pair of strong hands grabbed him by his left arm and dragged him out of the car.

Another pair of strong hands grabbed his right arm, and the two ape-men literally carried him to a location McNabb assumed to be in the interior of a building and seated him roughly on a hard, wooden chair. He heard a male voice from his front instruct the two kidnappers to remove the duct tape and handcuffs. McNabb rubbed his wrists, feeling a slight sense of relief he was no longer cuffed. He had no illusions, however, of his ability to overpower any of the supermen in the room, let alone three of them.

The male voice then directed McNabb to remove the sack over his head, which he promptly did. He squinted briefly as he adjusted to the light of the room. The light was not bright but was considerably more than he had experienced over the past thirty minutes.

He quickly took in his surroundings. It appeared he was in some sort of warehouse office. Empty racks and vacant warehouse space were vaguely visible in the darkness outside the office windows. The office was nondescript, with a few dilapidated file cabinets and a single, rusty-steel desk concealing the lower half of the man who was apparently in charge of this kidnapping.

As his eyes acclimated to the office light, he noticed the man behind the desk appeared to be wearing a Russian Military uniform.

"Who are you?" was all McNabb managed to say.

The uniformed Russian answered in broken, but understandable, English, "Perhaps I will tell you my name later, but, for now, all you need to know is I'm a colonel in the Russian Army. I apologize for the method used to bring you here. The risks to me, to you, and to the world are so high, I couldn't risk attempting to contact you in another manner. You see Mr. McNabb, I know who you are and who you really work for."

McNabb began to protest his innocence, still playing the game, but the colonel continued, "My intention is not to compromise or harm you in any way, sir. I have vital information your country needs. I want you to just sit there and listen to me. You can ask any questions of me once I'm through talking but not before. Listen carefully. What you do with this information is critical for the future of both our countries."

Litinov proceeded to outline the details of the Russian president's scheme to control the Middle East oil fields, including his own involvement in training the terrorist and facilitating the delivery of the nuclear bombs to America. He summarized the Chinese involvement in the development of the warheads and continuing participation in the furtherance of the plan.

In response to McNabb's obviously shocked expression, the colonel continued, "You're probably wondering why I'm telling you this. It isn't because I'm looking for any monetary gain or have any love for your country. I'm a Russian patriot, Mr. McNabb, and that's why I'm telling you this now. I'm convinced my president, Anitoli Lebedov, is crazy. He needs to be stopped before his insane ambition to rule the world results in its destruction.

"On Friday Lebedov will issue an ultimatum to the Israelis, warning them to pull all their troops out of the Arab countries they have overrun or face the consequences. The consequence Mr. McNabb, is a massive, nuclear attack on Israel the following Monday. I have no doubt he will do just that. As I said, he no longer views the world with a rational mind."

McNabb could wait no longer and asked, "What can I do?"

Litinov replied, "You must warn the Israelis. I know they have a substantial nuclear force and the means to deliver warheads to Russia. Now I, of course, don't want them to do that, but they've got to convince Lebedov they will do exactly that if he carries out his threat. Even in his crazed mind, he doesn't want the destruction of his own country, at least not yet."

McNabb stared into Litinov's eyes for a moment before asking, "Colonel, how can he be stopped?"

The colonel hesitated and then replied, "I don't know yet. I'm working on something, but I'm not convinced I can be successful. Whatever is done needs to be done quickly. Only eight Russians knew about our involvement with the terror attacks in America. Six of those, three generals, including Dimitry Yeremenko, and three nuclear scientists, have been arrested over the past two days and are being held incommunicado. They might even be dead. As I said, the president no longer thinks rationally."

McNabb blurted out, "One might say furnishing nuclear weapons to a terrorist group leading to the deaths of millions is not a rational act."

Litinov blushed, looked down for a moment, then raised his head and looked directly into McNabb's eyes. "For that, I'm truly sorry. I let my concept of duty rob me of my humanity and will pay the price for that mistake the rest of my life. That's the reason I've chosen to become a traitor to my country; to save it and, perhaps by doing so, ease my conscience, at least to some small degree."

After a pregnant pause the colonel raised his eyebrows and said, "Now go do what you need to do. I will contact you when I've decided on the next steps. In the meantime, I presume there isn't a need to cuff you for the trip back to your car?"

"I'll be a good boy."

"Unfortunately, Mr. McNabb, I will insist on the bag. You don't need to know this location."

"What is your name Colonel?"

"Perhaps, next time we meet, Mr. McNabb."

Chapter 77

It was a surprisingly bright, sunny day dawning outside the kitchen window, which reflected Benson's mood as he sat down at the breakfast table with Kristina and the kids. Benson was pouring himself the usual sugared cereal, which he would sweeten even more. He knew he faced a disapproving scowl from his wife, mainly because of the bad example he was setting for the children. Oh well, he figured, kids and sugar go together like waffles and syrup.

The debacle in Idaho ended yesterday about as well as could be expected, even though a lot of misguided Americans lost their lives in the process. The president certainly was not happy about the loss of any lives but had no regrets about ordering the military to end it. He felt sure his quick action saved innocent civilian lives. He sorrowed for the families of the law-enforcement personnel who were killed prior to the military action but felt he prevented even more law-enforcement deaths by ordering in the troops.

One other vexing issue on Benson's plate was also resolved satisfactorily yesterday. His confrontation with General Cooke in the afternoon resulted in a positive outcome, not just for Benson, but for the country. The short announcement to the national media late yesterday of Cooke's arrest hadn't resulted in any calls for the president's impeachment this morning. Perhaps the fallout would be manageable.

Benson's spirit was buoyed, not necessarily by the successful conclusion of both events, but by the realization he was capable as the country's new, albeit temporary, leader of making critical decisions quickly. Knowing the next few days and weeks would confront him with more critical choices, his confidence in his ability to make those decisions, when they needed to be made, had expanded significantly.

He was just about ready to pour a second bowl of mini-shredded wheat when the shrill ring of the business telephone interrupted him. He knew the business phone would not ring unless the off-hours switchboard operator knew the caller was on a pre-approved call list authorized to interrupt the president during non-business hours.

Benson rose from the table and walked the six steps to the counter and picked up the receiver. "Hello, this is President Benson."

"Hello Mr. President, this is CIA Director Bill Smith. I'm sorry to interrupt you and your family so early in the morning, but I've just been appraised of some vital information I must share with you personally, as soon as possible. I'm calling from my cell phone and am en route to your location, as we speak. I will be there in less than twenty minutes."

The president's curiosity was aroused, but, if the CIA director felt the information was of such importance he needed to personally present it to him, he wasn't going to pressure Smith to disclose any more information over the phone.

"Okay, Director Smith. I will make sure the calendar is cleared and see you in about twenty minutes."

He hung up the receiver, walked back to the table to finish his cereal and wondered what the new day was going to bring. As he sat down, Kristina asked, "Honey, you look perplexed. What was that all about?"

Benson looked at his wife and smiled, "Sweetheart, I don't know what it's all about. That's why I look the way I do. The CIA director is on his way here. In twenty minutes I'll probably know what kind of day it's going to be."

Twenty minutes later, William Smith sat in one of two brown-leather chairs arranged in front of the huge presidential desk. The president sat in the other chair, preferring that to sitting behind the broad expanse of desk.

Smith got right to the point. "Mr. President, two hours ago, one of our intelligence officers attached to our embassy in Moscow was abducted by two, unknown assailants and was taken blindfolded to a location in Moscow. There he met a uniformed Russian, who claimed to be a colonel in the Russian Army. This colonel then proceeded to tell him he worked directly for Russian president Lebedov and was instrumental in directing Lebedov's plans to take over the Middle East oil fields.

"He told our man part of that plan included supplying Al Zouri's terrorist organization with twelve nuclear warheads smuggled into the United States in September last year. The colonel claimed Lebedov was convinced the detonation of those warheads in twelve American cities would so devastate America we would no longer be a hindrance to his plans to control the world's oil."

Benson pondered for a moment and asked the director, "Was Russia just going to invade the Middle East?"

Smith answered, "No. According to the colonel, the plan was to arm the Arabs to the teeth and encourage them to attack Israel. The Russian president assumed Israel would eventually defeat the Arabs, destroying most of their armies in the process, and the Arabs would then ask Russia into their countries to confront the Israelis. Lebedov would pour in troops and equipment, force the Israelis to back down, and occupation of the oil fields would be a fait accompli.

"The plan has gone awry. The Israelis have defeated the Arabs faster than expected and are apparently intent on controlling the oil fields the Russians covet. Lebedov is livid about that and is ready to threaten the Israelis with nuclear annihilation if they don't withdraw."

The president frowned. "Is he serious?"

"Mr. President, our intelligence officer says the Russian colonel was adamant Lebedov has lost his senses; actually called him insane. He said Lebedov ordered the colonel to prepare Russian nuclear forces to launch a nuclear attack on Israel next Monday."

Benson cringed as he understood the gravity of what he just heard and stated, "Bill, we've got to warn the Israeli's immediately, so they can prepare however they can. Don't the Israelis have a robust nuclear force themselves?"

The CIA director replied, "Yes. Our latest estimates are they have over five hundred thermonuclear weapons at their disposal. As a matter of fact, the colonel indicated that just the threat Israel might target Russian cities with those warheads might be the only thing that would motivate Lebedov to call off his plan—if he truly believed the Israelis would do it."

"Faced with nuclear annihilation, does he not think the Israelis would respond? He must be an idiot," exclaimed Benson.

Smith smiled slightly and answered, "No Mr. President, not an idiot, but possibly insane. Lebedov apparently believes, by the time he issues his ultimatum to Israel on Friday, they won't have time to retarget their missiles."

Benson sighed, "Well, as I said before, we need to warn them to give them time to retarget their missiles and let them convince the Russian leader his country is risking suicide to attack."

Benson rubbed his chin, paused for a few seconds, looked into the director's eyes, and asked, "What about long-term? Assuming the megalomaniac can be convinced not to attack Israel with nuclear weapons, I still see this confrontation spiraling out of control."

The director shook his head before answering, "The Russian colonel also expressed similar reservations but indicated he was working on a solution of some sort. Short of threatening nuclear war, I don't see a lot of options at this point other than to let the colonel work out a plan. As you indicated in our cabinet meeting yesterday morning, we're already sending substantial military forces to the area should a military showdown occur between Russia and Israel."

"Who is this Russian colonel, Bill?" asked Benson, "Can we trust him? I mean, my gosh Bill, this guy has admitted a key role in killing millions of fellow citizens."

Smith replied, "We don't know for sure who he is. Possibly his name is Ivan Litinov, who has worked in special operations before. We just don't know, at this point, if Litinov had become that closely associated with Lebedov. Whoever he is, he has confirmed a lot about what we've suspected over the last several weeks, and the information he divulged is probably the best verification of whom he claims to be. As to whether or not we can trust him, I don't think we have much choice. There are no other options."

Chapter 78

What to do about Litinov? The Russian leader was mentally tying up loose ends, halfway between consciousness and sleep, while lying under his down-filled duvet. He had already ordered the termination of the only other six people who were privy to Russia's involvement in the nuclear horror unleashed on America, including the chief of the Russian general staff. Litinov was the only knowledgeable Russian participant remaining. Lebedov, however, still needed the talented colonel's services a little longer.

Lebedov knew his Chinese counterpart was doing the same thing in China, ensuring the world would never know how the Islamic extremists got hold of the weapons they used against the United States.

The one outstanding risk, other than Litinov, was the extremist leader Al Zouri, and Lebedov had initiated steps to eliminate that risk. Lebedov, as blinded by ambition as he was, realized the Russian public would rebel against his leadership if they knew he was responsible for the slaughter of millions of Americans in an unprovoked, surprise attack. They could justify, though never excuse, such behavior by blinded religious fanatics but would never accept their own country's involvement in such an atrocity.

As long as the Russian population remained ignorant, he was confident they would support forcing the Israelis to withdraw from the Arab countries.

Russia, since the fall of Communism three decades earlier, had developed enough of an informed and independent citizenry that public perceptions had to be taken into account, much more so than before. That would change, in Lebedov's view, as he was able to consolidate power, eliminate all political rivals, and completely control the communication outlets in the country. Such was not fully the case yet, however, so he still had to play his hand carefully.

If only the damned Jews had not been so efficient. I'll take care of those little bastards next week. With that thought, the President of Russia fell into a fitful sleep.

Prime Minister Ben Gurion, slowly hung up the phone. He knew in his heart sooner or later his small country would have to confront the Russian menace. He did not imagine it would be of the nature he was facing now. He could not fathom any leader in the civilized world resorting to nuclear weapons as a policy other than a last-resort self-defense, yet this Russian megalomaniac had already used them on the United States and was set to use them to destroy Israel.

During the telephone conversation, President Benson was most supportive, which Ben Gurion genuinely appreciated, but it was also clear Benson expected Israel to attempt to solve this problem without the need for the United States to threaten Russia with nuclear annihilation.

Both Ben Gurion and Benson knew if it ever came to a total nuclear exchange, the civilized world would cease to exist. The American president did not want to ratchet the pressure up to that level, at least not yet.

The Israeli needed good counsel, and he needed it now. Despite the fact it was midnight in Israel, he did not have the time to wait until the morning. He picked up the phone and dialed his night-time switchboard operator and instructed her to make immediate contact with his national security team and have them in his office within the hour.

Chapter 79

The plan put together on the spur of the moment was simple. Seal team Bravo would establish a close-in perimeter and cover all exits from the hostel with snipers. At the same time, Seal team Alpha would assault the hostel itself, hopefully with enough surprise Al Zouri could be taken before he or the other terrorists could react. Three-dozen Israeli commandos would form an outer perimeter supported by Apache helicopters to prevent any reinforcements from attempting a rescue.

The members of both Seal teams realized the extremely high risk of the operation and had no illusions about the difficulty of capturing Al Zouri alive. In any event, Al Zouri would not escape.

The Blackhawks disgorged their passengers at pre-set locations without incident and flew off to remote holding positions a mile, or so, to the west.

The nine members of Seal team Alpha gained entrance to the hostel through the open front door, quickly and silently dispatched the unarmed night-desk clerk, and fanned out to check each room. The hostel was small, similar in size to an American bed and breakfast, so there weren't a lot of rooms to check.

At the end of a second-floor, dank corridor, leading from the front-lobby stairs, three members of team Alpha kicked in the door to the last room in the hall to be met by two Arabs reaching for AK-47s. Both were dead before they could shoulder the weapons. Three other Arabs exited out the single window in the room and dropped ten feet to the ground below.

Seal team Bravo, peering through night scopes, quickly identified Al Zouri and subsequently drilled holes in the foreheads of his two companions.

Al Zouri, suddenly by himself, not knowing who or what he faced in the dark, did the brave thing and threw his automatic weapon to the ground and raised both hands over his head.

Ten minutes later, a bound, gagged, and blindfolded Al Zouri was secured onboard a Blackhawk helicopter headed south. The five

Apaches waited five minutes for the Blackhawks to clear the area and then unleashed their arsenal of Hellfire missiles and destroyed the hostel and surrounding buildings before heading south themselves.

"By Friday lead elements from both columns will be in contact with each other in Basra," surmised General Meier. "Perhaps, even by Thursday night."

"Then what?" asked the Israeli prime minister.

Meier continued, "Within a few days we will have achieved a solid defensive line extending from Mount Herman in Lebanon, through Damascus, all the way to Baghdad. From Baghdad the line continues along the Euphrates in western Iraq, and the Tigris in the east, to Basra, then south along the coast as far as the Arab Emirates. Israeli paratroopers, earlier, captured intact all of the major oil fields along the coastline in Saudi Arabia, Kuwait, and Basra.

"As a result, we also have all of the oil we need to keep our mobile forces going."

"What about resistance?" inquired Ben Gurion.

"Well", replied, Meier, "After some tough fights early in the Golan, we have met little resistance. It seems the enemy troops have chosen to join the millions of refugees headed north to get away from the 'Jewish monsters' from Israel."

The prime minister asked, "And the Russians?"

The general responded, "Nothing so far, other than a couple of reconnaissance over-flights. Intelligence photos from our OFEQ satellite suggest Russia is massing troops, armor, and air assets in Armenia and Azerbaijan, along the northern Iranian border. They appear about ready to move south. To reach the battlefield, they would have to pass through several hundred kilometers of Iranian territory. I suspect the fanatics in Iran might not willingly allow the Russians to move into, or through, their territory even to attack their greatest enemy. As we discussed last week, strangely, we have not encountered any Iranian troops."

The emergency cabinet meeting had begun shortly after 1:00 a.m. in the prime minister's residence in Jerusalem, and General Meier, at Ben Gurion's request, had been briefing the cabinet on the status of the war and latest intelligence.

The prime minister added to Meier's last statement, "I suspect the Russians are also waiting to gain Security Council cover before committing forces. The Council is scheduled to meet tomorrow. Our

American friends are confident, however, the British will veto any force resolution coming out of the sham meeting.

"The Russians have continued to prevent the American delegation from being seated, which would, you would think, lead to the other participants recognizing they are being setup. But it appears the Russians have them all so intimidated, or perhaps fooled into believing their own importance, they will proceed anyway.

"At any rate, I didn't call you all together here just for a briefing from General Meier, as important as that might be. Earlier this evening, I received an extremely disturbing call from the new American president."

The meeting did not adjourn until dawn was breaking over the eastern Jerusalem skyline. Options across a broad spectrum were considered, ranging from a pullout of forces to a suggestion, from the Likud member of the cabinet, to launch a preemptive, nuclear strike on Russia. The latter option was not considered overly enthusiastically.

In the end, a sober decision was made to immediately retarget 340 nuclear warheads, 70 percent of the Israeli arsenal. The number 340 represented virtually every missile Israel had in its inventory capable of carrying nuclear warheads, including the Jericho II, III, and the newly enhanced Shavit ballistic missile. Every significant Russian city west of the Urals would be in range.

Additionally, it was decided Ben Gurion would telephone Lebedov, after the Russian issued his ultimatum on Friday, to convince him that European Russia would be destroyed if Russia carried through on his threat. It was decided to wait until after the ultimatum was issued to protect the identity of the Russian informant, whoever that might be. It was felt his obvious access to Lebedov would be critical in the future if this crisis began escalating even further toward a massive world-ending nuclear exchange.

Chapter 80

The third Wednesday in February was really cold and miserable in Moscow. The howling wind found every little crack in the building housing the United Nations Security Council, and cold drafts wafted through the ballroom as the Security Council convened once more.

The Russian UN ambassador was in the middle of his harangue against the "Zionist hordes who are murdering thousands of innocent Arab women and children". He stressed emphatically, "Russia demands the world community authorize the immediate use of force to stop this criminal genocide.

"The displaced Arab governments of Syria and Iraq have already begged for our intervention to stop this catastrophe from continuing, and Russia will be forced to respond with or without this body's authorization. Any more delay is unacceptable. I implore your support!"

The Russian was followed by the French ambassador who, though somewhat more civil, was equally adamant in his denunciation of Israel's aggression against the Arab countries.

China's ambassador followed and even put the Russian to shame with his demagoguery. Speakers from Indonesia, South Africa, Venezuela, and Germany, in turn, all condemned Israel.

Finally the British ambassador, Sir Thomas Stanwick, stood to address the Council. He had a visible scowl on his face as he began to speak. "All of the nations represented around this table have joined in a unanimous condemnation of Israel, and it's obvious you all are about to endorse the Russian desire to enter into this war. Well my fellow world citizens, it seems you've all forgotten the events leading up to this current conflagration.

"Have you forgotten the buildup of Russian military hardware in the countries bordering Israel prior to the outbreak of hostilities? Don't you find it curious America was attacked by terrorists headquartered in those same Arab countries just prior to the war? Was that just coincidental?

"What about the absence of American representatives in this meeting today? Don't you find it strange they continue to be absent from such important deliberations, particularly when they were so brazenly attacked three weeks ago?"

The ambassador paused and slowly rotated his stare around the table. "No, my colleagues. I doubt any of you have considered any of this. It would be a little inconvenient to the philosophy of appeasement you've all so readily embraced."

A few delegates, including the French representative, voiced objections to the British ambassador's last comment.

Stanwick waited several seconds for the commotion to quiet and then continued, "Great Britain is not about to allow the Middle East, with such importance to the future of Europe, to fall under the control of a new imperialist Russian. That would be a world with no future at all."

The room erupted into pandemonium. The meeting adjourned without a vote. It was apparent Great Britain would have vetoed any resolution to authorize force.

Lebedov was incensed when a colonel on the president's personal, military staff apprised him of the news. His calculation to prevent the Americans from voting had backfired on him. He thought, *The damn smug British, still casting their lot with the Americans. Can't they see the Americans are no longer the world's superpower? Russia will take its place in spite of British objections.*

The president considered for a moment and then issued orders to the colonel to find Colonel Litinov and have him report in four hours to Lebedov's secluded dacha thirty-five miles southeast from Moscow.

Lebedov recently preferred holding meetings with Litinov at the dacha to avoid interacting with the ass-kissing military types constantly present in the Kremlin. In the future, until he made a final decision relative to Litinov, meetings with him to discuss *Hammer and Anvil* would be at the private residence.

He thought to himself. *It's time to take decisive action. To hell with the United Nations and the British boot lickers*. He reached for the phone and dialed.

Chapter 81

"Are we sure it's Al Zouri?" asked a doubting President Benson.

"Fingerprints have confirmed it," replied Director Smith over the telephone.

"Where is he?" inquired Benson.

"We have him secured in Israel," stated Smith. "At this point, I think we should keep it quiet. I don't think the Russians need to know we've got him. I also think we'll be able to get more information out of him in Israel than if we bring him back to the States."

"Bill," Benson sternly admonished, "under no circumstances do I want Al Zouri tortured. Any information we get out of him under those conditions would be useless. If he identifies Russia as the supplier of the warheads his organization used to destroy twelve American cities, it needs to be volunteered to be credible to the American public and the world at large."

"Yes sir," replied Smith. "I fully understand your concern and will ensure we get the information we need in a way we can use it."

The president nodded and said, "Thank you. Keep me apprised of any breakthroughs with him."

"Will do, Mr. President," replied the director.

"Bill, since we now have Al Zouri in custody, what about the organization he headed?" Benson, almost as if thinking out loud, asked, "Have we got enough information to pinpoint their headquarters and major training camps? If possible to do without killing unacceptable numbers of noncombatants, I'd like to eliminate the organization forever."

Smith, comprehending what the president was considering, replied, "The Israeli military has already destroyed the headquarters of Black October. It simply doesn't exist anymore in Damascus. The training camps in the Beqa'a valley and Syria have also been pretty much destroyed. Individual terrorists have either joined the refugee exodus or have melted into the Lebanese and Syrian populations to fight another day. That's why we were so lucky to find Al Zouri where we did."

Benson, who had been contemplating a strike, in kind, as appropriate justice for the terrorists who had so callously attacked his country, was not overly disappointed. He knew launching even a small, tactical nuclear weapon against a camp now populated mostly by women, children, and old men would make him no better than the criminals he wanted to eliminate. After pausing, he replied, "Okay Bill, I certainly have no desire to simply lash out and kill a bunch of innocent people. I appreciate your good work in these tough times."

Smith replied, "Thank you Mr. President."

After hanging up the phone, Benson returned to the bedroom where he had been dozing when the phone had rung ten minutes earlier. He observed his sleeping wife's beautiful, translucent profile highlighted in the soft, filtered light coming through the shuttered window.

How does she handle this? he wondered, knowing her compassion and love toward him meant she felt all of his stresses and fears, only she would never allow him to know she felt them. The events of the past few months meant he rarely had time for her or their children, yet she understood and provided a bulwark, against which he could face and overcome just about anything. He was truly blessed.

Chapter 82

As Litinov approached the president's dacha on the winding, spruce-lined driveway, he was awed at the opulence. In contrast to the wooden vacation dachas many of the Russian middle class owned, this was a palace. The driveway itself was 250 meters long and led to a massive three-story, granite building, at least a block wide at the front. An immense solid-wood, double-door entry was framed on both sides with massive copper-plated pillars.

The entire fourteen-acre estate was heavily forested with spruce and pine trees and was completely surrounded by a twelve-foot, steel-reinforced-concrete wall topped with concertina wire. Litinov was sure out-of-sight security personnel manned strategic locations all along the wall.

Closed-circuit TV cameras were visible as Litinov's limo passed through the secured main gate. The colonel suspected the two cameras he observed were a small fraction of the electronic surveillance equipment deployed throughout the compound. He made a mental note of how formidable the president's dacha would be in defense against any attack, short of an all-out, armored assault.

As the limo approached the circular drive in front of the entrance, Litinov noticed the steamy breath of two warmly-dressed security guards awaiting the arrival of the limo. He was sure it was below zero. The car stopped immediately in front of the entry doors, and one of the guards opened the car door and stretched out his left hand to assist the colonel out of the rear passenger seat. As he exited, the guard saluted Litinov who returned the salute smartly.

The second guard had already opened one of the entry doors, and Litinov strode briskly through the open door glad to be out of the biting cold.

The inside of the dacha was astounding. A huge foyer, perhaps a thousand-square feet, extended upward a full three stories and was illuminated by six massive chandeliers strung on thirty-foot-long chains.

The stone and plaster walls gave the impression of great age, yet the dacha was built within the last twenty years.

A tall, scrawny, uniformed butler greeted the colonel at the door and ushered him through two lead-glass doors on the right leading to the president's office. He said, "Take a seat Colonel, the president will be down shortly."

Litinov was admiring the opulent décor in the room, when the same doors through which he had entered moments before opened again as the President of Russia entered the room.

Lebedov nodded as he walked by Litinov around to the back of the equally-lavish, mahogany desk, paused a moment, then sank down in a heavily-padded, leather chair. He motioned with his hand for Litinov, who had stood when the president entered, to sit.

"Colonel," began the president, "It's time to finish what we began a year ago. The toothless Security Council no longer has any value to us. I had hoped to have its authorization before we launched military operations, but the bastard from England blocked that.

"Earlier today I issued orders for our military forces to initiate actions leading to our eventual occupation of the Middle East oil fields. The unanticipated early success of the Israelis will not last and will not stop my plans. Colonel, I assume you have also begun the steps necessary to, once and for all, eliminate Israel from the need for further consideration?"

Litinov, knowing he had initiated actions himself, unknown to the president, which would have exactly the opposite effect, replied, "Yes, Mr. President, our country's nuclear forces are prepared to carry out your orders on Monday, should you issue them."

Lebedov, rubbing his chin for a moment as if considering what to say to the colonel, added, "Colonel, you need to know we've hit some unanticipated roadblocks. Iran, who had initially indicated a willingness to participate in the attack against Israel, didn't do so and is now refusing to grant us permission to enter their country. That means before the bulk of our forces can even reach the Israeli lines in Iraq and Saudi Arabia, we might be forced to fight our way through Iran. While my generals tell me we can defeat the Iranian Army within a week, it creates a delay, which will only allow the Jews to build up their defenses before we can engage them.

"Another even more problematic development is the movement of American military forces into the area. Four carrier battle groups have arrived in the immediate theatre, two in the Persian Gulf and two more in the eastern Mediterranean. A Russian convoy loaded with military equipment and troops is sailing from Novorossiysk within a few hours and will reach Syrian and Egyptian ports in a little more than three days. The American naval presence poses an unacceptable risk to that convoy. Without the ability to land those troops and supplies, the success of our entire operation is in jeopardy.

"Apparently the Americans have also sent substantial supplies to the Israelis over the past week, and our intelligence sources are reporting American troops, including two armored divisions, are disembarking in Israel."

Litinov attempting as best he could to control a "what'd you expect?" smirk from forming on his face, stated, "I thought the United States was out of the game. After all we just killed ten million American citizens to keep them from responding militarily."

Lebedov's eyes opened wide in anger as he stared directly at the colonel and answered, "Litinov, I will excuse your sarcasm since I'm sure you share my frustration with the evolving situation. But, don't press me again. My patience with you is not limitless."

The colonel thought, *Yes. I'll bet it's not limitless. When do you plan on having me killed too you merciless son of a bitch?*

"Colonel, I will make you this promise. The Americans will be forced to back down, or their whole country will end up like the twelve smoldering ruins with which they're already dealing."

Litinov simply stared at the president, boring incredulous holes in his forehead, astounded by Lebedov's loosening hold on reality. "Mr. President, I don't mean to sound insubordinate, but the Americans have the wherewithal to destroy every single Russian city."

"And so be it, if that's how this ends," replied Lebedov matter-of-factly.

Ivan Litinov, the Russian patriot, who allowed his dedication to duty justify playing a leading role in the deaths of millions, now knew what he had to do. His country could not be sacrificed to the nightmarish whims of an egotistical maniac.

The world seemed to be caught in a whirlpool, spiraling downward beyond control. The international press was full of dire headlines proclaiming World War III was imminent, demanding the United Nations do something. They seemed oblivious to the fact the only members of the United Nations with military forces sufficient to do anything were belligerents in the current crisis.

Yesterday in a nationally televised speech by President Benson, the United States had announced to the world American troops and equipment were disembarking in Israel to provide support in the looming confrontation with Russia. Four aircraft-carrier battle groups were on station in the area, and a fifth was en route. Hundreds of fighter jets were also on their way.

China, for the first time, publicly announced it had deployed over two hundred fifty thousand troops in western Russian including four armored divisions. The deployments were, ostensibly, to protect against sneak attack from the West while Russia was engaged in freeing the Arab countries from Israeli tyranny. The European news organizations dutifully reported the Chinese announcement, omitting the fact the deployments had begun six months earlier.

Most editorials in Western Europe were condemning Israel and America, questioning why America was supporting Israeli aggression. The American media, for the most part, cautiously supported the president. Two of the most influential, traditionally anti-war newspapers, the *New York Times* and the *Los Angeles Times,* had not published since the attacks on January 30. A few others, led by the *Denver Post,* were asking editorially why the United States was about to engage in another conflict when so many assets were needed to rebuild the savaged American cities?

The cable TV talk shows were rife with opinions concerning the world situation. A few conservative pundits were actually very close to the truth without knowing why.

The public at large was fearful the United States was headed into war with Russia with a very uncertain outcome. While a vocal minority believed Russia was behind the attacks on January 30 and demanded retribution, most Americans realized the very real consequences of nuclear war and were scared to death.

No government spokesman had yet made any sort of public announcement or leaked confidential information regarding the government's suspicions of Russia's involvement in the attacks on America. Without proof, such conjecture could generate too many unanswered questions and lead to accusations of government manipulation of information to justify another war in the Middle East.

This morning, Russia issued an ultimatum to Israel, broadcast by virtually all major news outlets across the globe, warning that Israel must withdraw immediately from all Arab territory it has conquered or face dire consequences. The world assumed that meant Russian military involvement in the war. Israel and the United States knew what the Russians really meant.

Chapter 83

It was a cold, blustery, Friday evening thirty-five miles southeast of Moscow. Anitoli Lebedov, dressed in blue, fleece warm-ups, woolen socks, and no shoes, was cat napping on his favorite recliner in front of a crackling fire when the scrawny butler gently shook his shoulder.

"Sir, I'm sorry to interrupt, but there's an urgent telephone call. I believe the operator said it was from the Israeli prime minister."

Lebedov, shaking the cobwebs out of his head, was surprised Israel was responding so quickly. He had anticipated, almost hoped, they would have called his bluff, and he would then be rid of them forever. An Israeli pullback, however, was still preferable and would make the final implementation of his plan much easier.

He ordered the butler to bring the phone to him. A moment later the butler handed Lebedov the portable and, without being told, excused himself and left the study.

Lebedov answered the phone and, in his most pleasant manner, asked, "Hello, Mr. Prime Minister, what can I do for you this evening?"

The tone of Lebedov's heavily accented English bordered on jovial. He felt almost like a lion licking his chops before dining on a downed wildebeest.

Ben Gurion's reply in near perfect Russian sobered the president immeasurably. "Mr. Lebedov, let me tell you what you can do for me in Russian so there will be no misunderstanding."

"Misunderstanding about what?" Lebedov plaintively asked.

The Israeli with rising anger in his voice answered, "Listen carefully. You need to know right from the start of this conflict we suspected you were behind it. The frenzied Russian build-up of war materials, the Chinese military deployments, your own troop movements, and, finally, the terrorist attacks on America with nuclear warheads, which, I'm convinced, were supplied by you, were all part of your evil scheme to control Middle East oil."

Angered, Lebedov replied, "What are you talking about, you ..."

Ben Gurion, oblivious to Lebedov's attempted interruption, continued, "This morning you threatened my country with dire consequences if we didn't withdraw immediately from the Arab territory we have occupied over the past two weeks. If you had in mind a nuclear strike on Israel, you need to know, because of our early suspicions, we have retargeted all of our nuclear-tipped ballistic missiles to hit every Russian city west of the Ural Mountains. Should we detect even one missile launch from Russia, we'll pull the trigger on 350 of our own. That, Mr. Lebedov, is what I don't want you to misunderstand."

The prime minister of Israel abruptly hung up the phone.

Lebedov's shock and anger muted his ability to hear the click on the other end of the phone line. "You little Jewish bastard! Are you threatening me? Let me tell you. I don't need to use nuclear weapons to wipe your pathetic little country off the face of the earth. Do you hear me? Hello? Hello? Are you still there?"

Slowly the realization sunk in he was raving into a disconnected telephone line, which made him even angrier. He savagely tossed the portable across the study shattering it on the opposite wall.

Even in the depths of rage, however, Lebedov knew he had been checked. The destruction of the state of Israel, as pleasurable as that might be, would not further his goal of replacing America as the world's superpower if Russia ceased to exist west of the Urals. He would have to defeat the Jews on the battlefield.

McNabb tiptoed carefully over the ice as he gingerly made his way to his car. Grocery shopping in Moscow was always an adventure, and this particular Saturday afternoon was no exception. He questioned why he volunteered to shop for his wife, but realized it was because he loved her and didn't want her to risk breaking her neck. Besides, she was busy packing for herself and the children. He looked up into the heavens as he thought, *Thank God, they are flying out of Russia tomorrow morning.*

As he cradled two full grocery sacks in his left arm, he attempted to unlock the passenger side door with his right hand. Before he could withdraw the key a powerful, meaty hand grabbed his right arm. Both grocery sacks tumbled to the icy pavement, shattering glass bottles and scattering groceries in every direction.

He turned to the right and looked into the rugged face of one of the burly Russians who had kidnapped him earlier in the week. Before he could react, the Russian said in broken English, "Sorry about the food. The colonel needs to see you now."

This time McNabb drove with the Russian sitting next to him in the passenger seat; no sacks, blindfolds, or constraints. The Russian didn't say anything other than to offer directions as they drove. McNabb wasn't overly concerned about a possible FSB tale. The Russian equivalent of the FBI had, long ago, ceased following him to the grocery store.

After leaving upscale neighborhoods where embassy personnel and expatriates lived, they passed through several miles of rundown apartment buildings, and entered a dilapidated industrial area.

After having driven about twenty-five minutes, the Russian told McNabb to turn into a narrow driveway on the east side of an old, rusted-metal warehouse. As they approached an eight-foot high, chain-link fence at the end of the driveway, McNabb noticed a steel door into the warehouse being held open by another burly-looking man. The American assumed the man at the door was the second Russian he had met, under different circumstances, earlier in the week.

McNabb braked to a stop, turned off the ignition, and exited quickly. He strode around the front of the Volga and, without hesitation, entered through the open door followed by both Russians. Once inside he stopped, not knowing where to go next in the dimly-lit warehouse.

One of the Russians, with a smile on his face, touched the top of McNabb's arm and motioned for him to follow. He led the CIA spy to a small office in the interior of the warehouse. It was the same office he had been in earlier in the week.

Colonel Litinov welcomed him, stating, "Mr. McNabb, good to see you again. Please take a seat."

McNabb couldn't help but contrast this visit with his last one. Then he was in fear of his life. Now he was full of anticipation. He replied, "Good to see you too, Colonel. I just hope my wife is as happy to see me tonight coming home late without any groceries."

The colonel shot a glance at his Russian "henchmen", and the one who had accompanied McNabb from the grocery store simply said, "My fault, I owe him some groceries."

The colonel began speaking, "Mr. McNabb, I …"

McNabb interrupted, "Please call me Tyler. Could I get your name?"

Litinov smiled and replied, "Tyler you're right. There's no need for any more secrecy. My name is Colonel Ivan Litinov. For the past year I have served the President of Russia as director of special operations.

"As I told you earlier in the week, I carried out my duty as a Russian officer, which has now led to a crisis I didn't anticipate or want. I can plainly see where this is leading and am determined to stop it before my country, and, perhaps, the world is destroyed.

"Two days ago, I met again with President Lebedov. Now more than ever, I'm convinced he won't stop his ego-driven ambition to control the Middle East and become the world's new superpower, even if that means he destroys the world in the process. Tyler, he must be stopped at all costs"

McNabb replied, "Colonel, what are you proposing?"

The colonel hesitated and then answered, "I struggle greatly with this because I don't want to be a traitor to Russia, but I fear I have no choice now. Before I lay out my plan, you must promise me, Tyler, when this is over I will be returned to my country to face my fellow countrymen for what I'm about to do."

McNabb hesitated, realizing the American government might not be inclined to release the person responsible for smuggling twelve thermonuclear warheads into the country that caused the death of millions of Americans. His hesitation evaporated, however, when he realized there just might not be an American government to make such a decision without the colonel's involvement.

He stated, "Colonel, you know I can't commit my government as I sit here now. You can be sure, however, I will communicate your desire to them when we're done here, and I'm sure they'll agree with what you want. After all, there are no other real alternatives are there?"

Litinov nodded and answered, "I guess not. I trust you to do what you say, so let me proceed…"

Chapter 84

As dawn broke on Monday, the stillness of the cold morning was shattered all along the Iranian-Armenian-Azerbaijani border. Russian artillery had opened up a devastating barrage on Iranian defenses, reminiscent of Soviet barrages in the Great War seven decades earlier.

Russia had, up until the last minute, alternatively plead with and threatened the Iranians to allow passage of its troops and armor to engage the Israelis. The absolute irony of the situation was astounding. The Iranians and Israelis had become unwitting, de facto allies against Russia. The fanatics in Tehran did not trust the infidel Russians any more than the despised Jews.

By noon columns of T-90s and BMP infantry fighting vehicles were pouring into Iranian territory followed by hundreds of troop-carrying trucks. In all, ninety thousand troops were engaged in the breakthrough along the border with the task of eliminating Iranian resistance quickly and opening a safe route south for another two hundred thirty thousand troops massed in the rear.

The Russian military objectives did not include capturing Tehran or other Iranian cities or overthrowing the government. It did include carving out a huge swath of Iranian territory in the west, including virtually all of Iran's oil production capacity along the border with Iraq and the Persian Gulf. If the Russians were successful, Iran's Islamic extremists would, overnight, become leaders of just another beggar nation in a world of haves and have-nots.

What the Russians and the rest of the world did not know was Iran had progressed faster than anyone suspected in the development of nuclear weapons. Iran had actually produced two relatively small twenty-kiloton weapons and had fitted the warheads to the top of two North Korean supplied Shahab 3 missiles with a three thousand-kilometer range. Originally targeted against Israel, with the onset of the Russian attack, technicians were busy retargeting a new enemy. Common sense didn't seem to be high on the agenda of Tehran's zealots.

The mood around the oblong table was somber. The president had just outlined the stark options facing the country in the Middle East.

Benson was aware of the muted criticism beginning to coalesce in the American media, particularly on the network-TV talk shows. He desperately wanted to share with the American public his convictions about the course he had set, but knew, without conclusive evidence, he could only communicate in platitudes.

Earlier his hopes had been bolstered by a call from his CIA director, who told him the CIA operative in Moscow had held a second discussion with the Russian colonel. The colonel had a plan, which might end the crisis, but the risks were so seemingly insurmountable the prospects for success seemed remote at best. In the absence of any better options, however, the president had authorized Smith to take whatever action was necessary to make the plan succeed.

Benson solicited discussion with a question, "So, any suggestions or discussion on what I just outlined?"

The silence was deafening. Finally General Taylor, seldom at a loss for words, spoke, "Mr. President, I agree with you fully. We have two options; one to back down and the second to ratchet up the pressure. Nobody in this room would seriously entertain the first option, so we don't really have a choice. With the Russian invasion of Iran this morning, our options are down to one. I'm prepared upon your order to enforce a naval blockade in the eastern Mediterranean."

All six people in the room understood such action would mean, in all probability, within days the United States and Russia would be engaged in a shooting war. Each face registered the fear of the eventual consequences but also the determination to stay the course.

Benson stared straight ahead for a moment then looked directly at the general. "General, this evening I will announce that, as of midnight tonight, there will be a complete naval quarantine in the eastern Mediterranean. No ships of any country carrying military supplies or troops will be allowed to unload in ports in Egypt, Lebanon, or Syria. Your orders are to position warships as appropriate and initiate the embargo as of midnight, mountain standard time. I assume General you now have sufficient assets in the area to enforce the order?"

Taylor somberly replied, “Yes Mr. President. The USS Carl Vinson has just transited the Suez Canal and entered the eastern Mediterranean. We now have three battle groups, totaling fifty-five ships with 250 aircraft, in the area. Another three hundred jets are deployed in Israel and ready to fly, if needed.”

Benson slowly glanced upward, looking at the ceiling as if searching for some other answer there, and then, slowly scanning the other four faces, sighed, “We’ve certainly set the stage now haven’t we? May God bless us. Thank you all.”

Chapter 85

"The Americans have asked for our help to complete this mission. The risks are enormous. There is no way to minimize them, Colby. But the risks of failure are even worse," warned Colonel Dylan as he explained the mission upon which Engeman was about to embark.

Any good mission planner tries to cover gaps; areas where a plan can come apart. Contingencies in case this aspect or that goes awry are part of any good plan. The number of gaps, and the lack of contingencies with what the Americans were proposing were profoundly shocking.

As Dylan explained, Engeman was going to travel to Moscow under an assumed identity as an English physician. Once there, working through contacts within the Israeli spy network, he would rendezvous with a CIA officer named Tyler McNabb.

The two of them would be responsible for coordinating the assassination of the President of Russia and the subsequent defection of the director of special operations in Russia, a Colonel Ivan Litinov. It was a simple operation—the elimination of the president of the second most powerful nation in the world.

As explained by the Mossad colonel, Litinov would actually carry out the assassination. Engeman and McNabb's task would be to safely escort the Colonel out of the country, while the entire Russian internal security apparatus was looking for them.

Since the boiling crisis this mission was supposed to end was already boiling over, time was of the essence. Engeman was already scheduled on an Aeroflot plane out of Turkey tonight. He had ninety minutes to pack his gear and clothing, get to the Tel Aviv airport, and catch an early enough flight to make the connection in Istanbul. As he dashed out to his car, he wondered, W*hat am I going to tell my wife*? knowing full well it could be the last time he would ever see her.

Tyler McNabb, the American consular officer stationed in Moscow, sitting alone in a small diner a block from the embassy, contemplated the future; perhaps fretted over it was a better description. Too young to have experienced the stress older Americans routinely felt in the sixties and seventies, when one world crisis or another threatened to escalate into a nuclear confrontation with the Soviet Union, he was now full of an incomprehensible dread. His only solace was the knowledge his wife and children were out of Russia, even now on a United flight from Germany to the United States. Even that was not much of a relief, considering where this all could eventually end.

The improbable mission before him was likely the last chance the world had to avoid a cataclysm not seen in seventy million years. Back then, another worldwide catastrophe ended the reign of the dinosaurs and nearly exterminated life on earth.

Was he overstating the case? He hoped so. The gnawing in his gut and a palpable, unquenchable fear told him otherwise.

As he toyed with a plateful of mostly-uneaten goulash with his fork, he mentally plotted the rest of the evening. Between now and nine, when he would rendezvous with Dimitri and Nicolai, Litinov's two loyal kidnappers, he had to lose the sporadic tail the Russian security apparatus had assigned to him. That would not be overly difficult. The goons had become sloppy in their technique over the months of what had become a routine assignment.

He would accompany Dimitri and Nicolai to another remote location in the Moscow suburbs where he was to be introduced to a Mossad agent named Engeman.

Later in the evening or early morning, all four of them would connect with Litinov to plan the details of the mission impossible.

Dread or not, McNabb was a professional and a patriot. He would do whatever it took to complete this mission, even at the cost of his life. He plunked down sufficient rubles, took one last swig of the bottled Coke, and walked out into the darkness of the cold night.

Chapter 86

On TV screens all over the country, Americans observed a stern-faced president approach the podium emblazoned with the American eagle war bird across the front.

Never had the new president looked so somber, yet his eyes, as he bored straight into the camera, were hard. He began, "My fellow Americans, I have again requested some of your valuable time this evening to keep you informed of the continuing crisis we face in the world tonight.

"Early this morning, Russian military forces invaded Iran and have made substantial territorial gains already. While our country has no love for Iran's extremist leadership, we deplore the suffering of its people caused by Russia's aggression. Our primary concern is not just the fact Russian troops have invaded another country but of what their ultimate intent is.

"We're convinced the leadership of Russia has embarked on a course in the Middle East that, if unchecked, will lead to Russian control of virtually all of the area's oil production capacity. We believe their claimed desire to repel Israeli aggression is simply a subterfuge to become the world's next superpower.

"Some Americans have questioned why the United States is becoming involved in this crisis in the Middle East, when we have such a huge, overwhelming task ahead of us to recover from the terrorist attacks of January 30. It's precisely because of those attacks we must get involved. To do otherwise would justify the attacks in the eyes of the perpetrators.

"Are we 100 percent certain who was behind the attacks? Not yet; but let me present some startling coincidences that, when taken as a whole, paint a nearly complete picture of why we face this crisis now.

"Over the past several months, hundreds of thousands of Chinese troops were deployed in western Russia. — Was it just coincidence, during that same time, Israel's neighbors were supplied with millions of tons of the latest Russian military hardware? — Was it just coincidence, just prior to the nuclear attacks on our cities, Egypt, Syria, Saudi Arabian and Iraq deployed hundreds of thousands of troops on Israel's borders in offensive formations prepared to strike? — Was it just coincidence Black October carried out its inhumane strike on America on January 30? — Is it just coincidence the American ambassador to the United Nations has not been allowed to take his seat at the UN Security Council table in Moscow? — And, finally, is it just coincidence Russia is demanding UN authorization to deploy huge military forces into the Middle East for the first time in history?

"My fellow citizens, I'm convinced all these coincidences are actually part of a plan—a horrible, evil plan—to bring the civilized world under the yoke of tyranny on a scale never before seen.

"Some might ask me if I'm prepared to take America to war over a set of suppositions. My answer is an unequivocal yes. To answer otherwise would be to bury my head in the sand as has happened in the past to the world's chagrin.

"It's with somberness and trepidation I make the following announcement to the world, keeping in mind it's still not too late for President Lebedov of Russia to steer another course. Effective at midnight tonight, four hours from now, the United States will impose a naval blockade in the eastern Mediterranean preventing ships of any nation from delivering war materials and troops to Syria, Lebanon and Egypt.

"May God bless America. Thank you for listening."

The dacha's normally serene location did not provide any solace for Lebedov's troubled soul as the distant sun rose over the forested landscape. At every turn, more roadblocks appeared on the route to his vision for the new world.

Even though the operation in Iran was progressing as expected, the American president's announcement last night was particularly sobering. It meant deploying military forces through the Mediterranean shipping lanes was not possible without initiating a conflict with the United States. Lebedov wondered how he could have misjudged the Americans so totally.

If the Americans could ever prove conclusively he had furnished the warheads that destroyed the country's greatest cities, he feared what the reaction might be. Lebedov mused, *Litinov was right when he quoted Yamamato. 'I have only awakened a sleeping giant and filled her with a terrible resolve.' Today I must eliminate the last risk the Americans will ever know for sure.*

Chapter 87

Meanwhile in Tehran, the mullahs who ran the country had reached an ominous, though suicidal decision. With Russian troops pouring into their country, virtually slicing off the western quarter of Iran with all of its oil wealth, the fanatics had decided, with nothing to lose, to launch both nuclear tipped missiles. One was targeted on Russian troop concentrations just north of the Iranian border. The second was aimed at the southern Russian city of *Volgograd*, the scene so many years ago of the bloody battle of Stalingrad that proved the beginning of the end of another of history's tyrants.

The order was relayed to Iran's fledgling strategic nuclear command and within twenty minutes two bulbous-nosed, Shahab 3 ballistic missiles were arching skyward, from a previously unknown location, on a expanding base of billowing white smoke.

Eight minutes later, a huge mushroom fireball rose into the clear, cold sky in southern Azerbaijan, obliterating thousands of tanks, armored personnel carriers, mobile artillery, and tens of thousands of troops all staged and waiting for the orders to move south.

Ten minutes after that, a second fireball erupted one thousand feet over the center of the city of *Volgograd*, incinerating thousands of Russians going about their business in the middle of a cold, February workday.

Word reached the Russian president about a half-hour later. Two nuclear explosions had occurred. Early reports indicated the center of *Volgograd* had been destroyed with the loss of tens of thousands of citizens. Even more disconcerting to the Russian leader, however, was the news the most part of two armored divisions, waiting to move south through Iran, had been destroyed. *How ironic*, he thought to himself in a surprising moment of lucid thinking in spite of his uncontrollable anger, *the Iranians have done this to me. Russia helped them build their nuclear weapons!*

His plan to attack the Israelis was in shambles; his available forces now severely depleted. The long-term goal of controlling the Middle East oil reserves was now in great jeopardy as well. His only real alternative now was to defeat the American naval blockade, which could lead to all-out war.

Iran would pay regardless. Lebedov picked up the telephone to make a quick call to the Russian defense minister. Both the president and the defense minister possessed black briefcases containing launch codes and necessary information to launch nuclear missiles. The briefcase called the *Cheget* was the Russian equivalent of the American president's Football.

Within ten hours Tehran, twenty-four other major Iranian cities, and Iran's nuclear reactors and research facilities were nothing more than vast smoking wastelands. The mullahs in Tehran, in their extremist wisdom had just committed, along with millions of unwitting fellow citizens, national suicide. The Israeli plan to destroy Iran's nuclear capability had just been made superfluous.

The cat was now out of the bag. A nuclear exchange had occurred. The world waited, knowing the next exchange would be its last.

Chapter 88

Engeman had arrived at Sheremtevo International as expected the previous night and had been met by two Russians, one a real physician and the second a make-believe one. Introductions were formal, and appropriate medical terminology was used in case the conversations were overheard. Predetermined code words were also uttered during the introductions.

They subsequently rendezvoused with American CIA officer, Tyler McNabb, and two more Russians whom the American introduced as Dimitri and Nicolai.

Early the next morning, the CIA man, his two Russian friends, and Engeman drove to a rusty-steel warehouse in a rather decrepit section of Moscow, where Engeman met Colonel Ivan Litinov.

The plans discussed during the meeting were originally to be executed later in the day, but the awful events of the day in *Volgograd* and Azerbaijan changed the timing. A second meeting with the colonel was scheduled in the evening to initiate actions the following day. Events were cascading totally out of control. It had to bc tomorrow, or it would be too late.

Late in the day, the President of Russia asked for Russian national TV exposure to address the nation about the attack on *Volgograd* and Russian troops in Azerbaijan. His message was vintage Russian propaganda. He claimed Russian motives in attacking Iran were pure, simply to ensure safe passage of troops to the south, but Iran reacted insanely.

He did not attempt to justify the extreme overkill of Russia's retaliatory strike on Iran that repulsed much of the world and a considerable number of Russians. Many were beginning to openly question Lebedov's explanations of Russia's involvement in the Middle East war; a few actually wondering if Lebedov was behind the whole thing.

What really ratcheted up the concern, however, was the bombshell he dropped at the conclusion of the speech. After claiming blamelessness for all that was happening, he stated in an almost off-the-cuff manner, “A convoy of thirty troop ships and cargo vessels has sailed from the Black Sea port of Novorossiysk, protected by twenty-five warships. The destination is Cairo, Egypt and Latakia, Syria. Any attempt by the United States to stop or interfere in any way with the ships in the convoy will be resisted with force. The United States cannot dictate any longer to the world. War between our two nations is now in America’s hands.”

Litinov was scheduled to meet with Lebedov the next morning at 10:00. The colonel and his co-conspirators knew what they had planned had to be done then or never.

This evening’s meeting, the last to ever be held in the old warehouse office, was a gloomy affair. None of the participants held out much hope of success but knew the attempt must be made.

Litinov rehashed the original plan and updated it as needed. He said, “As I indicated yesterday the key to success is to get this done quickly and leave the dacha immediately, thereafter. My meeting with Lebedov is at 10:00 tomorrow. I don’t anticipate I will be searched for weapons or a microphone, since that has never happened.

“I normally carry a Makarov 9 mm pistol and have fitted a silencer to it. I also had my holster modified to handle the silencer, and I don’t think it will be noticed. Since Lebedov and I are the only two still alive who know about the nuclear bombs, I’m sure we will be alone.

“After I have killed him, I will try to find the *Hammer and Anvil* operations manual, if it still exists, but will not be able to search for long. Our only hope to survive this is to get far away from the Dacha as fast as possible. I should be able to leave the Dacha without any problems and drive out to the main gate. I have never been questioned or stopped before.

“Once his body is discovered, the entire security system in Russia will be mobilized to find me. If you two are not able to get me out of the country alive, then killing Lebedov will be for naught. I’m confident the Russian people will believe me if your countries can give me the opportunity to speak to the world’s news organizations. If we fail, the generals who will control Russia will proceed with the war and wherever that leads.”

Engeman spoke first, “Colonel, we’re as ready as we can be. Our network in Russia is extensive, much more so than you can imagine. We have transportation and interim safe houses set up all the way to St. Petersburg.”

"Safe houses are useless. If we have to spend one night in a safe house we'll be too late," interjected Litinov.

Engeman replied, "I realize that Colonel. The houses will only be used as safe places to exchange cars."

McNabb chimed in, "Once in St. Petersburg, our CIA assets will take charge. They have arranged for a helicopter pick-up and transfer to a sub in the Baltic Sea."

Litinov smiled at the two spooks and, in a somewhat exasperated tone, replied, "It all sounds so easy."

He looked at McNabb. "Tyler, is the microphone ready to go?"

McNabb replied, "Yes, Colonel. The latest stuff and all ready to go."

The colonel continued, "Alright. Dimitri and Nicolai will meet you tomorrow at 7:00 a.m. Plan on arriving at our rendezvous point near the Dacha at 9:15 where you can wire me up, Tyler. If by some small chance you're stopped in route, Dimitri or Nicolai can do the talking. As you might say in either of your countries, God be with you."

Chapter 89

Governments and media outlets throughout the world were calculating zero hour; the moment when American warships would confront the Russian ships. Depending on when exactly the Russian convoy got underway and who was doing the calculating, the most optimistic forecast was no more than forty-eight hours of world peace remained. Some even predicted the crisis would occur in less than a day, but that would require the Russian ships to sail at impossible speed.

In any case, the world was holding its collective breath, not seeing any way out of the looming war, and fearing the possibility of an ensuing Armageddon.

The American and Russian embassies in both host countries were busy shredding documents and cleaning out desks in preparation for imminent evacuations. The winds of war were swirling, and the world was braced.

A day and a half earlier, it had been relatively easy to disappear into the Moscow landscape. Now the Russians would be alerted, since McNabb had not shown up yesterday at the U.S. Embassy. He knew instinctively they would suspect something wasn't right.

It wouldn't take a genius to connect the dots to McNabb, once Lebedov's body was discovered. He only hoped he and Engeman could facilitate Litinov's appearance before the world's press, before the Russians concluded America was behind the assassination. That could be a trigger for nuclear war by itself.

He and Engeman ate breakfast together, a rather bland combination of eggs and ham. Little conversation occurred. Both were deeply immersed in private thoughts, perhaps the last time either would have the luxury to do so. McNabb and Engeman had instantly bonded with each other, both coming from professional backgrounds, Americans by birth, and family men in a profession where such values are rare.

After tipping the maid—they assumed she was a maid, but then who knew for sure, since they had spent the night in one of the Israeli safe houses on the outskirts of Moscow—they returned to their small bedrooms to brush their teeth and collect their gear.

Each would carry 9 mm Makarov pistols with three clips and silencers. Litinov furnished the pistols the night before. Use of the handguns would only be a last resort and would probably mean the mission had failed.

Precisely at 7:00 a.m. the two spies met Dimitri and Nicholai at a parking garage next to a large strip mall, which was becoming a more common feature in the Moscow landscape. Dimitri quickly changed the license plates on McNabb's Volga, and all four men piled into a similar looking Volga driven by Nicolai. It seemed most cars in Russia looked alike.

McNabb would never drive his Volga again, and it was hoped the new license plates would delay quick identification.

The drive to the rendezvous point near the dacha was uneventful. They passed through *Bronnitsy* and *Khorlovo* en route south, roughly following the *Moskva* River. Not much traffic was on the road, the weather was cold but clear, and the road itself was not icy. While en route, they passed a couple of local police cars parked on the side of the road, but neither made any attempt to stop them. The cops were apparently looking for speeders, a somewhat unusual activity for cops in metro Moscow.

Five minutes before the scheduled meeting time, while parked in a secluded area surrounded by spruce 150 yards off of the pavement, the four conspirators heard a vehicle approaching on the dirt road leading from the highway. They breathed a collective sigh of relief, as the colonel's sun-illuminated, broad face could be seen through the front windshield of the approaching sedan.

All four men exited the Volga and greeted Litinov with hugs and kisses on both cheeks.

Twenty minutes later, McNabb had covertly wired Litinov for his upcoming meeting with the Russian president. The CIA officer recognized the risk with the microphone, but both he and Litinov felt it was important to record his conversations with Lebedov. The recorded conversation could prove to be invaluable verification of Litinov's story.

At 9:45 Litinov slid behind the wheel of his black sedan, nodded to the two intelligence officers and his burly Russian colleagues, and drove through the trees back down the dirt road. It would take him about five minutes to arrive at the dacha front gate.

According to the plan, McNabb was to monitor Litinov's conversation with Lebedov from this location, since it was well within range and totally secluded. Once Litinov had finished his business with the Russian president, they would wait for him to arrive, camouflage his car, and all five would leave in Nicolai's vehicle.

Litinov arrived at the main security gate and was stopped by two Russian military guards, each armed with Kalashnikov, automatic rifles. A third uniformed guard was standing inside of the guardhouse, adjacent to the automatic gate. The colonel displayed his credentials to the guard on the driver's side of the car who looked up and nodded to his comrade in the guardhouse. The electric gate slowly swung open.

He drove up the long, winding drive and parked in front of the dacha's immense front doors. He noticed two more armed, uniformed guards standing at attention on both sides of the building's entrance. Neither guard made an effort to open Litinov's car door, as was normally the case. The colonel exited his car and walked toward the Dacha's entry. One of the guards reached for the door handle and opened the door for the colonel.

Once inside the foyer, surprisingly, Litinov was greeted by Lebedov himself. Litinov wondered where Lebedov's emaciated butler was. The Russian president ushered the colonel into the office where they had conducted business on previous occasions. Litinov marveled again at the luxurious décor. Lebedov uncharacteristically motioned for him to sit down before the president, himself, sat.

Lebedov said, "I appreciate your visit today, Colonel. Events in the world seem to be spiraling almost out of our control."

"They certainly do," replied Litinov.

The president, less than convincingly, stated, "Let me assure you, though, I'm still confident we're in control of our destiny, even now."

The colonel nodded his agreement, only thinking in totally different terms of what the president's own destiny was to be.

Lebedov continued, "As you know Colonel, within the next forty-eight hours our country will be facing a confrontation with the United States that could lead to a nuclear exchange between our two countries. While I certainly don't want that; after all, our own country would not survive such an attack, I will absolutely not back down to the Americans. If they still want to pursue war with Russia, even after experiencing first-hand the consequences of nuclear war, then they are more foolish than I could have ever anticipated."

Litinov, trying to draw out more specific information from the president, baited him. "As I said before, Mr. President, I thought that's why we furnished the warheads to the Arabs, so your plan would not lead to a confrontation with them."

Lebedov, displaying a flash of anger on his face, took Litinov's bait and replied in a controlled, though obviously irritated, manner, "Colonel, I warned you before not to press me on this. We were wrong in our judgment. I think we should have ensured more damage was done, particularly to their military infrastructure, but then it would have been very difficult to mask such an attack as terrorism.

"The Americans are foolish, but I don't believe they are willing to risk complete destruction in defense of the Jews."

Litinov couldn't believe what he was hearing. *Did Lebedov actually believe the United States was about to engage Russia in war simply to defend Israel?*

Lebedov continued, "The Americans already know I'm willing to use nuclear force. The former country of Iran is mute testimony of that. Let there be no mistake about this, however. I'm prepared to launch our strategic nuclear missile forces against the United States if they attempt to prevent us from reaching Egypt and Syria."

Litinov was dumbfounded, thinking, *Lebedov is willing to destroy the world if his grandiose ambitions are thwarted. He truly is insane.*

Lebedov reached down and pressed a small red button hidden from the view of anyone sitting to the outside of the desk.

"Now Colonel, I still have the support of the Russian people and will keep it as long as they don't know about our involvement with the Black October terrorist group."

The colonel, too late, recognized where the conversation was going and reached for his Makarov. Before he could draw, he felt a cold, steel gun barrel press into the back of his head. At the same time a muscular hand clamped down on his holster, preventing him from drawing his weapon.

The president, with a smirk on his face, said, "Nothing personal Litinov, but you're just one risk too many." He looked past the colonel's shocked face and ordered, "You know what to do. Get it done."

Chapter 90

The convoy, consisting of thirty, heavily-laden ships sailing southwest across the Black Sea, was scheduled to rendezvous with its Russian naval escort in less than an hour. The convoy had sailed eighteen hours earlier from the busy port of Novorossiysk, the largest Russian port on the Black Sea, after loading thousands of troops, hundreds of tanks, and tons of war supplies.

The naval escort, totaling twenty-five mostly ultra-modern warships, constructed during Russia's recent military expansion, had sailed from the Ukrainian port of Sevastopol. Once the rendezvous was completed, the lead ship in the convoy would reach the Bosporus five hours later.

The looming confrontation with the United States Navy would occur in less than two days.

"Oh shit! We've got a problem here," yelled McNabb to the three others standing outside the car. The two Russians were grabbing a smoke, and Engeman was relieving his bladder.

All three turned to the driver's side window where McNabb's contorted face was framed by a set of large earphones.

"Litinov's been arrested."

"What?" exclaimed all three in unison.

Engeman spoke first, "Can you tell where they're headed?"

Dimitri interrupted, "They'll go to Moscow. We've got to stop them here."

"What do you mean here?" asked McNabb incredulously.

Dimitri replied, "I mean the road leading from the dacha curves sharply just before reaching the dirt road upon which we're parked. We must block the road as they reach the turn and kill Litinov's guards before they can react. We must move now. We don't have time to wait."

Engeman volunteered, "Nicolai, you drive and block the car as it rounds the curve. Two of us will ambush them from the trees. Dimitri, you get the driver, and I will kill any remaining guards if there are more than one. Tyler, I think you need to keep listening to Litinov for any clues he can give us, at least up until the last few seconds. Agreed?"

McNabb nodded his head reluctantly.

The three outside quickly piled into the car. Nicolai turned the key and the cold engine sputtered and threatened not to start. He tried again, and the showpiece of Russian technology, finally, slowly turned over and began to whine sporadically. Nicolai waited twenty seconds to let the engine warm up, shifted into gear, and accelerated up the dirt road toward the paved highway.

McNabb, excitedly exclaimed, "We've got to hurry. They just got into Litinov's car. The colonel is driving. Based on what he has said, I think there are three guards."

Engeman cautioned the others, "We've got to make sure of our targets. The colonel must not be hit under any circumstances."

The three others had "no duh?" expressions on their faces.

Colonel Litinov kept talking, in spite of his captors' reluctance to talk back. He desperately wanted to give his co-conspirators as much information as he could, hoping it would be enough to save him and the mission. "Where are you taking me? Why does it take three of you to guard me, am I that dangerous? Which one of you gets to keep my car when we get to where we're going? I can't believe you're making me drive my own car to my execution. Did somebody cut out your tongues?"

The last remark drew a knock on the back of his head with a gun barrel, which caused him to pause for a few seconds.

As they exited the dacha estate through the secured gate and turned left, he began talking again, "Why did we turn north? Are we going to Moscow?"

Finally one of the guards in the back seat, who had heard enough, told Litinov in no uncertain terms, "One more comment Colonel, and I will put a bullet in the back of your head right now. It will be a shame to cause a mess in your car, but a mess is better than listening to your incessant drivel."

Not wanting to test the guard's resolve, Litinov kept his mouth shut.

After driving for a few minutes, the colonel recognized they were approaching the dirt road turnoff where they had set up earlier in the morning. He began braking, expecting if his four rescuers were going to attempt something, it would likely be here.

As he drove around the sharp corner he caught movement in his left peripheral vision as a black Volga suddenly shot across the road in front of his car. He buried the brake pedal as the car skidded to a halt. He braced himself on the steering wheel, while his three captors were thrown into the dashboard and back of the front seats.

As they tried to recover, looking forward toward the car blocking the road, shots exploded from the rear on both sides of the car causing Litinov to reflexively duck down toward his captor next to him. As he did so, a spray of crimson washed over him as blood and brain matter erupted from the occupant of the shotgun seat.

"Colonel, are you hit? Are you alright?" yelled Engeman through the shattered, side, front window. Litinov looked like a bloody mess, but slowly sat up, looked out the window at Engeman, and smiled, his white teeth in stark contrast to his bloody, red face. "I'm still alive, Colby."

Chapter 91

Extremes of emotions were raging inside the Russian president's mind as he sat relaxed on his favorite leather recliner in his study. On the one hand, he felt satisfaction at knowing Litinov's termination would almost eliminate any risk of Russian exposure in the terrorist attacks on America. On the other hand, the terrorist leader Al Zouri was probably still alive, though he had mysteriously dropped out of sight. Perhaps he had been killed during an Israeli strike against the terrorist bases in Lebanon, but the uncertainty was unnerving.

In spite of the Iranian nuclear attack on Russian troops in Azerbaijan, he still had close to fifty thousand troops approaching the Iranian / Iraqi border including one armored division and parts of a second. Coupled with a successful delivery of thousands of troops, tanks, planes, artillery, and heavy transports in Syria, within a week Russia would have more than sufficient forces to destroy or, at least, throw back the Israelis in Iraq and Saudi Arabia.

This optimistic scenario, however, was in serious jeopardy because of the damned Americans. He knew the Russian convoy did not have sufficient strength to force its way through the American blockade, and, if he could not land troops and equipment in Syria, *Hammer and Anvil* was doomed.

Lebedov had to force the Americans to withdraw. He would never concede he had overplayed his hand, even if it meant nuclear disaster. He had one option left, just short of all out nuclear war. The three American aircraft carriers and support vessels in the eastern Mediterranean, as powerful as they were, could not survive even a limited nuclear attack.

He would warn the Americans first, give them thirty-six hours to withdraw, but would not back down if they refused. If they didn't withdraw, he would issue orders to destroy the fleet.

Lebedov picked up the telephone on the end table beside his leather chair. He first dialed his defense minister who answered the dedicated direct line after three rings, "Hello, Mr. President, this is Defense Minister Yakov."

"Mr. Yakov, after careful consideration of the situation, I have made a decision we must implement forthwith to protect Russia's interests in the current Middle East crisis."

"What might that be, President Lebedov?"

"I'm about to telephone the American president on the hot-line and inform him if the American fleet in the Mediterranean doesn't withdraw within thirty-six hours, Russia will use nuclear weapons to destroy it."

The defense minister did not respond for several seconds. Finally, in spite of every effort to control it, his voice trembled in reply. "Don't you think the Americans will respond in kind? It could be a catastrophe for our country."

Lebedov sarcastically answered, "What have I got surrounding me, a cadre of cowards? No. I don't think the Americans will respond in kind. They aren't stupid. They will not risk the destruction of three carrier battle groups, nor launch a nuclear war they can't win to save the Jews. Do not question my judgment, Yakov. Just do what I say. Have a plan ready for my approval by 5:00 p.m. that will ensure the destruction of all three battle groups. We must be prepared to launch the attack not more than thirty-six hours from now. Is that clear?"

"Yes, Mr. President," Yakov meekly replied.

"One final thing," Lebedov added almost as if an afterthought. "You, and the Russian general staff, need to meet with me this afternoon at five at the Dacha. Bring your plans with you."

The president hung up without waiting for an answer.

He immediately dialed a second number. After waiting a couple of minutes for the general's aide to ring the call through, the newly appointed chief of staff answered the phone. Lebedov briefed the general on his plans. The general, who replaced the recently arrested—and executed—former chief of staff, Yeremenko, was totally loyal to Lebedov, owing him his current position. He agreed to the president's orders to bypass the defense minister if he balked at authorizing a nuclear attack on the American carrier battle groups.

Next, Lebedov picked up the red telephone and pushed the red button on the receiver, which automatically dialed the President of the United States.

Night had fully embraced the city of Denver when the red phone, the famous hot-line link between Russia and America established fifty years earlier after the Cuban missile crises, began ringing. The telephone link had actually been used only one time since the crisis in the Caribbean, during another crisis in 1967, when Israel was about to destroy the combined armies of Egypt, Jordan and Syria.

Benson, as was the norm recently, was working late in his office trying to catch up with piles of paperwork he never had time to review during the day. Due to having never used the phone, when it first rang he nonchalantly picked up the portable business telephone and heard nothing but a dial tone in his ear. He quickly turned and looked at the red phone, noticing a flashing amber button. In spite of a sudden dryness in his mouth, he picked up the receiver and crisply said, "Hello, this is President Benson."

On the other end of the connection, Lebedov greeted Benson in heavily accented English, "Hello, Mr. President, this is President Lebedov. Congratulations sir on your recent appointment to the presidency. It's so unfortunate it occurred due to such unpleasant circumstances."

Benson could not contain his contempt for Lebedov. "Cut the baloney Lebedov. I'm convinced you're the reason the 'unpleasant circumstances', as you put it, occurred in the first place."

"What are you saying Mr. Benson? Are you accusing Russia of having a role in the terrorist attack? I take personal offense at your accusation."

Benson's anger exploded and he continued on the attack. "I don't care if you take offence. Killing millions of innocent people in an unprovoked, surprise attack to further your ruthless ambition to take over the Middle East, places you ahead of Hitler, Ghengis Khan, and all the others as history's worst, most-ruthless despot. You are a malignant tumor to the world and should be removed like any other cancerous growth."

The pause in Lebedov's response evidenced his shock at Benson's accusations. Finally, he replied acidly, "Mr. Benson, you can't prove what you're saying. I'm sure of that. But listen carefully you Jew lover. I will not allow you to stop me. You have thirty-six hours to remove your ships from the eastern Mediterranean, or I will destroy them with nuclear weapons."

Benson replied with equal acidity, "You listen carefully, Lebedov. We will not withdraw one ship. A nuclear attack on our fleet will be the same as a nuclear attack on our country, and we will respond accordingly."

Benson slammed down the receiver, not wanting to listen to another insane word from the Russian tyrant. He looked upward to the darkened sky outside the window and uttered a plea, "Please God, if you are listening, help us out of this horrible mess."

Chapter 92

Halfway across the world, five other individuals were also hoping for any help they could find to get them out of a much smaller, but directly related, mess.

Litinov had cleaned up as best he could with the limited resources available. The five had decided they only had one alternative now, a direct approach to gain access to the dacha and finish what they started. Nicolai was the driver, Litinov the bait, and the other three were the shooters.

As they turned into the asphalt drive and approached the security gate, two uniformed guards greeted them with assault weapons aimed directly at the driver of the car. Nicolai slowly drove Litinov's car forward toward the gate with the window down as if to talk with the guard on the driver's side.

The guards were obviously confused and alerted since they had seen the same car exit just twenty minutes earlier with Litinov driving. This time Litinov was sitting in the front passenger seat. He had rolled his window down also.

The guard on the passenger side approached the Volga while the second guard stayed ten feet back covering the car with his AK-47. As the passenger-side guard peered into the window, his first and last vision was the barrel of a Makarov pointed at his head. The silenced shot caught him square in the left eye.

At the same time both rear doors opened, and Dimitri rolled out to the left and Engeman to the right, firing several shots, hitting the second guard multiple times in the chest and neck. Before the guard died, he squeezed off a three-round burst from his automatic rifle shattering the front window of Litinov's car.

McNabb, in the meantime, followed Engeman out of the car and with five quick strides entered the guard station. The third guard in the station was on the phone attempting to call in an alarm. He was stopped before he could utter a word by a bullet to his left temple.

An excited but inaudible muffled Russian voice was heard talking through the phone receiver. McNabb was about to hang it up when a bloodied hand grabbed it from him.

Litinov listened and said something in Russian over the phone. The conversation lasted about ten seconds and then Litinov hung up the receiver.

He looked at McNabb and said, "I told them we just shot a rabbit and called to make sure they didn't get alarmed."

"Did the other guy buy it?"

"He laughed, but I don't know if he bought my story. We've got to move quickly."

As the colonel and McNabb exited the guard station, they noticed Engeman and Dimitri leaning in the open driver's-side door. They rounded the front of the car and saw the object of their teammates' attention. Nicolai was slumped in the front seat, his unfocused eyes staring blankly upwards. A neat round hole an inch above his eye told them both he was dead. Blood was pooled under his head and was dripping off the front seat onto the floorboard.

Litinov, recognizing they did not have time to grieve, put his hand on Dimitri's shoulder and said in Russian, "I'm so sorry Dimitri. I know how much you loved your brother. I loved him too. But now we've got to finish this, for his sake."

"Dimitri looked up with eyes brimming with tears. All he could say was, "Okay."

Engeman and McNabb dragged the two guards around the back of the guard station into some heavy underbrush and hid them as best they could. Litinov entered the guard station and dragged the third guard to the same location.

Dimitri carried his brother to the rear of the Volga and placed him gently into the trunk.

Litinov drove, Dimitri was in shotgun, and Engeman and McNabb rode in the back. Litinov was reasonably certain the two guards who had greeted him earlier at the dacha were two of the three transporting him to Moscow. They were now dead. He hoped there were no others at the entrance to the dacha. His hope was fulfilled.

Litinov and Dimitri exited the car and approached the immense double doors. Engeman and McNabb stayed with the car.

The easiest option to gain entrance to the dacha was simply to ring the doorbell, which Litinov did. To their surprise, the door swung open, and the formerly missing butler was there to greet them. The look of shock on his face as he stared at the colonel didn't last long. Dimitri pumped a 9 mm round from his silenced pistol into the butler's right eye, and he crumpled to the marble floor with a thump.

Both strode quickly into the foyer, looked and listened for any movement or sound, and, when satisfied they were alone in the foyer, Litinov whispered to Dimitri to follow him. He figured Lebedov would be in his study, since it was still more than an hour before noon. He was not mistaken. As he and Dimitri approached the closed door, they could see a faint light underneath the door and could hear a muffled voice on the other side.

The colonel grasped the door handle and slowly turned it until the latch was free. He pushed slightly on the door and it slowly, quietly swung inwardly into the room.

Lebedov was standing over his desk with his back to the door, apparently about to complete a telephone conversation. Litinov heard the president angrily shout in broken English, "Mr. Benson, you can't prove what you're saying. I'm sure of that. But listen carefully you Jew lover. I will not allow you to stop me. You have thirty-six hours to remove your ships from the eastern Mediterranean, or I will destroy them with nuclear weapons."

Litinov watched as the president continued to listen for a few more seconds, the knuckles on his hand gripping the receiver going white as Lebedov squeezed harder and harder. The American president must have said something Lebedov didn't like, because he suddenly threw the phone receiver against the far wall, shattering the receiver. As he turned his face was bright red. Blood veins bulged at his temples. Lebedov looked up and, like a chameleon, the color in his face changed almost instantaneously to ashen white.

The president screamed, "Litinov! How can it be you? Why are you here?"

Both the colonel and Dimitri leveled their pistols at the president.

Litinov responded, "Lebedov, I don't know if I'll be able to stop the worldwide cataclysm from occurring that you've started, but I'm going to ensure you'll not live to see it."

Lebedov began to plead but had hardly uttered a word when bullets from both Makarovs slammed into his body. Lebedov was rocketed backwards onto his desk. Litinov walked up to the desk and stood over him. Lebedov looked into the colonel's face with glazed, pleading eyes. A final bullet from Litinov's pistol entered the nose and exited through the top of Lebedov's head, ruining the top of the beautiful, mahogany desk.

Litinov and Dimitri quickly searched through Lebedov's desk and file cabinets. One cabinet was still locked. Litinov blew off the lock with a bullet from his pistol, opened the drawer, and there it was, the operational plan for *Hammer and Anvil.*

He grabbed the manual, motioned for Dimitri to follow, and sprinted out of the study across the spacious great room into the foyer. They jumped over the prostrate body of the butler, ran through the open double doors, and slid through the open rear doors of the idling Volga. Litinov yelled, "Let's get out of here now!"

Engeman, who had shifted to the driver's seat, floored the accelerator and they shot down the long driveway. They stopped briefly at the front security gate so Dimitri could close it and then turned north on the highway toward Moscow.

A few minutes later, Engeman turned off the highway onto the dirt road and drove another hundred yards until they reached Nicolai's car. Litinov, McNabb, and Dimitri quickly got out of the car. Dimitri walked around to the trunk and gently removed Nicolai's body and placed it in the trunk of the second car. Engeman then drove Litinov's shot-up Volga to the right off the dirt road about thirty feet into a grove of trees. He piled brush haphazardly around the car to offer some camouflage and jogged back out to the dirt road.

Engeman climbed behind the wheel, Litinov slid into the passenger seat, and McNabb and Dimitri got into the backseat. Engeman turned the key in the ignition, and the engine cranked over a couple of times before idling smoothly. He shifted into gear, and the four conspirators headed north toward St. Petersburg on a 365-mile journey to save the world.

Chapter 93

Ninety minutes later, having not been able to make radio or telephone contact with guards at the main security gate to the dacha, two Russian soldiers and a leashed 120 pound German Shepherd cautiously approached the front gate. Utilizing a gravel path connecting all guard locations on the compound, the soldiers knew something was drastically wrong when the dog began whining uncontrollably. With AK-47s raised in firing position, the guards emerged from the tree-lined path ten yards from the gatehouse and slowly, carefully reconnoitered the area. After finding traces of blood but no guards, they followed the dog around to the rear of the station and discovered their three dead comrades.

The guard, without the dog, ran back to the guard station, picked up the emergency phone, and triggered a general alarm. Within eight minutes, a heavily armed, nine-man squad entered the dacha and found the butler's dead body on the foyer marble. Thirty seconds later, Lebedov's bullet-riddled body was discovered.

After having transferred to a second car in *Klin*, fifty miles north of Moscow, the four fugitives were breathing easier. The two-hour, seventy-five-mile drive to *Klin* had been uneventful. Possibly Lebedov's body had not yet been discovered, but they all knew such luck would not last.

Dimitri had left his brother's body at a safe house in *Klin* with promises it would be taken care of.

Fifteen minutes later the government radio station they were monitoring was interrupted by a special news bulletin. "The government has issued the following urgent message. A shooting has occurred near the president's dacha. There is no word on casualties, but the public should be assured, knowing President Lebedov is well and is now secured. The Russian security forces are looking for a person of extreme interest and need the public's help to find him. His name is Colonel Ivan Litinov. He is described as 183 centimeters tall, ninety-one kilos, muscular build, forty-four years old, with dark brown hair, graying at the temples. He has a heavy mustache and bushy eyebrows. He might be driving a black 2012 Volga sedan with Moscow license plate number 60871. Please tune to your local TV station. The colonel's photograph will be displayed every fifteen minutes."

McNabb spoke first. "Well, now it gets dicey. At least they haven't discovered your car yet Colonel."

"How long has he been out of contact?" asked General Cherlenko, the chief of Russia's military intelligence agency, the GRU.

The director of the FSB, Russia's equivalent of the FBI, and one of two agencies split off from the Soviet era KGB, answered, "We have not had contact with McNabb for almost four days."

"Don't you find it interesting he disappeared only three days before our president was assassinated?" inquired Cherlenko.

"Are you saying the Americans are behind the assassination?"

"No. I'm not saying that, at least not yet. I think it would be prudent, however, to broadcast his description with the colonel's. I assume you have issued an 'APB' with the local police throughout Russia?"

"General," a somewhat miffed FSB director replied, "We also know how to do our jobs."

Leaders of the GRU, FSB, and the SVR, Russian's foreign intelligence agency, had been meeting for the past thirty minutes at the "Aquarium", the headquarters for the GRU located outside of Moscow at the *Khodinka* Air field. None of the intelligence heads had any love for the dead president. His policies seemed to be leading the country toward a catastrophic war, and the primary motivation for each of them was consolidation of power and accumulation of wealth. A nuclear wasteland would provide neither.

The assassination, however, of the leader of their country, regardless of their personal feelings, could not be allowed to go unpunished or, at least, uninvestigated. All shared the fear of ignorance. Not knowing who or why left too many uncertainties. Colonel Litinov must be captured alive and questioned.

In the meantime, the huge Russian convoy was sailing toward the Bosporus strait and, unknown to the intelligence chiefs, the military was readying a nuclear attack on the American fleet.

The seven-hour drive from Klin to St. Petersburg, through the historic and picturesque cities of *Tver, Valdai, Novgorod,* and

Chudovo, was sketchy only because of icy roads in certain spots en route. At one point a few miles north of *Novgorod*, Engeman nearly lost control, taking a corner a little fast and losing the rear wheels on a patch of black ice. He recovered nicely, however, but not before the two in the back seat nearly lost it in their shorts.

It was early evening as they approached the St. Petersburg city limits. Engeman needed to locate the final safe house where they would hole-up for a couple of hours until nighttime darkness could mask their escape from the mainland by helicopter.

The black sedan was almost running on fumes, so Engeman pulled off the highway into a suburban petrol station. Litinov and McNabb both needed to relieve their bladders. They left the car and walked thirty yards to the single restroom. McNabb was in the lead. As they approached the putrid, filthy bathroom, a skinny Russian, who looked to be about thirty-five, exited the smelly hole and walked by them. A flicker of recognition flashed in his eyes as he passed Litinov.

The skinny man walked directly into the office, talked briefly with the proprietor, and was handed a telephone receiver. As he talked on the telephone, he glanced periodically out the window toward the restroom.

Dimitri, who was purchasing cokes and cookies, viewed the skinny Russian on the telephone and noticed him repeatedly looking over at the restroom where Litinov and McNabb had gone. He quickly paid for the food and gas and walked swiftly to the car. Litinov and McNabb returned a few seconds later and climbed into the back seat. Dimitri, with some urgency in his voice, stated, "Let's get out of here. I think we've been made."

For the past ten minutes the same set of headlights remained about fifty yards back regardless of Engeman's efforts to lose the car trailing them.

McNabb, worried about one set of headlights being joined soon by several more, stated what the others were thinking. "We need to eliminate the tail. We can't lose them, so we've got to kill them before they are joined by reinforcements. Colby, how far are we from the safe house?"

"I think we're now in *Kupchino*. As near as I can reckon, we're no more than a mile from it."

McNabb formulated a plan in his mind and said, "Slow down until they have closed the distance to several yards. Then stomp on the breaks, hit reverse, and slam into the front of their car. I remember watching demolition derbies when I was a kid. The winners invariably were the drivers who used the rear of their cars to ram the front of the opponents' cars. As soon as we've hit them Colonel, you, Dimitri, and I will jump out and kill the occupants. Then Colby, we'll need to book it to the safe house, because all hell will break loose out here."

Engeman slowed the sedan to a crawl causing traffic behind to slow and pull around them. More than one irate driver displayed the Russian equivalent of the bird finger. Their quarry closed to about ten yards when Engeman slammed on the brakes and immediately shifted into reverse. He punched the throttle, and the car accelerated backwards smashing into the tailing car before its driver could react.

The impact on both vehicles was severe but more so on the occupants of the trailing car, because they were not expecting the collision. As soon as the immediate shock of the crash was over, Dimitri, McNabb, and Litinov were out of the car firing 9 mm slugs into the following car, even as they approached it. There was no return fire.

Ten seconds later Engeman floored the accelerator, and the damaged, but still running, black sedan sped from the scene, leaving a crumpled, smoking hulk, the temporary tomb of two dead Russian FSB officers.

Chapter 94

The reaction was predictable. As in any law enforcement agency, once one of their own has been killed, the motivation to find the killers increases dramatically. The FSB was now focused on finding and killing Colonel Ivan Litinov and his three accomplices.

Multiple witnesses observed the carnage in *Kupchino*. Litinov was identified by at least one witness while illuminated in the FSB car's headlights. Others described two other shooters and a driver, though none could furnish anything other than general descriptions.

Local police were called in, scores of FSB officers were descending on St. Petersburg, and military resources were mobilized. Within two hours, over a thousand were on the hunt. The airport was blanketed, as were the train station and bus depots. Roadblocks were established on all highways leading to *Petrodvorets* to the west, *Chudovo* to the south, and all escape routes to the east and north.

The dragnet would find them. It was just a matter of tightening the noose.

When alerted, a Blackhawk helicopter would be dispatched from a U.S. Navy surface ship fifty miles northwest of St. Petersburg in the Gulf of Finland. It would land on a windswept, grassy field about three hundred yards in from the coast just north of *Ivanovka*, a town eight miles west of St. Petersburg. Timing had to be perfect. McNabb and Engeman both had radios tuned to the correct frequency to communicate with both the helicopter and a submarine lurking fifteen miles off the coast.

It was decided the chances to evade the dragnet would be increased if they split-up. Engeman and Dimitri would travel in one car. It was assumed their identities were not known, so the odds would be in their favor if stopped at a roadblock. Litinov gave Engeman the operations manual, figuring if he and McNabb were caught, at least Engeman would have the manual.

The colonel and McNabb would follow in a second car. If stopped and identified, they would attempt to shoot their way through the roadblock. It appeared no other options were open. The Russian convoy, even now entering the Mediterranean, did not allow further delay.

Thirty minutes past midnight, McNabb made radio contact with the submarine and informed them they were on their way and would attempt to rendezvous with the Blackhawk in one hour. Engeman and Dimitri left first followed thirty seconds later by Litinov and McNabb. Both cars were fresh. Driving a black sedan with a crumpled rear end would be a "come and get me" sign.

Dimitri navigated the way, working through several side streets, finally heading west on the highway to *Ivanovka*. Very little traffic was on the highway at this late hour. The drive was surprisingly smooth for the first several miles. Then, while still about a mile short of the pick-up point, the plan turned to muck.

Engeman and Dimitri crested a hill and observed flashing red lights a thousand yards down the road signifying a roadblock. A small string of taillights led back up the road from the roadblock. Dimitri, who was driving the car, felt their chances were good to make it through, but neither he nor Engeman believed Litinov and McNabb would be equally successful.

Engeman keyed his radio to talk with McNabb. After hearing his explanation of the situation, McNabb asked, "What do you suggest?"

Engeman, planning as he talked, said, "I believe Dimitri and I will make it through the roadblock. You'll be right behind us. Once we're through, the cops will be focused on your car and any cars behind you. We'll stop five yards past the roadblock and open fire on them. We should be able to kill several before they realize what's happening. You and Litinov wait until you see us start shooting and then join in yourselves. If there aren't too many of them, it might work."

McNabb looked over to Litinov in the passenger seat and briefed him on the plan. He nodded his approval. McNabb keyed his radio. "Okay, Colby, let's do it. I hope the man upstairs is watching over us tonight."

Four police cars were parked at the roadblock, two partially blocking the highway, leaving an opening big enough to allow one car through at a time. Eight men, all local police officers armed with automatic assault rifles, manned the roadblock. Any attempt to run through it would be suicidal.

Bright, almost-blinding, spotlights illuminated the eastern approach giving a clear field of fire to the officers positioned behind the cars and very poor visibility to those approaching from the east. Two officers questioned occupants of each vehicle stopped, while six others provided cover behind the cars.

Dimitri eased forward as the last car in front of him was waived through by one of the policemen. A burly, short officer, with a scowl etched on his face, approached Dimitri's open window. The second officer stood by Engeman's closed window and observed.

The burly officer gruffly asked, "Where are you going?"

Dimitri, nodding toward Engeman, answered, "I and my doctor friend here are headed to Petrodvorets to visit my mother. She is very sick and the doctor, who we got to know on a visit to England two years ago, was in St. Petersburg for a medical conference and agreed to examine her."

The policeman, not giving any indication whether or not he believed the story, asked, "Let me see your papers?"

Dimitri displayed his driver's license, and Engeman reached over and gave him his passport. He stared at the documents for a moment and grunted. Then he handed them both back to Dimitri and motioned for them to proceed.

Meanwhile, McNabb and Litinov hung back for just a moment to give Dimitri time to clear the roadblock. Then McNabb took his foot off the brake and allowed the sedan to slowly move forward.

The burly officer approached the vehicle. The unavoidably surprised expression on his face announced he had recognized Litinov.

At that instant exploding shots from in back of the roadblock caught both officers' attention for a moment, just long enough for Litinov and McNabb to dispatch them with shots to the sides of their heads.

The other six officers had turned and were attempting to defend themselves against the onslaught from the rear. Three were already dead. Automatic weapons fire shattered the dark night as the remaining officers sprayed randomly toward the flashes.

McNabb gunned the car through the opening and, once past the glare of the spotlights, both he and Litinov emptied their Makarovs into the hapless police officers. It was over in a matter of seconds.

They could see through the smoky darkness Dimitri and Engeman had not escaped unscathed. One was down on the ground and the other hunched over him. McNabb clicked on the high beams illuminating the scene. Dimitri stood up facing them.

"How bad is he?" yelled Litinov.

"I think he'll be alright," replied Dimitri. "He took one in the leg. I think it's broken. Our car is shot up pretty bad, though. I don't think it will go any further."

Litinov and Dimitri hefted the obviously hurting Engeman into the back seat of Litinov's car. McNabb slid into the other side, told Litinov to drive, and began to provide first aid to stop the bleeding. Dimitri barely got into the front passenger seat before Litinov accelerated the car east toward the pick-up point.

Fifteen minutes later the Volga was bumping over a rutted, dirt road leading to the rocky beach. They heard the beating rotors before they could make out the dim silhouette of the Blackhawk waiting like a giant grasshopper in the grassy field.

In two minutes all four were on board and the Blackhawk's blades began thumping faster as the bird slowly lifted off the ground. It dipped and turned north and headed out over the Gulf of Finland flying just off of the wave tops.

Chapter 95

The eight Mig 31 Foxhounds, dispatched fifteen minutes earlier from *Novgorod* Air Base, 150 miles southeast from St. Petersburg, were screaming northwest at mach 1.6 barely a mile above the wooded countryside. Common Russian citizens, unaware of the crucial events playing out nearby, were nearly shaken from their beds as sonic booms shattered the cold night.

The Russian pilots' orders were straightforward. Locate and destroy an American helicopter, which had taken off within the last five minutes from the southern shores of the Baltic Sea near *Ivanovka.* To motivate the fighter pilots even more, they were made privy to the information being withheld from the rest of the citizenry. The helicopter was carrying the assassin of the President of Russia. Additionally they were to attack any surface ships in the area, which might be supporting the Americans in their attempt to spirit the traitor out of Russia.

The Baltic Sea north of St. Petersburg was being monitored by a Russian A-50 AWACS system mounted on an Ilyushin-76 transport aircraft. The American Blackhawk's radar footprint, even though flying just above the waves, was already being tracked. As the fighter jets approached the coast, the squadron commander directed all eight jets to turn ten degrees to the north to approach the helicopter directly from the rear. In less than a minute the chopper would be in range.

"I've got a bunch of bogies coming in really fast from the south," screamed Colonel Joe Sylvester into his mike. Leading a small but potent force of five F-16 Fighting Falcons, Sylvester's mission was nothing less than saving the world. The F-16s had been thundering east just below the speed of sound for almost an hour. They had taken off from Orland Main Air Station, a NATO base located just west of Trondheim, Norway, with orders to ensure, at all costs, the successful extraction of a Russian colonel from Russia.

The Americans were flying high, almost thirty thousand feet, and were about thirty miles west of the bogies approaching at a right angle.

The focus of both fighter groups was plodding north just above the waves at about ninety knots. The future of civilization was riding on the outcome of this battle soon to be enjoined.

The Americans were already cleared all the way up to the Commander in Chief to engage any aircraft posing a threat to the helicopter. Eliminating the need for final authorization allowed Sylvester to order the squadron to attack the oncoming Migs without hesitation. One Falcon after another peeled off the formation and screamed downward toward the oncoming Russians.

The Russian commander saw radar blips at about the same time the F-16s began descending and ordered five of the Migs to break off and engage the Americans. The remaining three Foxhounds would concentrate on the Blackhawk.

The American colonel observed the Russian squadron splitting and calculated the smaller group would be going after the chopper. He split his group, sending three to face the oncoming Migs and two to attack the three Russians headed for the Blackhawk.

The Foxhounds were armed with *Vympel* R-33 air-to-air missiles with greater range but less speed than the American AMRAAM-Aim 120 D missiles. The Russians had the advantage in numbers, the Americans in training and tactics.

Benson was munching a Big Mac, brought to him by one of General Taylor's military aides. He, General Taylor, the CIA director, Treasury Secretary McClain, and Ambassador Simpson were ravenous, having not eaten since early morning. The five of them, and several other members of the military, had been holed up in the makeshift situation room at the Denver White House since 5:30 a.m.

As they were taking a short break to refuel, General Taylor received a call on his cell phone. His face paled as the conversation proceeded. The others in the room stopped eating and all stared expectantly at the general. He said, "Thank you" and slowly closed the cover of his phone. He looked up, obviously distraught, and said softly, "It's started."

The others almost in unison replied, "What's started?"

General Taylor looked from face to face before answering. "The skipper on the sub in the Gulf of Finland was just patched through and told me a massive dog fight is currently taking place between American and Russian fighter aircraft fifteen miles off the Russian coast. Apparently the Russians are attempting to take out the

Blackhawk carrying our Russian colonel, and our boys are trying to stop them."

The president, realizing the only chance to stop the momentum toward nuclear annihilation was now in critical jeopardy, asked, "What about the helicopter?"

"I don't know," replied Taylor. "Nobody on the sub has been able to establish a radio link with the chopper."

The Blackhawk pilot yelled over his shoulder to the four fugitives in the bay, "Get ready, you'll be jumping into the Baltic in less than thirty seconds." The four had donned U.S. Navy-issue wet suits and life jackets to keep them alive for the few minutes it would take for the sub to surface and retrieve them out of the frigid saltwater of the Baltic Sea. As they waited for the pilot's order to jump, they shivered as much from fear as the cold air rushing in from the wide-open, helicopter door.

The night sky above the helicopter resembled a Fourth of July fireworks show. Small flashes as missiles were launched were dwarfed by larger flashes as they found their targets. Trailing fire and smoke, missiles crisscrossed the sky.

Radar blip after blip disappeared off of the Russian commander's radar screen as missiles found their marks. The Russian jets, unfortunately, were also being decimated. After what seemed an eternity but was, in reality, less than five minutes, there were no blips left on his screen and no fighters, other than the commander's Mig, left in the air, American or Russian.

The commander took a deep breath, located the helicopter still ten miles in front of him, and proceeded to obtain a radar lock on the chopper. As he did so, he noticed the Blackhawk appeared to have slowed considerably and was turning toward the east. Once the radar lock was secure, he squeezed the trigger on his stick and launched the remaining two R-33 missiles. It would be over in a matter of seconds. Neither missile could miss at this range.

Litinov jumped into the blackness first, followed by Dimitri, McNabb, and Engeman. Even with the wetsuits, impacting the freezing water after a fifteen-foot drop sucked the breath out of each of them. Engeman winced as he hit the water, his broken leg taking too much of the impact.

As the Blackhawk veered away to the east, a sudden roar above drowned out the noise of the sea chop and helicopter blades, causing all four men to look up toward the chopper. As they did, the Blackhawk exploded in a huge fireball, momentarily illuminating the sea two hundred yards in every direction.

The Foxhound accelerated to just under mach one, headed south. The Russian commander radioed to his base at *Novgorod* and told them the helicopter was destroyed with no sign of survivors, and he did not see any American naval vessels. His satisfaction of completing his mission was tempered by the realization he had just lost seven of his comrades in the first battle of World War III.

Chapter 96

"How long before they arrive in London?"

An extremely relieved but tired CIA director answered the president with a brief description of the journey. "After being pulled half-frozen from the ocean, it took them about nine hours on the sub to reach Helsinki. There they transferred to a leased Bombardier Challenger business jet, which is scheduled to land at Heathrow in less than an hour."

Benson, almost as if talking to himself, replied, "It's 3:15 a.m. in Denver. The press conference is already set up at Heathrow airport. It should commence no later than 6:00 a.m. our time. That still gives us ten hours until the Russian ultimatum expires. God willing, Litinov's statement to the world press will end this madness."

The president paused then looked directly into the director's eyes. "Bill, if it doesn't, you need to know I've placed our strategic nuclear forces on DEFCON-1 alert. If our ships are attacked, I will respond with a massive nuclear attack on Russia."

Over ninety members of the international press were waiting in front of the hastily constructed, elevated stage at London's Heathrow International Airport, hoping to hear some news that might ease the gloom that had enveloped the world.

Just after noon, the large television screen flickered to life, and a hush quickly spread through the crowd. The now familiar face of the American president filled the screen, about to speak live from his Denver office. He began. "My fellow citizens of the world, three weeks ago my country was savagely attacked by terrorists using nuclear weapons in a display of brutality and callousness toward human life that will forever be viewed as the low mark of human depravity. Using nuclear weapons ensured the death of millions and suffering for countless others.

"We have been relentless in our effort to determine who was behind those attacks; who actually provided the warheads that killed so many. Today we now have irrefutable evidence the attacks were orchestrated, not by the terrorists who carried them out, but by the leader of a country we all considered as a trusted partner in our world community. The attacks were part of an ambitious scheme by a person so evil the dictators of the twentieth century pale in comparison.

"President Anitoli Lebedov, the leader of Russia, was the man behind this blood-soaked scheme. He entered into an alliance with the terrorist group Black October. With help from the Chinese, he supplied the terrorists with the warheads that destroyed twelve of America's cities.

"Even Alawai Al Zouri, the leader of Black October, didn't realize he was just a dupe. Lebedov used him, just as he had attempted to use the United Nations and the world's apathy, to gain control of the Middle East and become the world's preeminent power."

Benson stopped for a moment to allow the information to sink in, then continued, "What evidence do I have to make these accusations? One week ago an American Seal team backed by Israeli commandos captured Al Zouri in Lebanon. Since then, Al Zouri has furnished much information to corroborate what I have said. Even more convincing, however, is the evidence you are about to hear from Colonel Ivan Litinov. The colonel was Lebedov's former director of special operations and was instrumental in carrying out Lebedov's plan.

"I direct a special plea to those leaders in Russia who now are faced with continuing Lebedov's insane course. In light of what you are about to hear, you must cancel his orders to confront the American fleet. Mr. Lebedov is dead. He no longer dictates the course of events. I implore Russia's new leaders to reconsider, before it's too late."

As the image on the screen faded, a disheveled, tired Colonel Ivan Litinov ascended the stage to address the stunned world press. He gripped both sides of the lectern tightly, surveyed the crowd with his eyes, and began speaking in accented English.

He talked for twenty minutes outlining *Hammer and Anvil* in detail, describing Chinese involvement in the development of the warheads and subsequent smuggling of the warheads into America. His description of Lebedov's contempt for Europe's leaders as pacifistic appeasers elicited winces among some of the European members of the international press.

The crowd was shocked when Litinov described Lebedov's assassination.

The colonel held up the operations manual he had taken from Lebedov's office and offered it as corroboration to his story.

Finally, he indicated a need to speak directly to the Russian people. He spoke in Russian. "My fellow citizens, I love Russia as I know you do. I know you would never have allowed such an evil plan to be carried out had you known about it. No normal human being could ever conscience the murder of millions of innocent people simply to further the ambitions of a despot.

"I will forever regret my role in this atrocity and know I can never be forgiven by my fellow countrymen. I intend to return to Russia to pay whatever penalty you deem appropriate.

"Now, however, you must not allow our military leaders to go forward with the insanity Lebedov started. You must make your will known before it's too late. Your lives and the world's hang in the balance."

World reaction was quick. Governments across the globe condemned Russia and the ongoing military moves. They almost unanimously called for the immediate withdrawal of troops from southern Iran and the turning around of the Russian convoy now in the northeastern Mediterranean.

Events in Russia were even more stunning. Within an hour after the government media outlets ran with Litinov's entire Heathrow statement, crowds began gathering in cities across Russia. Three hours later, half-a-million Muscovites were marching in the street toward the Kremlin demanding the Russian military reverse course.

The pressure was immense on Russia's generals but was not really the overriding factor in their decisions. Once aware of what actually had happened, the military leaders, who were mostly sane individuals who had no desire to be the cause of the loss of their own power, enthusiastically issued orders to end the crisis.

About an hour before the deadline of Lebedov's ultimatum, a reconnaissance jet flying off the deck of the USS Carl Vinson reported the ships in the Russian convoy were turning and sailing back west. Cheers erupted on the bridge of the huge ship when the announcement was made.

Epilogue

One would have to be naïve to say the world was now a safer place to live. The nuclear threats from North Korea and Iran had been eliminated. That good news was offset by the millions of displaced, destitute Arab refugees now living in squalid camps in northern Syria and Iraq. Several million Iranians lived in similar conditions in eastern Iran. All still hated Israel and blamed the Jews for their current situation. The pool of potential Muslim extremists had been multiplied tenfold.

Israel was stretched to the breaking point trying to hold onto hundreds of thousands of square miles of occupied territory. It was not Israel's intent to hold onto to any of the Arab lands, save the Golan Heights and portions of the West Bank. It was the Jewish nation's intent, however, to trade land for peace, a somewhat familiar approach, only now on a much bigger scale. Oil pumping nonstop from the oil fields Israel now controlled, generated money— lots of money— which not only helped the small country in its negotiations but also financed its temporary occupation.

Russia finally withdrew its troops from Iranian territory but only after fighting small but deadly skirmishes with Iranian insurgents exacting revenge on the retreating Russian soldiers for the attack on Iran's cities.

Chinese troops quickly left Russian territory. They were jeered and mocked by the Russian population for their role in the crisis, and, in two separate instances, several were killed in skirmishes with irate citizens. The premier of China, Zhu Jiaboa, and his foreign minister, Chou En Lo, were unceremoniously replaced and never heard from again.

Colonel Litinov, as promised, was allowed to return to Russia to a mixed reception. Many hailed him as a hero for the courage to kill the insane Lebedov and stop a nuclear war. The military and intelligence agencies, however, could not forgive him for the deaths of many of their own, so he was put on trial and convicted of treason.

In a stunning rebuke of the military/intelligence establishment, the military judge at the trial sentenced Litinov to involuntary discharge from the military and five years probation. The Russian public was satisfied. Litinov decided, thereafter, to accept a publisher's offer and write a book.

Dimitri also went home to Moscow where he was able to attend his brother's funeral and, finally, grieve appropriately.

Tyler McNabb and his family were reunited in Virginia, where he was given a stateside assignment.

Colby Engeman returned to Israel and recovered from his wounds. He decided his real love was medicine, and, coupled with his desire to do what he could to help millions of Americans in desperate need, he resigned from the Mossad, packed up his family, and was in the process of moving back to the United States.

America was slowly recovering from the terrorist attacks. The cores of the destroyed cities would not be habitable for years to come. American ingenuity being what it is, new cities would be built on the perimeters. The impact on the economy, though initially severe, would be offset considerably by the massive reconstruction effort. The emotional scars on America would linger much longer. Trust in the federal government and global institutions and relationships had been shaken severely. A return to pre-attack normalcy would take years, most likely not until a new generation of Americans entered the scene. Perhaps this was a good thing, considering where blind trust had led.

New elections were scheduled to take place in July. The American Freedom Party, as well as Democrats and Republicans, were fielding a slate of candidates in all fifty states for Congress and the presidency. Nonelected President Benson had decided to make it official and declared his candidacy for the presidency representing his new party.

As if to prove the saying "nothing really ever changes", both the Democrats and Republicans were selling votes for money in an effort to overcome the lead in the polls enjoyed by the American Freedom Party. The election would prove to be very similar to past efforts, a lot of dirt and not much substance. It remained to be seen if ordinary Americans would still buy the sleaze.

Benson reclined on the comfortable patio loveseat, his arms encircling his wife Kristina as they snuggled in the warm spring evening in Denver. "Honey," Benson whispered in his wife's ear, in a reflective moment, "do you think it was all worth it?"

Kristina, understanding exactly what her husband was asking, replied, "Sweetheart, if you mean was saving the world from destruction worth a few months of awful stress, numbing fear, disrupted family life and zero romance, yes, Mr. President, it was certainly worth it."

www.ingramcontent.com/pod-product-compliance
Lightning Source LLC
Chambersburg PA
CBHW030821310726
48980CB00006B/575/J

* 9 7 8 1 4 5 8 3 3 2 8 7 5 *